Without warning, his lips came crashing down upon hers. She moaned in protest and made a belated attempt to escape, but to no avail. His arms tightened, holding her captive within his embrace while his mouth ravaged the sweetness of hers.

Lainey had been kissed before. Or at least she'd *thought* she had been kissed before. No man had ever swept her into his arms the way Ethan Holt had so masterfully done, and—heaven help her—no man had ever kissed her with such skill and passion.

His lips, warm and possessive, demanded a response. . . .

By Catherine Creel
Published by Fawcett Books:

WILD TEXAS ROSE
LADY ALEX
TEXAS WEDDING

Books published by The Ballantine Publishing Group
are available at quantity discounts on bulk purchases
for premium, educational, fund-raising, and special
sales use. For details, please call 1-800-733-3000.

WESTWARD ANGEL

Catherine Creel

FAWCETT GOLD MEDAL • NEW YORK

A Fawcett Gold Medal Book
Published by Ballantine Books
Copyright © 1995 by Catherine Creel

Library of Congress Catalog Card Number: 95-90430

ISBN 0-449-18280-0

Manufactured in the United States of America

First Edition: December 1995

10 9 8 7 6 5 4 3 2

To Craig, my fellow adventurer.
Thank you for making
so many dreams come true.

Chapter 1

Oklahoma Territory, 1889

Tomorrow, God willing, they'd cross into the promised land.

The promised land. The thought made Lainey Prescott's lips curve into a faint smile of irony. Not by any stretch of the imagination would the people back home in Missouri classify this grassy, undulating prairie stretching toward the horizon as a present-day Canaan, and yet for some it represented an earthly paradise like no other. To her, and even more so to her sister, Beth, Oklahoma meant freedom. It meant a completely different way of life, a new beginning. And heaven knew, they needed a new beginning.

She heaved a sigh and climbed to her feet beside the creek, then hoisted the filled wooden bucket to the bank. Her gaze flickered upward.

It would be dark soon; the cloudless April sky was already ablaze with the rich, pink-toned hues only a sunset could give it. There was a palpable tension in the air as the night approached. Even the babes in arms seemed to know that they were all—the rich and the poor, the refined and the ignorant—poised on the very brink of an event that would change their lives forever. The cool breeze carried with it the smells of wood smoke and food and horses throughout the camp, while

1

a quiet roar of mingled excitement and apprehension drifted upward.

Oklahoma. The sound of it evoked a wealth of emotion in even the most hardened of breasts. The name was Choctaw, a fitting combination of "okla" for people and "humma" for red. The Land of the Red Man, or Indian Territory, as it had officially been termed by Washington, was about to be invaded. Never mind that the government had promised it would belong to the Indians "for as long as the sun rose and the water flows." Come high noon on April 22, 1889, some two million acres in the very center of the unassigned lands would be thrown open to white settlement.

Lainey was happily ignorant of the politics involved. She was determined to be one of the fortunate few to claim the hundred and sixty acres guaranteed to each adult citizen under the Homestead Act. It would take her five years to obtain full title to the land, five years of working harder than she'd ever worked before, but it would be worth it. She and Beth and little Anna would have a home of their own. And they would never have to look back. *Never.*

Turning away from the water's edge, she started toward the hill. Another faint sigh escaped her lips. Beth would surely conjure up visions of disaster if she did not return soon. And there were still so many last-minute details to be worked out before morning.

The bucket was heavy and cumbersome, and her long, dark brown cotton skirts bore the evidence of a half-dozen spills by the time she reached the wagon again. At least the site they had managed to claim wasn't too far. Some of their fellow "rushers" had to travel a considerable distance to reach the camp's only source of water. Of course, she mused with a sudden frown, if any of them had had the good sense to remain back in Arkansas City and join the thousands of others planning to make the run via the Santa Fe Railroad, they just might have been able to spend this last night in the relative comfort of a hotel.

"Confound it all, I *knew* we should have taken the train," she murmured half to herself as she drew to a halt and lowered the bucket to the ground beside the canvas-topped prairie schooner. Like nearly everything else they had brought with them, it was brand new, purchased with the last of the money from the sale of their father's house.

"Nonsense," Beth Prescott retorted amiably, straightening from the cookfire with a big wooden spoon in one hand.

Older by two years, she was nevertheless shorter than her sister, her hair several shades lighter than the burnished gold of Lainey's, and her eyes a paler blue. Everything about her was softer and more refined, a fact that had frequently caused Lainey to bemoan her own voluptuous curves. It wasn't fair—Beth had had a child, and she still looked like a mere girl. Lainey gave an inward sigh. There was no accounting for the capriciousness of fate, which had decreed that *she* be the one with the kind of figure that drew unwanted and highly embarrassing glances from men.

"And you know it isn't at all ladylike to use language like that," Beth added in the next moment. The petite blonde tempered the rebuke with a smile and cast a quick, significant glance toward the adjoining campsite. "What on earth would Mrs. Gilbert say if she heard you? It is Sunday, after all, and—"

"—and Easter besides," Lainey finished for her. "But, I don't care a fig what Mrs. Gilbert thinks! She's bound to have heard far worse these past several days. *I* certainly have."

Lifting her chin to a characteristically defiant angle, she marched past Beth, to where a supper of bacon and beans sizzled in the huge iron skillet. She knelt and checked to make certain the coffee was boiling before crossing back to the wagon.

"Anna is still sleeping?" she queried, tossing a look over her shoulder.

"Yes." Beth's opal eyes softened and warmed with a maternal glow. "Poor darling. She was perfectly exhausted. I hate to wake her, but she'll have to eat something if she's to get a proper night's rest."

Lainey nodded in silent understanding. Her own sapphire gaze darkened as it traveled about the campsite, and she raised a hand to tuck a wayward strand of hair back into the single thick braid, which reached all the way down her back to her waist. A sudden frown of remembrance creased her brow.

Have you lost your mind, Lainey Prescott?

Matilda Sweeney's admonition still burned in her ears, still provoked a surge of anger and remorse within her. Matilda had always been a meddling old woman, it was true, but her words had struck home in the worst way. *Why, your father must be turning over in his grave! You cannot take your sister and her poor, innocent child to that godforsaken land of snakes and savages. You'll be killed, all of you, and it will be on your head!*

Ah, but a dead person can't feel any guilt, Lainey mused ironically. Her amusement quickly faded. God help her, she *did* feel guilty about bringing Beth and Anna to this wild, untamed country. It had been the most difficult decision she had ever made. And yet, what other choice did they really have?

"Oh, Lainey. I will be so glad when we have a garden, and maybe an orchard as well." Beth sighed as she stirred the skillet's thick, aromatic contents once more. "If I never see another pot of beans again, it will be too soon!"

"We should count ourselves fortunate to have plenty to eat," Lainey reminded her, unable to suppress a crooked smile. It wasn't often that Beth complained about anything. "At least we were able to buy enough provisions to last us for a while. I heard that some of the others are already going hungry."

"Do you really think that's true?" asked Beth. Her pretty, heart-shaped features took on an expression Lainey knew all too well. "If it is, then we must share—"

"We can't do that. If we start giving away our food, we won't have enough to last us until we get settled in." Noting the reproachful look in her sister's eyes, she grew a bit exasperated. "For heaven's sake, Beth Prescott! There must be over a thousand people in this camp. How can we possibly hope to feed all of them?" She didn't wait for an answer, instead reiterating quite firmly, "No. Absolutely not. I'm as ready and willing to help my fellow man as anyone else, but it would be utter folly to share what we have left. We're going to have to concentrate on looking after our own interests from here on out."

"I'm not at all sure that's the sort of example I wish to set for Anna."

"Anna is only a year old. She won't remember any of this."

"That still doesn't make it right, Lainey," Beth chided gently.

"Right or wrong, that's the way it has to be." She turned away and hastened to change the subject, all the while acutely conscious of her sister's disapproval. "It's certainly a lot quieter now, isn't it? I was beginning to think we'd never have an end to the revelry around here. All that shooting and yelling . . . I suppose we can thank the heat for calming things down a bit. You know, I do believe the night promises to be almost as warm as the day . . ." Her voice trailed away as she made a point of adjusting the rolled-up sleeves of her white lawn shirtwaist.

All day long, wagon after wagon had pulled up to the line, which was nearly forty miles from the Kansas border, fanning out in an unceasing stream to the east and the west. Most of the wagons were brand-new, or at least good and sturdy, and pulled by strong stock, but there were also a number of rickety, broken-down ones drawn by plodding oxen or horses that looked as if they should have been put out to pasture long ago. The collection included buggies as well, and fringed carriages, and even, amazingly, a few five-foot bicycles. Some didn't even have that; they had come on horseback or on foot. Whatever their mode of transportation, men would set up a cheer and fire several volleys into the air to celebrate their arrival.

The cowboys had been the worst, of course, recalled Lainey with a mental shake of her head. Enthusiastic to a fault, those rowdy young participants had proven responsible for more than their fair share of the commotion. And if dear Mrs. Gilbert found herself so easily shocked by a simple "confound it," she'd probably faint dead away at the words falling from *their* lips.

The sleepy, familiar cry of a child drifted out from the Prescotts' wagon. Lainey immediately gathered up her skirts and climbed inside, smiling down at the little girl whose angelic features were so much like her mother's.

"Good evening, sweetheart. Are you hungry?" Kneeling, she affectionately gathered the toddler close and pressed a kiss to the slightly damp, flushed smoothness of her forehead. "I'm sorry it's so hot. We'll have to see to it that you get a nice cool bath after supper."

"Mama," was Anna's only reply while she pushed crankily at her devoted aunt. Her limited vocabulary made any real conversation between them impossible; Lainey wished she knew how the little girl felt about leaving the only home she had ever known. But, just as she herself had insisted to Beth only moments ago,

Anna would never even remember the long journey—
nor the tragic circumstances that had prompted them to
leave Missouri.

She scooped the apple-cheeked baby up in her arms
and scrambled down out of the wagon. Beth hurried forward to take charge of her daughter.

"There you are at last, my little love. Come and sit
with me. Supper is almost ready." She sighed and
glanced at Lainey while murmuring, "I wish I had been
able to nurse her a bit longer."

"She's thriving just the same," Lainey assured her.
She watched as mother and child settled themselves on
a patchwork quilt spread upon the hard, sun-baked
ground. Beth looked incredibly lovely in her blue cotton
dress, while the white-gowned Anna was the very picture of a healthy, happy one-year-old. Gazing at the two
of them, she felt a sudden wave of homesickness. She
missed her father terribly, missed the house where she
had grown up and the people she had known all her life.
If only . . .

No! She silently cursed the self-pitying turn of her
reverie. There was nothing to be gained by thoughts
like that. What was done was done, and there was no
sense in looking back. It was time for them to get on
with their lives, to put the past behind them once and
for all. The future was theirs; all they had to do was
reach out and take it. And by thunder, that's just what
they would do, she vowed inwardly, the light of determination burning brighter than ever in her deep blue
eyes. Come hell or high water, they were going to make
a home for themselves in Oklahoma.

Darkness had long since fallen by the time she finished washing the supper dishes and putting them away.
Beth and Anna were inside the wagon, their voices in-
toning a humorous singsong in far from perfect unison.
The baby had been bathed, the horses had been fed, and

everything save the bare essentials had been packed in readiness for tomorrow's greatly anticipated event.

Lainey wandered restlessly about the campsite, her gaze flickering up toward the moonlit sky. She knew she wouldn't be able to sleep much that night. Judging by the sounds coming from the other wagons, neither would anyone else.

"Beth?" she called out softly, moving to the foot of the prairie schooner.

"Yes?" There was a faint rustling on the other side of the canvas, followed by a childish giggle.

"I think I'll take a walk."

"All right, but don't be gone too long. You'll need to get plenty of rest tonight. And Anna will no doubt awaken well before dawn."

"Yes, I know." A brief smile touched her lips. It didn't seem to matter how late the baby went to sleep, she was always the first one awake in the morning. And the little scamp didn't mind letting everyone know it.

Smoothing her long sleeves into place, she fastened the small pearl buttons on the cuffs and set off toward the creek. She started to catch up a lantern on her way, but decided against it. There was plenty of light from the moon. Its silvery radiance gave the rolling, shrub-dotted prairie an almost other-worldly look. Literally hundreds of campfires burned in the darkness, adding their dancing golden flames and curling smoke to the incredible scene. Wagons and horses and people were crowded together on the border for as far as the eye could see.

Lainey folded her arms across her chest and strolled leisurely past the neighboring campsites. Babies were crying, mothers were soothing, and men were discussing their plans for the next day. She breathed deeply of the night air and tried her best not to eavesdrop as she continued on her way. It struck her that she had never before encountered such a varied mass of humanity.

Having lived the entirety of her twenty-one years in the same small town—where everyone knew even the most intimate details of everyone else's humdrum existence—she was fascinated by the people who had come to seek their fortune in the West.

Gamblers and range riders, confidence men and honest nesters, horse thieves and skilled laborers, lawyers and merchants and all manner of saints and scoundrels . . . and women. There were certainly plenty of "scarlet angels" among the wives, widows, and spinsters. And plenty of men to appreciate their obvious charms.

She smiled to herself as her thoughts returned to the remarkable young woman she had met only that morning. Alice Bennett had been a librarian back in Virginia. Every inch a proper lady, Alice had nonetheless shocked her parents by declaring her intention to seek a new life in the Territory. She had braved their wrath to travel alone all the way to Oklahoma, only to realize that her chances of winning a homestead for herself were dishearteningly slim. Providence had thereupon tossed her into the path of one John McNeill, a widower with two young children.

The Minnesota farmer had made her a startling proposition—if she would but consent to marry him, he would make the run for them while she watched the children. Alice had thrown all caution to the winds and accepted. They had been married that same day. It was a marriage of convenience, to be sure, but it gave every indication of becoming so much more.

"How could you possibly marry a man you had only just met?" had been Lainey's inevitable response to the new bride's astonishing tale.

"John had the kindest eyes I had ever seen," Alice had explained, with a dreamy expression, then had blushed rosily. "And who knows where love may blossom?"

Love. Lainey frowned while turning the word over in

her mind. She had seen what love could do, and she wanted no part of it. No, thank you very much, she preferred to remain mistress of her own fate. Let the hopeless romantics like Alice believe what they wanted; *she* would never allow herself to become a slave to her emotions.

The creek lay just ahead now. She paused beside a cottonwood tree and idly raised a hand to the smooth surface of its bark. Someone was playing a fiddle nearby. The distinctive strains of a harmonica joined in, and it was only seconds before a chorus of voices, male and female alike, rose to serenade the camp with a lively rendition of "Clementine."

Lainey tilted her head back, her gaze momentarily fastening on the steady brightness of the North Star. Missouri seemed a world away at the moment. She closed her eyes and remembered how she and Beth used to lie on their backs in the grass and count the stars on a warm springtime night much the same as this one. They would speak of their hopes and dreams, girlish dreams that had been shattered all too soon.

Being the daughters of the town's only doctor meant being on their own a great deal, but they hadn't minded. They had been happy to take care of the house for their father, to cook and clean, and, occasionally, help him with his practice. Upon reaching the grand and enlightened ages of twelve and fourteen, they had even been allowed to accompany him on his rounds. It had been a good life, one Lainey wished could have gone on forever. Her wish might have come true, at least for a little while longer, if Beth hadn't fallen in love.

These past two years had proven difficult for everyone, but most of all for their father. Not that one word of reproach had ever passed his lips. No, he had been incredibly loving and supportive. But she knew his heart had been broken.

A sudden lump rose in her throat, and she was forced

to blink back tears. Would the pain of losing him never ease? she wondered disconsolately. It had been three months now, three months of uncertainty and anger and a bitterness of spirit she sought to conceal from Beth. Her sister had suffered enough already—

"Couldn't sleep?"

Lainey stiffened in alarm, a soft gasp escaping her lips as she spun about to confront the owner of the low, deep-timbered voice that had startled her. The first thing she noticed was that he was very tall. The second thing was that he was without a doubt the most all-out, wickedly handsome man she had ever seen.

She could make out the rugged perfection of his tanned and clean-shaven features in the moonlight. Her face flamed when she suddenly realized that his scrutiny was every bit as bold as hers. Bolder, actually, since his gaze dropped significantly to the full curve of her breasts before traveling back up to her face. She was unable to discern the exact color of his eyes—they were either green or blue, or maybe both—but he was standing so close she could feel the heat emanating from his hard-muscled body.

She took an instinctive step backward.

"I fail to see how that's any concern of yours." Her tone was one of cool primness. She folded her arms across her breasts again, almost as if to shield them from his steady and highly unsettling gaze. "And I would appreciate it if you would be on your way." She emphasized the request by turning her head sharply in the opposite direction.

"Sorry if I disturbed you. But I'm in no hurry."

He spoke with a distinct, warmly pleasant drawl that gave evidence of his Texas roots. The merest ghost of a smile played about his lips. He couldn't have been more than thirty, and yet Lainey immediately sensed that this man possessed the confident authority of someone much older. His next words only served to reinforce that impression.

"You shouldn't be out here alone."

"Why shouldn't I?" She lifted her head to a proud angle, her eyes flashing with irritation at being treated, however politely, as though she were little more than a child.

"Because it may not be safe." The tall stranger's own eyes narrowed imperceptibly. His attire was that of a cowboy—white cotton shirt, blue denim trousers, and leather boots—but he wasn't like the others. Lainey knew that right away.

"Not safe?" she echoed in disbelief, then bristled anew. "Of course it's safe! How could there possibly be any danger with so many—?"

"Crowds don't usually count for much in the dark."

She drew in her breath on another soft gasp when he suddenly lifted a hand to the tree beside her. His arm was stretched almost directly above her head. She felt her pulse give a wild leap at his nearness, and her eyes grew very round as they shifted back up to his face. The moonlight set his dark brown hair aglow, making him look even more rakishly attractive. He smelled faintly of soap and leather and coffee.

Lainey was thrown into a quandary as she stood there in the warm, smoke-scented darkness with the Texan who had materialized out of nowhere to provoke strange, and not entirely disagreeable, sensations within her. Everything about him was so vibrantly, unashamedly masculine. And although he was looking at her the same way other men had looked at her, his gaze held more than simple lust.

She couldn't make herself move away this time. A warning bell sounded in her brain, but her body refused to obey her instincts. Filled with an unfamiliar, breathless sort of expectation, she unfolded her arms and placed her hands nervously behind her as she leaned back against the tree for support.

"I—I suppose you're planning to make the run to-morrow?" she stammered.

It was a stupid question, of course, but she could think of nothing else to say at the moment. Her experience in making light conversation with men still on the green side of fifty was somewhat limited. As a matter of fact, she had never before been alone with a man, other than her father, for any measurable length of time. She had never really wanted to until now. *Why now?* an inner voice challenged. She chose to ignore it.

"Do you have a particular site in mind, Mr.—?" she asked before he'd had time to offer a reply to the first question. Her gaze met and locked with his.

"Holt. Ethan Holt. And yes," he confirmed, with another faint smile. "My brother and I are heading down to Guthrie." Taking his hand from the tree, he hooked his thumb negligently through one of his trouser's front belt loops. His other hand held a tan felt hat that was well-worn but brushed clean. "What about you?" It was his turn to inquire. "Will your husband be trying for a homestead?"

Ethan already knew the answer. He had made it a point to find out the first time he had set eyes on her back in Arkansas City. Her name was Lainey Prescott, there was no husband, and she was the first woman in years who had stirred his blood and his heart at the same time. Their meeting tonight wasn't a coincidence. He had followed her with the single-minded purpose of discovering what it would be like to stand this close to her . . . to let his eyes roam over her sweet, damnably alluring curves . . . to talk to her and see if she was even half as proud and spirited as she looked.

He wasn't disappointed. Not by a long shot.

"I'm not married, Mr. Holt," Lainey admitted, a dull flush staining her cheeks. "My sister and I have traveled all the way from Missouri. It so happens that we're hoping to settle near Guthrie, too. One of the men employed by the railroad was kind enough to inform me that the best land is there."

She didn't know why she was telling him this. Perhaps it was because she was feeling homesick and even a little lonely that night, or perhaps because there was something about Ethan Holt that made it easy to confide in him. Whatever the reason, she found herself compelled to tell him more.

"We have gambled everything on this venture. We sold our home and nearly all our possessions." She raised her eyes to his again before adding solemnly, "We cannot go back."

"Why did you leave?" He did not fail to notice the sudden shadow crossing her beautiful face. Wondering what had caused her pain, he was surprised at the way it affected him.

"My sister—my sister is a widow. Her daughter is still quite young. And when we read about the land rush in the newspaper, we decided to head West. We intend to start a farm, you see."

She had believed, mistakenly, that the lie about Beth would come more naturally to her lips by now. The whole thing had been her idea; Beth had only agreed to it after a great deal of persuasion. While the two of them might suffer an occasional twinge of guilt for the deception, it was necessary. They had to lie. For Beth's sake, and for Anna's, no one could ever know the truth.

"Have you farmed before, Miss Prescott?" Ethan asked next. The music and laughter continued in the near distance, but his wonderfully resonant voice cut straight through the other sounds. A number of seconds passed before the significance of his last words dawned on Lainey.

"How did you know my name?" She stiffened again

while her blue eyes narrowed up at him in suspicion. "We haven't met before. How——?"

"I asked."

His mouth curved into a brief albeit thoroughly devastating smile. He took a step closer, prompting her to straighten and bring her arms folding upward across her breasts once more.

Lainey was certain she glimpsed a roguish light in Ethan Holt's penetrating, blue-green gaze. The warning bell sounded louder than ever in her brain, but she stubbornly refused to run away like a coward.

"What possible reasons could you have had to ask about me?" she demanded.

"My reasons are my own," he parried enigmatically, then steered the conversation back to the previous topic. A slight frown creased his brow. "Even if you have farmed before, you won't be able to make it on your own out here."

"I don't recall asking for your opinion, Mr. Holt!" Infuriated at his presumption, she tilted her head back to confront him squarely. "And who the devil do you think you are, telling me what I can and cannot do?"

"Take my advice, Miss Prescott, and try for one of the town lots," he offered, unrepentant. "You're not meant for the kind of life to be found out on some hardscrabble little patch of earth." His eyes darkened with appreciation, and something else he couldn't put a name to yet, as they raked over the upturned storminess of her face. "You belong in town, with a real house and fancy clothes and a husband who'll cater to your every whim."

His words made Lainey see red. She planted her hands on her hips and fixed him with a look that would have withered lesser men.

"*You*, sir, can take your advice and——"

"Don't you understand, you little fool?" His hands shot out to close firmly about her upper arms. She gasped and blinked up at him in shocked amazement. "If you can't go back to Missouri, then at least don't make the mistake of ruining your chances here! Farming is hard even for those who've been doing it their whole lives. And for two women alone—"

He broke off abruptly and muttered something unintelligible beneath his breath. Then, as if suddenly realizing that he had lost his head—something he rarely did—he released the golden-haired young temptress who had been too much on his mind these past few days.

Damn it, he swore inwardly, he hadn't meant to touch her. He hadn't meant to let himself get so involved. What had happened to that iron self-control Travis was always teasing him about? And why the hell had he come after her in the first place? God knew, he was certainly old enough to know better—*in the living as well as the years*.

Lainey, meanwhile, remained speechless and becomingly flushed. No man had ever dared to lay hands upon her that way. She watched while Ethan, turning aside, tossed a quick glance up toward the sky. His features were inscrutable when he pivoted slowly back around to face her again.

"My apologies, Miss Prescott. I had no right to force my opinions on you."

"You—you most certainly did *not!*" she sputtered indignantly. Shock was replaced by righteous anger. "If you ever come near me again, I will summon the soldiers and have you arrested!" she threatened, referring to the cavalry troops stationed along the line to keep the peace and make certain no one entered the Territory ahead of time.

She uttered the warning with far more bravado than she actually felt. Plagued by a lingering, inordinate weakness of the knees, she finally gathered up her skirts to take flight. Ethan blocked her path.

"If you're so determined to claim a homestead," he told her in a low, even tone, "then make sure you ride the fastest horse you've got and head straightaway for the river valley at Guthrie. You'll need a section with few trees and plenty of water. And don't get too far from town. You'd end up regretting it when winter sets in."

"More advice, Mr. Holt?" she countered, with biting sarcasm. "It may surprise you to learn that I know *exactly* where I am heading tomorrow, and that I am also very well aware of the requirements for my claim."

"Good. I'm glad you've got it all planned out." There was more than a hint of sardonic amusement in his own voice as he took in the sight of her blazing sapphire eyes and high color. He resisted the sudden impulse to smooth a stray tendril of hair from her forehead. She looked incredibly young and lovely. And dangerous.

"Please get out of my way, Mr. Holt," requested Lainey, her manner now one of admirable composure. She hated losing her temper; she always felt so very foolish afterward. But confound it, Ethan Holt had pushed her too far.

Her arms still tingled where his strong fingers had gripped them. She swallowed hard and tried to set a course around him, but he still refused to let her pass.

"I'll walk you back." The offer was made partly out of the wish to prolong their encounter, and partly because she had aroused a strong protective urge within him. It had been a long time since he had experienced such a deadly combination of tenderness and desire.

"No, thank you." She met his gaze once more, only to feel a shiver dance down her spine at the warmth—not the least bit fatherly—she saw contained therein. Her voice was only a trifle unsteady when she said, "Good-bye, Mr. Holt."

"Good night, Miss Prescott," he corrected softly.

She didn't know whether to be relieved or disappointed when he stepped aside without another word. Following a brief hesitation, during which time a peculiar, highly charged silence rose up between them, she swept past him and walked swiftly back into the crowded, firelit darkness of the camp. She could almost feel his eyes burning into her back as she went.

Ethan stared after her for several long moments. Only after she had disappeared behind the first row of wagons did he raise the hat to his head and set off with long, unhurried strides toward his own campsite. He had given serious consideration to following her, but had reluctantly abandoned the idea. There was no use in stirring up more trouble, he told himself grimly. It was bad enough that he had behaved like some randy young puncher; why tempt fate by risking yet another flare-up?

His mouth twitched anew as he imagined what his brother would have to say if he knew about the incident. Travis wouldn't have settled for merely talking to her. He'd have made those few short minutes alone with her count for a good deal more than conversation.

But *he* wasn't Travis. And Lainey Prescott wasn't the kind of woman to be grabbed and pawed in the darkness. No, by damn—she was the kind a man either married or forgot.

Then you'd better hope your memory goes bad real fast, he mused wryly, only to sober in the next instant. The dilemma before him was a real one. His emotions, guarded carefully all these years, were playing havoc with his plans. The timing was wrong. Lainey Prescott had come into his life too soon—or too late.

Lainey, meanwhile, had reached the safety of her wagon again. She climbed inside, jerked the canvas flaps together, and immediately began undressing. Beth and Anna were already asleep. Thank goodness, she thought with an inward sigh of relief, she wouldn't have to face her sister until morning. Beth would be able to tell right away that something was wrong, and she was certainly in no mood to try and explain what had happened.

She frowned darkly as she slipped off her shirtwaist and skirt. Deciding it was too hot to bother with a nightgown, she quickly removed her shoes and stockings. She remained clad in a square-necked chemise of soft white cambric and a pair of white muslin drawers. Both undergarments, trimmed as they were with tucks and embroidery, had cost a pretty penny indeed from the mail-order catalog. "A lady must feel like a lady down to her toes," the advertisement had put forth.

Her eyes glowed with ironic humor at the notion. Maybe lingerie had something to do with it, and then again, maybe not. She seriously doubted that the quality of one's undergarments affected one's social behavior.

Ladies or no ladies, she and Beth had wisely agreed to dispense with corsets for the duration of the trip. It felt wonderful, almost sinfully so in a way, to be able to breathe and move about with such freedom. Petticoats had also been packed away in the trunk once they had reached Kansas.

A sudden, unbidden vision of Ethan Holt's handsome face swam before her eyes, driving the amusement from their brilliant blue depths. She wondered what *he* would think of her fine and fancy undergarments—or rather, the lack of them.

Her face flamed hotly at the utter wickedness of her thoughts.

"Lainey Prescott, you've gone and lost all sense of decency," she rebuked herself aloud, then shot a guilty, worried glance toward the wagon's other two occupants. They slept on, their faces looking positively angelic and their steady breaths mingling as they lay close together.

Lainey stretched out atop the quilt on the other side of Anna. She folded her arms beneath her head and stared up toward the bowed canvas topping the wagon. The natural cadences of the night joined with their more raucous, man-made counterparts in a symphony that wafted across the vast moonlit prairie. She listened to the sounds, her mind wandering while her body slowly relaxed.

Anna stirred briefly beside her. She looked at the child who was so like Beth and smiled softly. In spite of the tragic circumstances surrounding Anna's birth, the little girl had proven to be a blessing to them all. They could not regret her existence, though many of their "concerned neighbors" back home had certainly tried to make them.

Her gaze clouded with reminiscence once more. She had never understood how Beth could have tossed aside all her good sense and high principles to plunge into heartbreaking disaster with a man she scarcely knew. In truth, she conceded with another heavy sigh, she wasn't sure understanding would ever come her way.

But, standing close to Ethan Holt that night—being made so acutely, startlingly conscious of his manliness—well, she had at least gained a certain new insight into the age-old attraction men and women held for one another. And while her momentary confusion had been both alarming and inexcusable, it couldn't have possibly led to a thorough weakness of flesh and spirit. Nothing, and no *one* either for that matter, could ever serve to make her forget who she was and what she wanted out of life.

Her eyes swept closed as she muttered a highly unladylike curse. For heaven's sake, anyone would think she'd gotten all "hot and bothered" about a perfect stranger—and an insolent Texas cowboy at that. She would probably never see the man again, anyway. They might both be headed for Guthrie tomorrow, but then so were thousands of others. Anything could happen. Absolutely anything.

Rolling abruptly to her side, she wriggled her hips to find a more comfortable position in the makeshift bed. Sleep, however, remained stubbornly elusive. Her blood still ran too warm in her veins; she would never own up to the possibility that it could have something to do with Ethan Holt.

The long night wore on, offering up the promise of a new day and a new course of life for all those who shared the same fierce determination. History awaited . . .

Chapter 2

Lainey awoke to the sound of a familiar, mischievous voice close to her ear. The words were for the most part unintelligible, but there was little doubt as to the meaning of them. Anna Elizabeth Prescott had come to roust her.

It was with great reluctance that she opened her eyes and turned her head on the pillow. She had finally drifted off into a troubled sleep sometime around midnight, long after the music had stopped and the camp had settled into its own fragile tranquillity. Tossing and turning, she had tried, without much success, to clear her mind of its chaotic jumble. Thoughts of land and future crops and a bold, dark-haired cowboy with an unnerving way about him had crept into her dreams as well.

But the night was gone at last. She yawned and gave her niece a sleepy smile. A hasty glance toward the wagon's canvas told her that dawn had scarcely broken, and yet here was this devil-child exhorting her to leave a warm, languorous cocoon for the cold reality of the morning.

"Up!" The incorrigible Anna punctuated her demand with a shove.

"All right," murmured Lainey, pulling herself slowly into a sitting position. She smiled again and caught the little girl up to her for a quick hug. "Has anyone ever told you that you're a bit *too* cheerful in the morning?"

22

"Lainey?" Beth appeared at the foot of the wagon, her light blond hair already secured into a chignon. She was wearing a simple, primrose gingham dress that made her look far younger than her twenty-three years. "I knew Anna would do the trick," she remarked, with a soft laugh. "Breakfast is almost ready."

"Why didn't you wake me before now?" Lainey demanded, with a mock frown of reproach. "And I thought we agreed to have cold meals today. Christopher Columbus, Beth! We've already got everything packed and—"

"Then we can pack it again." Her sister cut her off good-naturedly. "It isn't much, really. We've hours yet before the rush begins, and besides, you're going to need a hot, nourishing breakfast." She frowned slightly, her eyes filling with a touch of renewed apprehension as she reached up to take Anna. "Oh, Lainey. I do wish you would reconsider about going alone. You're not accustomed to being on horseback for so long, and with so many people racing about, it's possible that you will be hurt or . . . well, I don't think it's entirely safe for you to be riding without protection of some kind," she concluded, with a faint blush.

"I have to go alone," insisted Lainey, flinging off the covers and rising to her knees. She began unbraiding her own hair. The thick, honey-blond curls looked wild, offering proof of the restless night she had spent. "And I certainly can't hope to win any land unless I ride. You know that. The wagon would slow me down too much."

She gave silent thanks once more for the advice given to her by the kindly young railroad clerk back in Arkansas City. He had told her where to head, how to get there, and what to do once she found a homestead she liked. She knew that many of the others intended to drive their wagons; she would have a definite advantage on horseback.

"We're going to keep things exactly as planned," she

reiterated. She took up the hairbrush and sat back on her heels, meeting Beth's worried gaze. "I'll ride ahead and stake a claim, while you and Anna proceed to Guthrie and wait for me there. Just think of it, Beth—before this day is through, we could finally own that farm we've dreamed about. One hundred and sixty acres of prime land, all ours. If determination has anything to do with it, it *will* happen."

Ethan Holt's words suddenly came to mind again. He had cautioned her against trying to farm. Worse than that, he had implied that she was suited to nothing more than decorating a rich man's parlor. The memory of his condescending, oh-so-masculine attitude made her eyes flash with irritation.

"Do you really think we can do it?" Beth asked, sighing. It was almost as though she possessed the ability to read her sister's mind. "Do you really think we can make it work, Lainey?"

"We can do anything we set our minds to." She believed that with all her heart. Why, a person had only to look at what they had accomplished thus far to know that there could be no stopping them. "You and Anna go have your breakfast," she directed with a preoccupied air. "I'll be along as soon as I'm dressed."

Beth nodded in silent agreement and carried her daughter the short distance to the cookfire. Lainey administered a few vigorous strokes to her hair, then hurriedly donned the same skirt and shirtwaist she had worn the day before. She had performed her usual daily ablutions in the wagon yesterday afternoon, but cleansing oneself with a sponge and a bowl of water could never hope to compare with a real, honest-to-goodness bath.

It would be sheer heaven to soak in a bathtub again, she mused wistfully. Hoping there would be an opportunity to do just that—and to accomplish the much needed task of washing clothes—once they reached

Guthrie, she twisted her long silken tresses up and secured them with a trio of deftly positioned hairpins. She slipped on a clean pair of white cotton stockings, buttoned on the sturdy kid walking boots she had purchased shortly before leaving Missouri, and sallied forth to meet the fateful new day.

This particular Monday in April had dawned bright and clear. The camp of hopeful, would-be settlers was just beginning to come to life as the sun's first tentative rays deepened into an all-out blaze. Women climbed sleepily down from wagons to cook breakfast, men saddled horses and harnessed teams hours before it was necessary, and children took full advantage of their parents' lack of attention to plunge themselves into a whirlwind of activity that knew no bounds. A gentle murmur quickly became a veritable roar again, with the familiar smells joining in to fill the cool morning air and remind everyone that today would see the end of their camaraderie. Whether forced or genuine, friendships had sprung up among them. But once the scramble for land began, it would be every man for himself.

The morning wore on in an endless bustle of excitement and confusion. Long before noon, the "boomers" were scurrying about in preparation for what was to come. Jockeyed into position, horses snorted and pawed impatiently at the ground. Men guided wagons into place along the starting line, anxious to be out front when the signal was given. A continuous row of horses, wagons, buggies, and carriages stretched from north to south, with a ridiculously small number of armed, blue-uniformed soldiers standing at attention directly opposite to hold back the palpitating throng.

Taking her place among the others for what would surely be the most remarkable and significant race of all time, Lainey knew she would never forget the sight before her eyes. It was almost beyond belief that she was here. She and Beth had certainly talked about this moment often enough, and yet it hadn't seemed real until now.

She stroked a soothing hand along her horse's neck, her thoughts drifting idly back over the morning. The hours had crawled by with agonizing unhaste. Anna had been unusually fretful, and her own head had begun to ache by the time she had finished double-checking the harness and securing the supplies inside the wagon. Walking down to the creek for one last time, she had been drawn into conversation with some of the other women who had gathered there. Nearly all of them were married—and therefore content to wait while their husbands took part in the run.

They had declared her to be wonderfully courageous—a few might have added "foolhardy" or even "shameful"—to be riding off across the wild Indian country in pursuit of a homestead. But she cared little for their opinions. The only thing that mattered was getting the land. To that end, she would ride like the very devil himself, endure any and all attempts to keep her from her purpose, and never forget that her future, along with Beth's and Anna's, hinged on what happened in the next few hours. *She had to succeed.*

Feeling as though her nerves were pulled tight as a bowstring, she frowned and tugged the front brim of the old black felt derby lower. It had been her father's hat; absurd though it looked, she hoped it would bring her luck. At the very least, she thought with a faint smile, it would serve to keep her from getting heatstroke.

She tossed a quick glance upward. The sun hung almost directly overhead now. Sitting astride her own mount, she shifted in the saddle and tried not to think about the thousands of others waiting as well. She adjusted her long skirts once more in an attempt at modesty, but was unable to cover her shapely, white-stockinged legs completely. Some distance behind the front line, in the midst of the strangely silent crowd, she knew Beth sat poised in readiness on the wagon seat with a squirming Anna beside her.

No one talked, at least not above a whisper. Tensions mounted, people and animals alike grew more and more impatient, and fingers clenched nervously about reins. Ahead lay a rolling, virgin prairie slashed by gullies and carpeted with bunchgrass. There were few trees, but a profusion of wildflowers bloomed everywhere, as if to say that Oklahoma could, indeed, be the earthly paradise many prayed it would be.

Lainey closed her eyes for a moment, took a deep, steadying breath, then allowed her bright sapphire gaze to wander across the faces of the riders beside her. She inhaled sharply when she saw the man, only a few yards farther down the line, who was staring back at her. His magnificent, blue-green eyes glowed warmly as they met the startled roundness of hers.

It was Ethan Holt.

She hastily looked away. What was *he* doing here? she wondered, flushing with annoyance. It couldn't be mere coincidence—or could it? No, she decided in the next moment, not when the line stretched as far as the eye could see. He must have been watching for her, spying on her. But why?

The question burned in her mind. She forced herself to refrain from stealing another glance at him. Just like the night before, however, she could feel his steady, penetrating gaze on her. Good heavens, was it possible that he was planning to follow her? The thought made her heart pound even more wildly.

She resolved to forget that he was here. Confound it, she had too much on her mind already! She couldn't think about him. She had to keep her attention focused only on the race. Ethan Holt could go to the devil for all she cared. *She* was going to Oklahoma.

The minutes ticked by on a decisive journey toward high noon. Horses were straining at the bit now, and some of the men were having trouble keeping their wagons in place. The sounds of babies crying, older children being hushed, and men muttering curses shattered the silence.

Lainey was caught up in the feverish anxiety as she gripped the reins more tightly. Tensed in readiness, she watched the cavalrymen, visibly nervous, break ranks at a passed-along signal from their commanding officer. Buglers quickly moved into position on either flank. It seemed that time stood still . . .

Finally the signal came. The buglers sounded the charge. Someone shouted "Go!"

And then all hell broke loose.

Exuberant cheers and whoops, fully equal to a band of marauding Indians, pierced the air and fairly shook the ground, sending echoes over every hill and plain. Whips cracked, horses screamed, and gunshots rang out in deafening unison as thousands of wild "boomers" charged headlong into the Territory. The great line surged forward with a mighty rush.

Lainey held on for dear life as her horse took off. Along with the other riders, she was in the very front of the throng, galloping hell-bent for leather across the prairie in a pounding of hooves and a rising cloud of dust. She had no time to think about where she was going; it was all she could do to prevent the frantically stampeding animal beneath her from colliding with one of the others.

Just ahead of her, a man screamed as he was thrown from his mount and trampled to death. She shuddered in horror and kept going. Some of the riders, unwilling to trust their luck any further, leapt from their horses only a short distance from the starting line and drove their stakes into the ground while everyone else went tearing by. Danger and disaster intensified as pandemonium reigned supreme.

Hot on the heels of that first furious wave of attack

came another and another. Prairie schooners lumbered and careened crazily, their drivers sawing away at the reins as other vehicles—buggies and carriages, buckboards and light-spring wagons—followed in confused haste. Several enterprising young men rode bicycles that wobbled comically across the uneven ground. There were those who trusted their own two legs to achieve their goal; they sprinted along in the midst of the great deluge, some of them, tragically, meeting their deaths on the same rolling countryside they had hoped to settle.

One bearded old-timer stopped just beyond the line and struck his tent, then waved cheerfully at the others who raced past. Still another hastened forward with a plow hitched behind his horse. The moment he crossed the invisible boundary, he began plowing a furrow around his new claim. But few were content with the land there at the border, believing it inferior to that which was farther south. Right or wrong, they were determined to wait, to press forward and hope that the fulfillment of their dreams lay ahead still.

The sound made by this immense caravan was like the roaring of thunder. It was a thrilling image indeed—the great Indian plains, rugged and boundless in their beauty, were dotted with covered wagons that resembled a vast fleet of ships upon a green and undulating sea. Other observers might have likened it to a massive army of ants swarming greedily across a plate of food. Whichever comparison came to mind, the sight was enough to make even the most jaded of witnesses feel an undeniable, heart-pounding excitement.

Lainey crouched low in the saddle while the wind tore at her hair and sent her skirts flying about her like a banner. True to her determination, she *was* riding like she had never ridden before. The dust stung against her eyelids, she had lost her father's hat, and she wasn't at all certain she was heading in the right direction. But still she rode on, praying that her own hopes and dreams would meet with favor that day.

She was only dimly conscious of the ear-piercing shrieks of the engine whistles as the long railway trains now steamed forth to join in the fray. Every coach was filled to overflowing with passengers crowded into the seats and aisles. People were hanging out of the windows, shouting and waving handkerchiefs. The more adventurous, or desperate, could be seen clinging to the sides and tops and platforms of the cars. Hundreds of them jumped down and scrambled off in search of claims while the train continued on its own mad dash over the prairie.

The land-hungry multitudes spread out, covering the plains for miles in all directions. Some headed due south for Guthrie, while others veered off to the east and west. The swiftest riders, most of them cowboys, disappeared from sight over the hills. The trains quickly overtook the wagons. Runners began to tire, their chests heaving and their legs feeling like lead.

A number of wagons broke down before they had carried their hopeful owners any distance at all. Some of the buggies and carriages, even those that had looked sturdy, cracked up in the deep gullies. Others overturned while the drivers were trying to avoid the treacherous holes and buffalo wallows. Horses and mules and oxen broke free from harnesses, axles snapped, and wagon poles split in two. The prairie floor was soon strewn with wrecks—and bodies, both human and animal.

Lainey was blissfully unaware of the extent of the death and destruction behind her. She had seen two men trampled, and a third seriously injured when his horse had fallen, but she was too far ahead of the wagons to know what was happening in their ranks. Her thoughts frequently drifted to Beth and Anna as she rode. She had every confidence in her sister's ability to guide the

wagon all the way to Guthrie. Beth was incredibly naive and trusting at times, but she was no fool. She
wanted a good life for Anna, and Lainey had little
doubt that she'd do whatever it took to ensure her
daughter's happiness.

*You're not meant for the kind of life to be found out
on some hardscrabble little patch of earth.* Once again,
Ethan Holt's words returned to hit her full force. She
turned her head on a sudden impulse, her eyes searching for him among the dozen or so riders who remained
about her. Most of the others had either outdistanced the
group by this time, or else had veered away in another
direction. Though scarcely fifteen minutes had passed
since the start of the race, the mass of humanity and
horseflesh had thinned considerably.

None of her companions wasted time or energy on
conversation. They all continued to ride along at a
breakneck pace, conscious of one another's presence
and yet almost completely self-absorbed. Two women,
both older than Lainey, had been a part of the group in
the beginning, but they were gone now. Lainey had
been tempted to drop out as well, to stake a claim along
the way and forget about her plans, but something deep
within her refused to surrender to the fear of ending up
empty-handed. There was still plenty of land left. She
had only to remain firm in her resolve, to be patient and
find the right place.

Facing forward again, she frowned and heaved an inward sigh. There was no sign of Ethan Holt anywhere.
She must have been wrong. Apparently, she reflected
with a nagging, unaccountable sense of disappointment,
it had never been his intention to follow her at all.

He was probably halfway to Guthrie by now. Yes, she
could well imagine him being the first man to arrive.
The one brief glimpse she had caught of him a few
miles back had told her that he was an expert horseman.

She couldn't help but wonder how much of his life had been spent in the saddle.

The irony of that particular thought was not lost on her. She ached all over. Every muscle in her body seemed to be offering up a protest for the pounding she was subjecting herself to. She had never spent so much time on a horse's back before, and certainly not while engaged in such a wild, desperate flight across the open countryside.

But she knew her own weariness was nothing compared to her mount's. The sweat-soaked animal was beginning to slow his frenzied pace. Although she would have liked nothing better than to pause and let him rest, she realized that to do so would be to risk failure of the worst kind. It was imperative that she keep going.

The minutes flew by. On and on she rode, oblivious to the fact that the other riders were pulling ahead. She was soon traveling by herself, maintaining a steady course for the land she had been told about. Too preoccupied to be concerned about her own personal safety—a woman alone in the middle of an untamed frontier, with no means of protection and all manner of men roaming the Territory—she never once bothered to look behind her. If she had, she'd have seen the lone rider who watched her every move . . .

Her hair was by now streaming down about her face and shoulders, making her regret her decision not to braid it. The sun beat down on her unprotected head, and she was very nearly unseated when the tiring horse stumbled.

But she would not stop. Not yet. Not until her instincts told her she had found home.

The landscape became greener as she journeyed farther south. The soil took on a rich, deep red color, while the sweet odor of shrubs and flowers combined with the more tangy aroma of the grass to fill the warm springtime air. Belts of timber—oak, walnut and cottonwood, blackjack and hackberry—interspersed the hilly, fertile prairie.

And then, miraculously it seemed, the Cimarron River valley lay spread out before her in all its natural glory, silently beckoning her forward. Thank God, she was here at last. *She had made it.*

"Guthrie!" she murmured in triumphant satisfaction when her gaze swept farther to view the small railroad town nestled on the banks of Cottonwood Creek. It wasn't much of a town really, but she'd known that already. And it wasn't the town itself that drew her attention; it was the land surrounding it.

" 'Head west along the river.' " She repeated the young clerk's instructions aloud. As if on cue, the faint sound of a train whistle echoed over the prairie. Her pulse raced in alarm when she spied a horde of canvas-topped wagons closing in on the town from the east. From her vantage point atop a ridge, she watched as horsemen materialized from all directions, spurring their weary mounts forward to swell the already monumental crowd of land seekers.

She looked farther and saw where the tents of Camp Guthrie had been pitched in neat rows a short distance from town. Hoping that the presence of the army signified peace and order, she hurriedly continued on her way toward the Cimarron River. There were scores of others riding across the fertile countryside as well, but she paid them no mind, not even when one of them shouted at her to stop. There was no time to waste. Wagons and horsemen and trains were converging on the town, their passengers threatening to snatch up every square inch of land.

She pressed onward still, urging the horse into a gallop that would consume his last burst of energy. She bypassed Guthrie, following a firm westerly course. Remembering Ethan Holt's advice—in spite of her annoyance with the way it had been given—she kept going until she had reached a place near the river where the landscape was particularly green and level. A creek wound its way across the site, glistening in the sunlight. There were few trees, except along the waterways, and a profusion of wildflowers bloomed in the grass-mantled fields. The air smelled sweet and fresh.

And perhaps, even more importantly, there was no one else in sight, nothing to indicate that the land had already been claimed. Far too many "sooners" had entered the Territory ahead of time and hidden themselves in bushes and ravines. They had sprouted from the landscape at the first notes of the bugle, making their own claims and thereby cheating the honest settlers out of the most desirable sections. At that very moment, all over Oklahoma, heated arguments between people claiming the same homestead or town lot were being settled with heated words and clenched fists—and even, in some instances, with drawn guns.

Lainey was relieved that, at least for the time being, her right to the land was not being questioned. She had known the minute she set eyes upon it that it was the perfect place for the farm she and Beth planned to start. There was no need to search any longer.

Her blue eyes sparkled with excitement. Reining her mount to a halt, she quickly swung down—and was dismayed when her legs buckled beneath her. She clutched at the saddle for support and cursed her own weakness.

"Easy, boy," she murmured to the horse when he tried to back away. It took several long moments for her to regain her balance; she glanced worriedly about, as though expecting someone to appear out of nowhere and challenge her claim. Once her legs felt steady enough, she led the exhausted animal the short distance to the creek and looped the reins about the branch of a cottonwood tree.

She quickly untied one of the saddlebags, withdrew the half dozen wooden stakes she had brought to mark the boundaries of the homestead, and set about driving them into the ground. Since she had no idea what one hundred and sixty acres looked like, she had to settle for merely placing the markers at regular, albeit far-spaced, intervals. They would at least serve to show that the land belonged to her. An official—more accurate—plan would be on record at the land office in Guthrie, where her claim would still have to be registered.

Feeling bone weary, and with the certainty that tomorrow would bring with it a soreness like she had never known before, she led the horse back to the creek. Her lips curved into a faint smile as she decided that the trip into Guthrie could wait awhile longer. Beth and Anna probably wouldn't arrive for hours yet. Besides, it could certainly do no harm to stay and see to it that the stakes remained undisturbed.

Belatedly lamenting the fact that she hadn't given any real thought about how the claim would be safeguarded in her absence, she sank down upon the grassy earth and swept the tangled mass of golden curls from her forehead. She saw that the horse was grazing peacefully now. After leaning forward to splash water from the creek onto her flushed face, she cupped her hands to take a drink.

The sound of approaching hoofbeats made her start in alarm. She sprang to her feet and instinctively raised a hand against the sun's blinding radiance, trying to make out the face of the rider—a man, if her eyes were any judge at this distance—who was bearing down on her. She had no gun, no way to protect herself, much less her claim. Dear Lord, what would she do if the rider turned out to be a claim jumper?

Her worst fears were realized when the man, fast closing the distance, angrily bellowed a declaration of prior ownership.

"This here's my land!"

Lainey did not immediately respond. Though her throat constricted with fear, she lifted her head to a proud angle and stood her ground as he jerked his mount to a halt before her.

"I said this here's my land!" he repeated in a menacing growl. He was big and rawboned, his dark eyes narrowed to mere slits and the lower half of his face covered by a beard of coarse, peppered black hair. From the look, not to mention the odor, of him, he had lived in the same clothes for the past week or more.

"I'm afraid you've made a mistake," Lainey pronounced, with admirable composure. "This claim is mine." Inwardly she was trembling with dread. Her thoughts tumbled and raced wildly as she wondered what she would do if the man took it in mind to reward her opposition with physical violence. It would be useless to call for help, for there was no one to hear her.

"Well then, looks like we got ourselves a little 'disagreement,' don't it?" He swung down from his horse and jerked his head toward Guthrie. "You get on out of here now, and I'll forget you was tryin' to steal my land."

"This is *not* your land. It so happens that I was here first, and I have no intention whatsoever of surrendering my claim!" Her voice held a telltale quaver, but she refused to back down. "The land was unmarked when I arrived," she pointedly informed him, "and I have a perfect right to stay. You will simply have to find another place."

She held herself rigidly erect, her blood pounding in her ears and a knot tightening in her stomach. Surely someone else would come along soon, she thought hopefully. If she could only remain calm and show this man that her determination was every bit as strong as his, then perhaps he would leave and seek another claim elsewhere. She couldn't give in. She couldn't! Heaven help her, she hadn't come all this way to have her land

stolen by some unscrupulous, foul-smelling giant who
sought to win by intimidation.

Her continued defiance sent hot color to the man's
coarse, ugly features. His gaze burned malignantly across
into hers, striking very real terror in her heart. His fingers clenched about the reins he was holding, and he
took a threatening step toward her.

"Damn your hide! Get out of here now, woman, or
else—"

"My husband is nearby, so you had better go!" she
warned breathlessly. The lie had flashed into her mind;
she prayed that it would have the desired effect. "One
scream from me will most assuredly bring him running,
and I doubt that he will think twice before killing you
where you stand!" she added for good measure.

"You ain't got a husband!" he countered, with a
sneer.

"Yes, I do! And what's more, he is an excellent
shot!"

She studied his face closely, waiting for his reaction
to this significant bit of information. He visibly wavered, trying to decide whether or not her words were
true. He narrowed his eyes at her in suspicion again.
She stood silent and still, her own gaze refusing to fall
before the furious intensity of his, her beautiful, somber
countenance betraying none of the awful panic that rose
deep within her.

Finally he turned to leave. She felt light-headed with
relief as she watched him gathering up the reins. But
her victory was short-lived. Suddenly and without warning, he ground out a blistering curse, spun back around,
and lunged toward her.

A shrill cry broke from her lips. She had no time to
escape, for the man's hands closed about her with brutal
force. He slammed her down to the ground, knocking
the breath from her lungs. She fought him like a wildcat, kicking and writhing, trying to claw at his face, but

he imprisoned her there on the grassy banks of the creek with his own body. His brawny, unwashed frame pushed her down into the fragrant earth.

"There ain't no husband!" he snarled. "And you should've run while you had the chance!"

Lainey had never known such a terrible, all-encompassing fear before. A wave of nausea threatened to overcome her as she struck out at her attacker. Trying to squirm free, she managed to scrape her nails down the side of his face. He swore again and retaliated by grabbing her wrist and yanking it cruelly above her head. His other hand began raking up her long skirts.

"No! Let me go!" she screamed hoarsely. *Please God, please don't let this happen!*

"You got this comin' to you!" His dark eyes gleamed with a sinister combination of lust and rage. "Yessiree, any woman with the gall to come out here alone's just askin' for some man to—"

"No!" She fought with all her might, but his superior size and strength, joined with the desire surging through his loins, made her struggles seem increasingly futile. He succeeded in capturing both of her wrists, and in the next instant he jammed a knee between her legs.

"Stop it!" Hot, bitter tears of defeat blinded her. She twisted frantically beneath him. "No, you—you can't do this! Please, don't!"

His only response was to take hold of the front of her shirtwaist and give a violent tug, ripping the fabric and sending the buttons flying. Lainey screamed once more and managed to pull one of her wrists free, but he quickly seized it again.

Choking back the sobs that rose in her throat, she prayed for deliverance. It never once crossed her mind to willingly submit; she knew that she would rather die than let this man have his way with her.

And then, with the same startling abruptness with which her ordeal had begun, it ended. The claim jumper's body was suddenly no longer atop hers, his weight no longer crushing her furiously defiant softness. She drew in a ragged breath and opened her eyes . . . just in time to witness the hard, punishing blow that sent him sprawling heavily into the creek.

Lainey blinked back the tears, her astonished gaze shifting to the man who had rescued her. His handsome face was a grim mask of deadly, white-hot fury as he stood ready to strike again, and the savage glint in his eyes left little doubt that he would not hesitate to finish the job.

"Mr. Holt!" She breathed in harshly with disbelief. She scrambled to her feet, clutching the torn edges of her shirtwaist together while Ethan hauled her attacker up out of the water.

"Come near her again, and I'll kill you," he promised. His voice was dangerously low and level, and he spoke the words with such conviction that the man decided, with the first evidence of wisdom he had shown thus far, to avoid an all-out battle.

"Hell, I didn't hurt her none," he muttered contemptuously. He jerked free, swiping the mud and water from his face. His eyes shot to Lainey. "But she's still on my claim!"

"That's not true!" she protested. She hastened to Ethan's side and looked up at him, her sapphire gaze wide and earnest. "I had already set my markers when he came along and tried to—"

"In case you ain't heard, there's a law against stealin' a man's land!" Her assailant bluffed loudly, still hoping to turn the situation to his advantage. "By thunder, I'll bring the law into this! The two of you'll be dancin' at the end of the rope if you don't get goin'!"

"Ride out now"—Ethan responded in a tone of deadly calm—"and you ride out alive." His hand had already inched down toward the gun holstered low on his hips.

Lainey caught her breath on a soft gasp. Her eyes widened with mingled apprehension and wonderment while they moved from one man to the other. She swallowed hard when her luminous gaze fastened on Ethan again. He looked entirely capable of carrying out his threat; it was as if a ruthless, cold-blooded stranger had taken the place of the insolent cowboy she had met the previous night. The thought made her tremble anew. She had never known anyone like him before. He was an enigma, this tall, lean-muscled Texan with eyes the color of the sea and a face that was far too handsome for his own good, and if she didn't do something, there was every likelihood that he would draw his gun and kill the man whose own coarse, mud-splattered features betrayed an alarming reluctance to back down a second time.

"Please, *go!*" she entreated, her fingers clenching within the shredded white fabric of her shirtwaist as she rounded on him. In spite of what he had tried to do to her, she had no true wish to see him dead. It never occurred to her that Ethan Holt might emerge the loser if the gunfight did take place. "You can notify the authorities in Guthrie of our 'dispute' if you like, but you can rest assured that I will also tell them about your vile, unwarranted behavior toward me!"

The bearded crook scowled darkly at her words, his eyes narrowing. Whether it was because of her warning, or because he sensed—correctly—that his opponent was not a man to be beaten, he decided not to take the risk. Muttering another curse, he spun about on his booted heel and stalked back to his horse. He hoisted his wet, foul-smelling bulk up into the saddle, then glared rancorously across at Ethan once more.

"You ain't seen the last of me, you interferin' son of a bitch!" he growled. With that one last bit of what was, in truth, only so much hot-aired bravado, he jerked on the reins and rode away.

Lainey stood watching until he had disappeared beyond the surrounding hills. When she finally turned to face Ethan, it was only to find that he was surveying her with a somber expression on his face and a strange, rather foreboding light in his eyes.

"I—I suppose I owe you a debt of gratitude, Mr. Holt," she stammered in a small voice, her gaze falling uncomfortably beneath his. She could feel the warm color flooding her face. Her hair was falling in a riotously tangled mass about her shoulders, her shirtwaist was torn beyond repair, and she winced involuntarily at a sudden, sharp pain in her hip.

"Are you all right?" Ethan asked quietly. He resisted the powerful urge to reach out to her. More than anything, he wanted to take her in his arms and give her comfort after the terrible ordeal she had suffered. But he had no right. No right at all. And after what that ugly, yellow-livered bastard had tried to do to her, he couldn't imagine she'd be too willing to let another man lay hands on her.

Ah, but his hands would be gentle, his touch soothing and warm. He would show her that not all men were like the one who, if not for his own desire to spare her further distress, would at this moment be lying in the creek with his face smashed to a bloody pulp. . . .

"I'm fine, thank you." She raised an unsteady hand to sweep the tumbling, disheveled golden curls from her forehead. Her eyes darkened at the memory of what had just passed. "I never suspected that I would be in any real danger."

"I tried to tell you it wasn't safe."

"Well then, I'm sure it must give you a considerable measure of satisfaction to know that your advice was well founded," she retorted, feeling at once foolish and defensive. Her eyes grew very round in the next instant. "How did you know where to find me? And how is it you were able to intervene so quickly when—?" She broke off, confusion giving way to renewed suspicion before he had a chance to offer a reply. "You were following me, weren't you, Mr. Holt?" she accused.

"Someone had to make sure you didn't get yourself lost. Or worse." There wasn't an ounce of contrition in either his voice or his manner.

"And so you decided to appoint yourself as my protector, is that it?" Her eyes flashed their blue fire up at him, while her whole body grew stiff with indignation. The discovery that he had been watching over her as though she were some helpless little flibbertigibbet provoked a wealth of emotions deep within her, none of which were particularly pleasant. "You didn't think me capable of looking after myself!" she went on to charge hotly.

"Something like that," Ethan allowed, with a faint smile of irony. He tried to ignore the way anger only served to heighten her beauty. She was without a doubt the most headstrong, quick-tempered woman he had ever known—and the most desirable. Even with her clothes dirty and torn and her hair looking all wild, he wanted to kiss the frown from her brow and make her forget what had happened. He swore inwardly, his traitorous heart and flesh refusing to heed his brain's determination to remain aloof. "You had no idea what you were getting into," he explained, with maddening equanimity. "I couldn't let you ride off alone."

"I see," Lainey replied through clenched teeth. Gratitude was completely forgotten now. She was furious at the thought that he considered her both naive and *his* responsibility. "Tell me, Mr. Holt—since you have been so busy chasing after me all day long, what about your own claim?"

"My brother's taking care of that."

"What do you mean?"

"He rode into Guthrie to file at the land office. Besides, you and I were headed in the same direction."

"I don't believe you!"

"It's true." His eyes made a broad, encompassing sweep of the land. "I've had my eye on this part of the Territory since I first saw it."

"And when was that?" she demanded, still far from convinced.

"A few years ago. Back when I was still wearing a badge." He gave her another brief smile. "It looks like we'll be neighbors, Miss Prescott."

"Neighbors?" Good heavens, that was impossible! And what was that he had said about wearing a badge? The thoughts whirled crazily about in her mind. Everything was happening so fast; her legs were starting to feel weak again, and she wondered if Beth and Anna were all right. As if all that wasn't enough to make her head ache, Ethan Holt was staring at her with a good deal more interest than she would have liked. *Neighbors?*

"It's getting late. The town will be a regular hotbed by now." He strode past her to his horse, which had joined hers beside the creek. Reaching into one of the saddlebags, he withdrew a clean, blue cotton shirt. He unrolled it and held it out to her. "Put this on."

"No, thank you," she declined, with a haughtiness that was in absurd contrast to her bedraggled appearance.

"Put it on," insisted Ethan. Although his expression remained perfectly serious, his eyes held a touch of wry amusement. "You'll cause bloodshed if you ride into Guthrie like that."

Her own gaze dropped to where her hands still clutched the torn edges of her shirtwaist across the full, delectably rounded swell of her breasts. Her ribbon-edged chemise remained intact, but it revealed almost as much as it covered up. And she had brought no extra clothing with her.

She glanced hastily back to Ethan. Once again, the

look in his gleaming turquoise eyes made her feel at once nervous and oddly excited. It was an entirely different sensation than what she had felt when the claim jumper had ogled her.

A liquid warmth seemed to start somewhere in the vicinity of her abdomen and spread slowly outward. She was thoroughly dismayed to realize that she *wanted* Ethan Holt to look at her the way he was doing. Dear Lord, had she left her modesty behind in Missouri?

Without another word, she marched forward, snatched the shirt from him, and whirled about so that her back was turned toward him. She could feel his eyes on her as she drew the shirt on over her torn garment and buttoned it up.

"We're not what you'd call a good match," he observed, noting that the sleeves hung several inches too long and the tail reached all the way down to her knees. She looked almost like a child standing there, all prim and proper, with that shirt of his swallowing her up. But there was certainly nothing childlike about her figure. No, by damn, she was all woman.

"Why, I—I should say not!" Uncertain whether his remark was about her disposition or her size, she chose to believe the latter. "I may not be as big as you, Mr. Holt, but I can certainly hold my own whenever the circumstances demand it."

"Can you?" He watched as she rolled up the sleeves and pivoted to face him again.

"I can indeed. That is, most of the time, anyway," she amended, recalling with vivid clarity her recent brush with disaster.

Gathering up her thick tresses, she wound them tightly into a coil and tucked the whole mass upward with a skillful twist of her wrist. She was thankful that he had refused to take no for an answer regarding the shirt; she felt more like her old self now that she was at least decently attired. In fact, she mused with a return of her usual good sense, she had probably only imagined the familiarity in her self-appointed champion's gaze. And his actions that day had in all likelihood been prompted by nothing more than an adherence to the code of the West she had heard so much about. He had been concerned about her the same as he would have been concerned about any woman traveling alone across the open countryside.

That was it, of course, she decided, taking comfort from the thought. He was a gentleman after all. Why, it was enough to renew one's faith in mankind— especially given the horrible misconduct of the man who had ridden away a few minutes ago.

"Are you and your brother planning to start a farm, too?" she queried in an attempt at a normal, less personal conversation. In spite of her conclusions about him, she instinctively kept a safe distance as she started toward her horse.

"No, a ranch. Cattle and horses." His smile this time was wonderfully disarming. "Where I come from, it's the only honorable profession for a man."

"And where *do* you come from?" Strangely enough, she realized she was curious to know more about his life—past, present, and future. Though why she would want to encourage any friendship between them was a complete mystery to her.

"Texas." That one word held all the pride and fondness he would always feel for his homeland. "Fort Worth, to be exact." Stepping forward, he reached out to help her mount.

She was determined not to let him see how much his proximity affected her, but she couldn't prevent a dull flush from staining her cheeks. The moment his strong hands curled about her slender, uncorseted waist, she felt as though an invisible current passed between them. Her eyes flew up to meet his.

"I think I can manage by myself, Mr. Holt," she murmured unevenly. She tried to move away, but he held fast.

"I think you're too independent for your own good, Miss Prescott."

He said it without a trace of criticism. As a matter of fact, Lainey could have sworn there was an undercurrent of affection in his voice. The thought made her color deepen again. She looked down toward the ground and silently cursed the returning weakness of her knees. It was all she could do not to clutch at Ethan's arms for support.

"Please, Mr. Holt. I—"

"My name is Ethan."

"Why, I couldn't possibly call you by your first name!" she protested, her wide, shocked gaze drawn up to his once more.

"Why not? We're neighbors now, remember?"

His fingers tightened about her waist, and he gently pulled her closer until they were almost touching. His eyes bored down into hers, the heat of his body scorching her skin even through the several layers of clothing. Her heart took to fluttering wildly, and although an inner voice warned her of an altogether different kind of danger than she had faced before, she couldn't seem to think clearly. She stood as if rooted to the spot, holding her breath while she waited for Ethan to say or do something to break the spell.

Her sapphire gaze moved with a will of its own to his mouth. *Was he going to kiss her?* She felt a twinge of mingled guilt and trepidation for even daring to consider the possibility, but nevertheless swayed toward him. She had no idea how close she came in that moment to being thoroughly and quite literally swept off her feet. . . .

"We're going to be seeing a lot of each other, Lainey Prescott," Ethan decreed softly. "You may as well get used to the idea."

She opened her mouth to answer, but was silenced when, with surprising ease, he abruptly lifted her to the saddle. Her hands shook as she gathered up the reins, and she refused to acknowledge the keen sense of disappointment she felt. She watched Ethan out of the corner of her eye as he mounted his own horse.

"Stay close," he commanded, with all the authority of someone who had a perfect right to do so.

"You've done enough 'looking after' for one day, Mr. Holt," retorted Lainey, bristling anew. "Once again, I am profoundly grateful for your assistance, but I have no intention of attaching myself to you!" To emphasize the point, she tossed him one last defiant glare, then reined about and urged her horse into a gallop across the rolling, sunlit grasslands.

Ethan swore underneath his breath, his eyes glinting hotly. With a determination that was more than a match for Lainey's, he jerked the front brim of his hat lower and took off after her.

Chapter 3

Guthrie was one gigantic, teeming mass of people and horses and wagons. Pandemonium reigned supreme there in all its bitter and unrestrained glory. Only that morning, the town had been nothing more than a watering stop for the Atchison, Topeka, and Santa Fe trains chugging across miles and miles of prairie wilderness; within the space of a few short hours, the tiny hamlet had been transformed into an exuberant city of more than ten thousand eager, land-hungry souls. Guthrie was certainly not unique in its frenetic birth upon the Western plains, but there would be few communities able to lay claim to the sort of genesis witnessed that day.

Lainey felt more than a trifle overwhelmed to be a part of it. She rode alongside Ethan in silence, her gaze very round and sparkling with fascination as they drew closer to the town proper. They had already passed too many fellow rushers to count. People were running and riding every which way, white tents and dusty wagon bonnets dotted the landscape like a huge flock of birds settling upon the hillsides and in the valley, and the new spring wildflowers had been crushed beneath a horde of contestants scrambling for quarter sections or the choicest town lots.

The small land office in Guthrie was visible in all directions—a singular beacon to all boomers scurrying about in the midst of the sun-drenched plains. Finished and painted a bright red earlier that same day, it was now besieged by a multitude clamoring to file claims. Even before the trains had rolled to a full stop at the station, the majority of the passengers had leapt off to pound their stakes and thereby seize the lots that had already been marked off by the federal surveyors. And immediately after that first train had come the horsemen and runners and wagons, swarming across the little town to erect a city of tents and ramshackle, pitched-up frame buildings, a city that swelled larger and grew more raucous with each passing hour.

The noise was almost deafening. Lainey was secretly glad of Ethan's presence beside her while her senses reeled at the commotion. In truth, she was ashamed at herself for having attempted to run away from him. She had half expected him to rail angrily at her when he'd caught up with her. But he had merely trained his mount's stride into an equal pace with hers, his handsome features inscrutable and his gaze fastened straight ahead.

Now that they had arrived in Guthrie, she realized that being the recipient of his "caretaking" wasn't such a bad thing after all. She swallowed hard and wondered how she would ever manage to find Beth and Anna in the crowd, wondered as well how she would be able to file on her claim when the irregular line that had formed in front of the land office stretched all the way down Guthrie's main, choked dirt street and around the corner.

"I had no idea there would be so many people," she worriedly remarked to Ethan, forced to raise her voice in order to be heard. "I don't know how I'm going to find my sister!"

Her heart filled with dread at the thought of shy, sensitive Beth trying to make her way among this throng, surging furiously across every square inch of the town. A number of fights had already broken out—the worst ones concerning the "sooners," who had somehow contrived to get there ahead of the others—and it seemed that everyone was arguing and shouting and generally raising hell. There was even a fierce, highly physical battle taking place between two women attired in bright-colored satin dresses that were scandalously short and low-cut. These soiled doves were far too intent upon scratching each other's eyes out to care that their heated disagreement was so public—not that they would have cared otherwise. Lainey shuddered at the sight while an appreciative audience of men urged them on with lewd comments and laughs.

"We'll find her," Ethan leaned closer to promise. He gave her a quick yet bolstering smile, then sobered again and ordered, "Come on!"

She obediently followed his lead as he guided his horse through the crowd, toward one of the few spots not occupied by anyone at present. It was on the other side of the depot, where the four surrounding lots were unclaimable due to the railroad company's right-of-way. Once there, Ethan dismounted, his hands already closing about Lainey's waist before she could decline his offer of assistance. He pulled her down before him and bent his head so that his lips were close to her ear.

"Wait here with the horses. You'll be safe enough if you stay put." His eyes made a brief sweep of the area before he suddenly frowned. "Do you have a gun?"

"Of course not!"

"Take this." He drew one of the six-shooters from his holster and thrust it into her hands. "If anyone makes a move toward you, shoot them." His mouth twitched before he added dryly, "Aim low."

"But what about my sister?" she demanded, her head spinning. "How will you know—?"

"I'll know."

He said it with such certainty that she could not doubt him. She recalled his confession that he had first seen her in Arkansas City; she could only suppose that he had seen Beth as well. Beth wouldn't recognize *him*, of course, since the two of them had never met, but she knew he'd think of a way to earn her trust.

She nervously fingered the gun in her hands and watched Ethan disappear into the crowd. Any guilt or resentment she felt as a result of his insistence upon finding Beth was dispelled by the certainty that he would be successful. And that was really all that mattered.

Releasing a long, pent-up sigh, she leaned against the side of the small wooden building and closed her eyes. It struck her again that she must have been completely out of her mind to have uprooted Beth and Anna . . . to have dragged them halfway across the country in pursuit of a dream that would probably turn out to be a nightmare. What in heaven's name had ever possessed her to think that *she*, of all people, could make a success of this mad venture?

She sighed once more and opened her eyes to peer toward the bustling crowd. It was useless to berate herself and regret the decision she had made. Beth and Anna were out there somewhere right now. Fervently praying that they would all be together soon, she was surprised to feel an ironic smile tugging at her lips. Ethan Holt was an unlikely guardian angel, but a forceful one. She could well imagine him doing whatever it took to find Beth.

"Have you a claim to file, young woman?"

Lainey turned her head to see a slender, well-dressed man of perhaps forty surveying her from behind a pair of thick-lensed wire glasses. She straightened, her brow creasing into a slight frown of puzzlement. He looked harmless, and anyway, she had forgotten that she was holding Ethan's gun.

"I beg your pardon?"

"Have you a claim to file?" he repeated, with all politeness. He eyed the revolver warily, but maintained his composure. "If so, then may I suggest that you allow me to represent you in your endeavor?" He handed her a small card upon which he had listed his occupation as lawyer and his name as Oliver T. Calhoun. "My esteemed partner and I have recently launched our practice here in Guthrie. For a small fee, we are prepared to file the necessary legal documents for our clients and therefore ensure that their interests are protected to the full extent of the law."

"Well, I—I *do* have a claim to file," Lainey admitted hesitantly.

"Then I would consider it an honor and a privilege to represent you, Miss—?" His inquiring gaze fastened on her face. She was one of the most beautiful young women he had ever seen, and yet he couldn't allow himself the luxury of thinking of her in that context. If she accepted his offer, she would be a client and nothing more. Still, he was only human.

"Prescott," she finally answered. "Miss Lainey Prescott." She sensed that she could trust the man. And the prospect of avoiding the hours-long wait in line at the land office was attractive in the extreme. A sudden image of Ethan Holt's disapproving countenance flashed into her mind. It made her all the more determined to accept the man's offer. "Very well, Mr. Calhoun. I should like to have your help. How much will it cost me?"

"A mere two dollars, Miss Prescott."

"Agreed."

Recalling a favorite saying of her father's about a fool and his money, she nonetheless took a small leather purse from her saddlebag and counted out the required amount. Oliver Calhoun produced a document for her to sign, then listened carefully to her description of her claim's whereabouts.

"The location does not have to be exact," he assured her. His mouth curved into a faint, wry smile. "Possession truly is nine-tenths of the law in the Territory, you see. I would advise you to return to your claim at once, Miss Prescott, and set about making the improvements required by the terms of the agreement. I will notify you of your claim's status in the near future."

"Thank you, Mr. Calhoun."

"The pleasure was all mine," he replied, meaning every word. He nodded at her before taking himself off to procure another client, all the while musing that, for him, the day had already proven a great success. It wasn't often that he encountered lovely, unattached women such as Lainey Prescott. The thought of seeing her again brought another rare smile to his lips. At least he'd have something to look forward to in the difficult days ahead.

Lainey, meanwhile, regretted her impulsiveness only a little. Her thoughts returned to Beth—and to the man she had entrusted to find her. Ethan Holt always seemed to be in the right place at the right time that day. Just when she needed him most, he materialized to take charge. It stung her pride to realize that she kept allowing him to do so. If they truly were going to be neighbors, she'd have to prove to him that she could be every bit as self-sufficient as she had claimed.

The heat became uncomfortable as the minutes crawled by. She grew increasingly tired of waiting, and the shrill whistle from the latest train caused her to jump. New arrivals were forced to battle their way across a mob of armed settlers, stakes and tents, and roped-off claims. Soldiers from Camp Guthrie were in attendance to keep the peace, but there was no hope of their being able to do much good in the face of such overwhelming odds. Already, the rough characters who had come to take advantage of the confusion were entrenching themselves in the city.

The roar of humanity intensified, the siege deepening into such chaos that Lainey began to fear Ethan would never be able to make it back. She slumped wearily against the building and fought against a loss of faith. And then, miraculously, she heard her sister's voice rising above the din.

"Beth!" she called back, her gaze anxiously searching. She felt light-headed with relief when she saw the trio advancing upon her. Beth was walking beside Ethan, while little Anna was riding high upon his broad, entirely capable shoulders.

"Lainey!" Beth raced forward to embrace her sister. "Oh, Lainey. I was afraid we'd never find you!"

"Thank God you're all right!" Lainey said, hugging her tight. She quickly drew away to study her face. "Did you have any trouble getting here? What about the wagon? How long have you—?"

"Everything is fine!" Beth assured her, with a soft laugh. She turned to direct a grateful smile up at Ethan, who had come forward to join them. He lifted Anna down from his shoulders and held her in his arms while Beth sang his praises. "Mr. Holt was truly a godsend! He rescued us before we met with disaster, which I'm quite sure we would have done if not for his intervention!"

Lainey's eyes flew up to his face. He relinquished the exhausted, quietly whimpering Anna into the care of her mother before looking back to her. His own eyes appeared to be brimming with humor, but he said nothing.

Confound him, she thought in annoyance. He was waiting for her to thank him. They both knew it. And she had very little choice in the matter.

"Well, Mr. Holt," she intoned dutifully, "it seems you've done it again."

"Have I?" came his nonchalant reply. He extended a hand toward her, his fathomless, blue-green gaze never breaking contact with the luminosity of hers. "I'll take that now."

"Take—?" she started to echo in bewilderment, then

realized that he was referring to the gun. She frowned at it in distaste as she placed it into his hand.

"Hit anything?" he queried wryly.

"No, nor did I attempt to!" she retorted.

"Mr. Holt told me you were successful in finding a claim," Beth remarked, her own features showing the strain of a difficult journey. "Do you suppose we might head there now?" She cradled Anna closer and smiled warmly at her sister. "I knew you would do it, Lainey. I am so very proud of you."

"You deserve more credit than I," contended Lainey. She battled sudden tears. "I was so worried about you!" She pulled her close again before asking, "Where did you leave the wagon?"

"Mr. Holt's brother is watching it for us," explained Beth, flushing slightly. "It isn't far."

"His brother?" Lainey repeated, her gaze moving back to Ethan. "But I thought he was—?"

"He was already on his way out of town when I came across him." Gathering up the reins of both horses, he told her, "I'll stay and file your claim for you. Travis will see that you get back out to your place."

"That won't be necessary," she replied. As though she knew what his reaction would be, she grew defensive. "It so happens that I have employed a lawyer to represent me at the land office. Mr. Calhoun is a perfect gentleman, and I have complete confidence in him!"

"I hope you're right," said Ethan, his tone skeptical. "You've still got two months before the deadline. If you haven't heard anything from this 'perfect gentleman' of yours by then, you might just find yourself facing a battle in the courts."

Without another word, he began leading the horses away from the depot, toward the outer fringes of the crowd. Lainey took Anna from Beth and followed quickly after him.

"My sister and I can find our own way back to the

wagon," she insisted. Her eyes flashed when he did not answer. "Did you hear me, Mr. Holt? I said—"

"I heard you, Miss Prescott." The merest hint of a smile touched his lips. "You'll ride with me."

Before she could ask him what he meant, he stopped and turned to Beth. She allowed him to place her on Lainey's horse. He gently but firmly peeled the fair-haired toddler, who had fallen into the sound sleep of the innocent by now, from her aunt's grasp and conveyed her upward into her mother's waiting arms.

"What are you doing?" Lainey demanded. "Beth said the wagon wasn't far."

"It will be safer this way."

Disregarding the rebellious expression on her face, he seized her about the waist and lifted her abruptly to the saddle. He wasted no time in mounting up behind her. She suffered a sharp intake of breath when her backside came into contact with the lean hardness of his thighs. He clamped one arm about her waist and reached around her with the other to skillfully maneuver the reins.

Though nettled by his dictatorial behavior, Lainey knew it was useless to argue with him. She consoled herself with the thought that Beth was much too tired to fight her way through the mob again on foot. So, for now, Ethan Holt's escort could not be avoided. But as soon as this day was through, she vowed silently, she would put an end to his unsolicited protection. She was already far too deeply in his debt.

Ethan avoided the more congested areas as they rode across Guthrie; still, it was no easy task. Thousands of people were jammed into a town that was never intended to hold more than a few hundred. And it was only getting worse.

Lainey strained forward more than once in an attempt to avoid being pressed into such shocking intimacy with Ethan's muscular warmth, but he merely tightened his arm about her. Her face flamed when, in the process of squirming about to find a more comfortable position, she felt the undeniable evidence of his manhood against her hips. She stiffened, naively hoping that he hadn't noticed.

He had, of course—all too well. With an inward groan, he battled a wave of pure, hot-blooded desire and cursed himself for a fool.

The trip, though relatively short in distance, took more than half an hour to complete. Lainey's face brightened when she spied the familiar wagon parked beneath the trees along Cottonwood Creek. A young man with light brown hair and rakishly attractive features hastened forward to greet them. The resemblance to Ethan was immediately noticeable.

"I was beginning to think you'd decided to stay on and treat the ladies to supper," he teased Ethan. Nearly as tall as his brother, Travis Holt was the younger of the two by some three years. His green eyes twinkled up at Beth when he moved to help her dismount. "Let me take her, Mrs. Baker," he offered, with a nod toward the slumbering Anna.

"Thank you, Mr. Holt," murmured Beth, a becoming color rising to her face. It always sounded odd to hear people call her by her mother's maiden name. It seemed particularly odd when *this* man did it.

She took care not to waken her daughter as she transferred her into Travis Holt's care. Once he had the child cradled in the crook of his arm, he reached up and slipped his other arm about Beth's waist. She swiftly disengaged herself the moment her feet touched the ground.

Lainey slid down without waiting for Ethan's assistance. Turning her back on him, she went to retrieve her horse. She glanced at the man standing beside Beth and found herself mentally comparing him to his brother. It

troubled her to realize that the conclusion ran unequiv-
ocally in the elder Holt's favor.

"Lainey, this is Mr. Holt. Mr. Travis Holt," Beth announced shyly. "Mr. Holt, this is my sister, Miss Lainey
Prescott." With a tentative smile, she took Anna from
him and headed for the wagon to place the baby on a
quilt spread inside.

"Pleased to make your acquaintance, Miss Prescott,"
said Travis. He replaced the hat atop his head, his gaze
following Beth. "I'm glad Ethan met up with you."

"I am grateful for your help with the wagon, Mr.
Holt," Lainey responded in all sincerity. She led the
horse over to the wagon and tied the reins to the back.
It was clear that she was impatient to be on her way.
The two brothers exchanged a quick look.

"We'll ride along with you," Ethan pronounced, already mounting up again. Travis hurried to fetch his
own horse from beneath the trees.

"No, Mr. Holt, you will not," Lainey disputed sternly.
"I will think of some way to repay you for everything
you have done, but it is time we parted ways. *For
good.*" She climbed up to the wagon seat, waited until
Beth had done the same, then gathered up the reins. The
horses, having enjoyed a much needed rest beside the
creek, snorted and pawed at the grassy earth in anticipation. "Good-bye," she said, her voice holding a ring of
finality.

Releasing the brake, she snapped the reins together
above the horses' heads and set off on a westerly
course. Ethan was torn between amusement and exasperation at her stubbornness. Remembering the way it
had felt to hold her against him, he frowned and settled
his hat lower on his head.

"Well?" Travis prompted, swinging up into the saddle. "Are we going after them or not?"

Ethan's only response was to mutter an ear-singing

curse. Unscathed, Travis gave a low chuckle and shifted negligently in the saddle.

"Who the hell would've thought we'd end up playing nursemaid to a couple of angels?" he drawled.

"Any objections?" Ethan shot back.

"Not a one, boss man. Not a one." Grinning broadly, he followed his brother's example as he touched his heels to the horse's flanks and gave unhurried chase to the wagon heading away from the brand-new frontier metropolis of Guthrie.

It was late in the afternoon by the time Lainey pulled the team to a halt beside the creek that meandered across their claim. She was relieved to see that the stakes she had set were still in place. She had no intention of telling Beth what had happened earlier; there was nothing to be gained by alarming her. And anyway, she reflected at the memory of Ethan's intervention, she seriously doubted the claim jumper would ever be inclined to return and face her "husband's" wrath again.

She set the brake and turned to her sister. A smile tugged at her lips as she swept a wayward curl from her forehead. She had almost forgotten how green the countryside was here near the Cimarron.

"Isn't it beautiful, Beth?"

"Why, it's everything I hoped it would be!" Beaming with pleasure, Beth cast a maternal glance over her shoulder to where her tiny daughter still slept. Tears glistened in her eyes when she met Lainey's gaze once more. "The three of us are going to have a good life here," she predicted, with emotion. "I just know it! Anna is certain to thrive in this fresh air and sunshine." She looked out over the fertile river valley and sighed. "It *is* beautiful, Lainey. And it will be even more so once we get a house built and a garden planted."

"We'll talk about that later. For now, we've got to make camp for the night."

She scrambled down from the wagon and set about unhitching the team. Intent as she was upon freeing the animals from the harness, she failed to take notice of the two riders disappearing over one of the nearby hills.

"Lainey, how did you meet Mr. Holt?" Beth unexpectedly asked. She gathered up her skirts to alight with a more graceful descent than her sister.

"What difference does it make?" She didn't want to talk about Ethan Holt. She didn't even want to think about him. Until now, Beth had seemed to realize that.

"You know, I was quite surprised when he called out to me in town today," the petite blonde confided, with a smile. "I had never seen him before, and yet he claimed to be a friend of yours. Friend or not, I was exceedingly grateful that he led me to you." She shook out her travel-worn skirts, only to cough gently at the cloud of dust that accompanied her efforts. In spite of the difficult journey she had undertaken that day, her appearance was not nearly so disheveled as Lainey's. "Where on earth did you get that shirt?" she now queried, her gaze alight with a mixture of humor and bemusement.

"I . . . Mr. Holt was kind enough to let me borrow it." Lainey decided to answer truthfully, then quickly changed the subject. "I'm afraid we'll have to continue sleeping in the wagon for the time being. I'll ride into town in a few days and see if I can arrange for the delivery of some lumber and nails, and find someone to help us with the building. Our house won't be much at first, of course, but at least we'll have a roof over our heads."

She led the horses the short distance to the creek and secured the reins with another long wooden stake. The hard-driven animals drank thirstily before starting to graze at the fragrant grass. Lainey returned to the wagon and untied the bucket that hung at the back.

"You can fill this while I fetch some wood for a fire,"

she instructed her sister in an undertone, mindful of the little girl sleeping inside.

"Surely you don't intend for us to build the house ourselves?" Beth challenged belatedly. It was clear from the tone of her own lowered voice that she viewed the notion as preposterous. "We know nothing about—"

"We'll have to hire someone. That might not be easy, given the fact that everyone else will be in need of reasonable laborers. But we'll have to manage as best we can. It's high time we learned to stand on our own, Beth."

"What about Mr. Holt? I'm sure he would be more than willing to lend assistance. After all, he did seem—"

"Absolutely *not!*" Lainey virtually shouted. Coloring at the unintentional vehemence of her words, she pivoted about with the bucket still in her hands and marched away toward the creek. Beth, however, would not be put off so easily.

"Perhaps this isn't the best time for us to discuss the matter," she conceded, with a sigh, following close behind. "I'm sure you must be exhausted, dearest Lainey. I certainly don't wish to add to your troubles. But since the Holt brothers are going to be our neighbors, what harm can it do to at least consider seeking their advice?"

"No," Lainey reiterated firmly. She knelt and dipped the bucket into the flowing stream. "We came to Oklahoma to start a new life. And that's just what we're going to do. On our own. Without the help of Ethan Holt or anyone else."

Beth was forced to admit defeat. She knew from a lifetime of experience that it was entirely futile to argue with her sister when she had set her mind upon a certain course. Just as their father had always said, she mused with an indulgent smile, Lainey should have been the firstborn. She was stronger and brighter and wonderfully self-assured. Lainey would never have let herself make the mistake of falling in love with the wrong man. The thought sent a shadow across her delicate, heart-shaped countenance.

"Oh, Beth. I'm sorry!" Lainey apologized, her eyes full of contrition as she stood in time to witness her sister's distress. Believing herself to be the cause of it, she hastily lowered the bucket to the ground and caught her up in a warm embrace. "You're right, of course. I—I *am* much too tired to discuss it rationally. I promise you, we'll talk about everything tomorrow."

"Does that mean you're going to tell me how you met Mr. Holt?" Beth parried, with an affectionately teasing smile.

Lainey took up the bucket again and frowned in mock reproof.

"I scarcely know the man," she declared evasively. Then she relented enough to disclose, "Our acquaintance is neither very long nor very close. I encountered him quite by accident only last night."

"What a startling coincidence then that he and his brother should be claiming land so near ours."

"Call it what you will," said Lainey in an obvious attempt to dismiss the subject as she headed back to the wagon, "I have no intention whatsoever of deepening our 'friendship' with them."

Anna chose that opportune moment to announce her awakening with a shrill cry that echoed across the surrounding plains. Beth hurried forward to soothe her daughter, leaving Lainey to battle the unbidden and highly disturbing memory of Ethan Holt's virile, hard-muscled body pressed against her soft curves.

Later that evening, after they had finished their supper and tucked Anna into bed beneath the wagon's canopy, the two sisters sat together before the fire and listened to the sounds of the night. Somehow, the stars appeared to be burning more brightly in the sky above now that they were home. Other campfires glowed in the distance, reminding them of the fact that they were far from alone on the newly settled prairie.

A coyote's mournful howl rose in the cool, smoke-scented air. Lainey's eyes widened, and she knew a moment's apprehension before she remembered the rifle that lay in readiness beneath the wagon seat. It was unlikely they would have need of it, but she was nevertheless glad she had learned how to handle it—not with any real degree of marksmanship, but at least with the basic skills necessary to get by.

Beth's thoughts evidently followed a similiar course.

"Perhaps one of us should fetch the gun," she whispered, prompting Lainey to smile. She doubted that either wild animals or vicious outlaws would care to eavesdrop upon their conversation.

"I'll get it."

When she returned with the rifle a few moments later, she found Beth stifling a yawn and making a visible effort to stay awake. The day had been long and arduous. Tomorrow would be difficult as well.

"Go to bed, Beth," she directed kindly. "I'm going to stay out here for a while."

"Are you sure you don't mind?"

"Not at all. Go on now. Anna may waken and need you."

Beth required no further persuasion. She kissed her sister good night and trudged wearily over to the wagon, where she soon joined her beloved daughter in a deep and dreamless sleep.

Lainey heaved a sigh and cast a swift, encompassing glance about her. One of the women back at the camp had warned her about snakes. She had seen none so far, but the mere possibility of sighting one was enough to send a shiver up her spine.

In spite of her own fatigue, she felt unaccountably restless. So much had happened within the past twenty-four hours; she couldn't help but wonder what other surprises fate had in store for her. There were so many things to be done—so many acres to be plowed, and seeds to be planted, and not nearly enough pennies to be pinched. In fact, their funds were now alarmingly low. She hadn't wanted to worry Beth, but the situation could turn desperate unless they managed to make their present supplies last longer than the week they had counted on.

What about Mr. Holt? Beth had asked in all innocence. The thought of running to him for help . . . well, she would be hanged before she'd do it.

Unwilling to examine her feelings for a man she had known such a brief time, or why those feelings already ran to the extreme, she climbed to her feet again and wandered away from the fire. She and Beth had washed up before supper, but she longed to do a more thorough job of bathing. Her gaze drifted toward the creek.

It took only a few seconds of contemplation before she turned her steps in that direction. Musing that she'd probably catch her death of cold, she impulsively leaned the rifle against a tree and began unbuttoning the fresh shirtwaist she had donned before supper. Ethan's borrowed shirt lay folded neatly upon the wagon seat. She would return it. Eventually.

Concealed within the darkness, and far enough away from the fire's illuminating glow to feel secure in her privacy, she stripped off her blouse and skirt, and then her shoes and stockings. She was tempted to remove her chemise and drawers, but told herself she was being quite daring enough for one evening. Her eyes made another vigilant sweep of the area. It was now or never.

She dipped a toe into the water. It was downright chilly, so much so that she nearly abandoned the whole idea. But she persevered, stepping carefully into the stream with both feet. Her hands moved up to loosen her hair. The luxuriant, honey-gold tresses came tumbling down about her face and shoulders. She shivered and smiled at the thought of what she must look like, standing there half-naked in the creek at that late hour of the night.

Beth would probably insist that she was suffering the aftereffects of too much sun and riding. And to lend further proof of her "madness" was the fact that it had sprung to life in the middle of a rugged, starlit wilderness that could be holding an untold number of dangers.

Perhaps she *had* taken momentary leave of her senses, thought Lainey. Whatever the case, it felt wickedly pleasurable to be so free. She knelt and began splashing the water across her arms, shivering all the more as her undergarments became soaked.

She had no warning before the deep, familiar voice sounded behind her.

Chapter 4

"I think you should get out now, Miss Prescott."

A gasp of shocked alarm broke from Lainey's lips. She jerked her head about, her heart pounding wildly as she spied the outline of a man standing only a few feet away on the creek bank. It was not so dark that she couldn't make out his face; she would have known him anywhere.

"*Mr. Holt!*" she said with disbelief. A fiery blush stained her cheeks while her eyes grew round as saucers. "What in heaven's name are you doing here?" She instinctively tried to rise to her feet, only to lose her balance. A small, strangled cry escaped her as she went toppling back into the water. She landed on her derriere with a loud splash, her long hair streaming across her face and her bare, shapely legs sprawling immodestly.

Ethan tossed his hat aside and crossed the distance between them in two long strides. Oblivious to the fact that his own clothing was bound to end up as wet as hers, he scooped her up in his arms and bore her back to the shadows beneath the trees.

"Put me down!" she demanded in a furious whisper. Her eyes flew toward the wagon. "Let me go!" She struggled against him, pushing at his broad chest in an effort to make him release her.

"Damn it, woman! Are you trying to get yourself killed?" Ethan challenged between clenched teeth.

All too aware of her damp and scantily clad charms

as she squirmed within his grasp, he was torn between the urge to lash out at her and the far more tempting desire to sweep her closer. He reluctantly set her on her feet, though his hands came round her upper arms. His warm fingers burned upon her silken flesh. He frowned down at her in the darkness, trying not to let his penetrating gaze stray downward . . . to where the thin white cotton of her chemise had been rendered virtually transparent.

"What if I hadn't been the one to find you like this?" he charged in a low tone edged with anger. "You little fool! You might have been—"

"How dare you scold me!" she hotly cut him off, trembling with both cold and indignation. "I have a perfect right to do as I please upon my own land, Mr. Holt, and if I please to take a bath, then I will most certainly do so!" She brushed the hair from her face and made another unsuccessful attempt to pull away. "*You* are the one deserving of a reprimand. What did you think you were doing, sneaking up on me like that? I can think of no good reason why you should decide to intrude upon me in the middle of the night."

"I came to make sure you were all right," he ground out. He suddenly released her as if the contact had truly scorched him. His eyes darkened as he watched her fold her arms across her breasts. When he spoke again, it was in a deceptively quiet, level tone. "I'm sorry if I frightened you. But I meant it when I said it's dangerous to let down your guard. There are far too many men around like the one who attacked you this afternoon."

"I don't need you to remind me of that!"

"What you *need*, Lainey Prescott, is someone to shake some sense into that pretty head of yours. You don't belong here. And if you weren't so naive, or just plain stubborn, you'd admit it."

Lainey was at first stunned into speechlessness by his words. In the next instant, however, her narrowed, blazing eyes shot invisible daggers up at him. She balled her hands into fists and planted them on her hips, too infuriated at the moment to realize that her wet garments concealed little from his smoldering, blue-green gaze.

"I've had quite enough of your high-handedness, Ethan Holt! No one asked you to look after me. I am a grown woman, and I certainly don't require a guardian. Find someone else upon whom to bestow your 'protection'—I'm sure there are scores of helpless females who would be eternally grateful for the honor. But I would appreciate it if from this day onward you would leave me alone!" She flung an arm in the general direction of the wagon where Beth and Anna slept on, ordering imperiously, "Now get off my claim!"

She had no idea how utterly beguiling she looked—or how much fuel her proud defiance added to the fire in Ethan's blood. For several long moments, he remained silent and motionless. The only indication of the battle that raged within him was a single muscle twitching in the clean-shaven ruggedness of his left cheek. His eyes raked hungrily over her, drinking in the sight of her near nakedness.

Her chemise and drawers were plastered damply to her body, outlining every voluptuous curve. Even in the darkness, her beauty was undeniable. And to make matters worse, he could see the way her full, rose-tipped breasts swelled beneath the clinging wet fabric.

Lainey crimsoned in angry embarrassment as a result of his bold scrutiny. In spite of her present, chilled condition, she felt herself grow warm all over. A warning bell sounded in her brain. She became desperate to avoid what they both knew to be inevitable.

Without pausing to consider the wisdom of her actions, she suddenly bent down and grabbed hold of the rifle she had left beside the tree. Her hands shook when she lifted it. She tried to aim it at Ethan, not entirely sure what she would do once she succeeded, but he wasn't about to let things get that far.

She cried out softly as he snatched the gun from her hands. He seized her wrist in an iron grip, then allowed the rifle to slip back to the ground. Everything happened so fast, Lainey had no time to struggle. She gasped as she found herself yanked roughly forward. Ethan's strong, sinewy arms wrapped about her, crushing her startled softness against his muscular warmth.

Without warning, his lips came crashing down upon hers. She moaned in protest and made a belated attempt to escape, but to no avail. His arms tightened, holding her captive within his embrace while his mouth ravaged the sweetness of hers.

Lainey had been kissed before. Or at least she *thought* she had been kissed before. No man had ever swept her into his arms the way Ethan Holt had so masterfully done, and—heaven help her—no man had ever kissed her with such skill and passion.

His lips, warm and possessive, demanded a response. She pushed weakly at his broad shoulders, her head spinning as her legs threatened to give way beneath her. Liquid fire coursed through her veins; the sensation was new and more than a little alarming. Another moan rose low in her throat, and she was dismayed to realize that, instead of fighting him like her conscience demanded, she was perilously close to melting.

The kiss deepened. Lainey suffered a sharp intake of breath when Ethan's hot, velvety tongue thrust between her lips. At the same time, one of his hands moved down her back to close about the well-rounded firmness of her bottom. She squirmed, her eyes flying wide at the shocking familiarity. Her movements prompted Ethan to groan and gather her even closer.

Her curves fitted against the hard planes of his body with rapturous perfection, her breasts pressed so tightly to his chest that her every heartbeat mingled with his.

The evidence of his manhood was as undeniable as her own womanliness. She felt a newly awakened yearning blaze to life within her, a deep, body-and-soul longing for something she could not yet put a name to. She strained upward against him, her arms entwining of their own accord about his neck as she began to kiss him back . . .

She shivered as a sudden gust of wind swept across her damp, thinly covered softness. It was enough to bring her crashing back to reality. At that point, she wasn't sure which she feared the most—Ethan Holt's passion or her own. But she knew she had to put a stop to the sweet madness before it was too late.

"No!" she choked out, tearing her lips from his. "Let me go!"

She renewed her struggles with a vengeance, bringing her hands up to push frantically at his chest. For a moment, it appeared he would not relent. He seized her wrists and forced her arms behind her back. His gaze burned down into the stormy depths of hers. A highly charged silence rose between them, the creek murmuring softly in the moonlight while the dwindling fire crackled and hissed, sending a shower of sparks flying heavenward.

Lainey stared up at him in breathless expectation. She was now acutely conscious of the fact that she was clad in nothing but wet, clinging undergarments—and that the night hid very little. Ethan Holt was seeing a good deal more of her than any man had seen before. But more importantly than that, he had dared to touch her with a boldness that, at least momentarily, had rendered her incapable of rational thought. She knew she would never forget the passionate, wildly provocative kiss they had shared. *Never.*

Tilting her head back so that she could meet his gaze squarely, she could feel her damp tresses cascading down about her hips. She swallowed hard and waited for him to speak, unable to move or look away. His eyes branded her with the same merciless intensity his lips had displayed, lingering on the delectable curve of her breasts before traveling back up to fasten on her flushed, beautiful face.

Already confused by what had happened, she was thrown into an even greater quandary when he suddenly released her without a single word of protest or explanation or apology.

He turned away, paused briefly to retrieve his hat, then strode back toward the spot near the fire where he had left his horse. Lainey stood as if transfixed while he swung up into the saddle. Her entire body still tingling warmly, she watched him take control of the reins and settle the hat upon his head. When he finally spoke, it was in a low, resonant tone that sent another involuntary chill dancing down her spine.

"I'll be back," he vowed. That simple promise held a meaning she didn't want to explore. But the very sound of it struck a chord of fear in her heart.

With a faint smile playing about his lips, Ethan reined about and rode away into the night.

Lainey released a long, ragged sigh and dropped slowly to her knees beside the creek. Dazed, she reached out to gather up the remainder of her clothing. Her eyes fell upon the rifle, which still lay where Ethan had placed it. The painful memory of her childish, impetuous behavior came back to haunt her, and she caught her lower lip between her teeth as a fresh wave of mortification washed over her.

Aghast at what she had done—or rather, at what she had allowed Ethan Holt to do—she closed her eyes and fought back sudden tears. She would never have thought it possible that she could be so weak-spirited. Shame and indignation mingled together within her breast, making her feel more miserable than she had felt in a long time.

But there was nothing to be gained from dwelling upon it, she told herself staunchly a few seconds later. The whole humiliating episode was over with, and she'd do well to put it out of her mind entirely. In fact, the next time she encountered her "neighbor," she would behave as if it had never happened at all. No, by thunder, she wouldn't give him the satisfaction of knowing how very much his kiss had affected her. She would not speak of it, not even to Beth.

Dear, sweet Beth, she thought with another sigh. Beth would surely find it difficult to believe that her practical, levelheaded sister had actually let a man, a virtual stranger no less, capture her in an ardent embrace and bestow a long, intimate kiss upon her lips, all while she was in such a shocking state of undress. Beth would certainly never understand how it could have happened . . . or would she?

Frowning darkly, she rose to her feet and clutched the dry clothing to her breasts. She snatched up the rifle, heading back to the fire to kick dirt over the already dying flames. Once certain the blaze was safely extinguished, she took herself off to bed at last.

After peeling off her soaked chemise and drawers and exchanging them for a clean white nightgown, she lay down and tried in vain to fall asleep. She was plagued by the memory of Ethan's mouth upon hers. Raising a hand to her lips, she brushed her fingertips across them before muttering a curse and rolling angrily onto her side. It occurred to her that, although she had only known the overbearing, impossible man for a single day, he had already managed to wreak havoc on her emotions.

"Lainey?" Beth murmured in a sleepy voice beside her.

"Yes?" she whispered in return, flushing guiltily. "What is it?"

"I just wanted to make sure you were here."

"I'm here. Now go back to sleep," she directed affectionately.

"I thought I heard a man's voice."

"A man's voice?" She felt a pang of remorse before stammering, "You—you must have been dreaming."

"The strangest thing is . . . it sounded remarkably like Mr. Holt," Beth persisted, yawning.

"Did it?" She groaned inwardly, her color deepening. "That *is* strange. But dreams are often that way, aren't they?"

"Do you have the rifle?"

"Yes." Relieved that the conversation had wandered onto safer ground, she smiled briefly to herself and said, "Don't worry. Everything's fine, just fine. Good night, Beth."

"Good night, dearest Lainey."

Lainey waited until she was certain her sister had drifted off to sleep again, then sighed and closed her own eyes. Her body ached from all the riding she had done, but it was the nagging, inexplicable ache in her heart that caused her to lie awake for a long time afterward.

The next day found her almost too busy to even think about Ethan—or his ominous parting words. She and Beth set to work immediately after breakfast, organizing a more permanent camp beneath the trees and taking inventory of their supplies. Anna toddled happily about in the sunshine. She had to be rescued on more than one occasion from the water's edge, but otherwise reveled in her newfound freedom.

Several riders passed by; none stopped. Lainey kept the rifle close at hand just in case. The most obvious danger facing them at present—a minimal one compared to what had happened the day before—arrived in the form of a veritable army of insects that seemed intent upon crawling over everything in sight. She and Beth took care to keep their sugar, flour, and other foodstuffs stored in a barrel with a hinged lid. They frequently inspected the baby for any sign of the pesky intruders, laughing at Anna's howls of protest whenever her play was interrupted.

Lainey recalled the stories she had heard from some of the women back in Kansas concerning the "bug palaces" their husbands planned to erect. Though inexpensive and a common sight on the frontier, these houses, built entirely of sod blocks, had come by their illfavored reputation honestly. Her own determination to build a real cabin grew even stronger as she swept a wicked-looking beetle from her skirts.

Beth wasted little time in beginning the task of clearing a small patch of land for their first garden. Anna did her part by planting herself on the ground and breaking up the clumps of rich, deep red earth her mother turned up with the hoe. Lainey, meanwhile, filled a huge iron kettle with water from the creek. She heated it over the fire, glad to finally have the chance to do the washing. It took the better part of an hour for her to scrub the mountain of dirty clothes that had accumulated throughout the past several days. She hung the clean garments out to dry across the length of rope she had strung between two trees, thankful that the afternoon was as bright and clear as the previous one had been.

Her eyes clouded with remembrance when she discovered Ethan's shirt among the other clothing. Musing unhappily that Beth must have put it there, she frowned and plunged it into the soapy water. Ethan's handsome face swam before her eyes. She snatched up the shirt and wrung out the fabric with an unnecessarily violent twist, feeling foolish and yet somewhat appeased.

The hours wore on in a never-ending whirl of activity. By midafternoon, the garden was well on its way to becoming a reality, the drying clothes flapped in the warm breeze, and Anna was napping peacefully in the wagon.

A tired but satisfied Beth leaned upon her hoe to survey her work.

"When summer comes, we should have plenty of good, nourishing vegetables," she remarked to Lainey. "We'll have to purchase a cow, of course. Anna will need milk. And I suppose you and I will eventually have to learn to hunt if we're to have meat. I don't expect you to encounter any difficulty learning," she added, with a crooked smile. "But I fear I may prove hopeless. Perhaps we can make an arrangement with one of our new neighbors to trade something from our garden for fresh game."

Though she was wearing a faded gingham dress and a pair of sturdy—an arbiter of fashion would have termed them hideously unattractive—boots, she still looked every inch a lady. Lainey, on the other hand, felt downright bedraggled in her own well-worn attire. She pushed several wildly rebellious locks of hair from her forehead and straightened from where she had just placed another armful of wood beside the fire. The water currently heating was for baths; she had already constructed a privacy shelter of sorts with a tarpaulin hung beneath the trees.

"Beth, I . . . there's something we should talk about," she said hesitantly.

"What is it?" Something in her sister's voice prompted Beth to stiffen.

"I don't know if we'll be able to afford a cow just yet. Or some of the other things we had planned to buy." She paused a moment, choosing her words carefully when she spoke again. "I don't want to worry you, but we'll have to exercise great caution with the money we have left."

"But I thought we had plenty—"

"I thought so, too. However, the wagon and horses and supplies cost more than I had anticipated." She forced a bolstering smile to her lips. "We'll be fine.

We'll simply have to be a bit more frugal than we've had to be in the past."

Her words lacked conviction, even to her own ears, but she refused to let her sister know the full extent of her worriment. Beth had never understood about money, she recalled with an inward sigh. Even before their father had died, she had been the one to handle the household finances. She had even assumed the task of keeping the books for his medical practice in those last few years. There had been times when her sister's aversion to mathematics had proven to be more than a little exasperating, but she had never been able to remain annoyed with her for long. Beth's kind and generous nature more than compensated for her lack of organizational skills.

"It's all my fault," the petite blonde now proclaimed disconsolately. "I shouldn't have insisted upon keeping so much. I'm sorry I didn't listen to you, Lainey. If we had sold everything—"

"Nonsense! You were right about that. Besides, it will all belong to Anna eventually. Our mother's jewelry, the china, the quilts and the books and the silver tea set— Why, she would never have forgiven us if we had dared to part with them!"

"What about your children?"

"My children?" Lainey echoed in bewilderment.

"Yes," replied Beth, her brow clearing again while her opal eyes sparkled. "You'll have a family of your own someday. And they will certainly wish to have keepsakes the same as my Anna."

"You needn't worry about that. I have no intention of marrying." She placed more wood on the fire and smoothed a hand down her navy cotton skirts.

"Oh, Lainey. You can't mean that!"

"I can indeed," she insisted firmly. Her face took on the obstinate expression Beth knew all too well. "I intend to remain unwed."

"You'll change your mind when you fall in love," her sister prophesied, with a sad little smile.

"No, Beth. I'm not going to fall in love."

"How can you be so sure?"

"Because I have never been so determined about anything in my life!" she declared a bit too vigorously. She colored, her troubled gaze falling beneath the indulgent warmth of Beth's. She stared at the dancing, crackling flames and explained in a dull tone, "I've seen what love can do. Papa was never the same after Mother died. And you have suffered terribly as a result of your own heart's 'entanglement.' "

"Yes, but that doesn't mean *you* shouldn't—"

"Shouldn't what? Shouldn't allow myself to be subjected to untold pain and humiliation? To be left feeling as though my whole life had suddenly come to an end?" She shook her head in an eloquent gesture of finality. "No, I won't do that. I can't!"

"I wish you could understand," remarked Beth, her own voice holding a telltale quaver. She turned to gaze out over the lush, rugged beauty of the surrounding prairie. A faraway look came into her eyes. "None of us wishes for pain. But it seems there can be no true happiness without it."

Lainey's frown deepened. She felt a pang of remorse for having stirred up the grief-laden memories again. It wasn't fair that her sister should be the one to suffer, she thought angrily. Was Beth to endure a lifetime of guilt and heartache as payment for a single transgression? If so, then there *was* no justice on earth. And if that was true, then Anna's father, wherever he was, would never feel the terrible anguish he so richly deserved.

They lapsed into silence as they resumed their work. A short time later, a lone rider topped the hill and advanced upon their camp in an easy canter. Lainey's heart stood still when she first sighted him.

Great balls of fire, she lamented silently. It was probably Ethan Holt, making good on his threat to return. Hot color flew to her cheeks. Praying that Beth wouldn't notice, she began edging toward the rifle. But as the rider drew nearer, she saw that it wasn't the man she had feared it would be. It was his brother.

Travis Holt reined to a halt and dismounted. His handsome, sun-bronzed features, so like Ethan's and yet far less seasoned, broke into an appealingly boyish grin as he led his horse forward.

"Ladies," he said by way of greeting. He swept the hat gallantly from his head. His eyes strayed to Beth before moving back to Lainey.

"Mr. Holt," she responded, with a polite smile. "To what do we owe this unexpected pleasure?" It was difficult to keep the sarcasm from her voice, for she suspected that his brother had put him up to the visit. Strangely enough, she was disappointed at the thought. Ethan Holt hadn't struck her as a coward. Far from it.

"Thought I'd ride on over and bring you these," he answered, presenting her with a string of fish. He looked to Beth again. She lowered the hoe to the ground and cast him a shy, tentative smile of her own while giving an unconscious pat to her upswept curls. It surprised him to realize how strongly that one simple feminine gesture affected him.

"Thank you, Mr. Holt," Lainey told him in genuine gratitude. Her eyes twinkled up at him. "However did you manage to catch so many?"

"We kept the other half for supper," he confided, with another grin. "If you like, I can show you how to catch all the fish you want."

"We would like that very much," Beth finally spoke up, then blushed at her own boldness. "I ... that is, if you can spare the time."

"I can spare it. And I'll teach you how to set a snare to catch rabbits. Prairie chickens, too."

"I'm sure you have better things to do than instruct us in the ways of the frontier," countered Lainey, her suspicions aroused once more. She was certain Ethan had devised the scheme. "My sister and I appreciate your generous offer, but we prefer to fend for ourselves."

"You'll be able to do that just fine once you've learned a few things," Travis good-naturedly persisted. He couldn't seem to keep his eyes off Beth, who was in turn quite alarmed by the way her pulse raced beneath his scrutiny. "Independence is a quality to be admired, Miss Prescott," he said, forcing his gaze back to Lainey. "But good intentions won't put food on the table."

"What a remarkable philosophy, Mr. Holt. I suppose your brother is responsible for your cultivation of it?" she challenged.

"I'm my own man." For a fleeting moment, his gaze filled with a steely light.

"Then you will certainly understand why we prefer to be our 'own women.' "

"Surely, Lainey, it will do no harm to let Mr. Holt assist us in this one small way," Beth saw fit to interject, earning herself a look of wounded surprise from her sister. She crossed gracefully to Lainey's side, all the while conscious of Travis Holt's mesmerizing, deep green eyes upon her. "We do need meat. Or at least Anna does. And I know you would agree that her welfare must take precedence over our pride in this matter."

Lainey flushed with a combination of guilt and irritation. She was tempted to tell Ethan Holt's brother precisely what he could do with *his* good intentions, but common courtesy prevailed. Feeling mildly betrayed, she lifted her head and gave him a curt nod.

"Very well, Mr. Holt," she capitulated, with obvious reluctance. "Since my sister has been kind enough to remind me that we have a young child to think of, I cannot in all good conscience decline your offer."

"I'll be over in the morning," he promised. His smile this time was for Beth alone. "We'll have that little girl of yours fattened up in no time, Mrs. Baker."

"In truth, Mr. Holt, that is not my objective," Beth parried, her own eyes shining softly. She cast a quick glance toward Lainey, only to see that her sister was surveying her with a frown of disapproval. "Good day, Mr. Holt," she murmured. Gathering up her skirts, she turned away and hurried off to check on Anna.

"How long has your sister been a widow?" Travis asked once she had gone.

"I fail to see how that is any concern of yours!" retorted Lainey. She had taken note of the way he looked at Beth—and the way Beth looked at him. Confound it, the last thing they needed was for this man or any other to start making a nuisance of himself. She was certain Beth had no real desire to be courted; their lives had finally settled into some semblance of orderliness. Complications, romantic or otherwise, would have to be avoided at all cost. "We have work to do. And I'm sure your brother needs your help," she put forth by way of dismissal.

"Ethan doesn't need anyone, Miss Prescott," he refuted, his eyes brimming with wry amusement. He lifted the hat to his head and flashed her a broad—appealingly crooked—smile. "He'd probably finish setting the logs by himself if I let him. Putting on the roof, too."

"You've already started building a cabin?" she queried in surprise. Travis nodded.

"We had everything sent ahead on the train." He swung up into the saddle and took an easy grip on the reins. "What about you? Are you planning to—?"

"We've made arrangements for our own house," she lied, then expanded upon the offense by adding, "I wouldn't be at all surprised if we were among the first to see completion of a permanent dwelling."

"I'm glad to hear it." If Travis doubted the truth of her words, he gave no indication of it. He merely smiled once more and touched the front brim of his hat. "I'll see you in the morning." Reining about, he tossed back over his shoulder, "Be sure and cook those fish before you eat them!"

Lainey's mouth twitched. In spite of her resolve not to like the man, she had to admit to herself that he possessed a certain undeniable charm. A "real character," her father would have termed him. It certainly wasn't difficult to envision him standing in the midst of a group of adoring young ladies, setting their hearts aflutter with that irresistible smile of his. His brother, however . . .

"Lainey Prescott, you *are* a fool," she muttered in furious self-recrimination. Rolling her eyes heavenward, she spun about and marched toward the wagon.

With the makeshift curtain closed about them for protection, all three Prescott women were able to enjoy a bath before supper. The bathtub was in actuality nothing more than a large wooden barrel, but it served its purpose quite well. Beth scrubbed Anna from head to toe, using some of the lavender-scented soap they had brought with them, then handed her over into Lainey's care so that she could take her own turn in the water's soothing warmth.

Once Beth had finished, Lainey added the last of the hot water and slipped within the canvas shelter to strip off her clothes. She lowered herself into the tub, then breathed an audible sigh of pleasure as she felt her tensed muscles relax. She had been dreaming about this moment for the past week. Now that it had finally come, she was determined to prolong it.

The water had begun to grow cold when she emerged from the tub. She wrapped a towel about her body and bent over to wash her hair, a task that required considerable patience. The long, wondrously thick tresses were still a bit damp by the time she and Beth and Anna had eaten their supper of fried fish and corn bread.

"Lainey"—Beth addressed her with a visible air of preoccupation—"I've been thinking about what you said. Regarding our financial situation, I mean." She cradled her well-fed, clean-smelling daughter in her lap and stared toward the fire. "Exactly how desperate are our circumstances?"

"I shouldn't have mentioned it at all." Lainey sighed. "I knew you'd worry."

"I have a right to know."

"Of course you do. A perfect right." She smiled at Anna, reaching out to rearrange the smocked, white cotton gown about her chubby little legs. "We're all in this together, aren't we?"

"Please, Lainey. Stop being evasive," Beth pleaded quietly.

"I'm sorry. But I can't know how bad our circumstances are until I learn how much money will be required for the house." That was true enough, she told herself. "We'll still have to purchase seed for the crops, of course, and we can't count on turning a profit just yet since it is already so late in the season. But at least we've plenty of wood and fresh water."

"And if Mr. Holt's instruction proves as beneficial as I fully expect, we won't be in any danger of starving," Beth obligingly added. She smiled at the expression of renewed annoyance crossing her sister's face. "Come now, he happens to be very nice. I can think of no reason why you should dislike him."

"I don't dislike him," Lainey protested. She frowned and murmured without thinking, "But his brother is one of the most infuriating men I have ever met." Her sapphire gaze fell hastily beneath the loving sparkle of Beth's.

"They do seem to be quite different. Not so much in looks as in temperament. But then, I haven't known them long enough to make a fair assessment."

"*I*, for one, intend to keep it that way," vowed Lainey. She climbed to her feet and plucked Anna from Beth's lap. "Come along now. It's getting late. I—"

She broke off abruptly when her ears detected the sudden, unexpected sound of approaching hoofbeats. Her throat constricted in alarm while the image of Ethan's face rose in her mind.

Surely he wouldn't seek a repetition of last night's madness, she thought breathlessly.

Once again, however, the rider turned out to be someone else. And he was not alone.

She watched the two horsemen drawing closer in the dull, silvery glow of the twilight. Her heart filled with dread when she realized that they were both strangers.

"Beth, take Anna and get in the wagon!" she directed in a sharp undertone.

"I won't leave you out here alone!" insisted Beth, rising to her feet. She accepted the baby into her arms once more. "They might be some of our neighbors," she suggested hopefully. "They might—"

"They *might* be anything! Now please, for heaven's sake—do as I say and take Anna to the wagon. And stay there until I tell you to come out."

Still hesitant to leave, Beth agonized over the decision facing her. She wanted to remain with Lainey, to be at her sister's side in the event of danger, and yet her maternal instincts demanded that she seek protection for her child. Finally she gathered Anna close and raced off toward the wagon.

Lainey clutched the rifle in her hands, offering up a silent prayer that she would remember how to use it if the need arose. She took a stance beside the fire, tensed in defensive readiness while the men bore down on the camp.

"Evenin', ma'am," one of the riders called out as he slowed his mount to a halt a few feet away. The other man did the same. Their gazes traveled boldly over Lainey before fastening on the gun she had raised to point in their direction.

"What do you want?" she asked, with deceptive calm.

Her own eyes narrowed at the sight of them. Their features appeared vaguely sinister in the firelight. They were both young, no more than five and twenty, and each wore a tooled leather holster buckled low on their hips. Their clothes were a cut above the usual well-worn trousers and faded cotton shirts favored by the cowboys back in the boomers' camp.

She stood proud and unyielding before them, refusing to allow them so much as a glimpse of fear. Inwardly she was a mass of nerves.

"We're lookin' for a man named Holt," the taller and darker of the two declared. "Ethan Holt."

Lainey swallowed the gasp of surprise that rose to her lips. Several conflicting emotions warred within her breast as Ethan's face swam before her eyes again. She sensed that these men, whoever they were, meant him no good.

Although it occurred to her that he might have done something dreadful enough to *deserve* whatever they had in mind, she knew she would not betray him, even in this one small way. Her personal feelings for him were of no significance. After all, she concluded with an inward frown, it was her Christian duty to help others avoid trouble.

"I said we're lookin' for Ethan Holt," the dark-haired gunslinger reiterated.

"Then I suggest you conduct your search for him in

the daylight hours," she countered in her best, primly small-town manner.

"Do you know where we can find him?"

"No. I do not."

"Someone told us he had a claim out this way."

"Indeed? Well, I'm afraid your source was mistaken. There is no one of that name among our many neighbors." Musing with a flash of resentment that she had never found it necessary to lie as often as she had done since meeting Ethan Holt, she forced a cool little smile to her lips. "You had best be on your way, gentlemen. My husband will be returning from town any moment now." That threat had failed dismally the day before. And to make matters worse, she couldn't count on Ethan Holt to rescue her this time.

"Husband?" the younger man responded, with a low, contemptuous chuckle. "Well now, he must be a real stupid son of a bitch to go off and leave you here alone."

"She isn't alone!" Beth's voice rang out from within the protective cover of the wagon.

Lainey's eyes flew wide in startlement.

"I have a gun as well, and I am not afraid to use it!" Beth warned on the other side of the canvas, her own lie uttered with amazing forcefulness and proficiency.

"Who the hell's that?" the rider in charge demanded tersely. His gaze sliced back to Lainey.

"My—my mother," she faltered, then quickly recovered her composure. "She is a bit 'touched,' you see, and has a fearsome temper. You would do well to go before she loses control of it completely."

"She's lyin', Rafe!" the younger man bit out.

"Shut up, damn it!" his partner growled. He looked at Lainey again, his eyes appraising her long and hard. Finally a slow, caustic smile spread across his face. "Tell that husband of yours he's a lucky man." He tipped his hat to her in an exaggerated display of politeness. "We'll meet again, ma'am."

"I think not," she disagreed, drawing herself up proudly once more.

The two gunslingers said nothing else before riding back the way they had come. Lainey waited until they had gone, then lowered the rifle to the ground with shaking hands and spun about to find Beth scurrying toward her.

"Oh, Lainey. I was so afraid they would do you harm!" She flung herself headlong into her sister's arms. "Thank God they left without incident! I'm not at all certain I would have known what to do if they had decided to remain any longer!"

"Whatever possessed you to interfere like that? Didn't you realize how dangerous it was?" admonished Lainey, trying to sound stern but managing only a half-hearted reproachfulness.

"I had to do something," said Beth, pulling away with a heavy sigh. "I suppose I thought they would be more impressed by the possibility of facing two guns rather than just one." Her eyes twinkled at a sudden thought, and her mouth curved into a smile of appreciative humor as she chided, "Your mad and quick-tempered mother? Surely, dearest Lainey, you could have assigned me a more attractive identity than that."

"It was the first thing that came to mind," Lainey defended, with an answering smile, then frowned when her gaze shifted toward the wagon. "Where is Anna?"

"She fell asleep a few minutes ago. Poor darling. I'm afraid she missed most of the excitement." All traces of amusement vanished from her own countenance in the next instant, and her eyes filled with renewed apprehension. "Do you think they'll return?"

"No," Lainey reassured her. "They have no quarrel with us."

"They apparently have one with Mr. Holt. I wonder

what they intended to do once they had found him. Perhaps we should warn him."

"We can tell his brother about it in the morning." She bent down to retrieve the gun. "But I think Ethan Holt can take care of himself."

Surprised to realize how fully confident she was in his abilities, she found herself gazing westward. She had watched Travis Holt ride away in that direction several hours earlier.

Ethan doesn't need anyone, he had said. Strangely enough, that thought troubled her . . .

Chapter 5

The next four days passed in a whirl of activity.

Travis Holt had made good on his promise to return. Ethan Holt had not. That particular fact did not escape Lainey's attention, even though she tried to pretend that it was nothing more than idle curiosity that prompted her to wonder—frequently—if and when he would finally put in an appearance.

She and Beth had determinedly charged ahead with their work, keeping themselves too busy to dwell upon the uncertainty of their future. In between a flurry of gardening and clearing and other time-consuming chores, they had managed to catch plenty of fish and small game. Travis had proven to be a kind and patient teacher in that respect, instructing them in the finer methods of setting trotlines in the creek and snares within the concealing thickness of the deep-rooted prairie grass. He had also shown them the proper way to skin and cook everything, smiling at their obvious and highly feminine reluctance to perform the bloody task.

Although Lainey was grateful to him for his help, she still couldn't help feeling uneasy at his marked attentions toward her sister. His eyes had sought Beth out at every turn. And Lainey had caught her stealing more than one oddly wistful glance at him. Beth had rarely spoken of him, but Lainey knew she had been affected by his flattering regard. Any woman would have been. Fortunately he had not called on them again.

On the third day following the run, Lainey had decided to try her hand at plowing. Her efforts had yielded a woefully small amount of turned-up earth. The horse had proven uncooperative, the plow difficult to maneuver, and to make matters worse, she had stumbled and fallen, only to be dragged unceremoniously along the ground while crying out to the accursed animal to stop. Beth had been sympathetic, as always, even going so far as to offer to spell her behind the plow. But Lainey had refused to give up. She would finish the job, even if it killed her. Sore and bruised afterward, she had been prompted to muse—with a smile of irony—that it might just be the death of her after all.

Now, some two days later, she was saddling the horse to ride into town. She had put off the journey for as long as possible, reluctant to venture into the chaos and confusion of Guthrie again. But the time had finally come to find out if their hope for a frame house instead of a dugout could be realized.

"Are you sure you should go alone?" asked Beth, her eyes full of concern. She lifted Anna in her arms and tugged the baby's calico sunbonnet into place.

"Yes," Lainey reaffirmed, pulling the cinch tight. "If Guthrie's even half as crowded as it was that first day, I would have to worry about losing you and Anna. The two of you will be much safer here. Only please, Beth, keep the rifle close at hand while I'm gone."

"Very well. But it won't do much good," she pointed out, with a dramatic little sigh. "I seriously doubt if I could ever use it."

"You could use it," insisted Lainey, a faint smile touching her lips. "You know you'd do anything to protect Anna."

"I suppose you're right."

"I know I am." She turned and gave her sister a quick hug, then pressed a kiss upon her niece's dimpled cheek. "I should be back before noon, but in case I am delayed for some reason, you and Anna should eat without me. I'll bring back more sugar and flour," she promised, hoping she would have enough money left over to get some coffee as well. It was the one luxury she had allowed herself when purchasing supplies back in Kansas.

Lifting a booted foot to the stirrup, she grasped the saddle horn and swung up onto the horse's back. She settled her long skirts about her and gathered up the reins. Her hair hung in a single long braid down her back, and she had wisely chosen not to wear any petticoats. Realizing that she had become spoiled these past two weeks, she wondered how she would ever grow accustomed to the tortuous restraint of a corset and the burden of numerous petticoats again.

Giving Beth one last warmly lit smile, she tugged on the reins and guided the horse away from the camp, setting a course for the town, which lay only a few miles to the east. She had no thought of encountering danger. The countryside was alive with the sounds and smells of vigorous new settlement, which added to her confidence. With so many people close by, she told herself, there was no reason to be afraid. She looked forward to meeting some of her neighbors in the near future. Perhaps, once the first wave of "settling in" had been accomplished, she and Beth and Anna could spend an entire afternoon visiting the boomers whose claims were near their own.

With one exception, an inner voice gleefully pointed out. She frowned, her sapphire gaze darkening as she shifted her hips in the saddle. Why the blazes couldn't she stop thinking about him?

She urged the animal beneath her into a gallop and went racing across the rolling, green-mantled hills as though the very devil were after her.

Guthrie, she soon discovered, had changed considerably in the five days since she had seen it last. It was a regular boomtown in every way—the construction of frame buildings had already begun, tents of all shapes and sizes stood everywhere, and the cool morning air was choked with a mixture of voices, the jingle of harness and creak of wagons, and the incessant pounding of hammers.

Outrageously high prices and long lines greeted the new residents at every turn. Lodging was very scarce, oftentimes nothing more than a bare spot of ground alongside dozens of fellow boarders. Hot meals were at a premium. The only source of water was the river; a single drink of this murky liquid was offered by a few enterprising, bucket-carrying souls for the sum of twenty-five cents. Merchants displayed their wares in a sort of massive, open-air emporium, while lawyers used crates and trunks as makeshift desks in their newly launched practices. Gamblers, having swarmed into town the very first day to set up their tents wherever space permitted, were enjoying a brisk and highly profitable business.

Lainey knew a moment's trepidation as she paused on the fringes of town. The scene before her was enough to make her wish she had let Beth come along after all. But she wasn't about to turn back. She took a deep, steadying breath, then plunged ahead into the crowd.

Heads turned and eyes widened as she rode past. There were scores of other women swelling the ranks, but they were outnumbered more than a hundred to one by the men. Families arrived daily to join their loved ones, so that children were becoming a more common sight. Their laughter was a welcome reminder of home.

Drawing her mount to a halt in front of the depot, Lainey swung down and looped the reins about the hitching post. She could only hope that the animal would be there when she returned. Men were busily unloading lumber and nails, glass and tools, and other building materials from the morning train. She took that to be a good omen for her own pursuit of a house.

Her gaze swept across the sea of people and tents, searching the vast array of hand-lettered signs for one that would indicate either a carpenter or a lumber dealer. She smiled to herself in satisfaction when she read the words BUILDINGS, COMMERCIAL AND RESIDENTIAL above a tent a short distance away. Gathering up her skirts, she set off across the street. It was difficult to walk with so many others milling about, but she managed a steady progress. She approached the tent at last and pulled the flap aside to enter.

A man with a full head of bright red hair and a beard to match sat perched on the edge of a crate. Engrossed in the latest edition of the *Oklahoma State Capital*, a newspaper printed in Kansas and shipped to Guthrie by train, he gave only a passing glance to Lainey when she stepped inside. In the next instant, however, he took a second look. He practically leapt to his feet.

"Good morning to you, ma'am!" He greeted her in a deep, booming voice that gave immediate evidence of his Irish roots. "Michael Flynn, at your service!" To prove it, he offered her the only chair in sight and stood at attention with a broad grin on his face.

"Good morning, Mr. Flynn," Lainey answered, with a brief smile. She shook her head at his offer of the chair. "My name is Lainey Prescott. My sister and I have need of someone to build us a house. We live just west of town, you see, and—"

"Say no more," he cut her off genially. "I'm a mite booked up at present, but I'm sure we can work out a schedule that will suit the both of us."

"And a price," she added.

"Well now, the price will depend on a good many things. Please, Miss Prescott, sit down and we'll get down to business."

She followed his advice, sinking into the chair while he resumed his own seat upon the crate.

They "got down to business" as Michael Flynn had said they should, but not with the results Lainey had expected. When she emerged from the tent a few minutes later, it was with a heavy heart and eyes full of fire. The price she had been quoted was completely unreasonable—it was *twice* what she had planned to spend!

Her temper flared anew at the memory of the Irishman's audacity and conceit. He had actually dared to suggest that she could make up the difference with certain "favors" directed his way. His meaning had been all too clear.

"Insolent, rattle-brained man," she muttered underneath her breath. She was fairly quaking with the force of her anger. If not for the fact that she never wished to set eyes on Michael Flynn again, she would have gladly marched back inside the tent and given him a well-deserved piece of her mind.

Telling herself that there had to be plenty of other establishments she could try, she wasted little time in seeking them out. She was fortunate enough not to encounter any more disreputable businessmen like the first, but her good luck in that respect did not extend to her pocketbook. Everyone she spoke with demanded far too much money. And heaven help her, there was no way to raise the additional funds.

She spent nearly two hours fighting her way through the crowd and arguing with men in a futile attempt to persuade them to lower their admittedly exorbitant fees. They were all of them determined to make as much profit as the demand would bear. They suffered little or no remorse for their greed. Guthrie was a boomtown, they reminded her. Why should they settle for less than what they could get?

Lainey was forced to admit defeat. Her hopes were shattered. More than anything, she had wanted to give

Beth and Anna a real home, not some awful sodhouse full of bugs and snakes and God only knew what else. They deserved far better than that.

She turned her steps back toward the depot, her spirits lower than they had been since leaving Missouri. There had to be some way to get the money, some way she could pay for the house and still have enough left over to see them through the winter. It would be next spring before they could count on a profitable harvest, and even that wasn't a certainty.

Her mind racing feverishly, she did not notice the horse and wagon careening down the street until it was nearly too late. . . .

"*Runaway!*" someone yelled, his voice ringing out above the roar. A woman's scream rose in the air.

Lainey stiffened, her eyes widening in alarm. The crowd, panicking, scattered every which way. She tried to move as well, but a man knocked her down before she could reach the front steps of the depot. A sharp cry broke from her lips as she fell to her knees in the dirt. She raised her head and immediately staggered to her feet again, only to watch in horrified disbelief while the riderless, out-of-control wagon bore down on her.

The next thing she knew, someone seized her about the waist and pulled her to safety. Gasping to feel herself lifted and swung up to the depot steps, she watched, stunned, as the wagon passed harmlessly by.

"Are you all right?"

She turned her head to gaze breathlessly up at the man who still held her against him. He was quite attractive, even handsome, with hair black as midnight and eyes that were an unusual shade of gray. His dark, pin-striped suit and brocade satin waistcoat identified him as something other than a farmer or cowboy or simple merchant. Though his frame appeared slender, he was decidedly fit and muscular, his head topping hers by several inches. And he was staring back at her with undisguised admiration.

"Yes, I—I'm fine!" she stammered, blushing. She hastily disengaged herself from his grasp and smoothed down her skirts, then cast him a tremulous smile. "I don't know how I can ever thank you. If you hadn't come along—" She broke off and glanced toward the street. "Thank God no one was injured."

"I thought I was the one who had earned your gratitude," he teased, returning her smile with a smoothly appealing one of his own. "You must be new to Guthrie. I don't recall having seen you before. And I *would* recall it," he added, while his gaze flickered significantly up and down the length of her body.

"I—I don't live in town," she murmured, her eyes falling beneath his unsettling scrutiny. He seemed nice enough, yet she had the distinct impression that he was something of a rascal. A charming rascal, to be sure, but a rascal all the same.

"My name is Neil Halloran," he told her, without being asked. It was difficult to detect any trace of an accent in his voice. "And yours?" he prompted, his eyebrows lifting expectantly.

"Lainey Prescott." Good heavens, not another Irishman! she mused with an inward smile of irony.

"Well then, Lainey Prescott, maybe you'll allow me to buy you some dinner. There's a restaurant only a short walk away." His teeth flashed white as he lifted a black felt hat to his head. "I'm sure the cuisine is not of the high quality you're used to, but—"

"No thank you, Mr. Halloran," she politely declined. "I have pressing business to attend to." Indeed she did, she thought, realizing the truth of her words. A jumble of details, large and small, filled her mind all at once. She had almost forgotten about the sugar and flour . . . her horse would need water soon . . . and there was still the matter of the house. She had to find a way to raise the necessary funds. She *had* to. "Perhaps some other time," she added, with a faint, preoccupied smile.

"I saved your life, Miss Prescott. The least you can do is share a meal with me."

Her eyes flew back up to his face in surprise. She couldn't tell if he was serious or merely teasing her again. Strangely enough, his offer was tempting. But she had other—far more important—matters demanding her time.

"I'm sorry, but I can't," she reiterated firmly. "Thank you again, Mr. Halloran." She offered him her hand, expecting him to shake it. But he surprised her further by raising it to his lips. She felt a small tremor of delight run through her when his warm mouth settled, briefly yet affectionately, upon her flesh.

"I'll hold you to your promise." He released her hand and favored her with yet another smile. This time, however, his eyes gleamed with a strange, almost predatory light. Lainey felt her face grow warm again.

"My promise?" Her silken brow creased in puzzlement.

"Some other time, Miss Prescott," he vowed enigmatically, his gaze boring across into hers.

He gave her a slight nod, then turned away to disappear into the crowd. Lainey stood and watched until he was out of sight. She was left feeling an odd mixture of pleasure and uneasiness. Neil Halloran wasn't like anyone she'd met before. But what did it matter? A man like that couldn't possibly have any real interest in pursuing an acquaintance with her, she concluded with an uneven little sigh. And an acquaintance with him was *not* something she needed.

Mentally shaking herself, she spun about and plunged into the enveloping turmoil of the city's main street once more. There were several general mercantiles from which to choose; she finally settled on one not too far from the land office. A long, impatient line of men waiting to file claims still stretched out front, serving as a pointed reminder that she hadn't yet heard from Oliver T. Calhoun. She would have to find him eventually and inquire as to the status of her own claim.

She was finally on her way back to fetch her horse when a young man thrust a handbill at her. Frowning in confusion, she tried to give it back to him, but he had already disappeared into the crowd once more.

Her eyes fell on the piece of paper in her hand. The bold-faced words printed on it seemed to leap right off the page at her.

" 'The Palace Theater,' " she murmured aloud, noting with great and sudden interest that it was an advertisement for a show featuring a variety of entertainment. The picture below the name of the theater featured the likeness of a curvaceous young woman clad in a short dress and tights. It was obviously meant to appeal to the overwhelmingly masculine element of the town.

" 'Trained musicians, thespians of international renown, and beautiful songstresses,' " Lainey went on to read.

Songstresses.

Her sapphire gaze lit with excitement. Why not? she mused triumphantly, her heart racing as the idea took hold. She and Beth had sung together every Sunday in church until they had no longer been welcomed by the congregation. And they had performed at an endless number of socials and picnics and weddings. Why, if the comments of their former friends and neighbors counted for anything at all, then there was every reason to hope they could turn their vocal talents to good—and profitable, God willing—use.

Provided, of course, she cautioned herself, that the management of the Palace Theater or some other such establishment could be prevailed upon to give them the chance. It was possible that no one would have need of any additional singers at present. It was also possible that the audience would not wish to hear the kind of songs she and Beth had sung back home.

There was only one way to find out. Squaring her shoulders and giving an unconsciously defiant toss of her head, she whirled about.

"Dear Lord, *please!*" she implored in a heartfelt whisper, her eyes tossing a quick glance heavenward before traveling back to the earthly paradise of Guthrie.

It was nearly two o'clock in the afternoon by the time she returned from town. She spied Beth kneeling beside the creek, apparently too lost in thought to take note of her approach. Her deep blue gaze shone with mingled warmth and anticipation as she pulled on the reins and dismounted.

"Beth!" she called out, startling the other woman from her reverie.

"Lainey!" Beth exclaimed, with a smile of relief. She set the partially filled bucket on the ground and climbed to her feet. Hastening forward, she lovingly admonished, "Oh, Lainey! Where on earth have you been? I was beginning to worry."

"I'm sorry to be so late," replied Lainey. She allowed herself to be caught up in an embrace for a moment before drawing away. "Nothing worked out quite the way I had expected." It was her turn to smile as she proclaimed, "I have the most remarkable news."

"Did Mr. Holt find you?"

"Mr. Holt?" she echoed, her eyes widening in surprise. "No. But—which Mr. Holt are you talking about?"

"The elder one, of course. He came looking for you some time ago."

"What did he want?" Ethan Holt had come looking for her, she repeated silently, dismayed to feel her pulse give a wild leap. So, after nearly a week's time, he had finally seen fit to pay another visit . . .

"I don't know," answered Beth. "He didn't say. But

he was on his way into town, and I thought perhaps your paths had crossed."

"No." She shook her head and frowned, then suddenly remembered what she had been on the verge of announcing. She pushed all thought of Ethan to the back of her mind. "Beth, I—"

"I wouldn't be at all surprised if he wished to speak to you about those men who were here the other night," the petite blonde suggested. "I'm sure his brother relayed the story to him, and—"

"Beth, do be quiet and listen!" Lainey directed affectionately, her hands closing about her sister's arms. "I think I may have just discovered a way for us to have that house after all. *And* a cow!"

"Really, Lainey?" She beamed with pleasure. "You were able to hire someone?"

"No. At least, not yet. But I *was* able to find us a job."

"A job?" Beth stared up at her as though she had taken complete leave of her senses. "Lainey Prescott, what are you talking about?"

"It isn't official yet. I'm afraid we'll still have to submit to an audition. But I have made all the arrangements, and Mr. Bloomfield assured me that we can earn twice what we could hope to earn elsewhere."

"What do you mean, 'audition'? And who is Mr. Bloomfield?"

"He is the proprietor of the Palace Theater. That's where we're going to sing. This might well turn out to be the solution to all our troubles!" she pronounced in a voice full of satisfaction.

"We're going to sing on the *stage*?" Beth asked in disbelief. Her eyes grew enormous within the delicate oval of her face. It was obvious that she was both astonished and scandalized by the idea. "But, we couldn't possibly do such a thing!"

"Why not? We've been singing for an audience since

we were children. What difference does it make where the performance takes place? Christopher Columbus, Beth! We certainly won't suffer eternal damnation just because we set foot on a stage. It will be completely respectable. I mean, it isn't as if we're going to be standing there in nothing but our shimmies."

"Why, Lainey Prescott!" her sister gasped.

"Mr. Bloomfield offered to provide us with suitable costumes," she continued, without any sign of repentance. "And he's going to allow us to select our own repertoire. He seemed much impressed by the fact that we have had some prior experience."

She did not add that he had also been impressed by her appearance. Her eyes clouded anew as she recalled his critical and highly embarrassing appraisal, but she told herself it was perfectly natural that he should be concerned. After all, as he had commented with a quiet, knowing chuckle, no one wanted to pay good money to see a woman whose face would stop an eight-day clock, even if she did have the voice of an angel.

"But, what about Anna?" Beth queried, her head spinning dizzily. "And what about the farm?"

"We'll have to take Anna with us. The job will only require three evenings a week to begin with. And I'm sure we can find someone to look after her while we're onstage. There will be plenty of other entertainers— perhaps we can strike a bargain with one of them. And, as for the farm . . ." Her voice trailed away while her brows knit into a frown. She sighed and decreed with far more self-assurance than she actually felt, "The farm will simply have to wait. The important thing is that we'll be able to build a proper house and store up plenty of supplies before winter comes. We might still be able to plant a few crops in the fall."

"This isn't at all what we had planned, Lainey," Beth observed in a voice that was little more than a whisper.

She looked down toward her apron. "I don't think I can do it. I don't think I can get up onstage and—"

"And *I* say that we'll do whatever we have to do!" snapped Lainey. She immediately regretted the defensive sharpness of her tone. Her eyes full of remorse, she lifted a conciliatory hand to her sister's arm. "I'm sorry, Beth, but I can think of no other way. It will only be for a few months' time. If we're even half as successful as I hope, then we won't be troubled with financial worries again. At least not in the near future, anyway."

"Do you really think so?" Beth asked wistfully. Her gaze traveled to where Anna lay sleeping in the wagon.

"I do." She smiled and began leading her horse toward the cool, glistening waters of the stream. "Now come on. We've got a lot to do before tomorrow. Mr. Bloomfield is expecting us at ten o'clock in the morning."

Beth stared thoughtfully after her. It had always been the same, she reflected with an inward sigh. Lainey was the one who made the plans, the one who took charge and looked after everyone, while *she* was the one who followed. That arrangement had been acceptable to the both of them—until now.

Things had started to change of late. Ever since they had set out for Oklahoma, she had felt an increasing desire to play a more active role in their decisions. She wondered if Lainey could understand. It was as if she had left a part of herself behind in Missouri, a part she was not eager to find again. Anna deserved a mother with the strength to meet life unafraid. And Lainey, she thought, her mouth curving into a soft smile while her eyes shone brightly, Lainey deserved a life of her own.

Ethan did not ride by again until much later that afternoon. Lainey was perched on the back of the wagon, engaged in the process of braiding her newly washed hair, when she became aware of his approach. She glanced up and caught sight of him just as he topped the nearby rise in the land. Her eyes grew very round while sudden, warm color flew to her cheeks.

"Why, it's Mr. Holt," Beth noted behind her. Unlike her sister, she beamed an earnest smile of welcome at him as he guided his mount down the hill toward their camp.

Lainey abandoned her efforts to bring her willful tresses under control. Leaving the thick, luxuriant mass of golden curls streaming freely about her face and shoulders, she hastily stood and caught Anna up in her arms. No matter how diligently she had tried, she had not been able to erase the memory of the kiss they had shared. It came back to haunt her full force while she watched him draw the high-spirited roan to a halt.

"How very nice to see you again, Mr. Holt," said Beth. "Did your trip into town go well?"

"Yes, Mrs. Baker, it did." He swung agilely down from the saddle, then lifted a hand to tug the hat from his head. His penetrating gaze moved to Lainey. "I'd like to have a word with you, Miss Prescott."

His deep-timbred voice was laced with amusement; she appeared to be holding the baby in front of her like a shield. There was nothing at all amusing, however, about the fire in his blood. By damn, he mused silently, seeing her again was both a pleasure *and* a torment. He had forced himself to stay away this long, even though he had known it would do no good.

"Alone, if you don't mind," he added quietly, his blue-green eyes flickering briefly toward Beth before fastening on Lainey once more.

"Of course," Beth consented, before her sister could offer a reply. She wasted little time in reaching for Anna. "Come along, sweetheart." Her brow creased into a mild frown of bemusement when she encountered resistance from Lainey, but she persisted. She scooped a loudly chattering Anna into her own arms and bore her away to the shade beneath the trees.

"What is it you want?" demanded Lainey, her own eyes flashing up at him. She felt uncomfortable in his presence. And strangely, alarmingly, breathless.

"Not here," Ethan insisted, with a slight shake of his head. "Let's go for a ride."

"You want me to go for a ride? With *you*?" Her eyes now widened with incredulity.

"What's the matter, Miss Prescott? Are you afraid?" The challenge was issued with an indulgent tenderness that made her color deepen.

"Why, I—absolutely not," she denied hotly.

"Good. Then come on. There's something I want to show you." He slowly advanced on her, his hand already reaching for hers. She instinctively retreated a step.

"I am not going anywhere with you, Ethan Holt!" Her voice rose in a near panic, and she cast a worried look toward the creek before declaring in a furious undertone, "I should think, owing to the humiliation you forced upon me the last time we were alone together, you would not now have the unmitigated gall to make such a request."

"Come with me," he cautioned, a dangerous smile playing about his lips, "or I'll stay for supper. And later."

Lainey's sapphire gaze narrowed and blazed. The threat was a subtle one, but she recognized it for what it was—blackmail, plain and simple. Resentfully telling herself that she had never before encountered such an all-out scoundrel, she battled to control her rising temper and glanced at Beth and Anna again.

She capitulated with an ill grace.

"Very well, Mr. Holt," she virtually hissed. "But if you dare to lay so much as a finger on me, I will not hesitate to make you pay."

"Your point is well taken, Miss Prescott," he drawled,

a light of devilment in his eyes when he reached for her once more.

"I will ride my own horse, thank you." Her words belied the angry vehemence with which she uttered them. Ethan suppressed a smile of wry humor, and, disregarding her protests, seized her arm in a firm but gentle grip.

"We won't be gone long. It will be faster if we ride double."

She held back, her mouth opening to fling a defiant— blistering—malediction at his handsome head. But she saw that Beth was looking their way. With an inward curse, she acknowledged defeat and allowed Ethan to lead her over to his horse. He tossed her up into the saddle. She immediately scrambled backward, making it clear that she had no intention of subjecting herself to the ordeal of being in his arms again. She settled her blue gingham skirts about her and silently dared him to object. His eyes glowed warmly as he mounted in front of her and gathered up the reins.

"Hold on tight," he instructed. It was his turn to mutter an oath when he caught the fresh, lavender scent of her. He was painfully conscious of her delectable curves behind him, and he suffered untold agony when her full breasts accidently brushed against the hard-muscled planes of his back.

Lainey frowned as she shifted into a more comfortable position. Though reluctant to touch Ethan, she knew she had little choice. Her arms slipped about his waist. He tugged on the reins and headed slowly toward the spot where Beth stood watching Anna examine a rock she had found on the banks of the creek.

"Where are you going?" Beth asked, with a smile. Resting a vigilant hand upon the toddler's head, she looked first to Ethan, then to her sister.

"Mr. Holt has something to show me," Lainey replied, her tone deceptively even.

"I'll have her back in time for supper," promised Ethan. He felt her stiffen behind him.

"Of course. But there's no hurry," Beth reassured him. They were already riding away when she thought to call out cheerfully, "Have a pleasant ride!"

Lainey groaned inwardly. She attempted to loosen her grasp once they had left the camp behind, but Ethan foiled her efforts. He touched his heels to the roan's flanks, thereby prompting the animal to take off like a shot. She was forced to hold tight in order to avoid plummeting to the ground. She flung a murderous glare at the man in front of her, all the while making a silent promise to herself that she would never, *ever*, allow Ethan Holt to bend her to his will again.

The first several minutes passed in silence as they rode. Finally Ethan slowed the horse to a walk. The waning sunlight cast a benevolent golden glow upon the landscape; it seemed to fall with particular favor upon the well-built log cabin and barn that Lainey spied in the near distance. The setting could not have been more picturesque.

"What a lovely place! I wonder who lives there," she murmured, her curiosity temporarily overcoming her anger.

"I do."

"You?" she blurted out in disbelief.

"And Travis." His low, splendidly resonant voice held a note of pride when he told her, "It's not much yet. But it will be."

"How on earth did you manage to finish everything so quickly?" She scarcely noticed when he drew the horse to a halt. "Why, we've not yet even—"

"That's what I wanted to talk to you about." He slid from the saddle, then turned to lift her down as well. She would have moved away the instant her feet met the ground, but his fingers remained curled possessively about her waist. "What about your own place?" His mouth twitched when he suggested wryly, "Maybe you're planning to live in a wagon the rest of your life, Lainey."

She gasped, her eyes flying wide at the sound of her name on his lips. It sounded remarkably like an endearment.

"That happens to be none of your business, Mr. Holt," she parried, pulling free at last. She hurried to put some distance between them, then swept a wayward lock of hair from her face and lifted her head proudly. "But since you seem to delight in trying to interfere with my life, you might as well know that I plan to have a house built as soon as possible."

"And when will that be?" He dropped the reins and hung his hat on the saddle horn. The horse obediently stayed put, bending its head to nibble at the sweet prairie grass.

"Soon," came Lainey's evasive reply.

She didn't know why she should feel compelled to tell him anything at all. He certainly had no right to demand any explanations. But it gave her some perverse satisfaction to think about what his reaction would be when he learned of her impending employment. She had little doubt that he would heartily disapprove.

"I have a proposition to make you," he startled her by announcing. He sauntered closer, his gaze never leaving her face.

"A proposition?" She eyed him warily. "What sort of proposition?"

"My brother and I will build you a cabin. In return, you can let us use your land for grazing this summer." He flashed her a brief yet thoroughly disarming smile. "We'll fence the yard so you won't be bothered with cattle on the front porch. And I'll even throw in a dog. You'll need one to help keep the rabbits out of your garden."

"Why, that—that is all completely out of the question," she sputtered, appalled at the very idea. The last thing she wanted was to be in Ethan Holt's debt!

"No it isn't," he masterfully disputed.

He came to a stop mere inches away, towering above her while his eyes burned down into the luminous, deep blue depths of hers. The late afternoon sunlight set her hair afire, and the simple but highly becoming dress she was wearing made her look all the more like she belonged in a rich man's parlor than on the wild plains of Oklahoma. Only she *was* here, he told himself, and he'd be damned if he could wish her elsewhere.

"It makes perfect sense," he pointed out. "The three of you will have a roof over your heads, and we'll have the extra pasture we need when the cattle arrive from Texas next week."

"I'm afraid you don't understand," Lainey pronounced in calm, measured tones. She folded her arms across her breasts and offered him a triumphant look, trying not to let herself be affected by his nearness. "My sister and I have no need of such an arrangement."

"Then you've found someone to build—?"

"No. But we should be able to do so in the near future."

"That isn't good enough," he opined curtly. "It isn't safe for you in that wagon. With four walls around you, you'd have some protection."

"Protection from what?"

"From the weather, for one. It isn't going to hold forever," he warned, flinging a quick glance up toward the sky. His features suddenly grew taut, and his eyes darkened. "And from the type of men who came looking for me the other night." White-hot rage filled him at the thought of what those two bastards had done. He had taken steps to make sure it didn't happen again; he wasn't about to let her get drawn into the trouble.

"Do you know who they were?" asked Lainey. She

was surprised to see a faint, mocking smile touch his lips.

"Let's just say they were 'old friends.' "

"They certainly didn't seem very friendly," she contended, her eyes narrowing up at him in suspicion. She recalled how he had once said he'd worn a badge. Perhaps, she thought, there was a connection. "Were they associates of yours when you were a lawman?"

"Associates?" He shook his head. "Not exactly. But they seem to think we've got some unfinished business to settle." It was obvious that he wasn't going to say anything more on the subject. His brow cleared in the next instant, and he told her, "Travis and I will get started on the cabin right away. It may take a few days to get the rest of the logs we'll need, but we'll go ahead with the fencing in the meantime."

"There isn't going to *be* any cabin," she asserted. "We don't need your charity, Mr. Holt, and—"

"It isn't charity." He cut her off with maddening authority.

"Call it what you will—the fact remains that we don't need your help!" Though ashamed of her cowardice, she obeyed the sudden impulse to turn away. She could feel his eyes on her as she crossed back to stand beside the horse. Gently clearing her throat, and reminding herself that his opinion shouldn't matter to her in the least, she revealed, "We have taken a job in town. The matter hasn't been officially settled just yet, but I am confident that it will be by this time tomorrow."

"What kind of job?" Ethan demanded.

"What difference does it make?" she retorted. Then she was surprised to hear herself confessing, "If you must know, Beth and I are going to be featured at the Palace Theater. We're going to sing." She spun about as if fully expecting him to criticize her judgment. "We needed the money, Mr. Holt, and I see nothing wrong with performing on the stage."

Ethan's only response was to stare across at her with an inscrutable expression on his face and a dull gleam in his eyes that gave her no hint of how the news had affected him. She felt a sharp twinge of disappointment. Several long, highly charged moments of silence passed.

"Well?" she finally prompted with angry impatience. "Aren't you going to tell me what you think? Heaven knows, you've certainly never been hesitant to force your opinion on me before!" She lifted a hand to the saddle, her fingers idly tracing a seam in the leather. "It doesn't matter what you think, of course. Beth and I—"

"You're not going to do it," he decreed quietly.

"What?" she gasped, jerking her head about. "Why, you—you have no right to say that!"

"I have every right."

"Indeed? And what the devil makes you think that?" she now demanded, her eyes fairly snapping at him.

"I care what happens to you." He swiftly closed the distance between them again. His hands shot out to grip her arms. "Damn it, woman, do you have any idea what you're letting yourself in for? The Palace is no place for someone like you!"

"And how can you be so sure of that?" she challenged, struggling within his grasp. "The theater doesn't even open for business until tonight. How can you possibly know—?"

"I know," he reaffirmed, his gaze filling with a harsh light. "Listen to me!" He gave her a quick, compelling shake, his fingers tightening about her soft flesh. "You can't do it, Lainey. It's too dangerous."

"Dangerous?" She temporarily ceased her struggles. "In what way?"

"The two of you will be traveling alone at night. Anything could happen. And then there're the men in the audience. I've seen it happen before—some of them won't be satisfied with just looking."

"I can take care of myself," she declared, with a bravado that was in direct contrast to the growing trepidation within her. In spite of her resistance, he had planted doubts in her mind.

"Even if you want to forget you're a lady," he continued brusquely, "your sister doesn't deserve that kind of treatment."

"Forget I'm a lady?" she echoed, her voice rising on a furious note. She brought her hands up to push ineffectually against the broad, immovable force of his chest. "How dare you! Let go of me!"

"Not until you agree to forget about this 'job' or any other."

"No! Damn you, Ethan Holt," she swore, the denunciation rolling off her tongue with surprising ease, "I don't have to answer to you." She suffered a sharp intake of breath when he suddenly yanked her up hard against him.

"Don't you understand, you little fool?" he ground out, his gaze smoldering down into hers. "I can't stand by and let you ruin your life."

"Take your hands off me!"

Infuriated beyond reason, she could think only of getting free. She lifted her arm and brought the palm of her hand stinging against Ethan's cheek in a loud, forceful slap.

Chapter 6

A loud gasp broke from her lips. Aghast at what she had done, she stared up at him in breathless dismay. Her gaze widened in horror at the sight of his cheek, which bore the faint red imprint of her fingers. His own hands fell slowly away from her arms.

"Well done, Miss Prescott," Ethan proclaimed softly, his deep voice laced with sarcasm. He told himself he'd had it coming to him, that he'd had no right to lay hands on her or even demand that she listen to him. And yet he knew there was no turning back. She mattered to him. She mattered a hell of a lot more than he wanted to admit. The thought of her standing in front of a bunch of rowdy, woman-hungry men while they undressed her with their eyes was enough to make his blood boil.

Lainey swallowed hard and opened her mouth to speak, but no words would come. She did not wait to see what his next move would be. Seizing the opportunity to escape, she pushed abruptly past him and fled down the hill. Her long skirts tangled about her legs, causing her to stumble. She made a desperate attempt to regain her balance, but to no avail. With a strangled cry, she fell to her hands and knees in the thick grass, her long, silken tresses cascading wildly about her.

The next thing she knew, Ethan was catching her up in his strong arms. He hauled her roughly to her feet. She gasped again and tilted her head back to face him.

Blanching inwardly at the near savage gleam in his eyes, she squirmed in his grasp—and was rewarded for her latest defiance when he locked her within his warm, fiercely masculine embrace.

"Stop!" she hissed. "Let me go!"

She could feel her face flaming. Her heart was pounding so loudly that she was certain he could hear it. She raised her eyes to his again, only to tremble at the way his gaze, dangerously intense and full of magnificent, blue-green fire, raked over her. Good heavens, she thought as a knot of panic suddenly tightened within her stomach, what did he mean to do?

She renewed her struggles, but Ethan swept her even closer against him. She was alarmed to feel her feet leaving the ground, and downright thunderstruck to realize that her arms had crept upward with a will of their own to entwine about his neck.

"Someday, Lainey Prescott . . ." Ethan vowed huskily, then captured her lips with his own.

The kiss was hard and almost punishing at first, but soon grew tenderly, rapturously, seductive. Lainey moaned low in her throat and felt her senses reeling. She clung weakly to him while the same liquid warmth she had felt before coursed through her body. She did not merely submit; she kissed him back with a sweet, beguiling ardor that caused him to groan inwardly and tighten his arms about her until she could scarcely breathe.

She inhaled sharply against his mouth when his tongue thrust between her parted lips to explore the moist cavern of her mouth. His bold, velvety tongue teased provocatively at hers, while his hand swept down her back to curl about her buttocks with a possessiveness that sent crimson flying to her cheeks. Reason was well and truly vanquished by passion as the kiss deepened.

All too conscious of her virile, hot-blooded "captor's"

arousal, Lainey squirmed restlessly in his embrace, unaware that her innocent movements provoked such a
blaze of desire within him that he had to call upon every
ounce of self-will he possessed to keep his own passions
under control.

Without warning, his mouth suddenly left off its
heated ravishment of hers and trailed a fiery path downward . . . to where her breasts rose and fell rapidly beneath the fitted bodice of her gown. The rounded,
lace-trimmed neckline offered a tantalizing glimpse of
the satiny flesh that seemed to beckon his caress. He
urged her farther upward. His other hand moved with
dizzying impatience to tug the blue-checked fabric
lower, so that he could press a series of warm and deliciously wicked kisses to the swelling curve of her
bosom.

"Ethan!" she gasped out. The touch of his warm lips
upon the tops of her breasts was so unexpected, so
shockingly pleasurable, that she trembled and felt herself becoming light-headed. His mouth branded her, his
hand closing upon one of her breasts . . .

"Ethan!"

He jerked his head up at the sound of his brother's
voice. Swearing in vengeful silence, he heard his
brother call his name again. His eyes shot to where
Travis was bearing down on them with purposeful
haste.

Lainey murmured a cry of startlement and pushed
frantically at Ethan's shoulders. Shaken and mortified in
the extreme, she would have fallen if not for his arms
about her. He quickly lowered her to her feet, but kept
a steadying hand about her arm as Travis slowed his
mount to a halt nearby.

"Sorry to crowd in on you like this, but I just ran into
Marshal Sutton. He's in Guthrie, at the land office. He
said to tell you he's calling in that favor you owe him,"
announced Travis. Grinning sheepishly at Lainey, he

touched the brim of his hat in a gallant gesture. "Miss Prescott."

Lainey merely nodded at him in response, still flushed with embarrassment at having been caught in such an intimate *entanglement* with his older brother. She was painfully aware of Ethan's fingers burning against the flesh of her arm. Refusing to so much as glance his way, she pulled free and spun about in an effort to compose herself.

"Did he say it was urgent?" Ethan demanded tersely, his gaze smoldering at the interruption.

"No." Travis shook his head. His own eyes were dancing with roguish amusement. "But I think that was the general idea."

Ethan's rugged, sun-bronzed features took on a grim look. He moved toward Lainey again, fighting the urge to say to hell with both Travis and Sutton and finish what they'd started. Though he'd certainly had no intention of letting things get too far—both the time and the place were wrong—he had wanted to prolong the exquisite torment until neither one of them could bear any more.

"I'll take you back," he said quietly.

"No, thank you," she declined in a voice choked with emotion. She pushed past him and hurried across to ask Travis, "Will you please take me home, Mr. Holt?" Her beautiful eyes were bright and full of an unconsciously desperate appeal.

"I'm the one who brought you here. And I'll be the one taking you home," Ethan insisted, earning him a wrathful scowl from her.

"Come on now, Ethan, it does make sense," Travis bravely intervened. "I'll see that Miss Prescott gets back safely, while you head on into town. I doubt Sutton's going to wait too long. Seeing as how he's in charge of the whole Territory, he's bound to have a lot on his mind."

"Thank you," Lainey told him in true gratitude.

Without waiting for Ethan's consent, she reached a hand up to Travis. He hesitated only a moment before taking it and hoisting her up behind him. Ethan's eyes narrowed imperceptibly as he watched her settle her skirts about her shapely, white-stockinged legs. Moving to his own horse, he transferred the hat to his head and swung up into the saddle.

"We'll start on Miss Prescott's cabin tomorrow," he informed his brother.

"You most definitely will not!" Lainey reasserted, her gaze filling with fire once more. She flung him a glare that made him smile to himself and recall an old saying about looks being able to kill. But he was still very much alive, and determined to stay that way long enough to show Lainey Prescott just how well-matched they were. *In every way.*

"Tomorrow," he repeated, his tone one of ominous certainty. He rode away, leaving her to stare after him in mingled outrage and confusion—and disappointment.

She was furious with herself as well as him. Confound it all, how could she have let it happen again? And with even more shamelessness than before. Chagrined at the memory of his lips upon her breasts, she closed her eyes and tried, without success, to forget what it had felt like to be kissed with such fierce longing.

Someday, he had said. What had he meant by that? she wondered, then angrily told herself it didn't matter. That day, whatever its significance, would never come. With heaven's help—and a determination that was in very real danger of crumbling—she would have to guard herself against Ethan Holt. . . .

"What do you think of our spread, Miss Prescott?" Travis asked conversationally, nodding toward the ranch he and his brother had talked about starting for years. If not for Ethan's damned independence and his own wildness, he told himself with an inward smile, they'd have been back home in Texas by now. But Oklahoma might just prove to be the right place after all.

"It—it's very nice," Lainey murmured, with a somewhat distracted air.

"The cabin's only got one room, but we'll add on later. I'm afraid yours won't be any larger."

"Please, just take me home, Mr. Holt," she pleaded. She had no desire to plunge into the same argument she had just played out with his brother; there had been quite enough confrontation for one day. Indeed, her head ached and her nerves felt as tightly drawn as a bowstring. She wanted nothing more than to return to the sanctuary of her newfound home.

Although Beth was quite surprised to see that a different Holt had returned her sister to camp, she wisely chose not to interrogate Lainey about it. Travis stayed only a few minutes. He complimented Beth on her appearance and tossed a gleeful Anna into the air, then announced that he had to be getting back to his own place.

Lainey thanked him again and took charge of the baby, disappearing into the wagon. Still too engrossed in the highly perplexing memory of her most recent encounter with Ethan, she did not realize the danger of leaving Beth alone with Travis until it was too late.

"I am grateful to you for seeing Lainey home, Mr. Holt," Beth proclaimed as they walked together for a moment. Her pretty, heart-shaped countenance was suffused with a becoming color, and her opal eyes shone softly up at him. "Perhaps, sometime soon, you and your brother would care to have supper with us. I feel that it's the least we can do to repay you for your many kindnesses toward us."

"You don't owe us anything, Mrs. Baker," he insisted solemnly, then flashed her a crooked smile. "But I'll take you up on that offer of a meal. Ethan's nearly as sorry a cook as I am." He glanced down at the hat in his hands. "Don't you think it's time we stopped being so formal? It's true we haven't known each other very long, but we're going to be seeing a lot of each other starting tomorrow and—"

"Tomorrow?" she broke in to ask with a frown of complete bafflement. "I'm sorry, Mr. Holt, but I don't understand what you mean."

"We're going to start on your cabin tomorrow. Ethan's got everything arranged." It was his turn to frown, his gaze momentarily clouding while it traveled over her face. "You didn't know?"

"No." She cast a bemused look toward the wagon. "I suppose that's what your brother wanted to talk to Lainey about."

"Among other things," quipped Travis. He watched in secret delight as her eyes grew very round. "We're going to build you a cabin in return for some extra grazing land."

"I see. Well then, Mr. Holt—"

"As I was saying a moment ago, I think it's high time we put a stop to this 'Mr. Holt' and 'Mrs. Baker' business. I don't think we'll be breaking any hard-and-fast rules if we step on ahead to a first-name basis, do you?"

"Well, I—I suppose not," she faltered, her color deepening at the warmth in his voice. She was wearing a rose-printed cotton dress that fit her slender curves to perfection, and her light blond hair was swept up in a loosely fashioned chignon. There was a tiny smudge of dirt on the silken smoothness of her left cheek—lingering proof of the long day's work.

To Travis, she looked incredibly fresh and lovely. She was more of a lady than anyone he'd ever known before; it struck him that she would put the other women of his acquaintance to shame. He told himself that he wasn't good enough to seek a friendship with her, let alone court her, but his stubborn heart refused to listen. He wasn't accustomed to feeling such uncertainty and yearning. He had never been plagued with a lack of self-confidence in the past. But now, for the first time in his life, he actually felt nervous in a woman's presence.

"How long have you been a widow, Beth?" he asked in a low, almost reverent tone. He had posed the same question to Lainey once before, but he was glad now that she hadn't answered.

"I . . . since before Anna was born," Beth murmured, surprised at how pleasurable it was to hear him say her name.

Pleasure, however, immediately gave way to guilt. She hated lying to anyone, but it bothered her most of all to lie to this man. He was so kind and personable, and she sensed in him a gentleness of spirit that belied his rakish, devil-may-care manner. The fact that he was handsome was of only secondary importance to her. She had been deceived by good looks and winning ways two years ago; she wasn't going to make the same mistake twice.

If only *she* weren't the one carrying out the deception this time. Travis Holt deserved better than that, she thought with an inward sigh of remorse.

"It must have been hard on you, losing your husband so young," he remarked. They had finally reached the spot where he had left his horse. He unlooped the reins from the tree and turned to face Beth with an earnest expression on his tanned, chiseled features. His green eyes darkened when he confided on sudden impulse, "I've never been married. I've never even come close. And God forgive me, I've done a lot of things I regret."

"Why, Mr. Holt—"

"Travis," he corrected, with a faint smile.

"Travis," Beth amended submissively. She gazed up at him in bewilderment, trying to ignore the fluttering of her own heart. "I don't understand why you should suddenly feel compelled to tell me this."

"Don't you?" His mouth curved into another smile,

even more captivating than the last. He moved closer, his gaze softening as it caught and held the wide, soft blue radiance of hers. "I think, Beth Baker, that I've been looking for you my whole life."

"But, how—how can you know that?" she stammered breathlessly. She retreated a step, but her back came up against the tree. Her pulse leapt wildly as she watched Travis advance upon her again.

"The first time I saw you, I could have sworn I'd been struck by lightning," he told her, his eyes brimming with tender amusement.

Travis realized that he no longer felt nervous—only impatient. He was impatient to find out if there was any hope of making her care for him. Still, he cautioned himself not to proceed too quickly. She needed time to examine her feelings, time to get used to the idea of having another man in her life. Although he experienced a sharp pang of jealousy at the thought of her husband, he was not one to dwell on the past. God willing, he would teach her to love again.

"What you describe could well be nothing more than mere physical attraction," Beth pointed out in a futile attempt to explain away what they had *both* felt. "And while I am naturally quite flattered by your . . . consideration, I think it would be best if you did not speak of it again."

"Why not?" He was so close now that they were almost touching. Noting her visible alarm, he longed to take her in his arms and offer her solace, to kiss away her doubts. But he didn't want to frighten her, and he knew Lainey might be watching them. "What harm can it do for us to talk about it?" he challenged softly.

"You wouldn't understand!" cried Beth, startling herself as well as Travis with her vehemence. "Please, if you have any regard for me at all, you'll offer me your friendship and nothing more." Fighting back sudden tears, she whirled about and fled across the campsite to the other side of the wagon. There, hidden from view, she buried her face in her hands and choked back the sobs that rose in her throat.

Travis frowned worriedly after her. It pained him more than he cared to admit to think that he had been wrong, that what she felt for him was truly nothing more than a cordial, wholly platonic interest. He cursed himself for a fool and angrily mounted up. Reining about, he stole one last rueful glance toward the wagon and urged his horse into a gallop. He rode away, too unhappy to think about anything other than the woman who had unintentionally captured his heart.

Lainey tried comforting her sister after he had gone, but Beth would not be consoled. Neither would she disclose what had happened. She wept as though she would never stop, casting herself facedown inside the wagon and pouring out her tears on the quilt. Anna, perturbed by the rare sight of her mother's crying, took to wailing in sympathy.

Lainey blamed Travis, of course, and vowed to discover exactly what he had said or done to cause her beloved, even-tempered sister such overpowering distress. She would have saddled her horse and given chase to him that very moment, but Beth implored her not to. She had little choice but to wait for the storm tide of weeping to pass and hope that an explanation would follow. Vengefully condemning both Holt brothers as black-hearted Texas scoundrels, she rocked Anna in her arms and swore underneath her breath as the image of Ethan's face rose in her mind.

Beth's eyes were still faintly underscored by shadows the next morning. She seemed much like her old self otherwise, however, and told Lainey she was looking forward to their trip into town. Disappointingly, she had refused to speak of Travis Holt. And neither one of them made mention of Ethan's promise to begin construction on their cabin that day. It was as if, by remaining silent on the subject, they could somehow prevent the inevitable.

They saddled their horses after breakfast and set out for Guthrie, each offering up a silent prayer that the audition for Mr. Bloomfield would not prove too nerve-racking. Lainey, being the more experienced rider of the two, held Anna in front of her as she rode. She smiled at the little girl's obvious pleasure at being on horseback for the first time. Anna's laughter was a balm for her own disquietude.

A few clouds had gathered on the western horizon, but the sun's rays stretched eagerly across the morning sky. Lainey eased her grip on the reins and lifted her face toward the warmth. Mr. Bloomfield wasn't expecting them until ten o'clock, but she had insisted that they leave an hour beforehand. Following the audition, she planned to go in search of Mr. Calhoun.

"What is the theater like?" Beth queried, her brows drawing together in a pensive frown.

"It's nothing more than a large tent at present," Lainey admitted. "But Mr. Bloomfield said they hope to have the two-story frame building completed by the end of next week. It's absolutely amazing, Beth, the speed with which everything is happening in town! There are tents everywhere, and so many buildings already taking shape. Guthrie doesn't look at all the way it did when we first saw it."

"I'm glad of that. I hope there will be a church soon. And a school. You do realize, don't you, that it is Sunday morning?"

"I suppose I hadn't really thought about it." Time had held no meaning for her these past few days.

"Well, I have," said Beth. Looking troubled, she released a sigh and opined, "It doesn't seem right, Lainey, that we should be conducting business such as this on the Sabbath."

"I'm sorry, but it simply cannot be helped. We should

be able to restore some order to our lives soon," she offered hopefully, her arm tightening a bit about Anna's waist. "For now, however, we'll just have to take advantage of the opportunities whenever they come along."

"Perhaps you're right," Beth murmured in uneasy concurrence. A shadow crossed her face, and she quickly looked away so that her sister wouldn't glimpse the sorrow in her eyes.

Guthrie was a tumultuous whirl of activity, despite the fact that it was Sunday morning. Few of its inhabitants either noticed or cared that the day had traditionally been a time of rest; there was no resting to be done in a boomtown.

Lainey was glad they had allowed the extra time, for it was nearly a quarter before ten when they finally reached the town's main business district. Beth was suitably impressed by the progress that had been made. Her widened gaze swept across the astonishing jumble of tents and humanity with fascination. She dismounted alongside Lainey in front of the depot and reached up for Anna.

"Why are we stopping here?" she queried in puzzlement.

"Because the horses will be safer here," Lainey explained with a brief smile. She waited until she was sure the baby was secured within Beth's grasp, then dismounted as well and hastily smoothed down her skirts. "It's even more crowded near the theater. That's where the majority of the construction is taking place."

"Oh, Lainey. Are you truly certain we should be doing this?" asked Beth, still plagued by misgivings about the venture. Her qualms were not eased by the sight of a man, obviously inebriated, staggering about nearby. The noise and smells and general air of pandemonium were enough to make her wish she had gathered the courage to say no to her sister. "Perhaps we can think of some other way—"

"No." She shook her head and finished looping the reins about the hitching post. "Please, Beth. You're just going to have to trust me."

Taking the other woman's arm in a firm, compelling grasp, she started off toward the Palace Theater. It was only a short walk away. Beth clutched Anna protectively to her bosom as they went and did her best to ignore the men who favored her with bold stares. She was relieved when Lainey announced that they had arrived at their destination, and her eyes grew round once more when they lifted to the bright, dramatically lettered sign hanging above the tent's doorway. The tent itself was positively gigantic, a massive rectangle of white canvas held aloft by an army of wooden posts and metal bolts.

"Mr. Bloomfield told me they can accommodate two hundred patrons at once," Lainey told her. She took a deep, steadying breath of her own before smiling again. "Come on. And try not to be nervous. Our surroundings may have altered, but singing here in Guthrie cannot be so different from singing back home. Except that our performances will be rewarded with a good deal more than applause from now on."

The audition proved to be mercifully brief. And completely successful.

They sang only two songs—one hymn, at Beth's insistence, and one popular ballad—then spent the remainder of the time talking with their new employer, an outgoing, rather portly man whose clothes were most assuredly on the flamboyant side. When they emerged from the tent a scant twenty minutes later, Lainey was glowing with pleasure and excitement.

Beth, on the other hand, was feeling even more uneasy than before. Mr. Bloomfield had been all that was gentlemanly, of course, although he *had* subjected her to a scrutiny that was a bit too familiar for her tastes.

He had pronounced their voices to be excellent, and had reconfirmed their freedom to choose their own material. But still, she remained unconvinced that the Palace was the right place for their talents to be displayed.

"Just think of it, Beth—we're to start tonight," Lainey happily reiterated. She caught Anna up in her arms and gave her sister an infectious smile. "I told you everything would work out. How fortunate we are that Mr. Bloomfield's wife will be on hand to watch the baby for us." She turned her loving gaze upon Anna and murmured teasingly, "Your mother and aunt are going to be wealthy women in no time."

"I know Mr. Bloomfield said he would provide us with costumes," Beth commented, with a distracted air, "but I do wish he had allowed us to see them beforehand. How can we be certain they will fit us properly?"

"Oh, there will be plenty of time for that later!" Lainey insisted, waving away her sister's concern. "We've got to find Mr. Calhoun now. And we must return home in plenty of time for Anna to have a good long nap. I'm afraid she'll be up well past her bedtime tonight." According to Mr. Bloomfield, their last performance would not begin until eleven o'clock, which meant they wouldn't get home until nearly midnight. The late hour worried her a bit, but she told herself they would simply have to adapt.

Oliver T. Calhoun's "office" was located following an intensive search through the melee of Guthrie's main thoroughfare. Lainey's eyes lit with triumph when she spied the sign above his tent. Still holding Anna, she swept inside with Beth close behind.

"Why, Miss Prescott," the lawyer exclaimed in pleasant surprise. He remembered her; in fact, she had been much in his thoughts these past several days. Although he had crossed paths with literally dozens of clients since the run, *she* was the one who had crept into his mind even at night. And not merely because her claim was in question. "Please, come in!" he urged, offering her a chair before smiling politely at Beth. "How do you do?" he said. "Allow me to introduce myself. I am Oliver T. Calhoun."

"I'm Miss Prescott's sister," Beth replied. "Mrs. Baker." She smiled at him in return and took a seat in the chair beside Lainey's. Anna scrambled down from her aunt's lap and toddled over to examine a crate in the corner of the tent, while Beth kept a maternal eye upon her.

"I've come to inquire about the status of my claim, Mr. Calhoun," declared Lainey. "I know it's only been a few days, but I was hoping you might have some news. Favorable or otherwise."

"I do have news, Miss Prescott. And I'm afraid it is not favorable," he admitted with visible reluctance. He frowned as he sank down into his own chair behind the oak desk he'd had transported all the way from Chicago. "True to my word, I have been in pursuit of the matter since the first day you agreed to my representation. Only yesterday, I discovered that no less than three other individuals have filed a claim on your particular quarter-section."

"Three?" she echoed in stunned disbelief. "But, that—that's impossible! I was the first and only one to set markers, and I have maintained an uninterrupted residence ever since!"

"I understand that. But it may turn out to be of no real significance. You see, the court could still recognize one of the other claimants as the true owner. It all depends on how convincing an argument they are able to present." His frown deepened when he confided, "Yours is not the only claim in question, Miss Prescott. And, to be perfectly honest, I suspect that the majority of these cases are being sought in an attempt to frighten the initial claimants away. The process can be quite lengthy, and costly as well. I myself have already been forced to dismiss a number of cases."

Lainey could scarcely believe what she was hearing. Dear God, she reflected numbly, surely they hadn't come this far in order to lose everything? It wasn't fair. It simply wasn't fair! Filled with righteous indignation at the mere thought of defeat, she sighed heavily and transferred her furious, blazing sapphire gaze to the neat stack of papers on the lawyer's desk.

Seconds later, she stole a quick glance at Beth. The look of apprehension on her sister's face only served to strengthen her resolve.

"You said there were three individuals, Mr. Calhoun," she remarked in calm, measured tones. "Very well. Who are they? And upon what do they base their claim to my land?"

"I am not privy to their evidence. But their names are a matter of public record now." He lifted one of the papers, quickly scanned its contents, and revealed, "There is a man identified as Joseph Smith. Another has listed his name as Thomas Payton. And the third calls himself Arnold Merriwether." A faint smile of irony touched his lips when he lowered the paper and met her gaze. "You must understand, Miss Prescott, that it is not at all unusual for a false name to be given whenever someone is involved in such questionable tactics—as I believe these tactics to be. Nor is it unheard of for the actual claimant to employ another man to act as 'the front,' if you will. I cannot make that judgment myself, of course, but are any of these names familiar to you?"

"No. None of them. I have no idea who these men are, or why they have selected *my* claim to contest." She sighed again and confided, "My sister and I do not have a great deal of money left, Mr. Calhoun. Although we have found employment, it will be quite some time before—"

"Say no more, Miss Prescott," he gently cut her off. "I will continue to handle the case."

"But I won't be able to pay you, at least not yet. And we must still build a house." She refused to acknowledge any thought of Ethan when she added this last.

"Then I will wait." He smiled, his bespectacled eyes gleaming warmly across at her. "It's much too soon to worry. And the matter may very well resolve itself. There is always the possibility that Mr. Smith, Mr. Payton, and—lest we forget—the esteemed Mr. Merriwether will realize the error of their ways and seek their fortunes elsewhere."

"I certainly hope so," she murmured.

"If I may be so forward, Miss Prescott," he requested, changing the subject. "You mentioned that you had found employment. Will you be working in town?"

"Yes, at the Palace Theater." Her brow cleared somewhat as she told him. "My sister and I have been engaged as songstresses. Our first performance will take place tonight." She was surprised to view his sudden, sharp frown. "Is something wrong, Mr. Calhoun?"

"Are you familiar with the Palace?"

"Familiar? Well, I suppose you could say that. We have just come from there. Mr. Bloomfield was kind enough to grant us an audition this morning."

"I see. And are you completely certain that you wish to provide entertainment in the sort of atmosphere the Palace offers?" he asked, choosing his words carefully.

"Of course. Why shouldn't I be?"

"Perhaps, Miss Prescott, you will allow me to offer you some advice. The advice of a friend." His kindly gaze included Beth as well. "I have no personal knowledge of the theater's reputation, yet I have been given to understand that it is not at all suitable for ladies. My sources have informed me that, beginning with the very first performance last night, there was such an overall tendency toward drunkenness and hooliganism that the local authorities were forced to demand an early end to the festivities. I fear you would not be at all comfortable in such rough surroundings," he concluded.

"I am grateful to you for your concern, Mr. Calhoun," Lainey replied in all sincerity, "but I cannot help but feel Mr. Bloomfield will take steps to ensure there is no further trouble."

"Perhaps we should heed Mr. Calhoun's advice, Lainey," Beth interjected at this point. The lawyer's words had struck fear in her heart; not only was she concerned about her own and Lainey's safety, but there was her daughter to think of. Her eyes flew to where the fair-haired little girl was still determinedly attempting to scramble on top of the crate. "I cannot bear the thought of placing Anna in the midst of such danger."

"Nor can I," Lainey emphatically agreed. "If the situation turns the least bit hazardous, then I promise you, we will leave."

She had always kept her promises to Beth. She fully believed, however, that she would not be called upon to keep this one. While Mr. Calhoun's remarks troubled her more than she cared to admit, she refused to be scared away so easily. No, she and Beth would perform as planned that evening, at which time they would be able to judge for themselves whether or not they wished to continue their association with the Palace Theater. It couldn't be as bad as all that, she thought.

Considering the matter settled, she rose to her feet and offered the slender, fortyish man her hand.

"Thank you, Mr. Calhoun. For everything."

"I consider it an honor, Miss Prescott," he proclaimed, clasping her hand with the appreciative warmth of his. "And once again, you can be certain that I will do everything in my power to help ensure your victory with the claim."

He said good-bye to her, and to Beth and Anna, then

watched as the three of them disappeared into the brightness outside. His brow creased into yet another reflective frown after they had gone. Bending his frame slowly back down into the chair, he smiled wryly to himself and realized that he would be among the fortunate audience at the Palace Theater when the beautiful Prescott sisters made their debut.

Upon reaching home once more, Lainey hurried to prepare a cold meal while Beth sought to keep a visibly drooping Anna awake long enough to eat. The sun hung almost directly overhead by then, and the wind had shifted to the northwest. There were still only a few clouds to mar the endless blue perfection of the April sky, but it was apparent that the weather was heading toward a change.

Much later that same afternoon, the Holt brothers finally showed up. Travis was in control of the long-bed wagon, which was fully loaded with logs, while Ethan rode alongside the wagon on horseback. Lainey and Beth exchanged looks of mutual consternation before hurrying forward to greet their uninvited guests.

Lainey, of course, made straightaway for Ethan. She was waiting for him when he reined his mount to a halt, her eyes full of fire and her color high. Wasting little time, she lit into him with a vengeance.

"I thought, *Mr. Holt*, that I had made myself perfectly clear," she charged. She folded her arms angrily across her chest and fixed him with a scorching glare. "There is no bargain between us—not now, not ever!"

"Have it your way," he startled her by conceding. With only the ghost of a smile playing about his lips, he swung down from the saddle and turned to face her. "But we're still going to build you a cabin." He said it with that maddening tone of authority she had come to know all too well.

"And I say you are not!" She planted herself squarely

in his path and lifted her head to a proud, defiant angle. "This is my land, and I demand that you leave it—"

"Step aside, Miss Prescott," he commanded softly. His gaze burned down into hers. At that moment, she had little doubt that he would use physical force in order to move her. And she, confound it, could do nothing more than swallow her pride and comply.

Beth, meanwhile, watched in anguished silence while Travis guided the wagon to a stop. He set the brake and jumped down, his face wearing a coolly distant expression when he sauntered toward her. Contained within his emerald gaze, however, was a mixture of love and pain.

"Good afternoon, Mrs. Baker," he murmured, sweeping the hat from his head.

"Mr. Holt." Her own voice was scarcely above a whisper. She stood before him with downcast eyes, feeling at once heartsick and full of joy at his presence. Anna provided a timely rescue of her mother by hurling herself at Beth's long skirts and demanding to be held. Travis bestowed a quick, endearingly crooked smile on the little girl, then excused himself and strode past them to discuss something with his brother.

Lainey did not accept defeat gracefully. When Ethan dared to ask her where she wanted the cabin to be built, she rounded on him as though he had just committed the worst crime imaginable.

"For the last time, Ethan Holt, will you please listen to me?" she ground out. Her traitorous gaze strayed briefly toward his mouth—the arrogant scoundrel was actually smiling at her—and the memory of their most recent kiss sent her temper flaring to dangerous levels indeed. "I will not allow you to barge in here and—"

"We won't be able to do anything more than clear the site today," he declared as if she hadn't spoken at all. He settled his hat on his head once more and nodded at Travis. "Let's get to it."

Both shocked and outraged at his presumption, Lainey found herself at an uncharacteristic loss for words. She watched as he and Travis moved away. They entered into a discussion of the best possible location for the cabin, leaving her, and her sister as well, feeling as if they had been caught up in a whirlwind.

"I know we never talked about it," said Beth, joining her beside the wagon, "but I was under the impression that you had refused Mr. Holt's offer."

"I *did* refuse it!"

"Then why——?"

"For heaven's sake, Beth! I don't see how I can stop them. I could order them off our land at gunpoint, I suppose, but even that probably wouldn't work." She remembered, with humiliating clarity, what had happened the last time she tried pointing a gun at Ethan Holt.

"Well . . . if they are so determined to help us, then I think we should let them," Beth concluded reasonably. She transferred a clinging Anna's weight to the other hip. "We do need a place to live, and I'm sure there must be some way we can repay them."

"They want to use our land for their cattle." Her mouth curved into a faint, humorless smile. "At least that's the arrangement Mr. Holt proposed." She found it difficult to believe that a few acres of grass were as valuable as an entire cabin.

"Then why not simply accept it? I know you had planned to wait until we had saved enough money, but, please, Lainey," asked Beth, her eyes soft and pleading, "couldn't we——?"

"I don't think we have any choice in the matter!" Lainey finally conceded. She flung another inflamed look toward Ethan. "Heaven help me, Beth, I know I should be grateful for his—for *their* generosity—but I resent having it forced upon me!" Releasing a long, ragged breath, she asserted in a low voice simmering with emotion, "We're going to keep our distance whenever they're here."

"We most certainly are," her sister concurred, having already decided much the same. Her own troubled gaze was drawn to the younger Holt.

"And you're not to mention anything about the theater, understand?" Lainey cautioned at a sudden thought. She was relieved when Beth nodded in agreement.

They watched while the two men surveyed a patch of level, thickly carpeted ground only a short distance from the creek. Lainey battled the impulse to call out another protest. It would do no good. Just as she had told Beth, they had little choice in the matter.

And with Ethan Holt, she fumed in silence, it would probably always be that way.

Chapter 7

There was a storm brewing.

Lainey cast a worried glance overhead at the darkening twilight heavens. The clouds had thickened considerably within the past hour, hanging heavy and ominous while the unmistakable scent of rain filled the air.

"We can't possibly venture into town now," said Beth, her apprehensive gaze following Lainey's.

"There's always a chance it won't rain until after . . ." She left the sentence unfinished; her words had lacked conviction anyway. A faint sigh escaped her lips as she frowned in resignation. She knew what she had to do. "You're right, of course. You and Anna must stay here. I'll have to perform solo tonight."

"Oh, Lainey. You cannot be serious." Her sister gasped in disbelief. "Why, not only is Mr. Bloomfield expecting the two of us, it will be much too dangerous for you to be out riding alone. What if the storm should break—?"

"I'll simply have to take that chance." She was already heading off to saddle her horse. A thoroughly dismayed Beth followed hard on her heels.

"Lainey, please be reasonable!"

"I am being reasonable. Perfectly reasonable. One of us has to go—and you have to stay here with Anna," she reiterated. "Mr. Bloomfield will no doubt be disappointed when he sees that I have come alone, but at least this way I might be able to persuade him to let us keep the position. As for the storm, I'll wear a hat and one of the slickers we bought in Arkansas City. Besides, I won't be traveling all that far." She lifted the saddle to the animal's back and leaned down to buckle the cinch into place. Behind her, Beth was still unconvinced.

"What if someone, some bloodthirsty ruffian, should accost you?"

"If it will make you feel better, I'll take the rifle."

"The only thing that will make me feel better, Lainey Prescott, is for you to abandon this reckless scheme and stay here where you'll be safe."

"I know you were reluctant for us to take the job, Beth," Lainey said gently, her face illuminated by the campfire's soft, flickering glow, "and I cannot help but think that same reluctance is now coloring your judgment. I do appreciate your concern for my welfare, but I will be all right."

"What will you do if the weather takes a violent turn?" Beth demanded. She knew it was useless to argue, but she had to try.

"Then I will seek shelter and wait out the worst of it. The storms here can't be so different than what we've seen before." She finished the task and led the horse forward. "Please, Beth, try not to worry. I should be back by midnight, but in the event that I am delayed for some reason, don't assume the worst."

"You have forgotten something."

Lainey watched while she scrambled up to the wagon seat and then climbed down again with the rifle in her hands. She presented it disconsolately.

"Here. I don't want you to go, but I *will* feel somewhat better if you take it."

"Thank you," Lainey murmured, with a brief, indulgent smile. Wondering where to store the gun while she rode, she settled for tying it behind the saddle. That done, she hastened across to one of the storage trunks, and, after a few moments of searching, withdrew a broad-brimmed hat and yellow canvas slicker. Donning the protective garments, she returned to her waiting horse and mounted up.

"Please tell Mr. Bloomfield I'm sorry about tonight," asked Beth. "And be careful, dearest Lainey." Sudden tears glistened in her eyes, but she valiantly blinked them back.

"I will," promised Lainey. With one last bolstering smile, she rode away. Beth stared after her, watching until she had been swallowed up by the cool, rain-scented darkness of the deepening night.

The trip was achieved with no real hint of danger, other than a worrisome tendency on the horse's part to jerk his head and fight against the reins. The animal was apparently skittish as a result of the approaching storm, which Lainey still prayed would not break until after she had returned home again. But the clouds looked more threatening than ever. Lightning flashed just beyond the horizon, while thunder rumbled across the sky and shook the earth below. It required all of her newfound equestrian skills to maintain a steady course. Relieved when she glimpsed the combined glow of the lamps and fires—literally thousands of them—burning in the darkness ahead, she murmured soothingly to the horse and rode down the hill into town.

Guthrie at night was different than in the daytime, but it was no less rowdy. The saloons and gambling halls and theaters were filled to overflowing, the streets crowded with revelers. Although the more domesticated members of the population were happily ensconced within their tents and makeshift quarters, the others seemed intent upon raising hell. The later the hour grew, the more uproarious they became, as if they felt some desperate, inexplicable need to pack a whole lifetime of wicked pleasure into the few short hours left before the dawn. Music and laughter, not to mention the distinctive aroma of unwashed bodies and strong spirits, choked the same air that had smelled so fresh outside of town.

Keeping her head bent low, Lainey rode through the frenzied merrymaking without incident. She reached the Palace, noted with some dismay the crowd spilling out into the street, and guided her horse around to the back of the massive tent. Recalling Mr. Bloomfield's assurance that it would be safe there, she was pleased when a young man came forward to take control of the reins. He led the animal away to a nearby shed.

She shrugged out of the slicker and pulled the hat from her head. Her hair was tumbling down out of its pins, and she cursed its waywardness, wishing she had braided it after all. She took a deep breath and smoothed down her skirts before heading toward the rear entrance. Slipping inside the lamplit warmth of the tent, she was met by Mr. Bloomfield himself.

"Good evening, Miss Prescott." He greeted her with a broad smile. His gaze immediately searched for Beth. "Where is your sister?"

"I'm afraid she was unable to come tonight, Mr. Bloomfield. The weather—" she started to explain.

"I hired a duo," he pointed out coldly. The smile had faded, and in its place was an expression of barely controlled anger. "Two singers with your looks is a novelty. One isn't."

Lainey swallowed a sudden lump in her throat as she watched the corners of his graying, neatly trimmed mustache turn down. Anxious to hold on to the job, she forced a winning smile to her lips and offered up yet another apology.

"I truly am sorry, Mr. Bloomfield. You have every right to be annoyed. But, it's only for tonight," she assured him. "Please, give me the opportunity to prove myself to you. If you are disappointed in any way, then you do not have to pay me for the performance."

She watched his face closely, holding her breath

while he considered the matter. Relief washed over her when his features relaxed and he allowed the merest suggestion of a smile to touch his lips.

"All right," he consented begrudgingly. "You've got yourself a deal. You'll find your costume in there." He nodded to indicate a curtained-off area just to their left. "Put it on and meet me back here in five minutes. Don't be late."

"Thank you, Mr. Bloomfield." She whirled about and ducked inside what apparently passed for a dressing room. A cracked cheval mirror sat in one corner, and nearby was a small table upon which sat an open box of face powder, various other cosmetics, a hairbrush, a collection of mismatched hairpins, a bottle of lavender water, and a lamp. There were two gowns—one blue and one red—draped over the one and only chair. Mindful of the time, however, she spared only a brief glance for them.

She could hear the sound of masculine voices raised in dramatic fury as the current performance, a scene from one of Shakespeare's tragedies, drew to a close. The audience was remarkably quiet. She thought of Mr. Calhoun's words of caution and smiled. It seemed that his warning was unnecessary after all.

Quickly tugging the remainder of the pins from her hair, she put them in the pocket of her skirt and started unbuttoning her white cotton shirtwaist. She had soon peeled it off, and the skirt as well. Casting a worried look toward the curtain, she hastily snatched up the red satin gown. The blue one would have suited Beth perfectly, she told herself with a faint smile.

She slipped the gown on and struggled to fasten the half dozen hooks and eyes that ran down the back. The fit was not as good as she would have wished. The bodice felt a bit too tight, almost uncomfortably so, prompting her to think of the corset packed away in the trunk back home. It wasn't until she had taken up the borrowed hairbrush to begin dragging it through the rebellious golden tresses that she noticed the "briefness" of her costume.

A sharp gasp broke from her lips when she turned toward the mirror and caught sight of her reflection.

"What in heaven's name—?" she muttered in horrified disbelief.

Her eyes fell to where the low, rounded neckline of the fitted bodice revealed almost as much as it concealed. Her breasts swelled enticingly upward, the décolletage offering a scandalous display of the satiny flesh. The skirt was no better; its shimmering fullness reached only to her knees. She could see her face crimsoning as she stared at herself in the mirror. Her sapphire gaze sparked with mingled embarrassment and outrage.

"Miss Prescott?"

She started at the sound of Mr. Bloomfield's voice. Spinning about on her booted heel, she flung the curtain aside to confront him.

"Surely you don't expect me to wear *this*!" she demanded, her hands folding across the décolletage with furious and instinctive modesty.

"Well now, the fit's not bad. Not bad at all." His eyes filled with lustful appreciation as they crawled over her in a slow, critical appraisal. "If you looked any better, I'd have to call in the soldiers from Camp Guthrie to keep things orderly," he remarked, with a leering chuckle.

"I don't happen to find this in the least bit humorous, Mr. Bloomfield." Wondering where the devil *Mrs.* Bloomfield was, she did her best to control her rising temper. "I'm afraid you don't understand. I cannot appear onstage while attired like some—some loose woman!"

"You will if you want the job," he countered tersely. "And you're on next."

"But, I—"

"Take it or leave it." Fully confident of his own victory, he could afford to be magnanimous. "If you stay on, I'll see about getting you another costume." He pointed her toward the stage and added as both a compliment and a directive for future performances, "Oh, and I think it's a nice touch, leaving your hair down like that. It makes you look even younger."

She opened her mouth to demand, with biting sarcasm, why the devil she should *want* to look younger than her advanced age of one and twenty, but she never got the chance. At that moment, the audience erupted into a near deafening roar of applause. Mr. Bloomfield said something unintelligible, then disappeared through yet another curtain. The "thespians of international renown" took their final bow and exited from the stage—a sturdy albeit rather narrow wooden platform with steps leading up the back.

Lainey found herself beseiged by several conflicting emotions. Naturally she wanted the job and the money that went with it. But how could she possibly appear in front of anyone dressed—or only half-dressed—as she was now? Plagued by indecision, she was almost glad when the matter was taken out of her hands.

Before she quite knew what was happening, Mr. Bloomfield launched a surprise attack from the rear. He seized her hand, pulled her up the steps, and forced her through the opening in the curtain. By the time it occurred to her to struggle, he had already managed to position her on the stage. A burst of raucous laughter greeted her less than regal entrance.

"And don't forget to cue the orchestra," her employer called out behind her.

Lainey, furiously sweeping the luxuriant, honey-gold tresses from her face, stood in the center of the stage and knew a moment's panic. Her eyes grew very wide as they traveled slowly across the two hundred masculine faces . . . the two hundred pairs of eyes that stared back at her. The laughter had died down, and the tent was now filled with an expectant silence.

Though tempted to raise her hands to her plunging neckline once more, she forced her arms to remain at her sides. She drew herself up proudly.

At a nod from her, the "orchestra"—comprised of only three musicians—began to play. The bold strains of a piano joined with those of a fiddle and an accordion. The tune was familiar to most of the eager patrons, and Lainey hoped that she had chosen well. Taking a deep breath, she opened her mouth and began to sing.

" 'In Scarlet Town where I was born, there was a fair maid dwellin', as all young men were well aware, her name was Barbara Allen . . .' "

The old English ballad was unabashedly sentimental. It never failed to provoke a wealth of nostalgia within many a homesick cowboy and newly arrived townsman. Lainey's presentation of the song certainly added to its emotional impact. She looked at once earthly and ethereal as she stood before them in the tight, red satin dress with her long golden hair streaming down about her— desirable, and yet innocent. Her beautiful voice grew clearer and stronger after that first verse, and she soon became so lost in the words herself that she forgot all about the embarrassing inadequacy of her costume.

When she had finished, she waited anxiously to see what the audience's reaction would be. There was nothing but silence. Her gaze filled with trepidation as it moved over the men who were either sitting on the ground in front of the stage or standing in the back. Some of them had undoubtedly been drinking; the smell of whiskey was strong within the closely packed tent. But there was still no sign of the disorderliness Mr. Calhoun had warned her about.

She clasped her hands together and felt her heart sink

as the strange silence continued. Painfully conscious of the hundreds of eyes fastened on her, she turned to make good her escape. That was when the applause finally broke out. It was a wonderful, vigorous outpouring of appreciation for her performance, loud enough to shake the canvas all about. Some of the men added cheers and whistles, and one young patron was so overcome with emotion that he flung a handful of gold coins onto the stage while shouting out a marriage proposal.

Lainey's features relaxed into a warm smile of gratitude. She bent down to pick up the coins, intent upon giving them back to their rightful owner, but Mr. Bloomfield suddenly materialized on the stage beside her. He raised his hands to quiet the audience.

"The little lady will be back tomorrow night!" he announced, his voice ringing out with supreme satisfaction. He turned to Lainey and smiled broadly. "You've got yourself a job, Miss Prescott!"

She favored him with a cool smile of her own and once again made an attempt to leave. The crowd, however, demanded another song. Her thoughts immediately flew to Beth and the storm that had not yet broken. Though reluctant to agree, she told herself that it could do no harm to stay a little longer.

By the time she had performed a second song—"The Gypsy's Warning," another heart-stirring ballad—and exchanged the accursed satin dress for her own clothes again, the rain had started to fall at last. She frowned at the sound of the drops pelting the canvas and silently berated herself for tarrying so long. The ride home would be a wet one. With that unhappy thought in mind, she gathered up her hat and slicker and hurried out of the dressing room.

A loud gasp broke from her lips as she collided with the man who had been waiting for her just beyond the curtain. She blushed at her own carelessness and hastily stepped away.

"Oh, I—please forgive me," she said in apology. Raising her eyes to his face, she was surprised to discover that he was someone she had met before. Surprise quickly turned to horror. "Dear Lord, *it's you!*"

Scowling down at her was the same bearded, raw-boned man who had assaulted her and tried to jump her claim. His dark eyes glittered with both lust and vengeance, while his hands raised to dig into her arms.

"Didn't know you was a singer," he muttered, then gave a malevolent chuckle. He yanked her up hard against him.

"Take your hands off me!" she said, struggling furiously in his grasp now. If possible, he smelled even worse than before. She battled a powerful wave of nausea.

"Your cham-*peen* ain't here now!" he snarled derisively. He tried to kiss her, but she lowered her head and was about to bring her knee jerking up toward his groin when another man's voice, even and authoritative, cut the ordeal short.

"Let go of the lady, Vince."

Lainey's eyes flew to where Neil Halloran stood calmly surveying them from a few feet away. Every bit as well-dressed and polished as she had remembered, he was in stark contrast to the man who held her captive.

With startling obedience, Vince released her. He didn't say a word, but shot Lainey a last, menacing glare before beating a hasty retreat.

"You—you know him?" Lainey stammered up at her rescuer in disbelief.

"Only in passing." He stepped forward now and lifted a solicitous hand to her arm. "Are you all right?"

"Yes, but that man—"

"Will never trouble you again." With obvious reluctance, he dropped his arm back to his side. "I was coming to tell you how much I enjoyed your performance tonight." He smiled and allowed his gaze to travel warmly over her. His gray eyes held the same predatory gleam of interest she had noticed before. It was flattering, of course, but all the same she felt an involuntary shiver run the length of her spine. In spite of his outward veneer of charm, she sensed that Neil Halloran could be quite ruthless when crossed. The thought was both intriguing and unsettling.

"Thank you, Mr. Halloran," she finally murmured in response to the compliment. "Now, if you'll please excuse me . . ." She started past him, but his words detained her.

"I told Bloomfield to increase your salary."

"You told—?" she echoed in bewilderment, only to break off when his mouth curved into a smile of sardonic amusement.

"I own the Palace, Miss Prescott."

"You do?" Astonished by the news, she gazed up at him with eyes that were very wide and luminous. "Why, I naturally assumed that Mr. Bloomfield was the proprietor!"

"He runs the place for me," the attractive, raven-haired man declared nonchalantly. "I own a number of businesses in Guthrie. I didn't know until tonight that Bloomfield had hired you. You can imagine my surprise when I discovered that my own Miss Prescott was one of the featured entertainers. And a talented songstress at that."

"I am not *yours*!" she denied, with unexpected vehemence, then colored anew. She averted her gaze from the hawkish steadiness of his and said with more composure, "I must be getting home. My sister will be worried."

"Where do you live?"

"It isn't far," she answered evasively.

"Then I will escort you," he insisted. With yet another smile, he clasped her arm once more and lifted his hat to his head. "How fortunate that I came prepared." He nodded slightly toward the rear entrance. Lainey turned her head and saw that a large black umbrella was resting against the canvas.

She was thrown into a quandary by his offer. On the one hand, she found it rather nice to be in his company. Yet, on the other, she was reluctant to be alone with him. Her eyes kindled with a spark of wry humor at the thought of what his reaction would be when he discovered the true location of "home." She seriously doubted that he would be enchanted with the prospect of riding several miles across the open countryside in the pouring rain.

"While I appreciate your thoughtfulness, Mr. Halloran, I'm afraid I must go alone," she told him. Gently but determinedly pulling free, she softened the rejection by inquiring, "Will you be present at tomorrow night's performance?"

"I will," he affirmed. Though his gaze had darkened with displeasure, he did not press the issue any further. There was plenty of time, he told himself. Soon, he'd be able to convince *his* damnably prim and proper Lainey Prescott to let down her guard.

"Then I will see you tomorrow." She managed a brief smile. "Good night, Mr. Halloran."

"Good night, Miss Prescott."

Just as he had done the last time, he caught her hand and raised it to his lips. The gesture was still pleasurable, yet she found herself resisting the urge to pull away. He released her hand at last and watched while she crossed to the back of the tent. Feeling his eyes upon her, she quickly donned the slicker and the hat, then disappeared through the opening in the canvas.

Once outside, she noted with some dismay that, instead of a nice steady rain, she would be riding into a veritable cloudburst. The thunder and lightning had subsided a bit, however, leading her to believe that the worst might already have passed. She pulled the slicker more closely about her body, bent her head against the downpour, and raced the short distance to the shed where her horse waited.

It never occurred to her to turn back. She knew Beth was waiting for her, and she was more concerned with her sister's and niece's welfare than her own. They had endured other storms since leaving Missouri, of course, but this was the first time they had been faced with one while camped in the wagon. Before, they had been able to watch the deluge from the safety of a railroad car or hotel room. The weather had remained blissfully favorable once they had left Kansas behind. *Until now.*

Lainey shivered and urged the horse into a canter. The cold, surprisingly forceful drops of rain stung against the unprotected skin of her face and hands. Riding farther and farther away from Guthrie, she encountered a darkness so black and relentless that it was difficult to see. The only light came from the occasional bolts of lightning, which shot down from the heavens to strike, vengefully it seemed, at the earth. Thunder rolled and rumbled, its ear-splitting clamor worsening again.

Belatedly realizing that she had been wrong about the storm, Lainey felt her heart pound with growing apprehension. The wind was the worst. She could hear it howling across the rain-battered landscape, and a particularly violent flash of lightning revealed the way the trees bent and swayed, their leaves literally ripped from the branches. She was certain her hat would have gone flying if not for the fact that she had tightened the chin strap.

She rode inexorably onward, longing for the shelter of the wagon. Her eyes filled with compassion for the unfortunate animal beneath her, but she knew they had to keep going. She prayed that Beth and Anna were all right, and prayed as well that she would be able to make it home.

The weather grew more and more threatening. Lainey was no longer sure she was traveling in the right direction; she had become disoriented in the storm-tossed darkness. Tears of frustration gathered in her eyes. She cursed her own stubbornness, bitterly telling herself that she should never have insisted upon going into town alone at night—particularly on a night when all the warning signs had been right before her eyes.

Her throat constricted in very real alarm now. She tried to prompt the horse to further haste, then gasped when he suddenly jerked to a halt and reared up on his hind legs. She lost control of the reins and grasped at the saddlehorn, but to no avail. With a sharp, strangled cry, she tumbled from the animal's back.

She hit the ground with such force that the breath was knocked from her body. Stunned, she lay on her side in the mud, unable to move or speak, watching in horror while the horse galloped away into the darkness.

Chapter 8

Lainey had no idea how long she lay there with the storm raging about her. When she finally recovered strength enough to pull herself to her feet, her skirts were completely soaked through and her hair was plastered wetly about her face and shoulders. Still dazed, she realized that she had lost her hat. Narrowing her eyes against the rain that beat mercilessly down upon her head, she staggered to the top of the hill and tried to get her bearings. Lightning streaked with taunting brilliance across the sky, illuminating a countryside that looked only vaguely familiar.

Dear God, what do I do now? she wondered, her heart crying out for help. She choked back the sob that rose in her throat and furiously directed herself to remain calm. It would do her no good to panic; she needed to keep her wits about her if she hoped to find her way home.

Wincing at the sharp pain that shot through her right leg, she set off again. The wind was a chilling, watery blast against her face, and her boots slipped on the muddy ground. She hadn't traveled far at all before she lost her footing. She quickly righted herself again, but had trouble maintaining her balance. Her skirts, heavy with moisture, threatened to drag her down, and it was difficult for her to keep going while being met at every turn by the terrible crash and roar of the storm's fury.

Suddenly the outline of a horse and rider loomed before her in the darkness.

She stifled a scream and stumbled backward. Lightning flashed again, setting aglow the grim, handsome features of Ethan Holt.

"Oh, Ethan!" Lainey gasped out. Overcome with relief, she felt her legs give way beneath her.

In one swift motion, he was off his horse and catching her up in his arms. He gathered her close for a moment, his embrace at once tender and fiercely protective.

"Thank God I found you!" he murmured close to her ear. His deep, resonant voice was brimming with raw emotion, and if she had not been so fatigued, she would have marveled at the sound of it.

He turned and swiftly carried her to his horse. Lifting her to the animal's back, he swung up behind her. He raked the hat from his head and pushed it down upon hers. His powerful arms encircled her, holding her securely before him while he touched his booted heels to the roan's flanks and rode back the way he had come.

Lainey's eyes swept closed as she leaned weakly back against him. Once again, he had come to her rescue. And once again, her heart was filled with a strange mixture of gratitude and relief . . . and alarm.

They rode in silence for a while. Oddly enough, Lainey was no longer afraid of the storm. She knew that Ethan would see her safely home; he wasn't the kind of man to accept defeat on any terms. That was something she had sensed from the very first. In spite of the rain, which continued to lash at her, she felt warm and protected within his arms.

Her eyes flew wide at a sudden thought. She stiffened, her heart leaping with dread.

"Beth and the baby!" she gasped out, her voice scarcely audible above the frightening roar. "Dear Lord, I've got to make sure—"

"They're all right," Ethan hastened to assure her. He bent his head lower so that his lips were close to her ear. "Travis took them back to our place."

"To your place?"

"I'll explain later." His gaze darkened at the memory of the hell she had put him through that night. He would explain all right. And now that he knew she was unhurt, he would make damned sure she did some explaining of her own.

The thunderstorm raged on, slamming across the prairie and making the ride seem endless. No other words passed between Lainey and Ethan until they had reached his ranch. He drew the horse to a halt in front of the barn and quickly dismounted. Lainey remained in the saddle while he swung open the doors and led the animal inside.

The building was warm, the air smelling sweetly of hay and fresh lumber. A lamp hung from one of the rafters overhead. Its burning glow filled the barn with a soft, comforting light, revealing the four other horses who stood nibbling at the hay within their stalls. Lainey's thoughts traveled to her own horse, and she prayed that the animal would find its way home.

Ethan closed the doors again and strode back to her side. Reaching up for her, he seized her about the waist and pulled her down. She hastily drew away and tugged off the hat, then unfastened the canvas slicker, which had at least served the purpose of keeping her upper body dry. She kept her back turned toward Ethan while she gathered up her long hair and twisted it to remove the clinging moisture. It troubled her to realize just how uncomfortable she felt at being alone with him. Now that their difficult journey had come to an end, she found herself sorely tempted to take immediate and desperate flight.

Ethan stripped off his own slicker and flung it aside. His dark, sun-streaked hair glistened wetly in the lamplight as he watched Lainey shake out her mud-stained skirts. He frowned, his rugged features tightening into a grim mask and his blue-green eyes smoldering with a dangerous, foreboding combination of anger and desire. Without a word, he moved past her to begin unsaddling the horse. The rain drummed loudly on the barn's tin roof, while the wind thrashed at the walls.

Lainey's gaze flickered briefly upward before traveling to Ethan's face. His expression offered her no hint of the battle raging within him. If anything, he looked surprisingly indifferent to her presence. That thought was not as comforting as it should have been. She drew in a deep, slightly ragged breath and smoothed a few stray, damp tendrils of hair from her forehead.

"I'm going to go inside and let Beth know we've arrived," she declared.

"Not yet." His tone was low and abrupt. He said nothing else, but merely pulled the saddle and blanket off the horse and set them on the top rail of the stall. He removed the bridle next, then guided the weary animal into the enclosure, where a generous supply of oats waited. Lifting a handful of straw, he rubbed briskly at the horse's sleek back.

Lainey's eyes sparked with resentment at his arrogance; he had just naturally assumed that she would obey. And why not? she mused irefully. He had been ordering her about from the first night they had met!

But he came for you tonight, her mind's inner voice saw fit to remind her. She sighed and felt her own anger evaporating. It was true. Ethan Holt had probably saved her life. At the very least, he had prevented her from wandering about in the storm for hours on end. She remembered the way her heart had leapt at the sight of him. Why was it that, every time she needed help, he was there?

"I want to thank you, Mr. Holt, for your assistance," she offered sincerely. "I—I don't know what I would

have done if you had not found me." His silence continued, prompting another perilous rise in her temper, but
she maintained her outward composure while asking,
"How did you know I—?"

"Your sister told me where you had gone," he cut her
off.

He stepped away from the horse and swung the stall's
gate into place. Turning to face her at last, he fought
against the sudden, powerful urge to turn her across his
knee. He was furious with her for placing herself in
such danger, and furious with himself for caring so
damned much. His gaze, simmering with barely controlled fury, bored down into hers as he moved closer.

"As soon as we saw that the storm was about to hit,
we rode over to your place," he divulged with quiet, deceptive impassivity. "We should have gone sooner, but
we kept hoping it would all blow over. And we didn't
want to disturb you unless it was necessary." He paused
for a moment, struggling to ignore the way his heart—
and body—stirred at her nearness. As wet and bedraggled as she was, she had never looked more desirable.
He swore inwardly, his muscles tensing. "Travis
brought Beth and Anna back here. I headed into town
after you."

"I know it was stupid of me to go with the weather
so threatening," she murmured, her gaze falling guiltily
beneath his, "but I thought—"

"Blast it, woman! You didn't think at all," he ground
out. His hands shot upward to close about her arms. His
handsome face was thunderous, his eyes holding a near
savage gleam. "I would have thought you'd have more
sense than to go traipsing off alone at night like that. I
warned you to stay away from the Palace, Lainey. Not
only did you disregard my warning, but you damned
near killed yourself in the process!"

"Maybe I did, but that still gives you no right to tell
me what I can and cannot do, Ethan Holt," she count-

ered hotly. Her gaze easily matched the vengeful fire of his. "Now let go of me! Beth must be worried sick about me by now, and I—"

"And how the hell do you think *I* felt when I found out you had gone into town?" he challenged, his fingers burning upon her skin.

She gasped when he suddenly yanked her up hard against him. His hand tangled in the damp, riotously curling thickness of her hair. With a roughness that caused her pulse to race in alarm, he forced her head back and allowed his smoldering gaze to rake over the upturned storminess of her face. His other arm tightened about her waist while she stared breathlessly up at him.

"Do you have any idea what you put me through tonight?" he charged. Driven by feelings he wasn't yet ready to acknowledge, he bent his own head so that his lips were mere inches from the parted softness of hers. "I nearly went out of my mind thinking about what could have happened to you. Damn you, Lainey Prescott. *Damn us both!*"

His lips descended upon hers in a kiss so passionate, so fiercely intoxicating, that she moaned and felt as though her whole body had gone up in flames. She raised her hands to push at his chest, but it was only a token struggle to avoid the inevitable and they both knew it. Following only a few embarrassingly brief moments of resistance, her arms crept up to entwine about his neck while she swayed against him in an unspoken surrender.

His lips thoroughly ravished hers, his tongue plundering the willing sweetness of her mouth. His hand relaxed its almost punishing grip on her hair and swept downward to her hips. His fingers spread boldly, possessively, across the firm roundness of her bottom, pressing her supple curves into an even more intimate contact with his virile, hard-muscled frame.

Swept away by a desire so rapturously forceful that it

threatened to flare out of control, Lainey wasn't inclined to try and analyze why Ethan's very touch set her on fire. She knew only that she wanted the kiss to go on forever . . .

Ethan's other hand moved up to the pearl buttons of her shirtwaist. With an impatience and dexterity that made her suspect, unhappily, that he was entirely too familiar with the fastenings on a woman's clothes, he freed the top four buttons and tugged the liberated edges aside. His mouth left hers to trail a fiery path downward, along the silken column of her throat, until finally coming to rest on the upper curve of her breasts.

She suffered a sharp intake of breath when his warm lips strayed hungrily across the pale, satiny flesh he had just exposed. Instinctively arching her back, she strained upward against him, her eyes sweeping closed. His hand moved beneath her breasts, and in the next instant his mouth closed about one of the delicate, rose-tipped peaks. His lips sucked at the ripe fullness through the thin fabric of her chemise, while his hot tongue snaked out to flick with light, tantalizing strokes across the nipple.

"Oh, Ethan!" She breathed raggedly. The sensation was wickedly—deliciously—pleasurable. She clung to his broad shoulders, her breath nothing but a series of gasps as the exquisite torment continued. Moments later, he moved to tease at her other breast, his lips and tongue bestowing their moist tribute with such skill and tenderness that she feared she would soon be reduced to begging for mercy.

The violent springtime storm raging outside was well matched by the storm of passion raging within the warm, lamplit interior of the barn. Ethan's lips returned to brand Lainey's with sensuous, irresistible persuasion. Her arms encircled his neck again as he crushed her to him, and she was only dimly aware of the moment when he scooped her up in his arms and lowered her to the ground. He immediately placed his own body atop hers, his muscular hardness pressing her soft, trembling curves down into the thick and wonderfully fragrant pile of hay.

As had been the case the two other times he had taken her in his arms, everything happened with such dizzying swiftness that neither of them was quite prepared for the intensity of their passions. It wasn't until Lainey felt Ethan's hand upon her leg that she realized he was tugging her rain-soaked skirts upward. Locked within his masterful, hot-blooded embrace, she squirmed in a belated protest, but he ignored her struggles and relentlessly gathered the wet fabric up about her thighs.

She shivered as a rush of cool air swept across her lower body. Her stockings and drawers were as soaked as her skirts, and she shivered again before Ethan's hand smoothed with bold, loving appreciation across her thinly clad buttocks. His fingers curled about the well-rounded flesh, exploring every saucy curve until trailing down along her hip. His hand suddenly moved between her thighs.

She gasped against his mouth, her eyes flying wide.

Good heavens, she thought in startled anticipation, *surely he wasn't going to—?*

But he was . . . and did. She stiffened when his warm fingers insinuated themselves within the open seam of her drawers. He touched her at the very core of her womanhood, his fingers stroking the silken flesh in a caress that was both gentle and demanding.

Lainey could feel her face flaming. She could also feel her blood turning to liquid fire within her veins. But the shocking unfamiliarity of the caress was enough to bring on a well-timed attack of conscience. Though still a virgin, she was not completely naive. No, by heaven, she was all too aware of what would happen if she didn't put a stop to the sweet madness now. *And sweet madness it was.*

She squirmed, half in protest and half in ecstasy, and tried to close her legs against the wildly provocative invasion, but he would not be denied. Summoning every ounce of strength and reason she possessed, she finally tore her lips from his.

"No! Please, I—we mustn't!" she cried brokenly. She fought against him in earnest now. Snatching her arms from about his neck, she pushed frantically at his shoulders and twisted beneath him. His hands seized her wrists in a forceful, near bruising grip and yanked them above her head.

"Stop it, Lainey," he commanded tersely. Flinging one leg across both of hers, he easily held her captive. Her breasts rose and fell rapidly beneath her unbuttoned shirtwaist, and two bright spots of color rode high on her cheeks. Her eyes were splendidly ablaze.

Ethan's own burning gaze filled with contrition as it traveled over her face. She looked furiously defiant, frightened, and close to tears. And he was to blame. He had lost his head—again.

Muttering an oath, he released her wrists and rolled to his back in the hay. He pulled himself up to his knees and reached for her. But she was in no mood to let him touch her again. Eyeing his hand as though it were a thing to be despised, she sat bolt upright and scrambled to her feet, jerking her skirts down into place. Telltale bits of hay clung to her hair and clothing, but she was much too upset to notice. She rounded on him as he slowly drew himself up to his full height before her.

"I think it's time we came to an understanding, *Mr. Holt*," she proclaimed, with an angry formality that was in direct, and rather absurd, contrast to the wild abandon she had displayed in his arms. She trembled now with both shame and indignation. Still breathless and flushed with passion's glow, she furiously blinked back sudden, inexplicable tears and retreated to a safer distance.

"I was 'Ethan' a moment ago," he was ungallant enough to remind her. A mocking light of amusement crept into his eyes, but there was nothing the least bit humorous about the way his body ached with frustrated desire. He knew he should regret what had happened, but he couldn't. No, by damn, he wasn't sorry at all. "We'd better go inside," he decreed softly.

"Not until we come to an understanding," she reiterated. She swallowed hard and opened her mouth to speak again, only to take note of the way Ethan's eyes were lingering on her breasts. Her gaze dropped. Discovering that she had forgotten to button her shirtwaist, she blushed fierily and took immediate pains to remedy the situation. Her fingers shook as they worked, but she drew herself proudly erect and accused, "You tried to take advantage of me."

"Advantage?" His mouth twitched. "If I had really tried, I'd have succeeded."

"Why—how dare you!" Trying desperately to ignore the warmth that filled her anew, she folded her arms across her heaving breasts and seethed, "You are without a doubt the most conceited, overbearing man I have ever met."

"And you, Miss Prescott, are more of a woman than you'd like to admit." He strode unhurriedly past her and directed, "Come on."

She glared murderously at his back as he bent to retrieve his hat and both of the slickers. He moved to the doorway and swung open the doors. The wind flung the rain inside, offering up evidence of the storm's unremitting fury.

Anxious to escape Ethan's presence, Lainey hastened forward to take the slicker he offered to her. She held it over her head and scurried outside without looking back. The cabin lay only a few yards away, but it proved difficult to reach with the ground turned into a river of mud and the clouds still emptying their bounty in a merciless downpour. When she finally arrived at the front door, she disregarded the impulse to knock before going inside.

Travis and Beth, seated together before the fire, started guiltily as the door opened and leapt to their feet. Beth's eyes widened at the sight of her drenched, sadly travel-worn sister. Her delicate features lit with joy and relief as she flew across the bare wooden floor.

"Lainey! Oh, Lainey. I was so afraid you wouldn't be able to get back." She caught her up in a warm embrace and demanded in a tumble of words, "Are you all right? You're not hurt, are you? Dear heaven, I imagined all sorts of terrible things happening to you."

"I'm fine, Beth," she assured her, with a faint smile.

Travis came forward to take the slicker from her. He hung it on a peg beside the door, oblivious to the water pooling on the floor below it.

"I'm glad Ethan found you, Miss Prescott," he offered solemnly. "It was a bad night to be out, that's for sure." He closed the door again and took himself off to fetch her a cup of the fresh coffee he'd just made, leaving her to face another barrage of questions.

"Why, look at your skirts," exclaimed Beth, her gaze filling with horror as it traveled downward. "What on earth happened?"

Without waiting for a reply, she led her sister over to the fire, where the two of them sank down upon the rough-hewn bench in front of the comforting warmth of the flames. Travis placed a woolen blanket about her shoulders, then gently pressed the cup of coffee into her hands. She murmured her thanks for his kind solicitousness and sipped carefully at the hot, aromatic liquid.

The cabin, though consisting of only a single room, was spacious and undeniably well-built. Lainey's troubled gaze made a brief, encompassing sweep of the room. It was sparsely furnished; there was a table and another bench nearby, several barrels and crates full of supplies, and two narrow wooden bunks. She saw that Anna was sleeping peacefully on one of them.

The door suddenly flung open behind her. She colored anew and refused to turn around, her eyes clouding as they moved swiftly back to the fire.

"Mr. Holt." Beth rose to her feet and turned to face him with a heartfelt smile of gratitude. "How can I ever thank you for what you've done?"

"I'm glad I could help, Mrs. Baker," Ethan replied in a low tone.

He closed the door behind him, then added his own dripping wet slicker and hat to the pegs. His penetrating gaze shot to Lainey, who was doing her absolute best not to cry. She had always had little patience with overly emotional females, and she certainly despised this sudden and inordinate tendency toward tears in herself. But her heart twisted at the memory of what had happened in the barn ... It was inconceivable that she could have been so lost to reason. God forbid, what if she had actually been seduced by Ethan Holt tonight? The thought was much too disconcerting—and thrilling, if she would but admit it—to be borne.

Feeling perfectly miserable, she took a deeper drink of the coffee and gave an inward groan for the lingering weakness of her knees. Beth sat down beside her again while Ethan and Travis spoke quietly together near the doorway.

"The Holts came none too soon!" Beth told her, with a shudder of remembrance. "I was nearly frantic. The wind had grown quite strong, and poor little Anna awoke crying with fear at the sound of the thunder. Tra—the younger Mr. Holt helped us gather up a few things and then brought us back here. It had already started to rain by that time, but we were spared the worst of it." She sighed and slipped an arm about her sister's shoulders. "I prayed that you would be kept safe, dearest Lainey. And yet, strangely enough, I somehow knew you *would* be once Mr. Holt set out after you. He promised to find you, you see, and I could not help but believe him."

"I might very well have made it on my own if the horse hadn't thrown me," Lainey insisted, her voice quavering slightly. She knew she would never forget the sight of Ethan's face in the storm-tossed darkness. . . .

"The horse threw you?" Beth echoed in breathless concern.

"Yes. But don't worry. I'm fine, and I'm sure the horse has found shelter somewhere." She pulled the blanket more securely about her and frowned. "I knew I should have left the Palace sooner, but the audience was wonderfully attentive and I—"

"Oh, my goodness. I forgot all about the theater," confessed Beth. Her eyes sparkled with interest as they searched Lainey's face. "It truly went well?"

"Even better than I had hoped," Lainey responded, with another wan smile. "Mr. Bloomfield, however, was less than gentlemanly. I fully intend to discuss the matter with him tomorrow. And I'm afraid the costumes were as dreadful as you feared. They will have to be altered or replaced without delay." Her gaze kindled at the unpleasant memory. "But at least we are assured of the job, Beth. And I—I met the man who owns the theater."

"I thought Mr. Bloomfield owned it."

"No. The proprietor is a man named Neil Halloran. He told me—"

"Halloran?" Travis suddenly repeated behind them.

They both turned to stare at him in surprise. Lainey noticed the cautionary look Ethan gave his brother. Travis hesitated only briefly before turning away to gather up the extra blankets he had taken from one of the crates.

Lainey's eyes met Ethan's. His gaze was steady and piercing, and she felt as though he could see into her very soul. She hastily averted her face again, wishing for all the world that she had not made the fateful mistake of staying in the barn too long. It was beyond belief that she was now faced with the prospect of spending an entire night in his company. The irony of the situation was not lost on her, but neither was the dull ache still gripping her heart.

"Do you know Mr. Halloran?" she asked Travis.

"It's getting late," said Ethan, his deep-timbred voice filling the lamplit cabin with its resonance. "We'd better try to get some sleep."

"Sounds like the storm's going to last all night," his brother remarked. He shifted the blankets higher in his arms and nodded toward the bunks in the corner. "They're not the most comfortable beds you'll ever sleep on," he told the two women, then smiled crookedly before adding, "but they're a far sight better than the floor."

"Where will you sleep?" Beth asked him. She colored faintly when his green eyes warmed with loving humor.

"You needn't worry, Beth. Ethan and I will bed down out in the barn."

Lainey detected the note of real affection in his voice. Casting a suspicious glance his way, she realized that he and Beth must have been alone in the cabin, with no one but Anna to serve as a chaperon, for an hour or more. She couldn't help but wonder what had passed between them in that time. Remembering all too well how Beth had wept inconsolably on the occasion of their last meeting, she frowned to herself and vowed to learn the truth about their relationship. She certainly wasn't going to stand by and do nothing while her sister's heart was broken again. And she could imagine Travis Holt, charming rogue that he was, doing precisely that.

"There's plenty of wood for the fire," Ethan pointed

out. He sauntered forward to pour himself a cup of coffee. Lainey tensed, acutely conscious of his proximity as he lifted the pot from where it had been warming on the stone hearth. He filled his cup and took a long drink, then looked down at her. "If you need anything, Miss Prescott, you know where to find me."

"Thank you, Mr. Holt," she murmured coldly. She didn't know if his words contained any hidden meaning or not, but she raised her eyes briefly to his face and saw that his mouth had curved into the merest suggestion of a smile. *"Good night,"* she proclaimed, hoping that he would take the not-so-subtle hint and be on his way. She was greatly relieved that he would not be in the cabin all night.

"We'll check on you first thing in the morning," promised Travis. He and Beth exchanged a glance of silent understanding. They had made their peace that night, although Beth still refused to listen to his words of love. But he wasn't going to give up. Not by a long shot.

"Good night, Mr. Holt," she told him softly.

The two men finally took their leave. As soon as the door had closed after them, Lainey sprang from the bench and flew across the room to slip the bolt into place.

"Why, Lainey," her sister exclaimed in surprise. "I'm sure that isn't at all necessary."

"I have no intention of allowing either of the Holts to disturb our privacy," she insisted firmly. She checked to make certain the shutters were drawn together across the windows, then crossed back to the fire and began stripping off her wet garments. "I do hope you thought to bring along a nightgown."

"A nightgown? Well, no," admitted Beth, her silken brow creasing into a mild frown of regret. "I suppose it never really occurred to me that we would be spending the night. But I *did* bring some dry clothing." She hastened to open the carpetbag that sat atop the table. Following a brief search, she pulled out a pretty, sprigged cotton dress. "I'm afraid I didn't think to bring undergarments, either," she apologized, handing the dress to Lainey.

"That's all right. These will dry soon enough." She removed her shirtwaist and skirt, then sat down to peel off her boots and stockings. Her drawers came next, leaving her clad in nothing but her white cotton chemise. She draped the wet clothing across the bench in front of the fire and headed toward the beds.

"Aren't you going to put on the dress?" Beth queried in puzzlement.

"No."

"But Lainey, it . . . well, it isn't quite proper for a lady to go to bed like that."

"Maybe I'm not a lady after all," she muttered, then smiled faintly at the shocked expression on her sister's face. "For heaven's sake, Beth, no one's going to know."

The remark came back to haunt her a short time later, after she had settled beneath the covers of the bed. The mattress was hard and lumpy, the ropes of the frame creaking softly in protest whenever she moved. Beth and Anna shared the other bunk. Their slumber was mercifully undisturbed by either the howl of the wind or the crackle and hiss of the fire, which would soon be nothing but a glowing mass of embers. The storm alternated between an uneasy truce with the battered earth and a turbulent, all-out clashing of rain and thunder and lightning.

Lainey's thoughts drifted with a will of their own to the man she knew lay stretched out upon the hay lining the barn floor. Her emotions had been thrown into utter chaos from the first night they had met. No one had ever had such a startling and thoroughly overpowering effect upon her. *Overpowering,* her mind echoed. Yes, she mused while a sudden tremor shook her, his kisses were certainly that.

It was useless for her to continue denying that she found him attractive. Heaven help her, all he had to do was touch her and she became a veritable wanton in his arms. The Lainey Prescott who had done that wasn't the same Lainey Prescott who, until now, had possessed nothing but an idle curiosity about the mysterious longings between men and women. What had happened to the young woman who had vowed never to be swept away by passion?

She released a long, ragged sigh and turned upon her side. It suddenly crossed her mind to wonder if the bed upon which she lay was Ethan's. The possibility that it might be was enough to make her grow warm all over. She doubted that he would mind the "improperness" of her present attire . . .

She blushed at the wickedness of her thoughts and closed her eyes again. In spite of the storm outside, and its equally troubling counterpart deep within her, she eventually drifted off to sleep.

An insistent knock at the door awakened her the following morning. She started in alarm at the sound of it, her eyes flying wide and then filling with confusion as they swept about her unfamiliar surroundings. She turned her head to look at Beth, only to see that her sister's arms had tightened protectively about the baby. Remembering then where they were, Lainey frowned and tossed back the covers.

"It sounds as if our gracious 'hosts' are demanding entrance," she observed sarcastically.

"Shh, Lainey. They might hear you," came Beth's whispered caution. Ever the lady, she had chosen to sleep fully clothed rather than follow her sister's scandalous example. She made a graceful exit from the bed and caught up an already quite vocal Anna, intent upon changing the toddler's soiled diaper and dressing her in a fresh gown.

Lainey's eyes flashed when the knock sounded again. She leveled a wrathful glare at the door, or rather at the man she knew to be on the other side of it, and hastened to don the sprigged cotton gown.

"One moment, please," she called out, her voice somewhat muffled as she pulled the dress down over her head. She fastened the buttons, which ran up the front of the heart-shaped bodice, while crossing to the table, where she searched in vain for a hairbrush. Forced to settle for whatever magic her hands could achieve, she twisted the silken, tangled mass of curls upward and tucked the single thick strand into a precarious chignon.

"Oh, Lainey. I—I've got to pay a visit to the 'convenience,'" Beth confided in an undertone. She flushed with embarrassment at the thought of answering the call of nature with Travis and his brother having full knowledge of her destination. Lainey, however, was much more practical about it. Though she and Beth were both daughters of a physician, she was the one who had helped him with the more personal aspects of his patients' care.

"So do I," she replied, with a brief smile. "Perhaps Eth—Mr. Holt and his brother have thought to build an outhouse. Here, let me take Anna." She lifted the baby in her arms and watched while Beth smoothed a critical hand over her own amazingly tidy hair. "We'll all go together."

Marching purposefully forward, she slid the bolt aside and opened the door. Ethan stood towering above her, just as she had known he would be. The soft glow of the morning sun outlined his tall, muscular frame. He looked devilishly handsome, his dark brown hair waving across his forehead and his magnificent turquoise eyes glowing with warmth. The faint, pleasant aroma of hay hung about him.

Lainey was nonplussed by the way her heart suddenly leapt within her breast, but she determinedly concealed her inner turmoil behind a facade of cool politeness.

"Good morning, Mr. Holt," she offered, with admirable calm. Now that she had faced him again without falling to pieces, she knew she could manage to put last night behind her. She would simply have to maintain a safe distance from him at all times . . .

"Good morning, Miss Prescott." His gaze darkened as it traveled boldly over her. He smiled and nodded past her toward Beth. "Mrs. Baker. I hope you were able to get some sleep."

"We were indeed, Mr. Holt, thank you." She joined Lainey at the door, her eyes scanning the front yard for any sign of Travis.

"My brother's saddling the horses," said Ethan. It seemed that he had read her mind—or simply put two and two together. Musing to himself that he'd have to be blind not to notice what was going on between Travis and the pretty little widow, he wondered how Lainey felt about it. "As soon as we've had breakfast," he told her, "we'll ride over to your place and inspect the damage."

"Damage?" she echoed, her eyes widening. She hadn't considered the possibility of any damage. Given the violence of the storm, which had finally ceased its fury in the early hours of the dawn, she should have realized the threat to their possessions.

"It might not be too bad," Ethan commented. Then he informed her with a perceptiveness that, in Lainey's opinion, was all too rare in members of the opposite sex, "You'll find what you need out back. I'll put on some coffee."

She murmured a word of thanks as she shifted the baby in her arms and set off with Beth close behind.

When they were on their way back to the cabin a short time later, Beth paused to speak to Travis, who had just emerged from the barn. Anna insisted upon remaining with her mother. Lainey's eyes clouded with a touch of apprehension when she noted the way her sister's countenance positively glowed, but she gathered up her skirts and continued inside.

Ethan was bent down on one knee in front of the fireplace when she entered the cabin. Bright flames already danced beneath the mantel, and the rich smell of coffee filled the room.

Lainey came to an abrupt halt just within the doorway. Warm color flew to her cheeks as her eyes moved with a will of their own over the lean hardness of Ethan's thighs and hips. His denim trousers were stretched taut across his lower body, while the powerful muscles of his back and arms bulged beneath a clean, white cotton shirt. She swallowed a sudden lump in her throat and forced her gaze away, only to pale when she saw that her clothes were still draped over the bench where she had left them to dry the night before.

Her sapphire gaze filled with dismay at the sight of her delicate, lace-trimmed drawers. Realizing that Ethan must have seen them as well, she gave an inward groan and raced across the room to retrieve them. It was one thing to have him know she was as human as the next person; it was quite another to offer him such intimate evidence of her femininity.

"The coffee's almost ready," he declared, his eyes brimming with humor as he watched her snatch up the offending garment and whirl away toward the bunks in the corner. All traces of amusement vanished in the next instant, however, when his gaze fell on the alluring sway of her hips. He found himself wondering if those fancy drawers she had been so anxious to hide were the only ones she had with her. The thought that she might not have anything on under the dress made his loins tighten anew. "I'll have some bacon and biscuits cooked up in a few minutes," he added, his voice tinged with a slight huskiness.

"I'm not hungry." She moved across to the table and pushed the folded pair of drawers down into the carpet-bag, then returned to fetch the rest of her clothing.

"Afraid to sample my cooking?" Ethan challenged mockingly. He drew himself upright beside her and frowned. "You need to eat something, Lainey." His eyes glinted dully at the sight of the shadows beneath her eyes. He didn't know whether he, or the storm, was to blame for her obvious lack of sleep, but he felt a sharp pang of remorse all the same. Resisting the urge to gently sweep a wayward curl from her forehead, he told her, "Maybe you ought to stay here and get some rest."

"You needn't concern yourself on my behalf," she murmured in response. Moving past him, she came to a sudden halt when the handful of gold coins she had secured in the pocket of her skirt the previous night fell to the floor. They clattered noisily upon the bare wood.

Coloring, Lainey gasped and immediately knelt to gather them up. Ethan bent to help her.

"Were these your pay for last night?" he demanded in a low, dangerously level tone.

"I fail to see how that is any of your business." She took the coins he held out to her and thrust all of them into the pocket of her dress. Her arms tightened about the bundle of clothing once more. Glancing toward the fire, she revealed on sudden impulse, "Someone in the audience tossed them onto the stage. In truth, it was my intention to return them, but—"

"But you decided you'd rather be rich." His voice was whipcord sharp now.

"No, it wasn't like that at all!" she adamantly denied, raising her eyes to his face again. She knew a moment's trepidation when she glimpsed the fierce light burning in his eyes, but she lifted her head to a proud, defiant angle and told him, "Money *is* important to me, but only because I want to give Beth and Anna the kind of life they deserve. What is wrong with that?"

"Nothing. Just as long as you don't lose sight of what it is you're after." He turned away and began adding the bacon to the iron skillet heating on the stone hearth. "I want you to stay away from the Palace," he surprised her by proclaiming in the next instant.

"I'm well aware of your opinion on that matter, Mr. Holt," she parried, with a sigh of exasperation.

"Damn it, Lainey. I mean it," he said, his features tensing. He stood and faced her with a grim expression. "Halloran's not a man to be trusted."

"So you *do* know him!" She recalled how he had prevented Travis from answering her inquiry about the man the night before.

"I know him," confirmed Ethan. "And that's why you've got to believe me when I say it's dangerous for you to be around him. He's nothing but trouble."

"Trouble? What kind of trouble?" she demanded, her eyes narrowing dubiously up at him.

"You'll just have to trust me."

"Why should I?"

"Because I wouldn't lie to you, Lainey. Not about this, not about anything else." His piercing gaze locked with the brilliant blue fire of hers. The urge to touch her was too powerful to be denied any longer. While a strange, highly charged silence rose up between them, he lifted a hand to her cheek. His warm fingers bestowed a caress that was at once tender and electrifying.

Lainey felt her heart stir with emotion, felt her body come alive with the deep longing he had recently awakened. Unable to move away, she stared up at him and waited for the spell to be broken.

Surprisingly, Anna was the one who did it. Her delightful, high-pitched voice drifted to Lainey from the open doorway.

"Eat!" the little girl called out, the single word clear and insistent. She toddled into the room, making straightaway for the fireplace.

Lainey flushed guiltily and lowered the pile of clothing to the bench. She hurried to intercept her niece. Scooping Anna up in her arms, she pressed a kiss to the baby's temple and assured her that she would have her breakfast soon.

Travis and Beth entered shortly thereafter. Their eyes held a secret understanding that would, within a few days' time, help alter the lives of everyone inside the cozy, firelit cabin.

Chapter 9

The campsite proved to be a disheartening sight.

The wagon was still intact, of course, but the canvas top had been torn off by the winds and sent flying across the plains. Travis found it nearly half a mile away, ripped to shreds. Everything inside the wagon was thoroughly soaked—the bedding, all the clothing that had not been secured away in the trunk, and even the silver tea set wrapped lovingly in an old quilt and stored beneath the seat. Outside, the tables and barrels and crates were strewn haphazardly about, and the garden, which Beth had worked so hard to plant, had been battered into nothing more than a pool of dark red mud.

Several trees had either been blown down or suffered a significant loss of leaves and branches. The entire landscape showed signs of the storm's devastating force. Although the rising sun had broken through the clouds some two hours earlier, drops of water still glistened on the remaining leaves.

"At least the horses are all right." Lainey sighed, her spirits dismally low. A faint smile touched her lips when she saw that among the animals grazing beneath the trees was the one who had abandoned her in the storm. Her rifle was still tied behind the saddle.

"We may as well get to it," Ethan decreed. He dismounted and reached up to pull Lainey down from the horse he had loaned her. Declining his assistance with a frown, she hastily slid from the saddle on the other side

170

and went to join Beth and Anna, who had been only too happy to accept Travis's help.

The first order of the day was to begin the drying-out process. While the men set to work righting the crates and barrels, Lainey and Beth carried the bedding out into the sunshine and draped it across the tables. They hung the clothing on the line and made a critical assessment of the damage done to their supplies. Things were not as bad as they had initially seemed, and Lainey assured her sister that they would be able to replace what had been lost.

"You'll have to stay on at our place for a while longer," said Ethan, joining them near the wagon. He and Travis had transferred their own efforts to the cabin site; they had already settled the first logs into place. "We should be able to finish the walls in a day or two, but we won't have you roofed in until the end of the week."

"The end of the week?" Lainey echoed, her eyes widening with visible dismay. She watched as Ethan's mouth curved into a brief, mocking smile.

"Was my coffee all that bad, Miss Prescott?"

"Your coffee has nothing to do with it," she snapped. She colored faintly beneath her sister's close scrutiny. "We are not going to 'stay on' at your place, Mr. Holt. We are going to stay right here."

"You can't do that," he insisted. "You've got no shelter."

"Well, I—I can ride into Guthrie and see if I can arrange for repairs to the wagon."

"No, Lainey. Mr. Holt is right," Beth asserted, with uncharacteristic firmness. "I certainly don't want to risk being caught in another storm. And as he said, it will only be for a few days." She smiled at Ethan. "We are grateful for your kind and generous hospitality."

"The pleasure's all mine, Mrs. Baker." His eyes moved to Lainey again, and she could have sworn she glimpsed a light of triumphant satisfaction within their fathomless, blue-green depths. "Travis and I will stay and work until sundown. If you'd like to go back sooner—"

"No, thank you," Beth answered for the both of them. "We have more than enough to occupy us here."

Lainey knew she had little choice in the matter. Once again, she would have liked nothing better than to tell Ethan Holt precisely what he could do with his "kind and generous hospitality," but she had no desire to create a scene in front of Beth. Besides, she told herself, she couldn't very well hold fast to her insistence that they remain at the camp, not with the bedding so wet it would take days to dry.

Still, the prospect of spending even one more night in Ethan's cabin made her cast her eyes heavenward with a silent, desperate plea for help. She had little doubt that he would attempt to assault her again. *Assault?* an inner voice taunted knowingly. She frowned and marched away toward the creek.

The hours flew by. Long after Lainey and Beth had prepared the noon meal and finished going through everything in the wagon, they sat down together on one of the nearby crates. Anna napped atop a bundle of dry clothing Beth had spread in the wagon bed. The two men were hard at work on the cabin—the four walls were beginning to take shape.

"Beth, I've been wanting to talk to you about something," said Lainey. She had brushed her hair and secured it in a braid, but the rebellious locks still gave every sign of escaping to curl about her face.

"What is it?" Beth asked in all innocence. Her light blue eyes strayed to where Travis was helping his brother lift one of the logs into place.

"It's about Travis Holt." Her gaze followed the direction of her sister's. She tried, without any real measure of success, to ignore the way her pulse raced at the sight of Ethan's broad back and powerful, sinewy arms. He had rolled up the sleeves of his shirt and removed his hat. The sun lit gold in the thickness of his hair, while his features were solemn in concentration. "I know there is something between the two of you, Beth," she accused gently, forcing her thoughts back to the subject at hand. "Something beyond mere friendship. Indeed, I haven't forgotten the way you cried after—"

"Please, Lainey. It doesn't matter." Beth cut her off with a rosy blush.

"Of course it matters. I don't want to see you hurt again, Beth. I couldn't bear it." She sighed and raised a loving hand to her sister's arm. Her eyes gazed deeply into Beth's. "You don't deserve to know any more pain. And while Travis is both attractive and likable, I fear he isn't the sort of man to take on the responsibility of a wife and child. At least not yet."

"Do you—do you think he is really so much of a ladies' man?" faltered Beth, her heart twisting at the thought.

"I do. In fact, I would not be at all surprised if he had left a trail of broken hearts behind him. Not that it was ever intentional, of course, but he is much too handsome and full of charm for his own good." Ironically, she had reached a similar conclusion about Ethan after their first meeting. Her opinion had not changed since then. If anything, it had been reinforced.

"Still, I cannot believe him to be like Jack," remarked Beth. It was odd, but she could scarcely remember what Anna's father looked like. His betrayal had been every bit as painful as Lainey had recalled, and yet the pain was nothing more than a dull ache now. "Travis is a decent man, Lainey, a man with principles," she avowed, with feeling, then looked away. "And even though I know he has probably received more than his fair share of attention—attention of a romantic nature, that is—I'm quite sure he has never willingly broken a promise."

"Has he made his feelings known to you?"

"Not in so many words."

"And what about you?" Lainey demanded quietly, searching her sister's face. "For heaven's sake, you haven't lost all reason and fallen in love with him, have you?"

"I can assure you that I have no intention of allowing our friendship to deepen." Her answer was both honest and evasive, but Lainey appeared to be satisfied with it.

"I am relieved to hear you say so," she proclaimed, with a smile. "We're going to be happy here, Beth. Why, just wait until next year, when the farm has become profitable and we have a big house, a beautifully furnished one with columns and gables and even a real bathroom. We'll look back upon these days and marvel at our own inauspicious beginnings."

"I hope so," Beth murmured. Her gaze fell once more, and she swallowed a sudden lump in her throat.

The sun hung low on the horizon by the time they returned to the Holts' ranch. Beth surprised everyone by taking charge of the preparations for supper. Travis offered to help her. He hoisted Anna up to his shoulders and somehow managed to get a fire started while her tiny fingers kept tugging playfully at his hair.

Lainey made the mistake of expressing a desire to bathe before heading into town for the night's performance. Within seconds, she found herself pulled unceremoniously outside by a grim-faced Ethan.

"You're not going anywhere," he told her, his low voice edged with anger as he towered above her in the gathering darkness.

"Whether you like it or not, Ethan Holt, my sister and I have a performance to give," she retorted. She jerked free and struggled to maintain control over her flaring temper. "You have proven yourself a good neighbor in every sense of the word, and I am truly grateful. But we have a job to do, and I will not break my word to Mr. Bloomfield by failing to show up."

"Is it Bloomfield you're worried about—or Halloran?" he demanded tersely.

"I scarcely know Mr. Halloran!"

"Good. See that it stays that way."

"Why should I?" she countered indignantly. Her flashing eyes narrowed up at him. "You persist in warning me against the Palace, and now Mr. Halloran as well, but you have yet to explain why I am supposedly in such dire peril. I encountered no trouble last night," she reminded him, "nor do I expect to encounter any tonight. Beth and I *will* be going—with your approval or without it!"

She refused to listen to him any longer. Spinning about, she hurried back inside the cabin and added her efforts to those of her sister's.

Ethan frowned after her. He told himself he had no right to stop her.

Damn it, he thought as he tossed a glance up toward the sky, he couldn't let the two women go riding off alone at night. The journey aside, he had little doubt that Neil Halloran was already trying to think of a way to get Lainey into his bed. She was much too beautiful to escape his notice, and the bastard had always possessed an almost lethal charm whenever it came to women.

His eyes smoldered with mingled jealousy and rage at the thought of Lainey being thrown into contact with Halloran night after night. Whatever else happened, he was going to make sure her relationship with her employer remained strictly business.

Lainey was surprised when Ethan announced that he and Travis would be accompanying them into town. Her eyes widened as they flew across the table to his face.

"But I thought you—?" she started to point out, only to be cut off when he abruptly stood from the bench. They had just finished supper.

"I still don't think you should go," Ethan reasserted in a voice laced with steel. He exchanged a quick look with his brother. "But since you won't listen to reason, we're going to make sure you get there safely."

"And home again," added Travis. He turned solemnly to Beth. "I hold the same opinion as Ethan about the Palace, that it's not the kind of place for someone like you." An appealing glow crept into his eyes. "But I must admit I'm looking forward to hearing you sing."

Lainey's pulse leapt in alarm. Recalling all too vividly how scandalous her costume had been the previous night, she could only hope Mr. Bloomfield had made good on his promise to either improve or replace the accursed dresses. She knew with a certainty what Ethan's reaction would be if he saw her so immodestly attired. And even though she told herself she shouldn't care in the least, she paled at the thought of his disapproval.

The five of them traveled into Guthrie beneath a clear quarter-moon. Anna insisted upon honoring Travis with her presence upon his horse. Beth rode beside them, leaving Lainey to pair off in the lead with Ethan. She stole an occasional, surreptitious glance at him, but he never looked her way.

The town was crowded, as always, but the atmosphere was more subdued on this particular night. The storm had destroyed many of the tents and scattered goods everywhere. A number of residents had been forced to seek shelter in the saloons and gambling dens. The circumstances had certainly swelled the profits of these often disreputable establishments, but had also made it necessary for the overworked town marshal to call in the troops from nearby Camp Guthrie to help keep the peace.

The Palace's huge tent had, miraculously, suffered

only minor damage. The tears in the canvas had been patched that morning, and the ropes had been stretched taut once more. Although the ground was a bit on the soggy side, the audience proved to be as impressively large as the night before.

Ethan and Travis drew to a halt out front, while Lainey and Beth guided their mounts around to the rear entrance. Following only a brief hesitation, Beth had accepted Travis's offer to watch Anna.

Beth's mouth curved into a soft smile at the thought of the tall, dashing cowboy trying to control her beloved and highly rambunctious little daughter during the performance. He was really quite good with children, she mused, her eyes shining. And Anna seemed to have grown genuinely fond of him ...

Alarmed to feel her heart stirring the way it had done all too often since Travis Holt had come into her life, she cautioned herself against such feelings. It could never be. Travis wouldn't understand about Jack. The very thought of revealing her shame to him was unbearable; she couldn't endure his rejection. She was unworthy of his love, but at least she could claim his friendship.

Filled with a mixture of anguish and longing, she drew in a ragged breath and dismounted beside Lainey.

"Well now, I can't tell you how glad I am to see the two of you!" Mr. Bloomfield's voice boomed out to them as soon as they stepped inside the tent. He offered his salutations, took a puff on his foul-smelling cigar, and hooked his plump, unoccupied thumb into the pocket of his brocade satin waistcoat. "Yes, sir. We've got a full house tonight. Word about you has gotten around, Miss Prescott."

"I'm glad to hear it, Mr. Bloomfield," Lainey responded cordially. She would never like the man again, not after the way he had treated her the night before, but she bore him no ill will. "I do hope you've kept your word about the costumes."

"Costumes?" he echoed, feigning bewilderment. His face broke into a slow, conspiratorial smile. "I'll tell you what, Miss Prescott. You and your sister there do a good job tonight, and I'll buy you the prettiest dresses Guthrie has to offer."

"That is exactly what you promised *last* night." Her eyes sparked with anger.

"Did I?" He raised his cigar to his lips again and cautioned them, "You'd better hurry up and get ready. I've got some business to take care of." He beat a hasty retreat, disappearing through the flaps.

Lainey frowned darkly. She slipped a hand about Beth's arm and led her inside the dressing room. The same costumes were waiting for them. And the same grandly dramatic actors were performing another Shakespearean tragedy on the nearby stage. From the sound of it, the audience was not quite as orderly as it had been the previous night. Whistles and catcalls accompanied the performance, and one unfortunate thespian found himself pelted with a handful of mud. Where there should have been appreciative silence, there were instead outbursts of raucous laughter.

Lainey and Beth, however, were preoccupied with other matters. They quickly changed, then stood together before the mirror. Their gazes filled with mutual consternation. Beth's blue satin was only slightly less revealing than Lainey's red, but it nevertheless prompted its wearer to blush rosily.

"For heaven's sake, Lainey, we look positively *indecent*!" she pronounced in a quavering whisper.

"I know." Lainey sighed. "They are dreadful, aren't they? We could make an appearance in our own clothes, I suppose, but they are honestly much too plain." And dirty, she added silently, her eyes flickering toward the cotton dresses they had left draped over the back of the chair. The skirts of both gowns were spattered with mud.

"In this case, I would much prefer the plain," Beth murmured unhappily.

"It's only for tonight," Lainey reassured her. "I promise you—if Mr. Bloomfield fails to keep his word again, I will simply tell him that we cannot perform."

"What will everyone think?" Beth lamented, tugging at the neckline in a hopeless attempt to cover more of her bosom. Her curves were more slender than her sister's, but the costume accentuated, in embarrassing detail, the supple shapeliness of her figure. "What will the Holts think?" Her thoughts flew to one particular Holt, and she groaned softly in dismay.

"They will think whatever they please." Her own face flamed, belying the nonchalance of her words. "It will be all right, Beth. Once you are out on that stage, you'll forget about everything else."

"I will do this tonight, Lainey," her sister declared in a slightly tremulous undertone. She raised her eyes to Lainey's and shook her head. "But never again. Not like this. Papa would have been aghast to see us reduced to such—such immodest circumstances."

Lainey experienced a sharp twinge of guilt. Her gaze fell uncomfortably before Beth's, whose words rang all too true. It was her fault that they were in this predicament. Nothing was working out the way she had planned.

She cursed her own headstrong nature. Confound it, she reflected with an inward sigh, she had always been given to impetuous behavior. It had always brought trouble, this inclination on her part to act first and think later. Would she never learn? She caught her lower lip between her teeth and lifted her hands to the upswept thickness of her hair, making certain that the pins were securely in place.

"You're on in five minutes, Miss Prescott!" Mr. Bloomfield called out.

She took Beth's hand and gave her a smile that was half apology, half encouragement. They left the dressing room and advanced to the rear of the stage, where they waited until it was finally their turn to perform.

Beth nervously held back when they reached the top step, but Lainey compelled her forward. They slipped through the opening in the curtain and moved to the center of the narrow platform. Their entrance was greeted by a roar of applause. Lainey, noting the expression of fear on her sister's face, hurriedly nodded toward the musicians.

The strains of a song originally composed for the opera, "Silver Threads Among the Gold," filled the air, and the crowd quieted in anticipation while the "two beautiful, golden-haired songstresses"—their appearance at the Palace heralded by a flood of new handbills all over town—clasped their hands before them and offered up a quick, silent prayer that the performance would go well.

They needn't have worried, at least not yet, for their voices blended together with perfection. Beth's sweet, high-pitched soprano complemented the richer tones of Lainey's, and the sight of them standing there together, one a heavenly vision in blue and the other a more earthly goddess in red, was enough to bring a lump of sentiment to many a man's throat. It was also enough to provoke lust among the less honorable.

Ethan and Travis, meanwhile, stood along the canvas wall just to the left of the stage, scarcely fifty feet away from where their "guests" struck a graceful pose before the overly appreciative audience.

Ethan's gaze darkened as it raked over Lainey's scantily clad form. Jealous fury shot through him. Beside him, Travis's response was much the same.

"What the hell—?" his brother ground out. His arms

tightened about the wriggling Anna, and it was evident
from the look on his face that he, like Ethan, was battling the urge to drag them off the stage. "I'll kill
Halloran for this!" he muttered vengefully.

"You'll have to wait your turn," Ethan countered,
with a faint, humorless smile. His smoldering gaze remained fastened on Lainey. She looked damnably desirable, what with her full breasts threatening to spill out
of the low-cut bodice and her eyes glowing brightly.
His heart swelled with admiration for her beauty, while
at the same time his passions flared hotly. It made his
blood boil to think that every other man in the room felt
the same way.

She was his. She had been his from the first moment
he had set eyes on her. Damn it, he swore silently, he
hadn't planned on feeling this way. He had never
wanted a woman as much as he wanted her, had never
felt such an intoxicating mixture of tenderness and desire . . . and love.

For better or worse, he told himself, it was too late
now. He had fallen in love for the first time in his life.
And the last. There could be no turning back.

The song drew to its plaintive conclusion. This time,
there was no baffling silence to greet Lainey afterward. She turned and smiled at Beth as the applause
and cheers rang out loud enough to wake the dead.

"See, Beth?" she remarked happily, bending her head
close to her sister's in order to be heard. "I told you
nothing else would matter once we were out here."

"There they are," Beth proclaimed, her searching
gaze finally lighting on the familiar trio. She lifted a
hand toward them, but her smile quickly faded when
she glimpsed the scowl on Travis's face.

Lainey sought them out as well. She inhaled sharply
when her eyes met Ethan's. Warm color flew to her
cheeks, and she felt scorched by the angry disapproval

in his gaze. She resisted the sudden impulse to try and pull the neckline of her costume higher again.

Someone in the audience yelled out an impatient demand for another song. Another man joined in, then another and another. Within seconds, the tent was filled with a clamoring, increasingly unruly crowd.

Lainey and Beth exchanged worried glances. There was a strange tension in the air that night, and the smell of strong spirits was almost overwhelming. Lainey's gaze widened with apprehension when she noticed that some of the men near the center of the tent had leapt to their feet and were being warned, with ear-burning profanity, to resume their seats or face the consequences.

Desperate to restore the order that was fast slipping away, Lainey motioned to the orchestra to begin the next song. Only the first few bars had been played when a heavyset man seated in the front row suddenly took it in mind to scramble up onto the stage.

A breathless cry escaped Beth's lips when she realized that the drunken patron was making a beeline toward her. She backed away in rising panic, but he caught her about the waist and tried to press a kiss—a gesture of "gratitude for her beauty," if his slurred speech was any indication—upon her flushed and highly unwilling cheek.

That was when all hell truly broke loose.

Travis thrust the baby into Ethan's arms and bolted for the stage. Lainey, at first too shocked to do anything more than gape in disbelief, came to life at that same moment and flew at her sister's assailant in an attempt to make him release a weakly struggling Beth.

But Travis got there first. Lainey gasped and drew up short as he seized the man, literally tore him away from Beth, and sent him flying back across the stage with surprising ease. In the very next instant, however, someone else barreled up to take his place. Beth screamed a warning just before the newcomer set to with an attack upon Travis from behind.

"Fight!" one of the two hundred eager witnesses shouted, his voice brimming with obvious excitement.

"Every man for himself!" came another clarion call for an immediate, rough-and-tumble battle.

Within a matter of seconds, the whole place erupted into a melee of violence as old quarrels and new were suddenly being settled beneath the huge white canopy. It was as if everyone had been waiting for the opportunity to pummel a fellow boomer with his fists—and be pummeled in return. Threats and oaths and howls of pain rose together in the night air while those anxious to avoid being pulled into the frenzy scurried outside into the street.

Lainey raced protectively to Beth's side and watched in horror while Travis grappled with two adversaries at once. It was her turn to cry out when still another man climbed onto the stage and wrapped his arms about her. She struggled with all her might to break free, but he lifted her off her feet and bore her away toward the edge of the platform. Kicking and twisting like a veritable tigress in his grasp, she clawed at his arms and flung a blistering array of well-deserved curses at his head.

"Put me down! Let go of me, you black-hearted idiot!" she demanded furiously. Her struggles had loosened her hairpins, so that her luxuriant golden tresses now cascaded riotously about her face and shoulders. "Put me down!"

Ethan, of course, had already sprung into action by this time. With lightning-quick speed, he leapt onto the stage, transferred a saucer-eyed Anna to the care of her mother, and moved forward to rescue Lainey. His handsome features were set in a grim mask of fury, while his eyes held a savage gleam that boded ill for the man who had dared to lay hands on his woman.

The next thing Lainey knew, she was tumbling freely downward. She landed hard on the stage, scrambled up into a sitting position, and stared—breathless and with eyes splendidly aglow—at Ethan.

He landed a forceful blow to the man's chin, then skillfully dodged the fist of another combatant who had decided to try his luck against him. That man joined the first on the ground, and would no doubt have been joined by dozens more if not for Ethan's concern that Lainey would be drawn into the fracas again. Intent upon forcing her to safety, he seized her arm, yanked her roughly to her feet, and flung her facedown over his broad shoulder.

"Ethan!" she squealed in protest. She squirmed and pushed against his back.

"Keep still!" he snapped. She gasped, her eyes blazing with indignation while he carried her toward the steps leading down from the stage.

The same tipsy, heavyset man who had started the whole thing launched himself at them now with a bloodcurdling yell. Lainey suffered another sharp intake of breath as Ethan, his arm tightening like a band of iron about her legs, swung about and knocked the man aside. She pushed herself upward a bit, only to witness yet another attack. Ethan made short work of that miscreant as well and continued on his way to the steps.

Travis, catching sight of his brother and Lainey, hurried to extricate himself from the fight. He threw one last punch, then took Beth's arm and urged her along with him to the curtained area at the back of the tent. Anna began to cry once they were all away from the commotion; she had apparently enjoyed the sight of grown men acting like bad-tempered children.

"Damn you, Ethan Holt; put me down," Lainey said, seething.

He complied at last. She rounded on him with a vengeance as soon as she was on her feet again. Angrily sweeping the riotous locks from her face, she folded her arms beneath her breasts and glared up at him.

"You had no right to treat me so—so uncivilly! I'm surprised you didn't simply go ahead and *thrash* me while you were at it."

"Don't tempt me," he warned, only half in jest.

"Lainey Prescott!" Beth admonished sharply, her color still high and her own hair a bit wild-looking. "You owe Mr. Holt a debt of gratitude. Why, I shudder to think what might have happened if not for his timely intervention."

"Are you sure you're all right?" Travis asked the petite blonde beside him. He gallantly tried to keep his eyes from straying to the revealing décolletage of her gown, but he was only human after all—and every inch a hot-blooded Texas male.

"Yes," Beth assured him, with a shy smile. Her gaze clouded with concern on his behalf. "What about you? My goodness, Travis. You're bleeding," she exclaimed, her eyes growing enormous again at the sight of his slightly battered chin.

"It's nothing." He grinned and raised a hand to his jaw. "Nothing that won't heal in a day or two."

"Get your clothes," Ethan ordered Lainey. "We're going home."

"But I—" she started to argue.

"Get your clothes."

Though she colored furiously, she was wise enough to swallow the scathing retort that rose to her lips. She hastened into the dressing room, snatched up the clothing she and Beth had left there, and returned. Travis took Anna from her mother again and led the way outside. Lainey was following in her sister's wake when she suddenly heard Neil Halloran call out to her.

Ethan tensed behind her, his gaze darkening anew. She stole a quick glance up at him before turning to face the man whose eyes traveled boldly over her as he strode forward.

"You're not hurt, are you?" he asked, his concern for her welfare apparently quite genuine. He disregarded Ethan's presence altogether and told her, "I was delayed and didn't get here until after the fight had started. I can't tell you how worried I was when I saw what was going on. I tried to find you." He moved even closer. "I had begun to fear that you were still in the middle of that terrible ruckus."

"It's all right, Mr. Halloran," she replied coolly. "My sister and I were not injured."

"I'm glad of that, Miss Prescott. I feel personally responsible for your safety. If anything had happened to you—"

"You'd have found yourself answering to me, Halloran," Ethan interjected, his tone one of deadly calm. "As of tonight, Miss Prescott and her sister are no longer working for you."

"This doesn't concern you, Holt," the other man countered smoothly. He smiled at Lainey. "Miss Prescott and I can take care of the business between us."

"Well, I—" she began, only to fall abruptly silent when Ethan's hand closed about her arm.

"Your 'business' is finished," he decreed. His eyes locked in silent combat with Halloran's.

Lainey looked from one man to the other, her head spinning. She bristled at Ethan's assumption that she would meekly allow him to step in and take charge of her life, and yet she was reluctant to continue singing at the Palace after what had just occurred. She knew Beth would never come back. And she wasn't at all certain that she wanted to risk the possibility of being drawn into another brawl like the one continuing out front. The marshal and his deputies had arrived on the scene by now, but it would be some time before their efforts

brusquely. "For now, you're going to keep quiet and
t on your horse."

"*What?* Why, how dare—?"

"I'm warning you, Lainey."

It was clear from the tone of his voice that it
wouldn't take much to push him over the edge. Lainey
clamped her mouth shut, raised her head to an angrily
defiant angle, and jerked free to go racing across the
muddy, dimly lit grounds behind the theater.

As soon as they got back to the ranch, Beth took
Anna inside to put her to bed. Travis stayed behind in
the barn to unsaddle the horses. Lainey found herself
virtually dragged from her mount by Ethan, whose grim
expression and dully glinting eyes warned of an impending storm.

"What in heaven's name do you think you're doing?"
she demanded as he pulled her outside.

"We need to talk." He gave her no choice. Leading
her along toward the creek that flowed only a short distance from the cabin, he finally drew her to a halt beneath the trees.

His hand fell away from her arm. She rubbed at her
tingling, slightly reddened flesh and tilted her head back
to peer up at him in the darkness. The night was lit by
the quarter-moon's soft glow, which turned the landscape into a silver-hued paradise. The cool, clear waters
of the nearby stream gurgled quietly on their way to the
Cimarron. Somewhere in the distance, the faint hoot of
an owl announced the nocturnal creature's readiness to
hunt.

Lainey's gaze dropped before Ethan's. Recalling her
vow never to be caught alone with him again, she
glanced nervously toward the cabin and consoled herself with the thought that Beth and Travis were safely
within earshot. Indeed, she acknowledged with considerable reluctance, the only real danger facing her was
internal . . .

to quell the whiskey-induced violence wo⌐
any success.

"I'm sorry, Mr. Halloran," said Lainey, ac⌐
scious of Ethan's strong fingers tensing about ⌐
"But I am in no mood at present to discuss the m⌐

"That's perfectly understandable," he replied. "⌐
what you've been through, I'm sure you're anxious⌐
return home and get some rest. You have my sincere
apologies for tonight, Miss Prescott. I give you my
word that it won't happen again." His gaze narrowed
imperceptibly when it traveled back to Ethan. "In case
you haven't noticed, Holt, you're no longer wearing
badge. Don't interfere again."

Lainey's eyes flew wide. For a moment, she
afraid the two men would come to blows. She watch⌐
as they stood facing each other in the lamplight, the
faces betraying little of the rancor they held for each
other.

"Wait for me outside," Ethan directed her quietly. She
opened her mouth to protest, but he was already compelling her through the rear entrance.

Thrust unceremoniously outside, she stopped and
whirled about to cast a scowl back toward the tent. She
waited, feeling only a trifle guilty for eavesdropping as
she tried to hear what was being said in her absence.
The roar of the battling crowd overpowered all other
sounds, allowing her nothing more than the unintelligible murmur of deep, masculine voices.

She started in alarm when Ethan suddenly materialized before her. He took her arm in a firm grasp once
more and began leading her toward the shed where Beth
and Anna waited with Travis.

"What happened?" she couldn't resist demanding.

"Nothing."

"What do you mean, 'nothing'? Confound it, Ethan
Holt. You—"

"We'll talk about it when we get home." He cut her

"Very well," she said calmly. "What is it?"

"You're not going back to the Palace, Lainey."

"That is my decision to make, Ethan Holt!"

"Not any longer," he disputed, giving a curt shake of his head. His eyes fell with burning significance to where her breasts swelled above the low-cut neckline of the red satin dress. "Damn it, woman; look at you. It's no wonder you started a riot."

"I didn't start anything," she denied, stung by his reproach. "Beth and I did nothing more than sing. Is it my fault that some poor, drunken fool decided to show his appreciation?"

"What did you expect?" His dark eyebrows drew together into a frown. "This isn't some quaint little town in Missouri. Things are different out here. Guthrie's wild and full of men just waiting for the chance to cause trouble."

"Well, I—I know that now," she stammered, growing uncomfortably warm. She released a sigh and averted her face from the piercing intensity of his gaze. Her long hair was streaming down about her like a curtain of honey-gold silk, and every breath she took emphasized the full, delectable roundness of her breasts. She was blissfully unaware of the white-hot desire that coursed through Ethan's body like wildfire. "I'm sorry Beth had to be subjected to such danger," she murmured, fighting back sudden tears. "Dear God, I never thought—"

"I know."

In spite of his anger, he felt his heart twisting at the sight of her distress. She was such an innocent in some ways—and remarkably shrewd in others. He battled the sudden urge to draw her into his arms. He knew that if he started out giving her comfort, he'd end up losing his head again. And that was something he wanted to avoid, at least for now. She wasn't ready to face the truth yet. Still, he thought while temptation called him onward, there was something to be said for speeding things up a bit.

"Mr. Halloran gave me his word that it would never happen again," she reminded him.

"Halloran's word doesn't mean a thing, Lainey."

"And how do you know that?"

"We've crossed paths before." A faint smile of irony touched his lips before he revealed, "I knew him back in Kansas. He ran a gambling hall there, just like he's doing in Guthrie now. I had the pleasure of arresting him a couple of times."

"Were you a sheriff?" She looked up at him again, surprised to realize how very much she wanted to hear about his past. In some ways he was still little more than a stranger, but there were times when she felt as if she had known him for years.

"No. I was a federal man." His eyes clouded at the memory of too many years spent watching his back ... too many years seeing nothing but the darker side of life.

"Why did you stop?"

"It was time," he replied, his gaze sweeping across the rugged, night-cloaked beauty of the surrounding plains. "Travis needed a partner. And I was tired of living in the saddle."

"Then you were running away from something, too," she remarked, half to herself.

"Maybe," he allowed, with another ghost of a smile. Noting the sudden shadow crossing her face, he frowned again. "What made you leave Missouri?"

His low, wonderfully resonant voice washed over her in the darkness. She shivered a bit and folded her arms across her breasts, her gaze falling once more.

"After my father died, there was nothing to keep us there."

"Nothing?" He found it difficult to believe that there hadn't been some man who would have given the world to make her stay. The thought of it sent a blaze of jealousy through him, even though he told himself it was a waste of time to worry about what had gone before. All that mattered was the here and now—and the future. God willing, her future would be his own.

"Beth and I . . . we decided it was best to make a new life elsewhere," she explained, choosing her words carefully. "When I read about Oklahoma, I somehow just knew we should come here." She tossed a glance heavenward, her eyes wistful as they focused on the brightest star in the sky. "It's strange the way things work out, isn't it?"

"Fate knows no master," he observed, his smile this time disarmingly crooked. He sobered in the next instant and moved closer. His gaze seared down into hers. "Whatever it is you're running away from, Lainey Prescott, it's time to let it go. Forget about what's past."

"And have you taken your own advice, Mr. Holt?" she challenged.

"I've given it my best shot."

"Well, there are some things that cannot be forgotten, no matter how hard we try," she opined, with another sigh.

She unfolded her arms and raked a hand through the tumbling thickness of her hair. Wandering toward the creek, she idly scrutinized its glistening, shallow depths. It suddenly occurred to her that this was the first real conversation she had ever shared with Ethan Holt. Until now, it seemed that they had always been at cross-purposes with each other. She was surprised to realize that she actually *liked* talking to him.

But the truce was shattered in the next moment.

"I've got some business in town tomorrow," said Ethan. "I'll tell Halloran you won't be coming back." He had communicated much the same thing during those few minutes alone with the four-flushing bastard a short time earlier, but he would do so again—with more vigor.

"But I haven't made my decision yet," protested Lainey, whirling to face him again.

"I thought—"

"That is exactly the problem, Ethan Holt!" she suddenly lashed out at him. "You are always thinking for me, trying to impose your will upon me when I have a perfectly good mind *and* the capacity to use it." She stormed forward to confront him, her eyes shooting deep blue sparks as she balled her hands into fists and planted them on her hips. "If I decide to return to the Palace, then I will do so whether you grant your approval or not. In the meantime, I'll thank you to let me speak for myself."

"You've got a tongue sharp enough to cut a man in two, Lainey Prescott," observed Ethan, his words more affectionate than condemning.

Without warning, his arm shot out to curl about her waist. He caught her up against him, his face mere inches from hers. Shocked into speechlessness, she struggled for breath and felt her heart leap wildly within her breast.

"You'll do as I say, you little wildcat," he decreed huskily.

His other hand moving up to entangle within her silken tresses, he lowered his head and captured her lips with the strong, burning warmth of his own. The kiss was sweetly savage—and brief. Lainey had done no more than moan and raise her hands weakly to his shoulders when he released her. She gasped and lifted trembling fingers to her well-branded mouth. Her wide, luminous eyes were full of confusion and a secret disappointment as she gazed up at him.

"Why, you—you—" she sputtered, her face flaming.

"The name's 'Ethan,' " he declared mockingly. "Get used to saying it."

He turned and sauntered away, leaving her to stare after him in helpless, fiery-eyed anger. She watched as he disappeared into the barn.

You'll do as I say. His words continued to burn in her mind, placing her common sense at furious odds with her pride. She had meant what she'd said about the Palace, that she had not yet made her decision. But now that he had so arrogantly *ordered* her to stay away, she was inclined to continue her employment there after all.

Another involuntary shiver danced down her spine. Flinging one last glance up toward the endless night sky, she scurried across the yard and into the cabin.

Chapter 10

Lainey waited until after Ethan had left for town the next morning before saddling her own horse. Beth followed her into the barn, demanding to know what she was about.

"I've got to speak to Mr. Calhoun again," she explained. She pulled the cinch tight and lowered the stirrups back down into place. "He may have some news regarding our claim."

"Why didn't you ride along with Mr. Holt?"

"Because I prefer to go alone." Her brow creased into a frown as she slipped a hand beneath the bridle to lead the horse outside.

"You're not planning to speak to Mr. Bloomfield as well, are you?" Beth asked, her opal gaze narrowing in suspicion at a sudden thought. "Oh, Lainey. Surely you are not considering—?"

"I certainly don't expect you to go back, Beth. Nor would I ask you to do so after what happened last night. But our situation hasn't changed. We still need the money."

"Then we will simply have to find some other way to get it!" Horrified at the thought of her sister returning to the Palace, she reached out to take Lainey's arm in an unusually firm grip. "Please, you must not do it! No amount of money is worth placing yourself in such danger."

"I won't be in any real danger," Lainey asserted,

though her words lacked conviction. She sighed heavily and moved forward into the sunshine, anxious to change the subject. "I know the Holts are planning to work on the cabin today. Ethan should be back soon." It seemed perfectly natural for her to use his first name, though she didn't pause to think about it. "I will ride directly to our place afterward. I hope you don't mind being left alone with Travis for a while."

"Of course not," replied Beth, her color heightening faintly. "Anna and I will be fine."

"Good. With any luck, my meeting with Mr. Calhoun will yield favorable results this time."

"Lainey, I still don't think—"

"Don't worry, Beth." She cut her off with a warmly indulgent smile. "I promise I won't agree to anything without giving it a considerable amount of thought first."

She mounted up, took hold of the reins, and settled her dark blue muslin skirts about her legs. The costumes she and Beth had worn the night before were rolled into a bundle and tied behind the saddle. She planned to return them to Mr. Bloomfield with a few choice words of reproach.

Reining about, she touched her heels to the animal's flanks in a silent command. She rode away across the sunlit prairie, completely unaware of the surprises fate had in store for her.

A short time later, Beth coaxed Anna into a sorely needed rest. She dropped a tender kiss upon her sleeping daughter's forehead, then straightened from the bed and turned away. Her eyes flew wide when she saw that Travis stood framed in the doorway, his own gaze filled with a strange, forebodingly intense light.

"Why, Travis. I—I didn't know you were there," she murmured, lifting a hand to her throat while rosy color tinged her delicate, heart-shaped countenance.

"I've never been a patient man, Beth," he declared

enigmatically, prompting her to stare at him in confusion. His next words brought a startling enlightenment. "I know we haven't known each other very long. And I know the timing could have been better, what with all of us just starting out here in Oklahoma. But timing be damned!" he proclaimed, flinging his hat onto the nearby table. "I love you, Beth. I love you, and I think you feel the same way."

Beth's heart leapt wildly. His declaration had taken her completely off-guard. It filled her with a joy more profound than she had ever known—and a terrible, almost unbearably painful feeling of remorse. She opened her mouth to say something, anything, but could not. Her legs suddenly threatened to give way beneath her. She sank down on the bed beside Anna as hot tears stung against her eyelids.

Travis crossed the room in three long strides and dropped down on one knee before her. He captured her hand with the strong warmth of his and compelled her to look at him. She caught her breath when her eyes met his, for he was gazing at her with all the love in his heart.

"You told me we could never be more than friends. Well, I can't accept that! Damn it, Beth! Ever since the night of the storm, I've been aware that there is something between us so powerful, so sweet and full of magic, that it's useless to fight against it anymore."

"Travis, you—you don't even know me," she stammered breathlessly. Her bright gaze traveled over his handsome, chiseled features, and she felt a delicious warmth spreading through her body. He was the most attractive man she had ever known, and yet she knew it was much more than that. He was so very kind and gentle, and, in spite of what Lainey had said, she knew he was an honorable man. Still, she told herself in silent anguish, it could not be. "You don't know anything about me, not really," she reiterated, shaking her head sadly.

"I know all I need to know," he insisted. He seized her shoulders in a firm but gentle grip and stood to his feet, pulling her up before him. A tender, wonderfully crooked smile touched his lips. "I told you once before—I'm no saint. But I've never loved anyone before. And I've never asked anyone else to marry me. I want to spend the rest of my life with you, Beth Baker."

"That isn't my name," she confessed, her voice scarcely audible. The color had drained from her face now, and her eyes fell guiltily before the searching emerald depths of his.

"What?" He gazed down at her in loving bemusement. "What are you talking about?"

"My name isn't Baker." She took a deep, ragged breath and told him in a voice quavering with misery, "I'm not a widow, Travis."

"But, Anna—?"

"Anna is my daughter. But I was never married to her father." She choked back a sob and raised her eyes to his once more. "Don't you see? That's why we left Missouri. I—I didn't want to deceive you. I didn't want to deceive anyone!"

"You haven't deceived me," Travis assured her, but she didn't seem to hear him. She took a deep, ragged breath while her gaze clouded with painful remembrance.

"Anna is only an innocent child. She didn't deserve to bear *my* guilt. But that wasn't truly the reason we left."

"Then what was?"

"Jack's parents were going to take her away from me. In spite of the fact that he—that he abandoned me, they decided to claim Anna. They insisted that she belonged with them, and that the only thing I could give her was shame." The tears spilled over to course freely down her cheeks at last. "They are wealthy and powerful, so much so that we had little chance of winning against them. Lainey said the only thing to be done was to leave, to start a new life elsewhere and forget about what was past."

"Lainey was right."

"Was she?" Dashing at her tears, she pulled away and crossed blindly to the fireplace. "I am truly honored by your proposal, Travis Holt, but now you understand why I can never marry you."

"Are you still in love with him?" Travis asked quietly. His gaze held a dull gleam as it fastened on her back.

"No. I did love him, once. We were to be married. But he left long before Anna was born." She stared downward at the glowing pile of embers and felt her heart breaking anew. "I can't marry you, Travis. I can't marry anyone."

Travis scowled and muttered a curse underneath his breath. He was filled with murderous rage toward the man who had betrayed her. But his feelings for her hadn't changed one bit. *Not one bit.*

"You'll marry me," he ground out, swiftly closing the distance between them again. He spun her about to face him and swept her beguiling, slender curves possessively up against his hardness. His eyes softened as they took note of her incredulity. "You'll marry me and no one else," he decreed once more. "What the devil do I care what your name is? You'll be a 'Holt' from here on out anyway!"

"But, you mean it doesn't bother you that I . . . well, that I loved another?"

"It bothers the hell out of me," he admitted. "But not for the reasons you think. I haven't got the right to judge you. No one does. Besides, how could I hold something like that against you when I've done far worse?"

"I can't believe you've ever done anything terrible!" she adamantly protested, delighting him with her unwillingness to believe him a sinner.

"Well, I have. And someday I might tell you about it. But right now, I don't want to dwell on the past. All I can think about is how much I love you. Marry me!"

"But, I—I am not worthy of your love," she faltered, still not daring to accept his easy forgiveness. She had never thought to find a man who would love her so much. *Dear God, was it true?* "Oh, Travis. I don't deserve—"

"Don't ever say that again." His arms tightened about her, and he smiled softly before telling her, "I'm the one who's unworthy, Beth. You're much too good for a no-account saddle tramp like me. You do love me, don't you?" he questioned, sobering again. His eyes anxiously searched her face for the truth.

"Of course I do," she admitted, without hesitation. "But we—"

"Then say you'll marry me," he demanded. "Please, Beth. Say it."

She clutched weakly at his shoulders, her head spinning. It was all happening so fast. She had only known him a week. But time didn't matter, she realized. She had come alive again . . .

"What about Lainey?" she asked, still trying to be calm and rational. "And your brother?"

"What about them?"

"They may not be so willing to give their approval."

"I don't intend to ask for it."

"But the farm, and the ranch! For heaven's sake, Travis, where will we live?" A thousand questions tumbled about in her mind as she instinctively entwined her arms about his neck and felt her very soul take flight.

"We'll have to build a place of our own. I certainly don't intend to share a cabin with my brother once we're married. But we'll work all that out later," he as-

serted, impatient to kiss her the way he had been longing to do from the first day they'd met. He was already
bending his head toward hers when she suddenly raised
a hand to stop him.

"Please, Travis. You've got to promise not to tell
anyone about this yet."

"Why not?"

"Because I need time to break the news to Lainey.
I'm afraid she will be terribly disappointed when she
learns that Anna and I won't be living with her after
all." She and Lainey had spent the entirety of their lives
together. It seemed odd to realize that they would be
parting ways. Her eyes clouded as twenty years' worth
of memories flooded her mind. She felt a bit like a trai-
tor. And yet, God help her, she couldn't bear the
thought of living without Travis.

"She'll be happy for you, Beth," he assured her, with
another heart-stirringly tender smile. His eyes gazed
deeply into hers. "I'll be a good husband to you. And a
good father to Anna. I'll love her the same as my own.
She'll never lack for anything."

The tears glistening in Beth's eyes this time were put
there by a happiness she had never thought to know.
Love had set her free. And this man, this captivating
Texas cowboy whose arms were at once strong and gentle, would be the one to hold her forever.

"I'll marry you, Travis Holt," she vowed softly. She
swayed closer, her lips parting in a silent yet well-
understood invitation.

Travis needed no further encouragement. While little
Anna slept on, her future father kissed her mother for
the first time. The embrace was so sweet and so splendidly passionate that its eager participants yearned for
the day when they would join together as husband and
wife. In the whirling depths of their minds they offered
up the same prayer—*let it be soon.*

At that same moment, a few miles away in the town

already rumored to be designated as the new Territorial Capital, Lainey reined to a halt behind the Palace Theater. She swung down from the saddle, untied the bundle of clothing, and set off toward the tent, where, according to Ethan Holt, she had started a riot the night before.

She frowned at the memory of his censure and headed inside with the intention of finding Mr. Bloomfield. The theater was deserted at that hour, except for a table and chairs set up near the front.

Neil Halloran was seated in one of the chairs, his arms folded negligently across his chest as he leaned back and surveyed his three companions with a faint, self-satisfied smile. He looked every inch a successful "knight of the green cloth" that morning: his dark suit was impeccably tailored; his shirt of the finest white lawn; and his patterned silk vest a bright, bold crimson.

He was undeniably attractive, yet Lainey found herself musing wryly that he was very likely a wolf in sheep's clothing. She recalled what Ethan had told her about him. It wasn't so difficult to believe him capable of illegal activity; she had little doubt that he could cheat a man without blinking an eye.

The moment he caught sight of her, his eyes gleamed hotly. With deceptive nonchalance, he stood and moved forward to greet her.

"Miss Prescott! This is an unexpected pleasure. I didn't think you'd be back until tonight." His hand closed about her arm with a familiarity that made her stiffen. He led her to the table. The other men rose from their seats now as well, their faces betraying an interest that was far too acute for Lainey's tastes. "Gentlemen, I'm sure you've already had the pleasure of listening to my new singer. Miss Prescott, these are some of my fellow investors."

"How do you do?" she murmured, casting a polite smile in their direction. Inwardly she bristled at Halloran's casual use of the word *my* when referring to her status as his employee. She wasted little time in declaring the purpose for her visit. "I came to return these to Mr. Bloomfield." She lifted her head proudly and offered him the bundle. "Please tell him that he may burn them for all I care!"

He gave a low chuckle, took the costumes, and tossed them to land atop the table. His gaze was brimming with amusement as it flickered intimately over her.

"My sentiments exactly, Miss Prescott. You deserve far better." Desire surged through him at the memory of how she had looked in the red satin dress. He would get her something less revealing to wear onstage—and save the red satin for when the two of them were alone.

"About last night, Mr. Halloran," she began, "I—"

"Let's go outside where we can talk privately." He took her arm again and led her back across to the curtained area at the other end of the tent. They stepped through the flaps and outside into the sun's warmth. Once there, she pulled free of his annoyingly possessive grasp. Her beautiful eyes flashed up at him.

"You do not own me, Neil Halloran," she declared in a low, angry tone.

"I never meant to imply that I thought so." He lied smoothly. He had already decided that she would be his. She would belong to no other man—in spite of Ethan Holt's words to the contrary. *Holt.* His gray eyes darkened at the thought of their brief yet volatile meeting last night. It was time he did something about the interfering son of a bitch. There was no badge to protect him now . . . .

Forcing his thoughts back to the far more agreeable present, he smiled and folded his arms across his chest. He allowed his eyes the pleasure of traveling downward to the curve of Lainey's breasts before meeting her gaze once more.

"Well, Miss Prescott? Are you going to give me another chance?"

"Another chance?" she echoed in puzzlement, coloring faintly beneath his scrutiny.

"At the Palace. I promise, there will be no further outbreaks of violence. I've already taken steps to ensure that."

"What steps?" she demanded mistrustfully.

"I've hired some men to guard the stage during all performances. And I've spoken with the local authorities." He had spoken with them all right; he had paid them well to forget about last night's calamity. "In two days' time, we'll be moving into more permanent quarters."

"You mean the building is already completed?" Her eyes widened in surprise.

"It will be ready by the end of the week," he assured her. Reaching out to enclose her hand within the uncallused warmth of his, he faced her with an earnest expression and requested solemnly, "Please stay, Lainey. I won't deny that my interest in you isn't strictly business. But I give you my word that I won't force my attentions on you. I care for you far too much to treat you with anything less than the utmost respect." He mentally congratulated himself on his own performance when he noted the softening of her gaze.

Lainey visibly wavered, torn by indecision. She was all too aware of Beth's feelings in the matter. And of Ethan's. His face swam before her eyes, provoking a chaotic whirl of emotions—some alarmingly pleasant and some most definitely not—within her. She had no desire to analyze what Halloran had meant when he'd said that he cared for her. Great balls of fire, she reflected crossly, the last thing she needed was another man to bedevil her.

"Very well." She relented, though still not entirely certain she was doing the right thing. She withdrew her hand and added a stipulation to her consent. "However, I will not return until the Palace opens in its new location."

"Agreed." His eyes lit with triumph, while his mind was already formulating plans that, had she been aware of them, would have sent her running. "We'll advertise your next performance to take place on Friday. That should give us plenty of time to put the finishing touches on the place."

"One more thing, Mr. Halloran," she insisted.

"Anything you ask, Miss Prescott," he countered generously.

"My sister will not be returning. And if you truly wish to continue our association, you will provide me with a more suitable costume. I think you understand."

"I do indeed. You'll have it by Friday."

"But how can you possibly know if it will fit?" she asked with another slight frown.

"I'll know." His gaze moved slowly over her again, memorizing every sweet, well-rounded curve.

Lainey blushed and hastily took her leave of him. She rounded the corner of the tent, heading back toward the town's main street. Another vision of Ethan drifted across her mind, and she wondered if he had returned home yet. She felt a certain perverse satisfaction at the thought of how he would react when he discovered that she was going to continue singing at the Palace after all. Strangely enough, she seemed to delight in provoking him. It had never been in her nature before to purposely seek conflict with another human being. But then, she mused with a sigh, her nature appeared to have undergone a startling transformation ever since she had met Ethan Holt.

She set off toward Oliver T. Calhoun's office. The street was as crowded as usual, but she scarcely noticed the other people, for her mind was now engrossed with thoughts of her legal difficulties.

"Lainey Prescott?"

She stopped and whirled about at the sound of her name. The woman who had called out to her looked vaguely familiar. Quickly searching her memory, she watched as the tall brunet made her way forward.

"Why, Alice Bennett!" she exclaimed, recognition arriving only an instant beforehand.

It was the librarian from Virginia she had met shortly before the run. She could certainly never forget Alice's incredible story—marrying a stranger, a widower with two young children, simply because she liked what she saw in his eyes. At the time, it had seemed absurdly impulsive, but she wasn't so sure of that any longer. She had wondered on more than one occasion if the marriage of convenience had brought Alice happiness. Smiling now, she hurried forward to meet her.

"It's Alice McNeill now," the other woman reminded her, with a soft laugh. She embraced her warmly, then drew away and said excitedly, "Oh, Lainey. I wasn't sure I would ever see you again! How are you? And your sister?"

"We're fine. And you?" She and Alice hadn't known each other long, and yet she suddenly felt as if their friendship had endured for years. It was so good to see a familiar face in Guthrie. Except for Ethan, she had encountered no one from the boomers' camp.

"I am doing quite well, thank you," replied Alice. She looked remarkably young and pretty in her red calico dress. Her hair was caught up in a loose chignon, instead of in the more severe style she had affected before. "John managed to claim one of the quarter-sections just north of town. And the children are thriving!" A rosy glow suffused her features when she confided, "John and I are very happy together, Lainey."

"I am so very glad to hear it, Alice," Lainey proclaimed with heartfelt sincerity. She would never have believed it possible that two people, acquainted for only a few hours' time before their wedding, could find a love to last forever. And yet, the evidence was here before her eyes.

"You must come and visit us soon," insisted Alice. "Are you living in town?"

"No. Our claim is only a few miles to the west." A shadow of worriment crossed her face, but she forced another smile to her lips and said, "Beth will be so pleased to hear of our meeting."

"Please give her my best." She cast a quick look over her shoulder. "I'm sorry, but I must go now. John is waiting for me at the land office." It was her turn to look troubled when she disclosed, "We had the misfortune to lose some of our stock last night. John insisted that we speak with the marshal without delay."

"The marshal?"

"Yes. Someone took advantage of the darkness and made off with our cow, and two of the horses. We've heard of other incidents, too. Some have even occurred in broad daylight! But there is really nothing much to be done, I suppose." She sighed in conclusion. "These outlaws, whoever they are, seem to know exactly when to strike." Her brow cleared when she hugged Lainey again and implored, "Please, come and visit us soon."

"I will," she promised. She watched until her friend had disappeared into the midst of the crowd, then continued on her way to visit with the lawyer. Recalling what Alice had said about outlaws, she thought of the two men who had come looking for Ethan several nights ago. She shuddered at the memory of their cold, sinister gazes and prayed that they would never return.

Oliver T. Calhoun was delighted to see her, as usual, and wasted little time in revealing what he had learned about the other claims. The grim look in his eyes warned her that the news would not be good.

"I'm afraid, Miss Prescott, that the case against you has strengthened."

"Strengthened? But how can that be?"

"One of the other claimants, Mr. Merriwether, has offered a sworn affidavit to the effect that he witnessed you removing his markers and replacing them with your own."

"Why, that is nothing but a bald-faced lie," exclaimed Lainey, her eyes blazing with indignation. "I was completely alone when I arrived at the claim, and there were no other markers!"

"Did you encounter anyone else after you had marked the claim?"

"Yes." Her eyes darkened at the awful memory. "A man came along shortly afterward and insisted that I leave."

"What did you tell him?"

"The truth, of course. I informed him that it was my claim and he had no right to it!"

"What happened after that? Did he reveal his name or motive for his actions, or perhaps even—?"

"No." She shook her head and took a deep, steadying breath. Dull color stained her cheeks when she told him reluctantly, "He physically attacked me, Mr. Calhoun. Indeed, if not for the intervention of—of someone else, I might have been killed!"

"And would this 'someone else' be willing to testify on your behalf?"

"I think so," she replied, with a frown. She loathed the very idea of asking Ethan Holt for help again, and yet what choice did she have? Neil Halloran was acquainted with the man, but apparently not well enough to be of any assistance.

"It could be that your assailant is the same man now calling himself Merriwether," suggested Oliver.

"The thought has certainly occurred to me, but I doubt if it is true. I should think that he would not want his own despicable actions so closely examined." She did not tell him of her second, more recent encounter—with the man she knew only as Vince.

"Perhaps not." His mouth curved into a faint smile when he remarked, "It is still my belief that the three are connected in some way. As a matter of fact, I received a bit of information only a short time ago that leads me to suspect the true culprit in this scheme is someone very prominent in Guthrie."

"Who is it?" she demanded, silently vowing to see the man punished for his lies.

"I'm not certain of his identity yet." Without further proof, he was hesitant to name Neil Halloran. If Halloran *was* behind the scheme, he mused silently, it was just possible that the man's primary interests lay far more with Lainey than with the land itself. It certainly wasn't difficult to believe.

"Then what am I going to do?" Lainey sighed. "For heaven's sake, I can't sit back and allow my land to be stolen from me."

"There might be a way . . ." he began, his voice trailing away as a pensive frown creased his brow.

"Please Mr. Calhoun, if you know of anything, anything at all, tell me!" she prompted in growing desperation. Dear God, what would she and Beth do if they lost their land? They had nowhere else to go.

"You could apply to Ethan Holt for assistance."

"*What?*" she gasped in stunned disbelief. "You know Ethan Holt?"

"Mr. Holt and I have been in contact with each other. He—"

"You had no right to discuss my personal affairs with anyone else!" she fumed. She rose abruptly to her feet, her sapphire eyes blazing. "I believed you to be trustworthy, Mr. Calhoun, and yet you have violated my confidence in you."

"Please, Miss Prescott, sit down and I will explain,"

he exhorted gently. He smiled across at her and indicated the chair in front him. "Please."

Still reeling from the discovery that he had told Ethan about her troubles, Lainey struggled to control her temper. She was sorely tempted to go storming from the tent and never look back. But there was such kindness, such genuine compassion in the lawyer's bespectacled gaze, that she found herself sinking back down into the chair.

"Very well, Mr. Calhoun—*explain*."

"First of all, I did not reveal the details of your case to Mr. Holt. He came to see me after he had read of the other claims at the land office. As I told you before, they are a matter of public record. Mr. Holt was concerned about the status of your claim. He knew of our professional relationship." He paused for a moment, watching her angry countenance soften a bit. "Mr. Holt's claim borders your own, is that not correct?"

"It is."

"Well then, Miss Prescott, there may be a way to strengthen your own case." He hesitated, his personal feelings battling with his duties as her legal representative. Ethan Holt's regard for her had not escaped his notice. It pained him more than he cared to admit to realize that she would in all likelihood return the other man's affection—especially if his plan were to be accepted. Still, he wanted to help her. And if that required an emotional sacrifice on his part, then so be it. "Mr. Holt's own claim is not in question. As a matter of fact, he appears to hold considerable influence in the Territory."

"What does that have to do with me?" asked Lainey, frowning.

"I have not discussed the particulars with Mr. Holt yet—only the general idea. I think he was at first reluctant to consider my suggestion, but then realized it is not so illogical after all."

"And exactly what did you suggest to him?"

"I think the majority of your problem stems from the fact that you and your sister are unmarried," he explained. "Women, unfortunately, are not treated with the same consideration as men in the judicial system. At least not here in the Territory. A substantial portion of the male population seems to believe that a woman alone has neither the stamina nor the actual right to claim a homestead. While I myself do not agree with this antiquated opinion, I cannot deny that the problem exists." He readjusted his glasses before meeting her gaze again and finally declaring, "I think, Miss Prescott, that you would encounter far less resistance to your claim if you were married."

"Married?" she echoed, her eyes widening with incredulity. "What in heaven's name are you talking about? I am not married, nor do I have any intention—"

"Please, hear me out," he appealed firmly. "Your marriage would not have to be a traditional one, merely a legal one. After a few months' time, I would be more than happy to seek an annulment on your behalf, which I can assure you, the court would be more than willing to grant under the circumstances."

"I am not going to marry anyone."

"I have made inquiries about Mr. Holt." Oliver continued as if she had not spoken. "He was a highly respected peace officer for many years, and a formidable gunman, so I am told—an asset in these violent, uncivilized lands. With a husband such as he, Miss Prescott, you would not be troubled by anyone. In fact, I would not be at all surprised if Mr. Merriwether and his cohorts dropped their complaints the very instant they learned of your marriage."

"I cannot believe I am hearing this," Lainey said shakily, her head spinning. *Marry Ethan Holt?* It was unthinkable! She leapt to her feet again and charged, "Have you taken complete leave of your senses?"

"It is not quite so outrageous as it sounds," he insisted. He stood to face her with another faint smile. "As I said, you will be able to seek an annulment once things have settled down. In the meantime, you and Mr. Holt will be able to maintain your separate residences."

"And Eth—Mr. Holt has actually agreed to this preposterous tactic?" She was outraged to think that the two men had gotten together and decided upon *her* future. A sharp, inexplicable pain sliced through her heart in the next moment. Ethan Holt was willing to marry her ... and yet it would be nothing but a marriage of convenience. Just like Alice McNeill, she told herself. Except that Alice and her husband had found love.

"No," replied Oliver. "Mr. Holt and I discussed the possibility, but he insisted that he would have to speak to you before making a decision."

"I cannot do it, Mr. Calhoun!" Lainey emphatically declined. A dull flush rose to her face. "I ... well, I simply cannot marry anyone, *particularly* Ethan Holt, knowing full well that I have no intention of honoring the vows. It seems so dreadfully coldhearted and dishonest, and—"

"Coldhearted perhaps, but not dishonest," he contended with a lawyer's practicality. "As long as you and Mr. Holt are in agreement upon the true design of the marriage, then I foresee no real problems. Please, Miss Prescott, will you not at least consider this action?" he now urged gently. "I believe it would ensure the success of your claim, and it will save you a great deal of sorrow in the end."

"I'm not so sure of that," she murmured. Her troubled gaze moved back up to his face; she released a long, highly uneven sigh. "But, very well. I will consider it, Mr. Calhoun." Confound it, why had she said that? She couldn't possibly give any serious thought to such a ridiculous, mercenary little scheme. The very thought of broaching the subject of marriage with Ethan caused a knot to tighten in her stomach. It was all so humiliating ... and unaccountably depressing.

"You will let me know of your decision in the next day or two?" Oliver prompted further.

"Of course," she agreed, with a preoccupied air. Her emotions had been thrown into utter chaos by what she had just heard. She wanted nothing more at the moment than to pretend the conversation had never taken place. Dear God, what was she going to do?

Your marriage would not have to be a traditional one. Her face flamed as those words, above all others, continued to burn in her mind.

"Are you sure there isn't some other way?" she tried one last time, desperately hoping that maybe Oliver had overlooked something.

"None that I know of, I'm afraid. We could continue on our present course and hope for a more favorable development. But frankly, I am not at all optimistic." He came from around the desk and lifted a consoling hand to her arm. The gesture was a rarity for him; he was always careful to maintain a distance between himself and his clients. "I know the prospect is disagreeable to you, Miss Prescott. But, speaking as your friend, I would advise you to act without delay. I'll remind you—there have been several instances where people have been forced off their claims by far more unlawful means. I would not want to see you hurt."

"Thank you, Mr. Calhoun." She managed a wan smile. "I—I appreciate your concern."

Moving dazedly out of the tent, she made her way back down the street to retrieve her horse. She did not notice Neil Halloran watching her from the front of the theater as she passed by. That same predatory gleam she had glimpsed in his eyes once before filled their gray, hawkish depths now.

The ride home allowed her ample opportunity in which to ponder everything Oliver T. Calhoun had said to her, but her mind was no clearer by the time she arrived at her claim. She was still plagued by indecision—and still oddly hurt by the realization that what Ethan felt for her was apparently nothing more than a passing interest.

He had kissed her. He had very nearly had his wicked way with her. But it seemed she was no different than all the others—and she had little doubt that there had been plenty of "others." Confound it, why did the thought cause her such pain?

Slowing her mount to a walk atop the nearest hill, she spied Beth and Anna seated together in the shade beside the creek. Her eyes traveled farther, only to spark with several conflicting emotions when they fell upon Ethan. He was working alongside his brother, and she watched as he raised his head and caught sight of her. Even at that distance, she felt scorched by his gaze.

She frowned to herself again and rode into the center of camp, then reined to a halt and swung down from the saddle. Her sister stood with the intention of approaching her, but delayed the greeting when Ethan strode forward.

"Where have you been?" he asked casually.

"I'm sure Beth has already told you." She brushed past him, leading the horse to the other side of the wagon. A brief smile of irony touched his lips when he followed her.

"You spoke to Calhoun, didn't you?"

"Why, how did you——?" she started to question, only to break off and lift her head to a stubborn angle. "Never mind. I don't wish to discuss it!" She turned away again.

"Discuss what?" His gaze raked hungrily over her. Knowing full well that his offer of assistance would be declined, he watched while she set about removing the saddle.

"You know perfectly well what!" she retorted hotly.

She had done no more than unfasten the cinch when she rounded on him. "How dare you interfere in my affairs, Ethan Holt! I know that you went to Mr. Calhoun behind my back, and that you—"

"You needed my help, Lainey. I knew you'd never ask for it."

He stepped closer, towering above her with a look in his eyes that was at once tender and forebodingly passionate. His nearness only served to add to her confusion. She could literally feel the warmth emanating from his hard-muscled body, and her own eyes strayed to where his bronzed, powerful arms were partially exposed by the rolled-up sleeves of his shirt.

"I don't need your help!" she insisted, her voice quavering ever so slightly.

"Yes, you do." He smiled to himself, his heart swelling with love and pride at her spirit. She was every inch a lady, and every inch the wildcat he had called her last night. By damn, he would be the one to tame her—*but not too much.*

Lainey swallowed hard and whirled toward the horse once more. She was dismayed to feel her cheeks burning.

"No, Mr. Holt, I do not!" she reasserted. Then she added vehemently, "And you are out of your mind if you think I'm going to agree to the devious, ill-begotten plan you and Mr. Calhoun have contrived."

"Devious or not, it makes perfect sense," Ethan decreed, with maddening calm. His eyes glowed warmly at the thought of what lay ahead.

He had planned to court her for another month or two, to give her time to accept the truth that he had already acknowledged. Hell, he still had to decide what to do about Travis, and Beth and Anna. But there was no more time. Fate had provided an unexpected catalyst, and he knew he couldn't be sorry for the way things had turned out. It would have required an incredible amount of patience, and self-control, on his part to wait any longer. Now all he had to do was convince her that Calhoun's suggestion was a worthy one.

"We'll get married tomorrow," he told her quietly.

"What?" She spun about, her own eyes wide and splendidly ablaze. "We most certainly will not."

"The sooner the wedding takes place, the sooner you can stop worrying about your claim." He frowned down at her before demanding in mild reproach, "Damn it, Lainey! Why didn't you tell me what was going on? I might have been able to put a stop to it before now."

"What difference does it make? I am not going to marry you!"

"Why not?"

"Because it would be wrong." She heaved a ragged sigh, her gaze falling before the steady, blue-green intensity of his. "I know it would be nothing but a—a business arrangement, but it would still be wrong."

"We'll be breaking no laws. And we won't be hurting anyone. Calhoun said you could file for an annulment after a few months." There would be no annulment, of course, he vowed silently. Once they were married, she would be his forever. And he wouldn't have to hold her by force, either. She cared for him; he would make her admit it. After the wedding, he would woo his beautiful, headstrong bride with a vengeance. . . .

"You can't be serious about this," she proclaimed, shaking her head at the absurdity of it all. "Why would you want to do it? What could you possibly hope to gain?"

"I have my reasons." He smiled again and finally raised his hands to her arms. Her eyes flew back up to his face, but she did not pull away. "We don't have to tell Beth and Travis yet. But I'm confident they'll understand."

"How can they understand? For heaven's sake, *I* don't understand!"

She had no idea how desirable she looked to him, what with her face all flushed and her eyes shining brightly. Her long, honey-gold tresses, wayward as always, appeared ready to escape their pins at any moment, while her breasts rose and fell rapidly beneath her white cotton shirtwaist.

"Christopher Columbus," she muttered, "I can't believe we're even talking about this!" Her eyes narrowed up at him in sudden suspicion. "Did Mr. Calhoun make it perfectly clear to you that our marriage—if indeed there *is* a marriage—would be in name only?" She felt her knees grow weak at the sound of his soft, vibrant chuckle.

"Are you afraid you might be tempted to forget?" he challenged mockingly.

"Of course not." Her blush deepened. She finally pulled free and retreated to the other side of the horse, feeling the sudden need for a barrier between them.

"Then you've nothing to worry about on that score. I give you my word—unless you want things to change, they'll stay the same as they are now." That was true enough, he told himself.

"And you won't try—that is, you won't demand your husbandly rights?" she asked, still doubtful. "I'm not merely referring to our living arrangements. I want to make sure you don't suddenly take it in mind to seize control of my claim."

"Why would I do that?" His heart soared with triumph, for he could see that her defenses were crumbling.

"Well, you said you needed the extra land for your cattle."

"We made a bargain."

"*You* made a bargain," she pointed out, her eyes bridling with annoyance at the memory. She tugged the saddle from the horse's back and lowered it to the ground. Acutely conscious of the fact that Ethan was watching her every move, she was determined not to let him see how upsetting the whole subject was to her. It was best to remain cool and levelheaded, she cautioned herself, to treat the "arrangement" with no more sentiment than it deserved.

"I don't want your claim, Lainey," he declared truthfully. No, by heaven, he wanted *her*. "You've nothing to fear from me. Whatever you decide, I'll stand by you."

There was something in his low, deep-timbred voice that made her heart flutter wildly. She turned to face him again, only to note with surprise that he was already striding away to resume his work on the cabin. He always moved with such an easy masculine grace, she mused. He was so strong and self-assured, so damnably capable of doing anything and everything he set his mind to. She had little doubt that his wife would be well-protected . . . and well-loved.

His wife. That's what she would be if she went through with this crazy scheme. But she wouldn't really be his. And she wouldn't really be loved.

"God forgive me," she whispered, finally accepting the inevitable. There was no other way. Her mind screamed that she was making a tragic mistake, and yet her heart, strangely enough, told her that it was right. She didn't know which to trust anymore.

She pulled the saddle blanket from the horse and led him along with her to the creek. Sparing a brief, rather distracted smile for Beth and Anna, she approached Ethan with the news of her decision.

"Yes," she said simply. She frowned and shot a worried glance toward Travis, who took the hint and willingly moved to join Beth and Anna. "But I don't want anyone else to know yet."

"All right. We'll head into town first thing in the morning." His tone was deceptively level.

"So early?" she questioned. Then she sighed and conceded, "I suppose we may as well get it over with right away."

"We're getting married, not shot," he quipped wryly, his eyes twinkling down at her.

"Just keep in mind, Ethan Holt, that this changes nothing!"

"I'll try."

Her pulse leapt with alarm, but she would not turn back. She recalled something her grandmother used to say—*Now you've made your bed, you'll have to lie in it.* The words rang all too true.

Chapter 11

Mrs. Ethan Holt. Lainey could scarcely believe it had happened, and with such dizzying swiftness besides. The ceremony had taken less than five minutes. Five minutes, and now she was someone's wife. Ethan Holt's wife.

She stole a look up at her new husband as they stood together before the justice of the peace. One of the local deputies had volunteered to serve as a witness to the proceedings, which had just reached their fateful conclusion in a back room of the land office. There were no flowers, no music, no sentimental flourishes of any kind. They were dressed in their everyday clothes— Ethan in boots, denim trousers, and a blue cotton shirt that made his eyes look more hypnotizing than ever, and Lainey in a ruffle-trimmed cambric skirt and matching basque.

Her ensemble wasn't even white.

She felt a twinge of sadness when she thought of the wedding dress, her mother's wedding dress, packed away in one of the trunks back at the claim. Though she had never planned to wear it at all, she couldn't help wishing she had surrendered to the impulse to bring it with her that day. She had told herself that she had no right; her mother had worn it while marrying for love, whereas she was marrying for the sole purpose of keeping her land. *The sole purpose?* a tiny voice deep in her brain challenged.

Her reasons no longer mattered, she thought with an inward, disconsolate sigh. It was done. They only wedding she would ever have was nothing but a memory now. The whole affair had seemed so cold-blooded, so terribly dispassionate—at least thus far.

She gasped in startlement when Ethan suddenly swept her into his arms and brought his lips crashing down upon the parted softness of hers. Fighting against the impulse to melt against him, she squirmed in protest. He kissed her long and hard. When he finally allowed her to draw breath again, she was perilously light-headed. But she pulled away from him in anger, her eyes shooting deep blue sparks up at him while her cheeks colored warmly.

"What in heaven's name—?" she started to demand.

"Tradition," he explained simply. The merest hint of a smile played about his lips.

"Congratulations," the justice of the peace offered, shaking Ethan's hand and nodding politely toward Lainey. He seemed a bit too rascally to hold such an important position in the community, but there hadn't been a long list of applicants for the job. "I hope you'll both be very happy," he added for good measure.

"The same here," concurred the young deputy.

Lainey watched, simmering in silence, as the two men strode together from the room. Finally left alone with her husband, she wasted little time in taking him to task for his actions.

"Don't you ever do that again, Ethan Holt," she stormed indignantly. They both knew exactly what she meant. "Nothing has changed. You have no right to—to touch me."

"I have the right," he disputed, with alarming complacency. "We're married now, remember?"

"In name only!" She felt her heart leap at the strange gleam in his eyes. "We had an agreement," she reminded him. "We both understood that the marriage wouldn't be a real one. Therefore, I would appreciate it if, from this day forward, you kept your distance."

"What are you afraid of, Mrs. Holt?" he challenged softly.

"Don't call me that. And I'm not afraid of anything," she denied. "It's just that—" She broke off in confusion. Drawing herself rigidly erect, she frowned and insisted in a cool tone that belied the turmoil within her, "We should be getting back now."

"After we pay a visit to Calhoun."

"Very well. But I don't think it is necessary to inform anyone else of our marriage at this time." It was bad enough that Beth and Travis would know. Dear God, how was she going to explain it? She wondered what Beth would say when she discovered that her practical, normally levelheaded sister had plunged herself into this lunacy.

"You're wrong, Lainey," Ethan told her, with a slight frown of his own. He lifted the hat to his head and took her arm in a firm, possessive grasp. "I'm going to make sure the whole damned countryside knows about it. That way, anyone wanting to give you trouble will know they've got to deal with me." His gaze darkened vengefully at the thought of the three men who were trying to steal her claim.

"You wouldn't shoot them, would you?" she asked, her own thoughts following a similar course. The possibility that *he* might be the one hurt, or even killed, made her throat constrict with dread.

"Not unless I have to."

He led her from the building. Once outside, she pulled her arm free. Ethan smiled to himself and allowed his thoughts to drift toward the evening ahead.

Oliver T. Calhoun offered his felicitations and assured them that he would spread the news. Though pleased for Lainey's sake, he could not help feeling a pang of jealousy. He reddened in delight when she pressed a warmly grateful kiss upon his cheek, and his eyes were wistful as he watched her leave with her new husband. He doubted very seriously that he would ever be called upon to file that annulment . . .

As fate would have it, Neil Halloran strolled out of the Palace Theater's nearly completed frame building just as Ethan and Lainey were riding past. The smile on his face vanished; his gaze suddenly glinted like cold steel. He looked first to Ethan, then to Lainey.

Lainey felt herself color guiltily at the sight of him. She hadn't yet told Ethan of her decision, and she feared Halloran would see fit to mention it if they stopped. Turning her head away, she stiffened with growing trepidation when Ethan reined to a halt beside her. She had not choice but to do the same.

"Good morning, Miss Prescott," Neil offered, forcing a smile back to his lips. He ignored the other man altogether—but not for long.

"It's 'Mrs. Holt' now," Ethan informed him in a dangerously low and level tone. His handsome face wore a grim expression.

"What are you talking about?" the gambler demanded sharply, his eyes narrowing.

"We were married this morning. Lainey is my wife." His own piercing gaze held a mixture of satisfaction and wariness as he watched Halloran's features tense in barely controlled fury.

"I don't believe you!" Neil ground out. His eyes shot back to Lainey. "Miss Prescott—"

"I'm afraid it's true, Mr. Halloran," she confessed, her color deepening when she finally met his gaze. She inhaled upon an audible gasp. His face wore a look of sheer, bloodthirsty malevolence as he transferred his attention to Ethan once more.

"You always were full of surprises," he gritted between clenched teeth. "Some would say sneaky and underhanded."

"Hold whatever opinion of me you want," Ethan countered in a tone of deadly calm. *"But stay away from my wife."*

Lainey's pulse leapt in alarm. She was sure Halloran would say something about their agreement now. But, miraculously, he did not. His lips curled into a contemptuous sneer, and he gave a soft laugh.

"What's the matter, Holt?" he taunted in derision. "Are you afraid your bride's head is going to be turned by someone else? Maybe you're not man enough to—"

"Careful, Halloran," Ethan warned, with a faint, humorless smile of his own. "I'd hate to have to kill you on my wedding day."

"You're the one who'd better be careful," Neil drawled unconcernedly. His eyes fastened on Lainey again. "You wouldn't want to make your pretty little wife a widow just yet, would you?"

"Save your threats. Just remember what I said—come near her, and I'll kill you." It was a promise they both knew he would not hesitate to keep.

Lainey was relieved when Ethan urged his mount forward again. She stole a quick look back over her shoulder before following her new husband's lead. Neil Halloran was staring after them, the fierce scowl on his face giving evidence of the hot, vengeful rage boiling within him.

He was furious all right, furious at the thought of Ethan Holt bedding the woman he had intended to make his own. But marriage or no marriage, he vowed determinedly, she would still be his. His old enemy's time had nearly run out. And the grieving widow would have to be comforted—a duty he would fulfill with great pleasure. Yes, indeed, he told himself as a slow smile of evil intent replaced the scowl, he would make her forget all about Holt. Before he was through, she'd be begging him to take her.

His eyes gleaming lustfully at the prospect, he turned

and headed back inside the building. The theater would officially open in its new quarters that same night; he planned to advertise Lainey's return for the next. There was always a chance she wouldn't show up, but he had never been one to avoid a gamble. And in spite of Ethan Holt, he was still certain his luck was about to change—for the better.

Lainey was glad for the fact that Ethan didn't try and engage her in conversation as they rode back to her claim. She shuddered at the memory of his brief, fury-charged clash with Neil Halloran. It troubled her greatly to think of returning to the Palace after what had just happened. She had sensed from the very beginning that there was "bad blood" between the two men, yet she hadn't realized until now just how deep their animosity ran.

Mrs. Ethan Holt. Why the devil did she keep turning those words over in her mind? She was married, but she felt no different than before. Just as she had reminded Ethan, nothing had changed.

That's what she would tell Beth, too.

When they rode into camp a short time later, it was to find Beth offering Travis a well-earned drink of water in front of the unroofed cabin. Anna was scampering about with her usual wide-eyed curiosity. The day promised to be a warm one, though the sweetly scented breeze held its own promise of a respite from the heat.

Anxious to get the disagreeable task over with, Lainey dismounted and immediately called to her sister. Beth exchanged a quick, warmly lit glance with Travis before moving gracefully forward. Ethan's mouth curved into the merest hint of a smile as he led the horses away.

"Yes, Lainey? What is it?" asked Beth.

If Lainey had not been so preoccupied, she would have taken note of the soft, telltale glow in her sister's eyes. As it was, she frowned thoughtfully and drew Beth along with her to the back of the wagon.

"I have something to tell you," she announced, with obvious reluctance.

"Wasn't Mr. Calhoun able to give you good news about the claim?"

"No. I mean, it isn't about the claim. Well, it *is*, but—" She broke off and tossed a helpless look toward the heavens, then smiled faintly at Beth's expression of loving bemusement. "I had to do it, Beth." She sighed. "Mr. Calhoun said it was the only way to ensure that we did not lose the land."

"What are you talking about? What have you done?"

"I have married Ethan Holt." She held her breath and waited for Beth's reaction.

"Oh, Lainey. That's wonderful!"

Startled, she found herself caught up in an enthusiastic hug. This wasn't at all what she had expected. She seized Beth's arms and set her firmly away. Her brow creased into another frown as she shook her head in an adamant denial of her sister's conclusion.

"No, you don't understand," she insisted. Searching desperately for the right words, she blurted out, "It isn't a real marriage. Oh, it's legal, of course, but it's only a marriage of convenience. Mr. Holt and I were married so that the claim would not be taken away from us."

"A marriage of convenience?" the petite blonde echoed, visibly baffled.

"Yes! You see, Ethan was generous enough to grant me—no, to *loan* me—the use of his name for a few months. I didn't want to do it, but I could think of no other way. We aren't really husband and wife. Well, we are, of course, but in name only. In a few months' time, I'll be able to file for an annulment and we can forget that any of this ever happened." There was a slight catch in her voice when she said this last, but she refused to acknowledge its source. "Our circumstances have not altered in the least, save for the fact that we should no longer have to face the prejudices associated with being two unwed females. Mr. Calhoun assured me that, through my association with Ethan, we will no longer be troubled by anyone trying to steal our claim."

"How could marrying Mr. Holt ensure that?"

"It seems his reputation is such that only a fool would dare to cross him." Neil Halloran's face swam before her eyes, but it was quickly replaced by a vision of Ethan as he had looked when cautioning the gambler to stay away from her.

"Then you aren't really in love with him?" There was a note of sadness in Beth's voice.

"In love with him?" repeated Lainey, her own voice rising. Her eyes grew round as saucers, while two bright spots of color stained the smoothness of her cheeks. "Great balls of fire, where did you ever get such a ridiculous notion?"

"There is no need to shout, Lainey," Beth scolded gently, her opal gaze full of a knowing look now. "When you told me the two of you were married, I naturally assumed it was for the usual reasons."

"Well, it isn't." She spun about and folded her arms almost angrily beneath her breasts. "There is nothing between us, Beth, nothing whatsoever. As a matter of fact, I find Ethan Holt infuriating in the extreme!"

"That is a good deal more than 'nothing,' " Beth pointed out.

Her spirits had soared at the news of Lainey's marriage, but now sank again. For a moment, she had dared to believe that she and Travis could be together right away. If Lainey were indeed married to Ethan—a *real* marriage—then there would be no reason to wait. Apparently, however, it was not to be.

Her heart ached at the realization that nothing had changed. She still suffered a sharp pang of remorse whenever she thought of leaving her sister alone. It would have solved all their problems if only Lainey could have loved Ethan. From the very beginning, she had suspected that their feelings for each other ran toward the passionate. How could she have been so wrong? What she had believed to be a mutual regard was evidently nothing more than extreme dislike, at least on Lainey's part. She released a plaintive sigh and allowed her eyes to stray toward Travis.

"I'm sorry, Beth," said Lainey, regaining her composure now. "I knew you wouldn't approve. I'm not proud of myself for my role in the deception. But as Ethan himself insisted, we aren't breaking any laws, and we aren't hurting anyone."

"Perhaps not," murmured Beth.

"And the wedding took place at the land office, not in a church," she added, trying to convince herself as well as Beth that, somehow, the unspiritual location would make it all less sinful.

"I'm sure your motives were unselfish ones. I know you were only thinking of me and Anna. You always have."

"Then you're not . . . disappointed in me?"

"Why, how could I ever be disappointed in you? You have been so very good to me, dearest Lainey. I love you with all my heart. And if you think marrying Mr. Holt was the best thing to do, then I will certainly support your decision." She feared it would bring even more trouble, but she did not tell Lainey that. Embracing her once more, she smiled and took her hand. "Now, come and see the cabin. Travis told me they should have the roof completed by tomorrow."

"So soon?" Lainey responded in surprise. Beth's words had brought sudden, inexplicable tears to her eyes, but she resolutely blinked them back and looked to where the two men were already climbing up to the topmost logs with a bundle of cedar shingles.

"I think they are anxious to see us settled in our own

place," said Beth. In truth, she knew that wasn't the case at all. Travis had let her know in no uncertain terms how sorry he would be when she began spending her nights elsewhere, but he had consoled them both with the promise to build yet another cabin as soon as possible. Once it was completed, they would get married . . .

"That will happen none too soon for me!" Lainey opined feelingly. She was puzzled by Beth's soft laugh, but she did not question her about it as the two of them strolled together across what would soon be their front yard.

By the end of the day, the cabin was able to boast of nearly half a roof. Travis had driven Beth and Anna over in the wagon that morning, and the three of them set out for the ranch with Ethan and Lainey following behind on horseback.

The two men had loaded the bathtub into the wagon; at the sight of it, Travis had remarked teasingly that it was a good thing he and Ethan did all their bathing in the creek, for the blasted thing wasn't big enough to hold either of them. Beth had blushed rosily, her eyes sparkling in secret delight when he had whispered into her ear that once they were married, he'd be more than happy to introduce her to the pleasures of moonlight swims.

Lainey refused to look at Ethan in the gathering darkness. Her thoughts drifted back to their quick, unromantic wedding. Was it possible that, only a few short hours ago, she had stood before the justice of the peace and promised to love, honor and obey the man riding beside her? The memory of the kiss he had given her to seal the ill-fated bargain made her shift uneasily in the saddle.

Supper proved to be an unusually quiet affair, except for the baby's energetic chattering. Travis and Beth stole frequent looks at each other across the table, while

Lainey mainly just pushed the food around on her plate. Ethan, however, appeared to have suffered no loss of appetite. His bride noted with some resentment that he ate heartily.

The irony of the situation struck Lainey when she finally excused herself from the table to escape into the fresh air outside. It was her wedding night, and she would be spending it in a cabin with her sister and niece, while her husband and his brother slept in the barn.

Wedding night, an inner voice echoed as she tilted her head back to peer up at the starlit sky. This certainly wasn't the way she would have envisioned it. But then, she reminded herself with an inward sigh, she had never really envisioned it any way at all. So far, nothing was working out the way she had planned. She had never intended to marry, and she had certainly never intended to marry Ethan Holt. Her life seemed to be careening wildly along an uncharted course—and her emotions were in an absolute uproar.

The night wore on. After the meal, the men took themselves off to the creek while the women put the bathtub to good use. Anna toddled happily about once she had been scrubbed clean, only to fall asleep before her mother had even emerged from the tub. Beth hurried to finish, her mouth curving into a tenderly maternal smile as she put the little girl to bed.

The water was starting to grow cool by the time Lainey took her turn, but the fire's blazing warmth chased away the chills. She scrubbed at her skin until it was pink and glowing, then washed her hair with Beth's help.

"What are you doing?" she asked when her sister buttoned on a primrose cotton dress instead of a nightgown.

"I thought I would take a walk," said Beth. "It's still early, and I . . . well, I'm not sleepy yet." She tied a ribbon about her clean, light blond tresses and sat down to lace on her boots.

"Neither am I." Lainey sighed. Donning a freshly laundered chemise and a pair of drawers, she took a red calico Mother Hubbard wrapper from the replenished carpetbag and slipped it on over her head. "I'll go with you," she announced, belting the loose, high-necked garment.

"No!" Beth protested a bit too vigorously. A dull flush crept up to her face. "I mean, I would prefer to spend some time alone if you don't mind."

"Is something troubling you?" She eyed her sister closely, frowning at the peculiarity of her behavior. Beth hadn't been herself lately, she realized.

"No, of course not. I simply feel the need for a walk," insisted Beth. She hated the little deception, and yet she longed for a few moments alone with Travis. "It wouldn't be safe to leave Anna," she pointed out truthfully. "What if she awakened and tumbled into the fire?"

"You're right," agreed Lainey, her sapphire gaze full of contrition. "I wasn't thinking." Strangely enough, she had been absentminded all day. But then, she told herself with a faint smile of irony, it wasn't every day she gained a husband. *And what a husband he is,* that mischievous inner voice of hers observed. She offered up a silent curse.

"I won't be long," her sister promised. With one last smile, she turned and left the cabin.

Lainey sank down upon the bench in front of the fire. She slowly combed her fingers through the damp, luxuriant thickness of her hair and stared at the dancing flames. Falling into a troubled reverie, she did not hear the door open and close behind her.

"Mind if I join you?" Ethan asked softly, though it was more of a casual remark than an appeal for permission.

She leapt to her feet, her eyes flying wide at the sound of his rich, mellow voice. She whirled to face him and saw that he was smiling. It was a dangerously captivating smile, and the affection contained within his turquoise gaze made it all the more so. Alarmed to feel her heart pounding wildly, she concealed her disquiet behind a facade of cool indifference.

"Do as you please. It is your cabin, after all." She sat down again and raked her unbound tresses away from her face.

Ethan's eyes were brimming with wry amusement as he sauntered forward. He took up a stance beside the bench, lifting a negligent hand to the mantel and gazing down at the fire.

Lainey ventured a quick glance up at him, only to note that his dark hair still glistened damply. He stood only a few inches away; the fresh scent of soap hung about him, and he had changed into clean clothes as well. He looked disturbingly—wickedly—handsome.

"Beth should be back soon," she mentioned on sudden impulse.

"I wouldn't count on it."

"What do you mean?" she demanded sharply, frowning up at him.

"I mean, Mrs. Holt, that your sister and my brother are probably stealing a few kisses in the moonlight," he told her, another crooked smile playing about his lips as his fathomless, warmly lit gaze traveled to her face.

"Why, that—that isn't true!" she stammered in disbelief. She drew herself up from the bench once more and folded her arms angrily beneath her breasts. Her eyes flashed up at him. "How dare you say such a thing about Beth!"

"They're in love, Lainey," he informed her in a low, splendidly resonant tone. His smile this time was tender, his eyes full of compassion as they moved possessively over the upturned storminess of her face. "Surely you've noticed that—?"

"No." She shook her head in an adamant denial, refusing to acknowledge the truth of his words. "Beth assured me that there is nothing between them but friendship."

"I guess things have changed."

"She would have said something." *Beth and Travis?* No, it was absolutely impossible.

"I'm sure she will when the time's right," he remarked quietly. The urge to touch her was near painful in its intensity, but he forced himself to resist it. By damn, he swore inwardly, this wasn't the way he wanted them to spend their wedding night—arguing about Beth and Travis. Especially not when their own relationship was so furiously unsettled.

His whole body burned with desire. More than anything, he wanted to carry his beautiful, headstrong bride out to the barn and make love to her. He longed to possess her, to kiss and caress every inch of her sweet curves and show her in the most effective way known to man that she was his and his alone. His eyes gleamed hotly at the thought of it, but he offered up another silent curse in the next instant.

Patience, his mind cautioned. He had to give her a little more time ...

"Dear God, how did this happen?" Lainey murmured tremulously, stunned at the thought of Beth in love with Travis. The signs had been there all along, she now realized. A ragged sigh escaped her lips as so many telltale memories flooded her mind. How on earth could she have been so blind? She had been too wrapped up in her own problems, her own tumultuous feelings, to notice what was taking place. *Beth and Travis,* she repeated silently, sudden tears starting to her eyes.

"They're perfect for each other," said Ethan. "Travis will be good to her, Lainey."

"How can you be so sure of that?" she challenged, her gaze kindling anew as it met his again. "Confound it, Ethan Holt! Your brother is not at all the sort of man Beth needs! Why, she's refined and gentle and—"

"It doesn't make any difference what you think. Or what I think, either," he pointed out solemnly. He looked back to the fire, his eyes reflecting its bright golden blaze. "Love doesn't always have to make sense."

"*Love?*" she echoed, her voice edged with a scornful bitterness. "From what I've seen of love, it brings only pain and heartache. I can't believe Beth is willing to put herself through that torment again."

"Pleasure doesn't mean much without pain," Ethan declared in a vibrant tone. "Maybe that's why I know they'll be happy together. They've both already known more than their fair share of troubles."

"You don't understand! Beth isn't—" She fell abruptly silent and looked away. Sinking back down on the bench, she closed her eyes for a moment and revealed in a voice that was little more than a whisper, "My sister was betrayed by Anna's father. I couldn't bear to see that happen again. I *couldn't!*"

"It won't. Travis is as human as the rest of us, but you'll never find anyone with a better heart."

"You're his brother. I would expect you to rush to his defense."

"He's more than a brother," Ethan confided, with another faint smile. "He's a loyal and trusted friend. And you can rest assured that he'll never let anything happen to Beth."

"But we—we had such plans," she lamented brokenly. She told herself she should be happy that her sister had found someone else to love, but she couldn't help worrying. Jack had hurt her deeply. What guarantee was there that Travis Holt wouldn't do the same?

"Plans have a way of changing."

"Not mine," she denied, with fiery-eyed vehemence. Her long golden hair swirled riotously about her shoulders as she shook her head. "I'm going to have that farm, with or without Beth. And I'm going to build the biggest, fanciest house in all the Territory." In truth, her determination had suffered a terrible blow. She was heartsick at the prospect of losing Beth and Anna—they wouldn't really be lost to her, of course, she mused sorrowfully, but nothing would be the same once they had gone.

"You can't run the place alone," insisted Ethan. The firelight played across the rugged perfection of his countenance, and his eyes were smoldering with mingled love and passion as he gazed down at his wife's bent head. "You'll need help."

"I don't need anyone's help," she retorted hotly, too upset to be rational. "I should never have listened to Mr. Calhoun."

"What does that have to do with Beth and Travis?"

"Everything! If I hadn't married you, your brother wouldn't have believed it so easy to—to take advantage of her."

"That isn't true and you know it," he told her, frowning. His eyes glinted dully now. "What's between them didn't just spring to life today. And our marriage had nothing to do with it."

"Say what you will, but I still wish none of this had ever happened." She stood and headed for the door.

"Where are you going?"

"I'm going to find Beth and put a stop to this nonsense before it's too late," she vowed rashly.

"The hell you are," Ethan ground out. He crossed the room in two long, angry strides and caught up with her before she had done anything more than reach for the doorknob. She gave a soft, breathless cry as he spun her around to face him. His hands closed about her arms.

"Let go of me," she fumed. She struggled weakly within his iron grasp.

"Damn it, you little fool! Don't you see what you'd be doing if you went out there?" He yanked her closer, his eyes searing down into hers. "Stop thinking of yourself and think of Beth."

"I *am* thinking of her."

"No, you're not. How do you think she'd feel if she knew you wanted to deny her this chance at happiness? Don't make her choose, Lainey. Don't make that mistake."

"I'm not trying to deny her happiness," Lainey insisted, the tears gathering in her eyes once more. "I just don't want to see her get hurt again."

"The decision isn't yours to make. She's a grown woman, not a child. She's got to live her own life. And you've got to live yours."

She opened her mouth to argue, but no words would come. Suddenly she could hold the tears back no longer. They spilled over from her lashes to course down her cheeks. She dashed impatiently at them and felt a sob well up deep in her throat.

Ethan's heart twisted at the sight of her misery. He drew her tenderly against him, his arms enveloping her with their strong warmth. She did not resist. Her head rested upon his hard-muscled chest while her hands crept upward to curl upon his broad shoulders.

He held her for several long moments, until the furious storm of weeping had passed. She had never been one to cry for long—at least on the rare occasions when she *did* cry—and it was with admirable strength of will that she finally composed herself again. She had no idea how much hell she was putting Ethan through; holding her in his arms made him want her all the more. But he forced himself to release her, then watched as she drew a handkerchief from her skirt pocket and wandered back to the fire.

"I'm sorry. I—I don't know whatever possessed me to behave like that," she murmured, a lingering catch in her voice. She did not turn to face him.

"It's tradition for a bride to cry on her wedding day," he commented wryly. Tradition, his mind echoed. He remembered the kiss he had given her that morning. His gaze simmered with passion as it traveled lovingly over her.

"Perhaps. But I'm not really a bride." She released a long, pent-up sigh and conceded reluctantly, "You're right about Beth, I suppose. If she is truly in love with your brother, I cannot hope to gain anything by interfering."

"Let nature take its own course, Lainey," he advised. Groaning inwardly at the fire in his blood, he warned himself to leave before it was too late. His eyes strayed toward the sleeping Anna. If not for the child, he might very well have surrendered to the temptation to make their wedding night what it should have been. *Soon*, he promised himself. "Good night, Mrs. Holt."

"You're leaving?" She pivoted to face him at last, declining to take offense at what he had called her. Her own eyes were full of a longing she did not yet recognize.

"I could stay if you like." There was something in the way he said it that made her pulse leap alarmingly.

"No! No, that's quite all right. I'm sure Beth will be in soon. And we've a lot to talk about," she concluded, with a pensive frown.

"Then I'll see you in the morning." He turned and opened the door.

"Good night, Ethan."

The sound of his name on her lips made him pause. Muttering an oath underneath his breath, he stepped outside and closed the door softly behind him.

Lainey resumed her place on the fire-warmed bench. The memory of what it had felt like to be held by

Ethan, to be comforted by him while the tears flowed, was more compelling than she wanted to admit. She had never felt so safe and secure as when she had been in his arms . . .

Beth slipped inside the cabin a short time later. She was surprised to find Lainey still awake, and she hurried forward with a slight frown of worriment.

"Lainey? I thought you'd be in bed now."

"We need to talk, Beth."

"What is it?" She sank down beside her.

"Are you in love with Travis Holt?" Lainey asked, cutting to the very heart of the matter. She watched as her sister colored guiltily and looked down.

"Yes," Beth confessed, nodding her head. She quickly raised her shining eyes to Lainey's again. "I was going to tell you today, but after you and Mr. Holt—"

"That doesn't matter."

"Of course it does. I do love Travis, I love him more than I ever thought possible, but I don't want to leave you alone."

"Oh, Beth, I don't deserve a sister like you." She hugged her close and asked in a voice quavering with emotion, "Are you sure?"

"Absolutely," confirmed Beth. She drew away and smiled, her face positively glowing. "I told him the truth about Jack, Lainey. I told him, and he didn't care."

"Was it because of Jack that you insisted the two of you could never be more than friends?" It was all becoming clear to her now. She watched as Beth nodded again.

"I think I loved Travis from the very first, but I was afraid he could never love me if he knew the truth."

"And is what you feel now . . . is it different than before?" Lainey probed gently, still fearing that history might repeat itself.

"Oh, Lainey, it is completely different," affirmed

Beth. Her eyes filled with tears of joy. "I suppose I loved Jack, but it is nothing compared to what I feel for Travis. I'm not sure if I can explain it," she admitted, with a soft laugh. "I want to be with him every minute, to watch his face and hear his voice. I feel alive when I am with him; it's almost as though he holds half of my heart in his hands. And he is so kind. I know he will be a wonderful father to Anna. I could never marry him if I believed otherwise."

"He has asked you to marry him then?"

"Yes. But the wedding will not take place until after he and Ethan have built another cabin. Travis insists that it will be soon." Her eyes sparkled brightly at the thought.

"I see." She tried, without success, to keep the lingering uncertainty from her voice.

"Please be happy for me, dearest Lainey," implored Beth. "I know you can't help but feel disappointed about the plans we made together, but I promise you nothing will really change between us."

"Everything will change," she predicted, with a brief, ironic little smile. "How could it not?"

"But we can still see each other whenever we wish."

"Of course we can." She smiled again and raised a hand to her sister's face. "It's just that I'll miss you terribly. We've never been apart before. I pray that Travis is every bit as wonderful as you believe him to be."

"He is, Lainey. And I'll miss you, too. I—I don't know how I could have managed these past two years without you." Her eyes shadowed with painful reminiscence. "If not for you, I don't think I could have endured all that happened after Jack left."

"You give yourself too little credit. And besides, Papa was there to lend the both of us support," she recalled, her own gaze momentarily filling with sadness.

"That's true," said Beth. She smiled softly. "I'm sure Papa would have liked Travis. I wish he could be here."

"So do I."

"I suppose I can ask Ethan to give me away. I do wish Guthrie had a church. But it doesn't really matter, just as long as you and Anna are there with me."

"And Travis, too, of course," Lainey added, rising to her feet in conclusion. "Well then, if we're to have another wedding in the family, we should start making a few plans. *This* one is going to be done properly."

Beth gave another quiet laugh and looked toward Anna, who had slumbered blissfully through all the excitement. They changed into their nightclothes, then talked for quite some time longer, calling up cherished memories and marveling at the way their lives had turned out. Lainey knew their bond would always remain strong, but she also knew their sisterhood would enter a new, less intimate phase once Beth married Travis.

It seemed Ethan wasn't the only Holt capable of turning a Prescott's world upside down, she told herself, then frowned as her new husband's face swam before her eyes. Heaven help her, it was going to be a long night . . .

Chapter 12

"We are going to stay here tonight," Lainey insisted firmly. "Now that the roof is completed, there's no reason why we can't—"

"You haven't got any beds," argued Travis, reluctant to leave them alone. He wanted Beth and Anna close by; he had heard that the troubles around Guthrie were escalating. And truth be told, he had selfishly hoped to spend another night or two making plans and sharing sweet, stolen kisses with Beth out in the moonlight.

"We have managed without beds since purchasing the wagon," Lainey pointed out. She turned and flung an appraising look at the cabin behind her. "We'll be perfectly fine here."

"Lainey is right," Beth unexpectedly concurred. She smiled at Travis's frown. "You and Ethan have slept in the barn long enough. Besides, if you are still set on marrying me, Mr. Holt," she added, with a teasing light in her eyes, "then I will require some time in which to make the necessary arrangements with my sister."

"I'm set on it," he reaffirmed, his own gaze filling with passion's glow as he moved closer and slipped an arm about her waist. She blushed and tried to pull away, but he vowed not to release her until she had granted him a kiss.

Anxious to give the two lovers a few moments of privacy, Lainey caught Anna up in her arms and wandered toward the creek. Afternoon was quickly giving way to twilight, the sun's rays turning the sky into a last, magnificent burst of color. Another day had nearly passed . . . the first full day she had spent as Mrs. Ethan Holt.

Her eyes strayed eastward. Ethan had received another message from the Territory's federal marshal. He had ridden off to town nearly two hours ago, promising to return before nightfall. Unhappily, it occurred to her that he might be involved in something dangerous. She told herself it shouldn't matter so much—*but it did*.

An audible, strangely restless sigh escaped her lips. She and her "husband" had spoken little throughout the day. He and Travis had been occupied with finishing the roof, while she and Beth had busied themselves with sorting their things and moving them into the cabin. The spell of good weather had fortunately held, at least so far. She spied a few clouds on the horizon, but she could detect no change in the wind. Perhaps, she mused as she lowered Anna to the ground, life would proceed along a more even course for a while.

Ethan had still not come back by the time Travis mounted up with the announced intention of returning home to wash the day's sweat and dust from himself and see to the horses. The cattle would be arriving any day now, he told them, and there were still fences to be built. His first priority, however, was to build a cabin where he and Beth would live once they were married. He leaned down to kiss his future bride good-bye, then assured her that he would return later to make certain everyone had settled in for the night.

Once he had gone, Lainey hastened inside the cabin to change into a fresh gown and pin up her hair.

"What are you doing?" asked Beth, her eyes widening in mingled surprise and bewilderment as she watched her sister strip off the gingham dress.

"I am going to sing at the Palace tonight." She had very nearly abandoned the whole idea, particularly when she considered the prospect of running into Ethan on her way into town, but she cursed her own cowardice. She had to perform. Confound it, she couldn't let him think he could control her so easily.

"But—you can't go," Beth protested. She paled at the thought of it. "Oh, Lainey. I was under the impression you had abandoned that foolishness."

"It isn't foolishness." She drew on her best ensemble, a two-piece suit of peacock blue silk, fully intending to wear it onstage if the new costume proved to be as unsuitable as the old one. "We still have to repay our debt to the Holts. Even if you *are* betrothed to Travis, I am not going to accept their charity."

"But I thought you and Ethan had settled that."

"Ethan and I have settled nothing." Her silken brow creased into a frown of displeasure as she fastened the skirt and raised her hands to the buttons running down the front of the tightly fitted bodice. "And anyway, I gave Mr. Halloran my word. The theater is opening in its new location, and I promised to be there."

"Good heavens, what will Ethan say when he finds out you have—?"

"I don't care what he says. After all, he isn't really my husband. He has no right to interfere." She said it with a good deal more bravado than she actually felt. Recalling how he and Neil Halloran had made no secret of their mutual animosity the day before, she felt an involuntary shiver run the length of her spine. But she lifted her head in a gesture of proud determination and started unbraiding her hair. "I'm still going to need the money, Beth. If I have any hope of turning this place into a farm, I—"

"It's because of me, isn't it?" submitted Beth, looking perfectly miserable. "If I were not leaving, you wouldn't be so desperate."

"No, that isn't it at all," Lainey denied quickly. Whirling away from the mirror she had hung on the wall only a short time earlier, she raised her hands to the other woman's arms and declared earnestly, "I am simply trying to live my own life, just as you must live yours." Ethan had said much the same to her last night.

"But you could very well be placing yourself in danger again."

"There are no storms to blow me off course tonight," she remarked, with a brief, wry smile. "And I expect the audience to be considerably more well-behaved. Mr. Halloran has assured me that every precaution will be taken."

"Travis told me that Mr. Halloran is a dishonest man."

"I know he's something of a scoundrel." Lainey sighed, her eyes clouding once more at the memory of the hatred in his eyes when he had looked at Ethan. She told herself it didn't matter, that what was between the two men should not concern her.

It did, of course. Her heart twisted at the thought of the gambler carrying out his subtle threats about making her a widow. If she truly believed him capable of harming Ethan, she could never have continued their association. But, naively, she decided that he was not the sort of man to kill someone because of an old grudge—or because he was attracted to another man's wife.

"It isn't imperative that I like him, or even trust him," she insisted. "I will fulfill my obligation, and then I will ride straight home again."

"And what will happen when Ethan finds out?" demanded Beth. In spite of what Lainey had claimed, she knew there was something more than dislike between the two of them. A great deal more.

"I refuse to be intimidated by Ethan Holt or anyone else." She lifted the hairbrush and began dragging it through the shimmering golden curls with forceful, angry strokes. "I will return before midnight. It isn't necessary for you to wait up for me."

"Of course it is," Beth emphatically disagreed. "Why,

I couldn't possibly sleep until I knew you were safe. And if you have *not* returned in a timely manner, I will send Travis after you."

Lainey smiled at that. She swept her thick tresses upward, pinned them securely, and gave her sister a quick hug. Gathering up her skirts, she sailed purposefully from the cabin.

She cast frequent glances about her as she rode into town. Half expecting to see Ethan—and filled with a nagging apprehension at the prospect—she urged the horse into a swifter pace and arrived at her destination in near record time.

The newly completed building that housed the Palace was ablaze with light and filled with smoke, laughter, and music. Lainey reined to a halt in back of the theater. She was surprised to discover Neil Halloran waiting for her just outside the door.

"Good evening, Miss Prescott." He greeted her with a slow—undeniably triumphant—smile.

She could not tell if his use of her maiden name was accidental or deliberate. Preparing to dismount, she stiffened when she felt his hands closing about her waist. She swung down, then immediately pulled away.

"I promised my sister I would be home before midnight, Mr. Halloran," she informed him, smoothing the gathers of her skirt. She raised her eyes to his. Light streamed out into the darkness from the nearby windows, setting his swarthy features aglow. She could have sworn the expression on his face was one of improper regard.

"Then we'll have to make sure you keep that promise." He took her arm in an easy grip and led her toward the doorway. "I think you'll be impressed with the place, Lainey. The theater's downstairs. A real stage awaits you," he said, his teeth flashing in another smile. "And although some of the furnishings haven't arrived yet, there are tables and chairs for the customers." The certainty of huge profits caused his eyes to gleam in satisfaction. And the certainty that he would soon have the beautiful, golden-haired temptress at his side provoked a surge of lust within him.

"And what is upstairs?" asked Lainey, her inquisitive gaze traveling to the second floor.

"Rooms for the men who want to pursue a serious game of chance," he explained, with a low, sardonic chuckle.

"There will be gambling on the premises?" Her eyes widened in dismay.

"Only upstairs."

She preceded him inside the building. He took her arm again, announcing that he would show her to the dressing room. There were other performers wandering about backstage, and she was shocked to see that one of the women who passed by was clad in a low-cut satin gown even more immodest than the ones she and Beth had worn.

"I do hope, Mr. Halloran, that you have provided me with more suitable attire," she remarked.

"I have indeed, Miss Prescott."

"It's Mrs. Holt now," she reminded him impulsively, then felt sudden color staining her cheeks.

"Of course it is." His features tensed, and his gray eyes darkened ever so slightly. "But we don't have to be so formal any longer." He opened a door and told her, "You'll have complete privacy in here. Bloomfield's scheduled your performance to take place in half an hour."

"Very well." Her gaze traveled swiftly about the room. It was small but well-lit, and like everything else, smelled of fresh lumber and paint. "And is this my costume?" she asked, crossing to where a full-length, emerald green velvet gown hung from a brass hook on the opposite wall.

"I hope you like it."

"If not, I will wear my own clothing," she warned.

"You look beautiful just as you are," he parried, his gaze moving boldly over her. "But wear the velvet." And then, quite unexpectedly, he closed the distance between them and lifted his hands to her shoulders. "I had it made especially for you, Lainey." His fingers smoothed lightly, provocatively, down her arms.

"Don't do that!" she snapped. She would have pulled free, but his grasp tightened.

"Afraid you'll like it too much?" he challenged, the gleam in his eyes burning hotter.

"Not in the slightest!" It was true, she realized. His touch provoked only outrage in her now, without so much as a trace of pleasure. "Now let go of me, or—"

"Relax." With a mocking smile still playing about his lips, he released her and sauntered back to the doorway. "Someday, *Mrs. Holt*, you and I are going to come to an understanding." Before she could offer a retort, he left, closing the door on his way out.

Lainey frowned after him, still shocked and angered by his behavior. What kind of "understanding" had he been talking about? And how in heaven's name could she ever have found him attractive?

The strains of a rather bawdy drinking song wafted into the room, adding to her disquiet and prompting her to wonder if she might possibly have gotten herself into mischief after all. Unable to prevent her thoughts from turning to Ethan again, she hurried to change into the new costume before her qualms sent her running.

She was pleasantly surprised to find that the green dress fit her to perfection. The low, rounded bodice was tight, yet it offered only a tantalizing glimpse of her breasts. The skirt was not gathered; it hugged the curve of her hips before flaring gently outward. Her arms were covered by nothing more than a set of puffed half sleeves, making her wish she had brought along a pair of gloves. She encountered some difficulty in fastening the row of tiny pearl buttons that ran up the back, but finally succeeded and turned to face herself in the cheval mirror.

Eyeing her reflection critically, she decided that she looked exactly as she would have wished—like a lady. Or at least a lady who earns her living on the stage, she amended with a faint smile of irony.

She spied a pair of matching velvet brocade slippers near the dressing table, and she quickly sat down to unlace her boots. A knock sounded at the door just as she finished.

"Yes?" she called out.

"It's me, Miss Prescott," Mr. Bloomfield proclaimed in his usual ear-ringing tones. "I need to know what songs you've settled on for tonight."

"Well, I—I suppose I can follow the same repertoire as the first night," she told him, opening the door. She grew uncomfortable beneath his long, silent scrutiny. "Did you hear me, Mr. Bloomfield?"

"Oh, yes—yes, of course!" he blustered. He cleared his throat and grinned broadly. "We've got a full house again tonight. Standing room only at the bar."

"The bar?" she echoed. Her brows drew together in a frown of total bewilderment. "What bar?"

"Why, the one out front. We're charging two bits a shot tonight, in honor of our grand opening." He impatiently turned away and flung back over his shoulder, "Fifteen minutes."

Lainey closed the door again, then sank down into the chair with a troubled sigh. She'd had no idea that the Palace would be offering drinks. Good heavens, it was little better than a saloon! she realized in dawning horror.

"What the devil have I done?" she murmured, her sapphire gaze kindling with self-reproach. She was sorely tempted to change back into her own clothing and take flight, but she told herself it was too late.

She stood to her feet again and paced distractedly back and forth in front of the mirror, her countenance stormy. What would Beth say when she discovered that her sister had performed in a place that offered gambling and strong spirits? *What would Ethan say?*

Another knock startled her from her unpleasant reverie.

"I'd like a word with you, Lainey," came the familiar voice. It was Neil Halloran.

She muttered an oath and wrenched open the door. Her eyes blazed resentfully up at him.

"Why didn't you tell me you were planning to turn the Palace into a—a den of iniquity?" she accused. Her temper flared to a dangerous level when he threw back his head and laughed in pure amusement.

"This is a theater, Lainey, not a bordello." His eyes gleamed anew at the sight of her fiery blush. She looked ravishing in the dress he'd bought her.

"Perhaps not, but you never told me you intended to—"

"Does it really make any difference?" he challenged smoothly. He lifted a hand to sweep a stray tendril of hair from her forehead, but she angrily retreated a step. Her defiance only seemed to amuse him further. "With your spirit and my know-how, we could make quite a team," he told her, edging closer.

"You can keep your know-how, Mr. Halloran," she retorted in a low, simmering tone. "I would *not* have agreed to come if I had known of the changes you've made."

"Well, you're here now, so why don't we just make the best of things?"

He continued to advance on her. She instinctively backed away until her hips came up against the dressing table. Her throat constricted in sudden alarm as she gazed up at his smiling yet faintly menacing features. Her eyes grew very round while his own narrowed with intent. Strongly suspecting that he meant to kiss her, she resisted the urge to scream and instead settled for drawing herself haughtily erect and subjecting him to a furious, withering glare.

"Get away from me, Mr. Halloran!"

"I told you my interest in you was more than just business," he reminded her, his voice tinged with an unsettling huskiness. Though he stood mere inches away, he made no move to touch her. "You're quite a woman, Lainey. And you're wasted on a son of a bitch like Holt."

"Why, you—what a despicable thing to say," she sputtered indignantly. "Ethan Holt is a good, decent man, and unlike you, he is completely honest."

"I can see I'm going to have to improve your opinion of me," he countered, with deceptive nonchalance.

"That would be impossible."

She gasped when his hands suddenly shot out to close upon her shoulders, his fingers tightening about her flesh in a hard, punishing grip. He allowed her no time to struggle before his mouth came crashing down upon hers.

The kiss was almost brutal. She moaned in outrage as a wave of revulsion washed over her. The sensations he provoked within her were in direct contrast to what she felt whenever Ethan kissed her. There was nothing pleasant about the way Halloran's lips moved upon hers, nothing pleasant about being locked against his slender but wiry frame.

She struggled furiously, pushing at his chest and twisting within his ruthless grasp. When he finally released her, she fell back against the dressing table. A bottle of perfume, placed there as a gift by the same man who now stood gazing hotly down at her, tumbled to the floor and shattered into a dozen sharp-edged pieces.

"How dare you!" she seethed, her eyes full of venge-

ful fire. So enraged she could scarcely speak, she lifted a trembling hand to her lips and choked out, "If my husband knew what you had just done—"

"Tell him," gritted Neil. His lips curled into a malevolent sneer. "It would give me the greatest of pleasure to kill him."

Appalled by his response, she watched as he turned and began sauntering unconcernedly back to the doorway. He paused briefly on his way out.

"You're going to be mine, Lainey," he vowed, supremely confident of his victory.

"Never!" she denied, with heartfelt vehemence. His quiet, sinister chuckle filled her with dread.

"Oh, and in case it's crossed your mind to forego your performance this evening," he warned, inclining his head toward her one last time, "I think you should know I'm fully prepared to take whatever action is necessary to make sure you honor the commitment."

With that, he was gone.

Pale and shaken, Lainey sank down upon the chair. She shook her head in horrified disbelief at what had just happened. Her lips felt bruised, and she was sickened by the memory of his hands upon her. Fighting back tears of helpless fury, she thought of Ethan.

It would give me the greatest of pleasure to kill him. Halloran's words burned in her mind. Dear God, he couldn't have meant it, she told herself numbly. He couldn't have!

"What am I going to do?" she wondered aloud, her voice nothing but a ragged whisper. She had been aware of the fact that Neil Halloran was attracted to her, but she would never have suspected that his feelings ran to such an extreme. Did he truly want her so much that he was willing to risk Ethan's wrath? She had little doubt what her husband's reaction would be once he learned of Halloran's loathsome behavior toward her. A tremor of fear shook her.

"You're on, Miss Prescott!" Mr. Bloomfield announced from his post nearby.

She had to comply. Neil Halloran's threats had been uttered with far too much conviction to ignore. No matter how desperately she wanted to flee, she couldn't bear the thought of anything happening to Ethan. She had no time in which to examine her feelings, no time to think of anything other than keeping her part of the bargain. The decision had been made for her the moment Halloran had warned of retaliation.

Moving as if in a daze, she rose to her feet and left the dressing room. Mr. Bloomfield was waiting for her. She listened to the music swelling to a crescendo, then traveled forward with slow, measured steps to the center of the stage.

She suffered a sharp intake of breath at the startling sight that met her eyes as she turned toward the audience. To her right was a long, polished oak bar where men stood enjoying their two-bit shots of whiskey. Behind the bar, between numerous shelves laden with bottles and glasses, hung a large painting of a full-figured, redheaded woman wearing nothing but a smile. Tables and chairs filled the rest of the room, where men sat nursing their drinks and talking beneath brand-new chandeliers. Half a dozen women, their faces heavily painted and their shapely curves encased in bright, low-cut satin dresses, wandered about the room flirting and laughing and generally making certain that the Palace's well-paying customers had a good time.

Fighting down another wave of nausea, Lainey nodded toward the musicians and began to sing. Silence fell over the crowd as her beautiful voice offered up the plaintive ballad. She stood regal and lovely before them, a vision in emerald green velvet, as, for a few brief minutes, the harsh world receded and they were transported to another time and place.

To Lainey, the performance seemed to last forever.

Her troubled gaze frequently scanned the room, but there was no sign of her employer. She waited until the applause had thundered to its conclusion, then whirled and made her way back to the dressing room.

Fearing that Neil Halloran would seek her out again, she snatched up her clothing and hurried to escape through the back door. The long velvet skirts tangled about her legs as she raced feverishly outside, across to the stable behind the theater. Her horse snorted at her approach, and she smoothed a hand along the animal's neck before leading it out into the softly lit darkness.

She thrust her boots inside the folds of her blue silk suit and tied the bundle behind the saddle. Her hands shook, and she cast another worried glance back toward the theater. Finally she mounted up and reined about, praying that she would not be followed as she set a course for home.

She did not allow herself to breathe a sigh of relief until she had left Guthrie far behind. And even then, her sense of security proved to be short-lived.

Her eyes flew wide in renewed alarm when she spied a lone horseman riding hell-bent for leather toward her in the pale moonlight. She tugged abruptly on the reins, pulling her mount to a halt. Realizing that she had forgotten to bring the rifle, she held her breath and cast a fearful, indecisive look back toward town. But as the rider bore down on her, her gaze sparked with welcome recognition.

"Ethan!" she said, relieved.

Her tensed muscles relaxed; her mouth curved instinctively into a smile. The smile, however, faded in the next instant when Halloran's words came back to haunt her. And to make matters worse, she belatedly recalled the fact that she had defied her husband's orders by going into town in the first place. She swallowed a sudden lump in her throat and watched in growing apprehension while he swiftly closed the distance between them.

He didn't say a word as he reined to a halt before her. His handsome face was thunderous, his blue-green eyes smoldering with barely controlled violence. He swung down from the saddle, moved to Lainey's side, and dragged her down as well.

"What in heaven's name—?" she gasped out, shocked by his rough treatment. She tried to jerk away, but his hands closed like bands of steel about her arms.

"Is it true?" he ground out, filled with white-hot fury as he recalled what Beth had told him only a short time ago. "Did you go to the Palace tonight?"

She blanched at the savage gleam in his eyes. Dazedly reflecting that she had never seen him so angry before, she nodded her head.

"Yes, I—I did. I gave my word to Mr. Halloran."

"By damn, woman! You've gone too far this time!"

Another sharp gasp broke from her lips as he suddenly scooped her up in his arms and tossed her onto his saddle. She tried to scramble down again, but he mounted behind her and clamped an arm about her waist to hold her captive. He took hold of the reins, gave a silent command with his booted heels, and tightened his grip on his errant bride as the animal beneath them galloped back across the rugged prairie countryside. Lainey's horse pawed impatiently at the ground, then followed after them.

Lainey knew it was useless to protest. More frightened than she cared to admit, she held her tongue throughout the wild ride. She frowned in confusion when she noted that they were passing her homestead. Her pulse leapt in very real alarm when she realized that Ethan was heading toward his ranch.

All too soon, he was dismounting in front of the cabin and pulling her down. She found herself thrust unceremoniously inside. The only source of light was the moon above; its beaming radiance filtered down through the trees to fill the room with a soft, silvery glow.

Lainey whirled about. Trembling with a combination of fear and outrage, she was further dismayed to see that the cabin was empty. *Dear God, where was Travis?*

"Take me home," she demanded breathlessly.

"You are home," Ethan shot back. He closed the door and began advancing on her with deceptive calm.

"Confound it, Ethan Holt, you had no right to bring me here." She backed away, fighting down panic as her wide, fiery gaze darted about the room in a frantic search for escape.

"I warned you to stay away from the Palace, Lainey," he reminded her, his tone low and dangerously level. "I warned you to stay away from Halloran."

"I am free to do as I please!" she cried defiantly. She flew to the table and scurried behind it.

"Not anymore. We're married now. For better or worse. It's time you learned what that meant." His burning gaze, at once furious and possessive, raked over her in the moonlit darkness. He reached the table and knocked it aside as if it were little more than a child's toy.

"We're not really married," denied Lainey, her voice rising almost shrilly now. "You—you agreed that it would be in name only." She fled to the opposite side of the room, her fingers twisting within her long velvet skirts while she looked toward the door. "You don't own me, Ethan Holt. You never will!"

"You're my wife," he decreed masterfully. "And I'll be damned if I'll let you work for a man like Neil Halloran."

"Then be damned." She hastened back across to the pile of boxes and crates, still intent upon reaching the doorway. She had no idea what Ethan meant to do with her; she certainly wasn't going to stay and find out. "If you come one step nearer, I'll scream," she threatened, daring to hope that his brother was outside somewhere.

"Go ahead. There's no one to hear you. Travis is at your place."

They were completely alone.

That was all the impetus she needed to make her move. Gathering up her skirts, she raced for the door. Ethan caught her easily. As she would soon learn, his patience had run out. His good intentions had been conquered by jealousy and anger—and a desire so strong that even his love for her could not make him wait any longer.

"Let go of me," she cried, struggling furiously within his grasp as he swept her back against him. Her hair tumbled down out of its pins, the silken tresses cascading about her face and shoulders while she balled her hands into fists and struck out at him.

She managed to land a stinging blow to the clean-shaven ruggedness of his cheek, then gasped to feel herself being lifted bodily. He carried her, kicking and squirming like some wild, golden-maned tigress, across the room—to the narrow bunks in the corner.

Hot, bitter tears of angry frustration stung against her eyelids as she fought him. She was surprised when he suddenly set her on her feet again, but surprise turned to heart-stopping alarm in the next instant when his hand moved to the rounded neckline of her costume. His other arm tightened about her waist, imprisoning her before him.

"Did Halloran give you this dress?" he demanded in a tone edged with raw emotion.

Before she could answer, his warm fingers insinuated themselves between the layers of velvet and cotton and her full, heaving breasts. He gave a forceful tug downward, ripping the bodice of the costume, as well as the chemise underneath it, all the way down to her waist.

Lainey gasped, her eyes flying wide in stunned disbelief. She looked down, only to color rosily when she saw that her breasts were almost completely bared. A strangled cry broke from her lips as she instinctively raised her hands to snatch the torn edges of the bodice together, but Ethan was in no mood to be denied.

He seized her wrists and forced her hands behind her back. She cried out again when his head lowered toward her exposed bosom.

"No!" She renewed her struggles with a vengeance. His mouth roamed hungrily across the swelling curve of her breasts, offering only a taste of things to come before trailing a fiery path upward to her lips.

A moan rose low in her throat when his mouth took possession of hers. The deep, rapturous kiss demanded a response, a response she was determined not to give. His lips moved sensuously, passionately, upon hers, while his tongue plundered the moist sweetness of her mouth. She tried to pull her wrists free, tried to resist the intoxicating persuasion of his embrace, but soon found herself swaying weakly against him.

She was scarcely aware of the moment when he released her wrists. His arms enveloped her with their sinewy warmth, crushing her against the full length of his powerful hard-muscled frame. Her hands crept upward to his shoulders, and she clung to him as if she were drowning and he the only means by which she could be saved. Indeed, her legs threatened to give way beneath her at any moment.

"Lainey," he whispered hoarsely, his lips ceasing their fierce possession of hers long enough for him to sweep her up in his arms and lower her to the bed.

"No! No, please! Let me go!" she gasped out. She pushed at him again, defiance flaring anew when she felt her hips making contact with the quilt-covered mattress.

"Damn it, Lainey, you're mine," he murmured, passion turning his voice husky and making his fathomless, blue-green eyes glow hotly. *"You're mine!"*

With a bold swiftness that quite literally took her breath away, he stripped the velvet gown from her body. She was aghast to find herself clad only in her torn chemise and drawers. Her hands moved protectively to her breasts once more, and she blushed crimson before trying to scramble from the bed.

Ethan pushed her back down. He lowered his body atop hers, caught her wrists again, and yanked them above her head, then imprisoned them within the iron grip of his hand. She squirmed wildly beneath him, unaware that in doing so she only made his desire flare hotter.

"Let me go! Damn you to hell, Ethan Holt! You have no right to do this," she stormed, her eyes blazing venomously up at him.

"I have every right," he insisted, with quiet authority. His smoldering gaze locked with the deep blue fire of hers while his other hand swept downward to the gaping edges of her bodice.

"Whatever else I thought of you, I never believed you to be capable of—of *this*!" The sentence ended on a sharp intake of breath when his fingers closed about her naked breast.

"I'm going to make love to you, Lainey." His voice, deep timbered and splendidly vibrant, sent a shiver up her spine. "You're my wife. And by heaven, I hold what's mine."

He was through talking. His lips descended upon hers once more in a kiss every bit as fierce and compelling as the first. His hand roamed across her breasts, branding their satiny fullness while she gasped and felt a familiar, delicious warmth spreading through her body. His mouth thoroughly ravished hers, making her senses reel and her skin grow flushed.

The battle was already lost, and she knew it. What

was happening between them was inevitable; it had been ordained from the very first. In the most secretive recesses of her heart and soul, she had always yearned for him to touch her like this. And now, defeated by her own passions as well as his sweet mastery, she ceased her struggles at last. She responded with all the answering fire he had created within her, kissing him back and arching her back instinctively beneath him.

Moments later, his mouth left hers to trail feverishly across the glowing smoothness of her face, then down along the graceful column of her neck. He pressed a kiss to the spot where her pulse beat so rapidly, then lowered his head purposefully to her breasts.

"Oh, Ethan—" she gasped out, only to fall abruptly silent when his mouth closed about one of the rose-tipped peaks. His hot, velvety tongue swirled about the nipple with tantalizing movements, his lips suckling as greedily as a babe's. She bit at her lower lip to stifle a cry and threaded her fingers within the sun-streaked thickness of his hair. Her eyes swept closed, and she gave herself up to the wickedly pleasurable sensations as he continued the delectable assault upon her breasts.

His hand moved to the waistband of her drawers. With thrilling impatience, he tugged them downward, his other hand slipping beneath her hips so that he could pull the lace-trimmed cotton undergarment all the way off. She blushed when she felt a cool rush of air on her bared skin, and her color deepened as his fingers proceeded to urgently, hungrily, stroke and explore the firm roundness of her bottom. His lips returned to claim hers, while his other hand moved to the triangle of soft, golden curls at the apex of her slender thighs.

She inhaled sharply against his mouth when his warm fingers parted the silken flesh. He touched her at the very core of her femininity, offering a caress that was at once gentle and boldly, hotly, stimulating. She found her legs parting wider of their own accord. Her hips moved restlessly while her hands curled almost convulsively upon his broad shoulders. Her blood turned to liquid fire as it coursed through her veins. She moaned, feeling herself swept away completely on a flood tide of desire and longing. Passion built to a fever pitch within her; the deep yearning grew near painful in its intensity.

Everything was happening with such tempestuous haste, she had no time to think, no time to realize that nothing would be the same after this night. There was only Ethan, only the sweet madness the two of them were sharing in the darkened privacy of the cabin . . .

Finally Ethan could endure no more of the exquisite agony. His own passions burned almost out of control. He had never wanted a woman as much as he wanted Lainey. Loving her as he did, he was determined to make her realize that she needed him every bit as much as he needed her—in every way. *She was his.*

Raising his head, he gazed down at her beautiful face and felt his heart stirring with more love than he had ever thought possible. His hand moved to the front of his trousers. Swiftly unfastening them, he drew out his aroused manhood. His fingers then slipped beneath Lainey's hips once more, lifting her for the ultimate ecstasy of completion. He positioned himself between her legs, anxious to spare her pain and yet unable to wait any longer. Watching as her luminous sapphire gaze widened up at him in confusion, he plunged into her, his throbbing hardness sheathing perfectly within her soft, honeyed warmth.

A breathless cry of startlement escaped her. The pain was sharp but mercifully brief. She moaned again as the burning sensation between her legs gave way to a pleasure so intense that she feared she could not bear it. Her eyes swept closed as Ethan's hips tutored hers into the age-old rhythm of love. She grasped weakly at his arms, her breath nothing but a series of short gasps while his thrusts grew harder and faster. Their union was all flash and fire, full of passion's heat, and yet she sensed that Ethan had stormed a good deal more than her body.

Almost too soon for the both of them, the wild, fiery splendor came to an end. Another cry broke from Lainey's lips as the final completion sent her passions spiraling heavenward. The sensation was like nothing she had ever experienced before. It was as though she had been poised on the very brink of death and then had been snatched back to the glorious land of the living. Only dimly aware of Ethan tensing above her in the next instant, she felt herself flooded with a new, highly potent warmth.

His eyes gleaming with tenderness, and a touch of wholly masculine triumph, Ethan rolled to his back in the narrow bunk and pulled his well-loved bride close. She lay complacently in his arms for the moment, too overwhelmed by what had just happened to do anything else. She struggled to regain control of her breathing, and struggled as well to try and understand why she had been so powerless to prevent her husband's fierce, almost violent outpouring of affection.

I'm going to make love to you, he had vowed. Well, he had certainly done that, she mused in wonderment. Her whole body still tingled deliciously. Now she understood why Beth had succumbed to Jack's betrayal. Indeed, it wasn't at all difficult to see how a woman could let herself be tempted into a disaster of that sort. She'd always possessed a general idea of what was involved, of course—helping her father in his medical practice had seen to that. Only, until Ethan had demonstrated otherwise, she never would have believed it possible to feel so thoroughly captivated.

A sigh of utter contentment escaped her lips. But her languidness soon gave way to a returning sense of reality. It suddenly occurred to her that she was lying there almost completely naked; the torn chemise and a pair of black cotton stockings were all that remained of her attire. Her modesty was a trifle belated, and yet she now hastened to do something about her shocking state of undress.

"Please, I—I must go," she murmured, her face flaming as she pulled away from him and sat up. She snatched the torn edges of her chemise across her breasts. Feeling awkward and embarrassed in the extreme, she tried to rise from the bed. Ethan's hand closed about her arm.

"There's no hurry," he decreed softly. "Travis will stay with Beth and Anna until—"

"I promised to be home before midnight."

"You'll be late." He drew his tall, muscular frame up from the bunk and lifted his hands to the buttons of his shirt.

"What are you doing?" she asked, her heart leaping once more as she sat perched on the edge of the quilt-covered mattress.

"Exactly what it looks like." He stripped off the shirt and tossed it aside. Temporarily fastening his trousers, he moved across to the table and lit the lamp.

Chapter 13

"I am going home," declared Lainey, rising from the bed now as well. Careful to keep her breasts covered, she bent down and snatched up the green velvet gown. She frowned at the sight of it, and her eyes filled with dismay when she remembered that her silk suit was still tied behind her horse's saddle.

"I told you before—you *are* home." He turned to face her again in the warm golden lamplight. Her gaze widened as it traveled in fascination over his bronzed, powerfully muscled chest and arms. She swallowed hard and felt her traitorous knees weaken.

"What are you talking about?" she demanded in growing exasperation. "I don't live here."

"You do now." Bracing his lean hips against the edge of the table, he tugged off his boots and socks. He started toward her again, his steps slow and purposeful. The gleam in his eyes set off another warning bell in her brain. "Travis can sleep in the barn until he and Beth are married. You'll be moving in here with me."

"What?" she gasped, incredulous at the thought. She angrily draped the torn costume about her and fixed him with a narrow, reproachful look. "What the devil makes you think anything has changed?"

"I believe the evidence speaks for itself," he drawled lazily, his eyes flickering over her with bold significance. His mouth twitched at the sight of her fiery blush.

262

"Well, I—I know *something* has changed, but it doesn't matter. We had an agreement," she reminded him in a cool, almost haughty tone that seemed very much at odds with her alluring dishevelment. "I have no intention of allowing tonight to alter my plans. We will maintain our separate residences, and then in a few months' time, I will file for an annulment."

"No, Lainey," he disagreed, towering above her while she battled a fresh wave of panic. His gaze burned down into the stormy depths of hers. "There will be no annulment."

"Then I will seek a divorce," she retorted hotly. She was furious with herself, furious with him, and still so confused by the night's startling turn of events that she didn't know whether to make another bid for escape, or remain and hope that she could reason with him now that he had finally had his *wicked way* with her. First Halloran had dared to lay hands on her, and then Ethan had done the same—only with far more pleasurable and meaningful results. Dear God, what else would happen before morning?

Within moments, her husband provided the answer to that unspoken question.

"There will be no divorce, either," he vowed, his features dangerously grim. "You might as well accept the truth. You're my wife now—in every sense of the word."

"Only because you forced yourself on me." She flung invisible daggers at his handsome head when he gave a low, vibrant chuckle.

"As I remember it, there was very little need for force once I got you into bed."

"I hate you, Ethan Holt!" she cried impulsively, anger and humiliation making her reckless. She knew she didn't mean it, and yet she wanted to hurt him, to make him pay for being so damned irresistible.

"Hate me then," he ground out. His eyes smoldered

anew as he reached for her, his hands closing about her bare arms. He yanked her up hard against him. "But know that I'll never let you go."

She gasped in alarm and disbelief when he started pressing her back toward the bed.

"But you have already . . . done this," she pointed out unnecessarily. Warm color stained her cheeks.

"And I will again," he promised, disregarding her protests as he tumbled her down upon the bunk. She cried out softly to feel herself sprawling on her back atop the quilt. Her hands came up to push ineffectually at Ethan's broad, naked chest, while her anxious gaze flew toward the lamp.

"But the light—"

"Precisely. It's high time, Mrs. Holt, that I saw for myself what manner of woman I've married."

With no further warning, he jerked the velvet gown away from her and sent it flying downward to land in a heap on the floor. Her chemise, or rather what was left of it, followed shortly thereafter. She fought him, of course, but to no avail.

He released her briefly in order to unfasten his trousers again. Pulling them off, he stood before her, naked and unashamed, in all his masculine glory.

She crimsoned, but was unable to tear her eyes away from the rigid length of flesh that sprang forth from a cluster of tight black curls. Though she had seen only a few naked men in her life—and they had been ill at the time—she knew with a certainty that Ethan was a magnificent specimen of healthy, hot-blooded manhood. There wasn't an ounce of fat on his hard body. His stomach was flat, his thighs lean and muscular, his legs quite long. His upper body, as she had already noted, was powerfully sculpted, his skin tanned to a deep golden brown from a lifetime spent outdoors. He looked entirely capable of getting whatever he had set his mind to; she shivered at the realization that *she* was what he had set his mind to.

Groaning inwardly, she made one last desperate attempt to flee. She dragged the quilt over her own nakedness and made it as far as the foot of the bed. Ethan toppled her backward again.

"No!" she exclaimed breathlessly, squirming in his grasp. "You can't—"

"I can and will."

She cried out in defeat when he yanked the quilt from her. There was little doubt that he liked what he saw. His eyes darkened with appreciation and desire as they raked over her exposed charms: full, rose-tipped breasts that seemed to beg for a man's touch; a slender waist and delectably rounded hips; a triangle of soft, downy curls that were only a shade darker than her hair; legs that were long and shapely. Her skin was smooth and silken and glowing. She was even more beautiful than he had imagined. And she was his for the taking.

Embarrassed, and also strangely excited, Lainey folded her arms across her breasts in an effort to shield them from his burning gaze. The ghost of a smile touched his lips before he seized her by the shoulders and rolled her facedown upon the mattress.

"What are you doing?" she gasped. His only answer was to kneel beside the bed, sweep aside her luxuriant mass of hair, and press his lips to the nape of her neck. She tried to rise, but he pushed her down once more and allowed his mouth to wander. His warm lips trailed a slow, fiery path across the beguiling curve of her back, down along her spine, and then settled boldly upon her naked backside.

Her face flamed anew. She gave a soft, strangled cry and clutched at the pillow beneath her head. Ethan's hands curled about her waist, holding her captive for his pleasure—and hers. His mouth roamed hotly, wickedly, across her bottom, his lips and tongue exploring the pale, well-rounded flesh with a thoroughness that made her blush all the more. His teeth gently nipped at her buttocks, bringing no pain but a delicious tingling that prompted her to moan. Her hips moved restlessly beneath his caresses, and she caught her lower lip between her teeth while passion blazed to life deep within her.

His hands moved to her black cotton stockings. He began rolling them downward, his lips following as he bared her satiny limbs. Once he had dispensed with the very last barrier of clothing between them, he turned her onto her back. He finally lowered his body atop hers.

Lainey's eyes flew wide as bare flesh met bare flesh. The sensation was absolutely breathtaking. Her hands came up to grasp weakly at his shoulders. The rock-hard planes of his lithely muscled body fit perfectly against her soft, voluptuous curves. She was acutely conscious of his arousal; his manhood was pressing against her thighs.

He gave her no opportunity to protest. His lips descended upon hers, his strong arms wrapping about her body with such fierce possessiveness that she trembled from head to toe. She moaned again when his tongue plunged between her parted lips. Welcoming the sweet invasion, she kissed him back, her tongue meeting each provocative swirl and thrust of his. Her arms smoothed feverishly across the bronzed expanse of his back, and she clutched him even closer while the kiss rapidly intensified.

She was disappointed when his lips abandoned hers a few moments later, but her sense of loss turned to rapturous delight when he lowered his head to her breasts. He paid them moist and loving tribute, his lips and tongue working together to send desire coursing through her like wildfire.

His hands swept around to close about her breasts, then glided down to her hips. His fingers delved underneath to hungrily knead and stroke her buttocks before moving to her thighs. She waited anxiously for him to touch her in the place that yearned for his warm, knowing caress, but he surprised her by sliding his body lower. His mouth followed an imaginary path downward from her breasts to her abdomen, and lower still.

She gazed down at him in confusion when his hands parted her thighs. Before she could ask him what he was about, his lips were nuzzling at the soft curls between her thighs.

"Ethan!"

Hot color flew to her cheeks. She tried to close her thighs, but he pried them apart again and slipped his hands beneath her hips to hold her still. The shocking intimacy of his caress was in direct contrast to her ladylike sensibilities. Though a part of her longed to experience it, she told herself it was simply too wicked to be endured. She squirmed and pushed in earnest at his head. Ethan took mercy on her, silently promising to conquer all her inhibitions in the days ahead. Soon, he vowed to himself with an inward smile, he'd make her forget about being a lady in bed.

His fingers replaced his mouth, stroking at the delicate, deep pink flesh until passion's fire raced through her once more. He kissed her breasts again, then finally thrust into her. This time, she was an eager participant. Her legs tightened about the lean hardness of his hips, and she held on to him for dear life as the two of them soared together to a final, explosive completion that left them both fully sated and gasping for breath.

Afterward, Ethan reluctantly drew himself up from the bed with the announced intention of seeing to the horses. He knew Lainey needed some time alone. His eyes were brimming with a mixture of love and tender amusement as he watched her blush and look away.

She remained silent while he pulled on his clothes and strode outside. Once he had gone, she released a long, highly uneven sigh. Her emotions were still in utter turmoil, and she was certain that, come morning, she would ache in places she hadn't even known to exist before.

She sat up and climbed slowly from the bed, feeling an urgent need for a hot, soothing bath. Her legs were still plagued by an irritating weakness, and she frowned as she draped the quilt about her. Wondering if Ethan had truly meant what he'd said about forcing her to move into his cabin, she sank down upon the bench in front of the fireplace and swept the tangled, wildly streaming golden locks from her forehead.

No matter what she thought, no matter how she felt, there was no escaping the reality of her situation—she was Ethan Holt's wife. His kissless bride wasn't kissless anymore. No indeed, she told herself with a faint, humorless smile, she had been wedded and bedded and would now have to face the consequences. Her eyes flashed at the memory of her husband's lovemaking, while her accursed, embarrassingly disloyal body warmed with pleasure. She couldn't deny that she had enjoyed what he had done to her. Heaven help her, it had been even more wonderful than she would ever have thought possible . . .

She rose abruptly to her feet, hurried to the door to throw the bolt into place, then swept across to where a bowl and pitcher rested atop one of the nearby crates. Pouring water into the bowl, she dropped the quilt and took up a cake of soap and the sponge beside it. Her wide, anxious gaze shifted frequently toward the doorway while she bathed. She scrubbed hard at her skin, almost as though she were trying to scrub away the disturbing memory of Ethan Holt's touch.

When she had finished, she wrapped the quilt about her again and moved to unlock the door. She stepped outside into the pale moonlight. Ethan was in front of the cabin, adjusting the cinch on his horse's saddle. His mouth curved into a soft smile when he caught sight of her.

"I'll ride over and let Beth know you're with me," he said.

"Dear God, Beth!" she gasped, her eyes widening in sudden dismay. How was she possibly going to explain all this to her sister?

Well, you see, dearest Beth, I couldn't resist Ethan's lovemaking, and so now I'm afraid I can never come home again. Yes, she mused in bitter sarcasm, that would do the job nicely.

"I am not going to stay here," she declared, with considerable feeling.

"Yes, you are."

Holding the reins in one hand, he sauntered toward her. She stiffened in alarm, but resisted the cowardly urge to run.

"I'll be gone when you get back," she insisted. She clutched the quilt more tightly about her as he came to a halt mere inches away. His hair glistened damply in the moonlight; she realized that he must have washed up in the creek.

"Try to leave, and I'll come after you," he promised, with maddening, authoritative, calm.

"And then what?" she challenged on a sudden, reckless impulse. "You cannot force me to remain."

"You're my wife, Lainey. I'll do whatever it takes to make sure you don't forget it." It was clear from the look in his eyes that he would not hesitate to make good on his threat.

He did not reach for her as she thought he would, but merely turned and swung up into the saddle. She watched in silent, simmering fury while he reined about, and her eyes seared into the broad target of his back as he rode away into the night.

In spite of her determination to remain awake, she was sleeping peacefully when he returned less than an hour later. She had found her horse in the barn, retrieved her blue silk suit, and put it on before finally surrendering to the temptation to lie down. Her last thought before drifting off into blissful unconsciousness had been of Ethan . . . and his sweetly savage loving.

It was well past midnight when he slipped into the cabin. The lamp had burned down into nothing but a faint, flickering glow by then. Travis had dutifully remained out in the barn; overjoyed to hear Ethan's news, he lay atop the fragrant cushion of hay and yearned for Beth. Realizing that they could be married right away, he smiled at the prospect and gave silent thanks for his big brother's impatience.

Ethan quickly undressed and took his place in the narrow bunk beside his wife. There was scarcely room enough for the two of them, but he wasn't inclined to complain. Still, he mused while his turquoise eyes gleamed with satisfaction, he'd have to see about getting a real bed the next time he rode into Guthrie.

He smiled tenderly down at his beautiful, passionate bride as he drew her pliant curves against him. She stirred softly and snuggled closer to his naked warmth. Offering up a silent curse for the fire in his blood, he forced himself to close his eyes.

Lainey awoke to the rich, pleasant aroma of coffee. Her eyelids fluttered open, and she knew a moment's bewilderment when she looked down and saw that she was fully dressed. Enlightenment dawned as memories of the previous night came flooding back with a vengeance.

"Good morning, Mrs. Holt."

She started at the sound of Ethan's voice. Her gaze flew across the sunlit room to see that he was lifting the coffeepot from the hearth to pour her a cup of the hot brew. He was already dressed. She noted with a touch of resentment that he seemed to be in unusually good spirits.

"Thought I'd let you sleep in awhile," he remarked as he watched her struggle into a sitting position. "I'll see about breakfast as soon as you're up. We've got a cook-stove coming in on the train any day now."

"Have we?" she snapped. She dragged herself from the bed, only to feel an embarrassing soreness. She winced a bit, but raised her head to a proud angle and stood to her feet. Her golden hair fell about her face and shoulders in riotous disarray, while her suit was woefully creased.

"We'll ride over and get your things later." He crossed the room in two long, easy strides and offered her the cup. Suppressing a smile at her visible wariness, he ordered, "Drink it. It will make you feel better."

"Nothing will make me feel better," she retorted hotly. Nevertheless, she took the cup and raised it to her lips. Painfully aware of Ethan's eyes on her, she colored and looked away.

"A hot bath would probably help, too," he told her, with remarkable perception. Though he would have liked nothing better than to take her right back to bed and love the living daylights out of her, he knew she was in no mood to let him touch her at the moment. And after all, he consoled himself, they'd be spending the next fifty or sixty years together. He could spare a little patience now that she was his at last.

"I suppose you would insist upon watching," she countered in a flash of anger, her eyes blazing up at him now. She felt a sudden warmth steal over her at the sight of his slow, disarmingly roguish smile.

"I'd be lying if I said I wasn't tempted."

"Damn you, Ethan Holt! The least you can do is grant me some privacy."

"You can have all the privacy you want after breakfast. Travis and I need to get an early start on the fences today."

"How is my sister supposed to manage without me?"

she demanded, her thoughts turning to Beth again. "She and Anna are all alone, and—"

"Not for long," he informed her.

"What do you mean?"

"Beth and Travis are getting married tomorrow."

"What?" she said in startled disbelief. "Why, that's impossible! Confound it, Beth never said anything to me about—"

"Beth doesn't know yet," he confided, with a brief smile of irony. "Travis rode over first thing this morning to tell her."

"But, I—we still had so many things to arrange," she stammered, her head spinning at the news. She glared vengefully up at him. "You Holts are all alike!"

"Should I take that as a compliment?" he drawled wryly.

"You should not. It is unforgivably selfish of Travis to rush Beth into marriage this way, just as it was unforgivably selfish of *you* to deceive me."

"I never lied to you, Lainey," he disputed, his gaze narrowing imperceptibly. "I told you things wouldn't change between us unless you wanted them to. And by damn, you little spitfire, you wanted it every bit as much as I did."

"I did not," she vigorously denied. She wanted to hit him, to wipe the smug, satisfied look from his devilishly handsome face, but she knew there was every likelihood he would hit her back. She paled at the memory of his threat to punish her defiance. "How dare you say such a thing."

"You wanted it," he reasserted, with no sign of contrition. "And did you ever stop to think that maybe your sister's as impatient as Travis for their wedding to take place?"

"I would expect you to hold that opinion. After all, you're a man and—"

"And you're a woman. There's no shame in admitting that you have needs."

"The only 'need' I have is to forget I ever set eyes on you."

"Travis and Beth will live at your place after they're married," he announced, oblivious to the sparks her beautiful eyes were shooting at his head. "It will be a big help having him over there once the cattle arrive."

"I'm planning to start a farm, not a ranch," she saw fit to remind him.

"We'll have both eventually. But for now, we've got to put all our time in on the stock. There's good money to be made in cattle, Lainey. And this country's right for it."

He turned away and headed toward the doorway. She found herself at a sudden, perplexing loss for words as she watched him open the door.

"Breakfast can wait awhile," he said, pausing to face her again. A faint smile touched his lips. "I'll bring in some water for your bath."

Touched by his thoughtfulness in spite of her lingering annoyance with him, Lainey sat down and took another drink of the coffee. Her brows knit together into a pensive frown.

Beth was getting married tomorrow. Everything was happening so fast; had the whole world gone crazy? She still didn't understand how or why she had come to her present circumstances. And now her sister was getting married. To Ethan Holt's brother, no less. God help her, it was all simply too much to comprehend.

After Ethan had set the water on to heat for her bath and left her alone again, she took the precaution of drawing the bolt. She suspected that it would prove useless if he actually took it in mind to come inside, but she told herself a locked door could at least buy her some time.

She added the hot water to the partially filled tub,

then stripped off her clothes and immersed herself in the soothing liquid warmth. Her tensed muscles relaxed as she closed her eyes, but there was no such respite for her mind. It seemed odd to think that she was home now. She knew Ethan would never let her go; he had made that painfully clear. And anyway, she realized with an inward sigh, after tomorrow she would have no place else to go.

She couldn't very well move in with Travis and Beth. A faint smile of irony played about her lips when she envisioned the younger Holt's face upon hearing that his bride's sister would be sharing their one-room domestic bliss. Her amusement quickly faded. There was always the chance of securing accommodations in town, especially with so many hotels and rooming houses sprouting in the midst of the mayhem, but Ethan would only find her and bring her back again. No, she concluded unhappily, she would either have to leave Oklahoma altogether, or remain exactly where she was and try to make the best of things.

"Why?" she wondered aloud. Why did Ethan want her as his wife? That he wanted her in his bed was painfully obvious. Perhaps that was the only reason he had decided to make their marriage a "traditional" one. Perhaps when he had tired of her he would agree to a divorce. Having so little experience in such matters, she could only suppose that he *would* eventually tire of her. What kind of marriage could it be if it was based on nothing more than lust?

Trying to ignore the dull ache in her heart, she took up the soap and sponge. The fire crackled and popped beneath the mantel, sunlight streamed in through the windows, and the sounds of an awakening prairie paradise drifted on the cool morning breeze. It promised to be a beautiful day, but Lainey was too troubled to offer it suitable appreciation.

When Ethan knocked at the door a short time later,

she had finished her bath and was in the process of fastening the last button of her suit. Her chemise was torn beyond repair, but at least her drawers were still intact. She smoothed down her skirts and walked slowly across to open the door.

"Travis is back," Ethan announced casually. He strode inside, crossing to the fireplace. Lainey frowned after him, then turned back to find her new brother-in-law grinning down at her.

"Good morning, Lainey."

"Good morning, Travis," she responded, coloring faintly. She was unable to prevent a note of resentment from creeping into her voice. Though she honestly liked him, she was troubled by his insistence upon rushing Beth to the altar. And it didn't help matters any that he was Ethan's brother . . . Guilt by association, she mused caustically.

"Beth sends her love. She wants you to ride over as soon as you can this morning. I guess Ethan told you about the wedding." He appeared anything but repentant as his green eyes twinkled down at her.

"He did indeed." She tried to look stern, but her mouth curved into a begrudging smile. "I suppose I should offer you my best wishes. This is all quite sudden, but if it is what Beth wants, then I will be happy for you." Releasing a sigh, she sobered again and implored him, "Please, Travis. Treat her gently. She has endured so much—"

"I love her, Lainey. And I swear before God, she'll know nothing but kindness from me," he reassured her earnestly. He smiled again before entering the cabin at last. "I hope you'll be doing the cooking from now on. If I never have to sample Ethan's biscuits again, it will be too soon."

"It so happens that I am an excellent cook," she informed him loftily. Outlined in the doorway by the soft morning light, she raised her hands to her hair. "But if your brother has decided upon this little arrangement for the purpose of securing himself a cook and house-keeper—in general, a 'bondswoman'—then he will be sadly disappointed!" She shot a defiant, challenging look toward Ethan as she twisted up the thick curls.

"I don't think that's why he married you," Travis opined, then had the grace to look a trifle shamefaced.

Lainey bristled when she glimpsed the roguish amusement in Ethan's gaze. Muttering something unintelligible, she spun about and marched outside.

"I get the distinct impression your wife's not too happy to be here," Travis noted wryly. He poured himself a cup of coffee and watched as his brother set the bacon on to cook. "I hope you know what you're doing, boss man."

"You take care of your woman, and I'll take care of mine," Ethan parried, with only the ghost of a smile.

"Fair enough. But keep in mind that they're sisters. If Lainey's unhappy, it's bound to affect Beth. And I can't say I relish the prospect of finding your bride on my doorstep some night."

"It won't happen." He drew himself up to his full height beside his brother and pointed out in a voice laced with sarcasm, "You're a hell of an authority when it comes to women."

"I've had my share of problems with them," Travis willingly conceded. "But not anymore. I never thought I'd find anyone like Beth. And now that I have, I'm going to make damned sure I don't lose her." He took a long drink of the coffee, then changed the subject. "When are you supposed to meet with Sutton again?"

"He won't be back for a couple of days."

"You're not really going to let him deputize you, are you? Damn it, Ethan, we've got a ranch to run. And you've got a wife now. You can't go running off—"

"I don't want the job. But he needs my help." He

frowned and transferred his steady, penetrating gaze to the fire before adding half to himself, "I owe him."

"Maybe so, but you've served your time keeping law and order," insisted Travis. "Ten years is long enough. You'd had your fill of it, remember? I thought that was one of the reasons we came here. And now Sutton shows up and wants you to start riding with him again."

"He saved my life," Ethan reminded him.

"I know. And he gave you your start, too. But that doesn't mean you have to keep on paying. It has to end sometime."

"It will." It was evident from the tone of his voice that he considered the matter settled.

"Do you still think Halloran's involved in the claim stealing?" Travis asked, changing the subject again.

"That, and a whole lot more," replied Ethan. His eyes darkened while his features tensed in vengeful fury. "I know he's got a hand in everything that's been going on around here, but I can't prove it yet."

"Have you told Lainey any of this?"

"No. But I've made it clear she's never to go near the Palace again." His blood boiled at the memory of Halloran's eyes when they had fastened on Lainey. "Once I've got the proof I need, I'll make sure the bastard gets what he deserves," he vowed grimly.

Lainey materialized in the doorway soon thereafter. Unfortunately she had returned too late to hear anything of the brothers' conversation. Wrinkling her nose in distaste at the smell of burning bacon, she closed the door and swept forward to take charge of breakfast.

"I can see why Travis is so intent upon avoiding further exposure to your cooking!" she proclaimed, sparing a brief, accusatory look for her husband. She knelt before the hearth and used a towel to snatch the overheated skillet from the fire.

"We've managed to survive so far," Ethan drawled lazily. His eyes were brimming with indulgent humor as he watched her set the skillet aside and move across to the table.

"The two of you may take yourselves outside," she insisted, pouring flour into a bowl. "I will call you when breakfast is ready."

"Yes, ma'am," agreed Travis, another grin tugging at his lips. "Better do as she says," he advised Ethan, with mocking gravity. "There'll be hell to pay if you dare to cross a woman in her own house."

"This isn't *my* house," Lainey denied impulsively. She frowned and dropped her gaze back to the table.

Ethan and Travis exchanged a quick glance, then followed her bidding and strode outside. She expelled a long, pent-up breath once they had gone, and her eyes were clouded with renewed disquiet as she worked to prepare the meal.

After breakfast, she informed Ethan that she was going to visit her sister. He gave his permission without hesitation, and he promised to drive the wagon over to fetch her things later that afternoon. After saddling her horse for her, he led the animal out into the sunshine. She was hoping to avoid any physical contact between them, but he clasped her about the waist and lifted her up to the saddle.

"Are you planning to stay all day?" he asked, reluctantly drawing his hands away.

"I—I haven't made any plans." It wouldn't do her any good to make plans, she thought with a flash of annoyance. He would only overrule them anyway.

"Just make sure you don't take it in mind to head into Guthrie."

"If I *were* planning to go, Ethan Holt, you'd be the very last to know."

"I mean it, Lainey," he cautioned, his tone low and level. His eyes glinted dully as they met and locked with the stormy, brilliant blue of hers. "Stay away from the Palace—and Neil Halloran."

Her face paled at the mention of Halloran's name. She had completely forgotten about him. A knot of trepidation tightened in her stomach at the memory of his brutal kiss and subsequent threats, but she revealed nothing to Ethan. She knew he would seek the other man out; if he knew what Halloran had done to her, he might very well kill him. She shuddered at the thought of it. She had no wish to be the cause of bloodshed . . . And dear God, there was still always the possibility that Ethan would be the one killed. A sudden, sharp pain sliced through her heart.

"I'm not going into town today," she murmured truthfully, her gaze falling beneath his.

"Good." He stepped away from her at last and settled his hat lower on his head. "Travis and I will be setting fence posts along the western boundary of our land. Like I said, I'll be over with the wagon later."

She nodded mutely and did not look at him again before riding away. Urging her horse into a gallop, she raced across the rugged, sun-drenched countryside beneath a sky nearly as blue as her eyes. She reached her homestead in a matter of minutes. Beth and Anna were outside in front of the cabin. Their faces wreathed in smiles, they hastened forward to meet her as she pulled her mount to a halt and swung down.

"Oh, Lainey!" exclaimed Beth, hugging her as though she had been away for days instead of hours. "I was hoping you would come right away."

Anna was equally emphatic in her greeting; she flung her little arms about her aunt's legs and set up a constant, happy jabbering. Lainey gave a soft laugh and bent to catch the apple-cheeked toddler up in her arms.

"I've no idea what you're saying, sweetheart," she confessed, her eyes shining with tender affection. "But I am so very glad to see you."

"Can you stay for a while?" asked Beth.

"As long as I please," replied Lainey. Her voice was

underscored with a touch of defiance. "And, from what I've heard, we have a great deal to talk about." She watched while a rosy blush stained her sister's cheeks.

"I suppose Travis told you about tomorrow?"

"Ethan told me," she admitted, with a sigh. Her brow creased into a slight frown as she searched Beth's face closely. "Are you sure about this? I know you love Travis, and I know he loves you, but it seems to me that the two of you are rushing things terribly!"

"No more so than you and Ethan did," Beth pointed out, with a fondly amused smile.

"Yes, but that . . . well, that was different."

"Was it?"

"Of course it was! I never intended to live with Ethan, and I certainly never intended to—" She broke off abruptly. It was her turn to blush while Beth treated her to a quizzical scrutiny.

"Then why are you living with him now?" the petite blonde asked in bemusement.

"Because he is giving me no other choice." She frowned darkly and lowered Anna to the ground. Her eyes, kindling with a variety of emotions, followed the toddler as she ambled over to the steps of the cabin. "Ethan Holt has decided that we are to be husband and wife—and *not* in name only. Confound it, Beth—I'm beginning to think he never had any intention of keeping his part of the bargain."

"So you—you are truly his wife?" Beth probed delicately.

"Yes, damn it."

"Lainey Prescott!"

"It's Mrs. Holt now," she corrected, with bitter sarcasm. "And you needn't look so shocked. My language is entirely in keeping with his treatment of me."

"Good heavens, he hasn't harmed you in any way, has he?" Beth demanded, her light blue eyes filling with horror at the thought.

"Well, no," Lainey conceded reluctantly. Her color deepened again. "And *yes!* Great balls of fire, I am so terribly confused about all this. I didn't want it to happen, but it did, and now I don't know what I'm going to do." She felt a sharp twinge of guilt when an inner voice reminded her that she had wanted it to happen very much once Ethan had taken her in his arms. "Oh, Beth," she whispered tremulously, "I am so ashamed."

"There is nothing to be ashamed of," insisted Beth, her gaze full of understanding as well as compassion. "What you felt was perfectly normal. After all, Ethan is your husband now. It is a wife's duty to—"

"Duty?" She shook her head in an unhappy denial and revealed in all honesty, "My behavior was anything but dutiful." Wildly abandoned would be a more apt description, she added silently, then gave an inward groan.

"Well then, I suppose I must confess to the same lack of decorum," Beth declared, with a smile, her eyes sparkling softly. "I feel anything but dutiful whenever Travis kisses me." Wicked or not, she was impatient for tomorrow to come.

"Yes, but you are in love with Travis."

"And can you truly deny that you feel nothing of the same for Ethan?"

"I—I don't know what I feel anymore," she stammered, then sighed heavily. Her luminous sapphire gaze drifted toward the glistening, tree-lined waters of the creek. "There are times when I am convinced I dislike him in the extreme, when I am certain I cannot endure another minute of his infuriating arrogance and high-handedness, and other times when I . . . well, when I find myself actually *wanting* to be near him! I've never felt this way before, Beth. And God help me, I never want to feel this way again."

"I am afraid, dearest Lainey, that such a thing is unavoidable."

"What do you mean, 'unavoidable'?"

"I have suspected all along that you and Ethan shared something quite unique—and passionate. Ethan Holt is in love with you," she opined, smiling again. "And I think, if you will but search your heart, you will realize that you return his affection."

"In love with me?" Lainey echoed, her eyes widening in stunned disbelief. "Why, he most certainly is not! Nor do I feel anything of the sort for him."

"Are you really so certain of that?"

"Of course I am."

"Oh, Lainey. Why else do you think he married you? As you yourself pointed out, it does seem as though he always wanted your marriage of convenience to be a great deal more than that."

"Yes, but he has never made any declarations of love," argued Lainey. Several conflicting emotions played across her face as she considered her sister's words. *Ethan in love with her?*

"Perhaps he doesn't think you are ready to hear them yet," Beth suggested gently. "From what I have seen and heard, I don't think you would have been too receptive—"

"Receptive? For heaven's sake, I don't see how I could be any more *receptive* than I was last night," she blurted out, only to color fierily again in the next instant. "You don't understand, Beth. The only thing he cares about is the physical attraction between us."

"If that were true, I doubt he would have given you his name. My own unfortunate experience has taught me that men do not marry women for that reason alone." A shadow of painful remembrance crossed her delicate, heart-shaped features. "Ethan Holt, in particular, does not strike me as the sort of man who would allow a passing fancy to prompt him into a lifelong commitment. No, Lainey. I think he is in love with you. The evidence is there every time he looks at you. I cannot understand why you are refusing to face the truth of his feelings, as well as your own."

Lainey opened her mouth to speak, but closed it again while her heart took to pounding fiercely within her breast. She told herself that Beth was wrong—and yet her emotions held no more clarity than before. Nor did Ethan's behavior toward her. Dear God, what was she to think?

"It has all been quite sudden, hasn't it?" Beth commented, with a sigh of her own. "You may be in a quandary at the moment, dearest Lainey, but I know it will work out. Once you've had a bit more time to accustom yourself to the situation, I'm sure you can find the happiness you so richly deserve. In any case, you are Ethan's wife now. He has every right to insist that you live with him."

"And I have every right to seek a divorce," she countered rashly. All too well, she remembered Ethan's vow that she would be his forever.

"A divorce?" Beth's eyes grew round as saucers once more. "Surely you aren't serious? I cannot imagine your husband would ever agree to such a scandalous—"

"He might, in time," she insisted, though her words lacked conviction even to her own ears. "But whether he does or not, I have no intention of spending the rest of my life with a man who seems determined to . . . *enslave* me!"

It was a thoroughly unfounded accusation and she knew it. But her whole world had been turned upside down, and though she secretly yearned for her sister's opinion to prove correct, she would not let herself dare to hope that Ethan cared so much.

As to her own feelings, she still refused to acknowledge anything more than a startling, forceful ambivalence—on the one hand, she was furious with Ethan Holt, while on the other, she wanted him to make love to her the way he had done last night. His very touch had set her afire; she felt a renewed warmth stealing over her when she remembered how his lips and hands had boldly explored her naked body. She cursed her own wantonness, then sighed again and looked back to her sister.

"Let's go inside," said Beth, slipping an arm about her shoulders. "Travis and I are going to be married tomorrow afternoon. The ceremony will not be a formal one, of course, but that doesn't matter. I thought I would wear Mother's wedding dress. That is, if you think it would be appropriate under the circumstances."

"Of course it's appropriate. How could it not be?"

"Well, it is white," Beth reminded her, looking uncomfortable, "and I suppose I haven't the right—"

"Beth Prescott, you have *every* right!" asserted Lainey. "Mother would be proud to have you wear it. And perhaps, someday," she added, her gaze softening as it traveled to the fair-haired toddler once more, "Anna will be married in it as well."

"Or one of your own daughters."

"My daughters?" Good heavens, she hadn't even thought about *that*! Her pulse raced as it occurred to her that she might already be carrying Ethan's child. The possibility filled her with consternation—and a strange, warm pleasure.

Beth called to Anna, who obediently came running as fast as her tiny legs would carry her. Lainey smiled as she watched her sister scoop the child up in her arms.

"I hope Travis and I are blessed with more children," Beth confided, her eyes wistful. She returned Lainey's smile with a soft, self-conscious one of her own. "But I suppose it's foolish to talk of such things when we aren't even married yet. Oh, well. Come inside. I'll put on a fresh pot of coffee, and then we can see for ourselves what needs to be done to the dress."

Lainey stayed for the remainder of the day. More than once, she toyed with the idea of leaving before Ethan arrived with the wagon, but she was reluctant to part from her sister. It had occurred to her that this would be the last time they would be together without the mutual responsibilities of marriage. After tomorrow, everything would change. They would both be wives, and they would both have an impossible, irresistible Holt to contend with. Fate was truly capricious, she reflected, mentally shaking her head.

Ethan drove the wagon over late that afternoon. Travis rode alongside. Lainey was surprised to see that they had loaded one of the bunks into the wagon. She stood framed in the doorway of the cabin with Anna in her arms while Beth hastened gracefully forward to greet her future husband and present brother-in-law with a welcoming smile.

"We brought this for Anna," explained Travis, nodding toward the narrow bed. He dismounted and swept Beth against him for a quick, hard kiss. She was flushed and breathless when he let her go. "You and I, sweetheart, will be buying a bed of our own when we're in town tomorrow."

"But, won't you be needing it?" Beth asked Ethan in all innocence.

"Not anymore," he assured her, a wry smile playing about his lips while his gaze moved to Lainey. He climbed agilely down from the wagon and set about helping Travis unload the bunk.

Lainey set the squirming Anna on her feet and watched them. She had packed all her clothing and personal belongings in one of the trunks resting just within the cabin doorway. Beth had insisted that she take some of the special mementos they had brought from home. Several photographs and books were packed amid the clothing, and she had been grateful for her sister's generosity in including half of the china and one of the two chairs their grandfather had made more than thirty years ago. She knew that these things would make Ethan's cabin seem more like home—even if she *was* living there against her will.

Once they had carried the bed inside and loaded the trunk and chair in its place, Travis announced that he would be staying for supper. Ethan, however, declined Beth's kind invitation and said that he and Lainey wanted to get back to the ranch before nightfall.

"But, we are in no hurry," Lainey protested.

"I am." He took a firm grip on her arm and led her over to the wagon. She flung him a speaking glare, but he merely lifted her up to the seat, tied the reins of her horse to the back, and turned to Travis and Beth with a brief, appealingly crooked smile. "Don't let him stay too late, Beth. It's hard enough getting a full day's work out of him as it is."

"I hold my own," Travis parried smoothly.

"And you'll hold it even better after tomorrow," quipped Ethan. He paused to stroke a quick, affectionate hand across the top of Anna's head before taking his place beside Lainey and gathering up the reins.

"I'll see you in the morning, Lainey," said Beth. They had nearly finished the alterations to the dress, but there was still a bit of hemming and tucking to be done.

Lainey managed a smile as she murmured a response. Swallowing a sudden lump in her throat, she lifted her hand in good-bye, then clutched at the side of the wagon seat when Ethan snapped the reins together. The team started forward, the wheels rolling and bouncing over the grassy earth.

She was acutely conscious of Ethan's proximity as they drove homeward in the fading light of day. And no matter how desperately she tried, she was unable to prevent her thoughts from straying to the night ahead.

Chapter 14

Lainey scrambled down from the wagon the very moment Ethan drew the team to a halt near the barn. He smiled to himself as he watched her scurry inside the cabin.

She closed the door, then leaned breathlessly back against it for a moment. Dismayed to realize that she was trembling, she chided herself for her lack of courage and resolutely straightened her shoulders. She crossed to the table, maintaining at least an outward composure, and struck a match to light the lamp.

By the time Ethan came inside with her trunk, she had already managed to start a fire and was in the process of mixing the ingredients for corn bread. She spared only a brief, surreptitious glance in his direction as he set the trunk down and lifted his hat to the peg on the wall beside the doorway.

"Unless I miss my guess, we'll have rain before morning," he remarked casually. The look in his eyes, however, was anything but casual.

Lainey said nothing. Her nerves were strung tight, and she could not keep her anxious gaze from straying toward the bed in the corner. She gave serious consideration to offering up some excuse—a headache, or perhaps even the more time-honored plea of her "monthly curse"—that would prevent Ethan from claiming his husbandly rights that evening, but she knew it was hopeless. He would take her to bed again. And *she*, confound it, would thrill to his lovemaking with the same shameless enthusiasm she had displayed the night before.

"I'm going to wash up in the creek," he announced. Then he startled her by inquiring in a low, splendidly vibrant tone of voice, "Care to join me, Mrs. Holt?"

Her eyes flew to his face. She felt her stomach do a strange flip-flop at the sight of his soft, tenderly roguish smile.

"Definitely not!" she retorted, with a trifle too much vehemence.

"Why not? It's nearly dark. And there's no one around to see." That was true enough. He wouldn't risk it otherwise; the thought of any other man gazing upon her naked charms made his gold-flecked eyes darken with jealous fury. "The water might feel a bit cold at first, but you'll get used to it once you're in."

"Are you actually suggesting that we—that we take off our clothes?" stammered Lainey, her own eyes growing very round at the thought.

"Guilty as charged."

"Why, I would never do such a thing," she denied, with prim indignation.

"I remember a time when you came pretty damned close," he was ungentlemanly enough to remind her. Another disarming smile tugged at the corners of his mouth. "As I recall, that was also the night I first kissed you. I think I knew even before then that you were mine."

"Why in heaven's name do you keep saying that? I am not *yours*, Ethan Holt!"

"Aren't you?" He sauntered across to the fireplace and lifted a hand to the mantel. Though he stared down at the flames, she knew he was not yet finished bedeviling her. Not by a long shot. "It's no coincidence that you and I ended up together, Lainey. Call it fate, or Providence, or whatever else you like—we were destined to be together. Even if I hadn't already known it, last night would have been enough to bring me around to the truth."

"What happened last night was a mistake," she was quick to proclaim, her cheeks crimsoning at the mention of it.

"It was no mistake." He transferred his penetrating gaze to her face again. "Damn it, woman! If you'd stop being so hardheaded, you'd see that we're perfect for each other," he insisted. His voice brimmed with wry, loving amusement, and his eyes were warmly aglow as he watched her struggle to pretend cool indifference. "The last thing I had counted on was getting married. I won't deny that the thought crossed my mind once or twice through the years, but nothing ever came of it. Even after I had decided to take off the badge and hang up my guns, my plans didn't include a wife. Not yet. But you changed all that."

"I can assure you, it was completely unintentional," she countered, only to feel her knees weaken at the sound of his quiet chuckle.

"Are you sure about that?"

"Of course I am." Her fingers clenched angrily about the bowl as she finally looked at him. "You have no doubt been the object of many a woman's romantic designs, Ethan Holt, but you cannot count me among their number." Dismayed at the turn of their conversation, she took up the spoon again and started beating at the thick yellow batter. "I thought you were on your way to the creek."

"I am," he confirmed. But instead of heading toward the doorway, he set an unhurried, purposeful course in her direction.

"What are you doing?" she demanded, her stormy gaze narrowing in suspicion. There was a strange little smile playing about his lips as he advanced, and his eyes gleamed dangerously.

"I'm taking my wife for a swim."

"You most certainly are *not!*" Her pulse leapt in sudden alarm. "I am not going with you!"

"Yes, you are." Pausing to tower ominously above her, he reached out and took her arm in a firm but gentle grasp.

Thrown into chaos by his stated intentions, Lainey did not stop to think. She acted solely on impulse—a childish one, she would later admit. Lifting the bowl in her hands, she thrust it forcefully at her husband and jerked free.

Ethan glanced down at the wet cornmeal splattered across the front of his shirt, then turned to see his errant bride wrenching open the cabin door. With a faint smile of ironic appreciation for her proud, indomitable spirit, he strode after her, instinctively snatching up his rifle on the way out.

The chase was a short one. Lainey had only made it as far as the barn when he caught up with her. She cried out as she felt his strong arm clamping about her waist from behind. He easily swung her off her feet, sent her flying facedown over his shoulder, and bore her away to the creek.

"Put me down," she demanded furiously. Her long hair came unpinned, and the shimmering golden tresses spilled down across his back while she kicked and squirmed in a futile attempt to make him release her.

Without a word, he carried her to the water's edge and set her on her feet. She pushed against him, but he captured both of her wrists and held them behind her back with one large, powerful hand as he began deftly liberating the buttons that ran down the front of her bodice. Almost before she knew what was happening, he was stripping the embroidered cotton gown from her body. It fell in a heap about her ankles.

"No," she whispered, clad only in her undergarments now. She had changed into fresh clothing during her visit to Beth and Anna; she wondered dazedly if she would soon find it necessary to order a new supply of lingerie. "Stop it, Ethan!"

It soon became apparent that he would not be swayed. He tumbled her down upon the grassy creek bank, pulled off her boots and stockings in spite of her more than halfhearted resistance to his efforts, and tugged at her drawers. She managed to roll over and scramble up onto her hands and knees, but then gasped sharply when he yanked the ruffled white garment downward. Crimsoning with embarrassment to have her bottom bared to him in the twilight, she was unable to prevent him from removing her drawers altogether. Her chemise was all that remained; it soon joined the rest of her clothing.

"Please, don't!" she screamed in earnest as he scooped her up in his arms and tossed her, naked and struggling, into the creek.

She landed with a loud, accompanying splash. Her eyes flew wide at the shock of the cold water. Her hips made hard but not painful contact with the creek's sandy bottom before she spluttered to the surface again and found her footing. Standing waist-deep in the water, she raked the wet curtain of hair from her face and folded her arms modestly across her breasts.

"What a—a perfectly unchivalrous thing to do," she sputtered wrathfully.

"The water feels good, doesn't it?" he drawled, without any remorse whatsoever. His eyes smoldered with passion as they traveled over her pale, glistening curves. He quickly stripped off his own clothing and waded in to join her. Her face flamed anew at the sight of his nakedness. She hastily turned her back on him. He wrapped his arms about her from behind and pulled her close, so that his manhood pressed intimately against the firm roundness of her bottom.

"Ethan!"

"It strikes me, Mrs. Holt, that we should make these swims a nightly ritual," he suggested in a husky tone.

She groaned inwardly and tried to pull away, but he spun her about to face him. Her wide, luminous gaze met the gleaming warmth of his as he crushed her to him. A shiver ran the length of her spine—and it had nothing to do with the chilling temperature of the water.

Locked against him in breathless expectation, she instinctively parted her lips and waited for him to kiss her. But he was of a mind to tease her a bit first, to show her that he was capable of more than the inevitable conquest. She squealed in protest when he suddenly bent his tall frame downward, hauling her into the water with him. He leaned back until he was immersed up to his chest, then plunged her underneath the surface. She came up spluttering and coughing, only to bristle at the sound of his soft, mellow laughter.

"Why, you—" she muttered. She launched herself at him in retaliation, threading her fingers within the wet thickness of his hair and trying to force his head under the water.

"Hasn't anybody ever warned you about playing with fire?" he challenged. His deep-timbred voice was laced with an intoxicating mixture of amusement and desire. While she maintained her efforts to repay him, he swept her up against him and stood to his feet. Once again, she was certain he would kiss her; once again, he offered a dunking instead of a kiss.

"Damn you, Ethan Holt," she seethed when she emerged from the clear, gently flowing waters.

Unchastened, he reached for her. She succeeded in evading his grasp this time.

"I have had quite enough of your particular brand of 'swimming.'" With that, she crossed her arms over her breasts again and made her way to the bank. She had never witnessed this playful side of him before. Part of her wanted to remain and see how far things would go, but the more practical voice inside her brain cautioned her to leave before it was too late.

Ethan made no move to stop her—at least not yet. He watched as she stepped carefully out of the water. Her supple, shapely body gleamed white in the gathering darkness. His fathomless turquoise gaze smoldered anew as it roamed possessively over her naked backside.

Lainey snatched up her chemise and pulled it on over her head. The thin white garment clung to her wet curves, and she shivered again as the cool evening air swept across her near nakedness. Aware of Ethan's burning gaze, she hastened to retrieve her gown.

She never got the chance to put it on.

Ethan swiftly closed the distance between them and seized her about the waist again. She could do nothing more than gasp in startlement as she found herself toppled unceremoniously backward to the pile of clothing beside the creek.

"What—?" she started to demand, only to break off when her husband suddenly lowered his hard, naked body atop her scantily clad softness. Shocked by the realization that he apparently meant to make love to her right there and then—the prospect of doing *that* outside in the open air seemed downright wicked—she brought her hands up to push at his chest.

"You're a beautiful woman, Lainey," he told her quietly, his eyes searing down into the wide, sparkling depths of hers. "But that isn't why I married you."

"It isn't?" she whispered. Her weak struggles ceased altogether, and she lay breathless and trembling beneath him while he treated her to a slow, devastatingly tender smile.

"I won't deny it wasn't what first caught my interest," he confessed, his arms tightening about her. He seemed oblivious to the way the night wind danced across his bronzed, naked skin. "But a man's a fool if he marries a woman for that reason alone."

"Why, that's exactly what Beth said," she blurted out, then colored in embarrassment. Now he would know that she had been discussing him with her sister.

"She was right. I fell in love with your spirit, with your courage and your pride and your damned stubbornness. I've never known a woman like you before. And God help me if I ever do again," he said, with a mock frown of exasperation.

"You—you're in love with me?" she stammered, visibly incredulous. Her heart fluttered wildly in her breast, while at the same time her whole body tingled beneath the masterful, breathtaking pressure of his.

"Yes, Mrs. Holt, I am." His handsome face grew solemn, and his gaze reflected what was in his own heart when he declared softly, "I love you, Lainey. I think I loved you from the very first, even though I sure as hell didn't want to. I told myself I'd get over it." His mouth curved into a faint smile of irony. "I was a fool, plain and simple. In spite of all my plans, in spite of everything, I love you. And I always will."

"Why didn't you . . . tell me this before?" Lainey faltered in a small voice. *Dear God, was it true?*

"Would you have listened?"

"I don't know," she admitted in all honesty. Her temper flared in the next instant. "But you still should have told me."

"I'm telling you now."

"Yes, and I suppose you expect me to surrender to your every wish as a result." Her eyes flashed defiantly up at him as she renewed her struggles. She couldn't have said why she fought him; strangely enough, she felt a sense of betrayal, as if by keeping his feelings for her a secret until now he had somehow violated her trust. It would have troubled her far less to respond to a man who had professed to love her than one who had

merely proven himself to be a captivating lover. She
still didn't know if she believed him . . . She was almost
afraid to believe him. "Will you please allow me to get
up?" she asked, though it was much more of a demand
than a request. "I am cold and—"

"I know a way to get us both warm."

She opened her mouth to offer up a suitable retort,
but he silenced her with his lips. There was no playful-
ness in him now. The kiss was deep and hungry and
sweetly rapturous, prompting her to moan in passion instead of protest. He swept the hemline of her chemise
impatiently upward, so that his strong, knowing fingers
could caress the rose-tipped fullness of her breasts. Her
arms lifted of their own accord to glide across the
broad, muscular expanse of his back, and she felt a
delicious tremor shake her as her naked flesh made contact with the scorching hardness of his.

It wasn't long before she was arching her back instinctively beneath him. But he was determined to prolong the delectable torment. He loved her. God knew,
he loved her more than life itself. Yet her response to
his declaration had hurt him more than he cared to admit, and he vowed to make her want him so much that
she would forget about her damned pride and beg him
to take her.

It was to this purpose that he tore his lips from hers
and slid his body downward. She was left gasping for
breath, both confused and disappointed by his abandon-
ment, but not for long. Her eyes flew wide when he
suddenly parted her legs, slid his hands underneath her
hips, and lowered his head toward the inviting triangle
of soft golden curls between her thighs.

"Ethan, *no!*" came her shocked, breathless cry of protest. This time, however, he was in no mood to be mer-
ciful. Desire, hot and forceful, blazed through her at the
first touch of his mouth upon her delicate, rosy flesh.
She closed her eyes, her fingers threading almost con-

vulsively within his damp hair while his lips and tongue worked their sensuous magic. She caught her lower lip between her teeth to stifle a scream of pure pleasure as her inhibitions were well and truly conquered.

"Oh, Ethan," she gasped out, her head tossing restlessly to-and-fro upon the bunched-up clothing. "Please."

Satisfied that she was near mindless with longing, he finally raised his head.

"Please what?" he challenged, his voice laced with a passion every bit as intense as her own.

"Ethan."

"Tell me what you want, Lainey," he commanded. When she did not immediately comply, he bent to his highly enjoyable task once more.

"Ethan," she implored, her whole body on fire. "Damn you! I—I want you to—to *please!*"

That was good enough. His eyes gleaming with triumph, he wasted little time in granting them both release. He positioned himself between her quivering thighs, lifted her hips, and slid easily within her moist, velvety warmth. The final blending of their bodies was wild and sweet, and, in truth, a little bit of heaven on earth.

Afterward, he swept her up in his arms once more and waded back into the creek. She was feeling far too contented at the moment to resist. This time, however, there was no playful battle to be waged. He lowered his body into the water and held her close for a while, then ducked his head beneath the surface and came back up to press a slow, wet kiss upon her mouth. She moaned softly, entwined her arms about the corded muscles of his neck, and parted her lips beneath the intoxicating possession of his. . . .

When they finally emerged from the water again, Ethan pulled on his trousers and gathered up the rest of his things. Lainey, on the other hand, donned every stitch of her clothing, save for her stockings and boots.

She scurried barefoot across the yard and into the cabin, feeling a trifle self-conscious now that the fiery enchantment had given way to reality once more.

She was glad that Ethan did not choose to speak of personal matters during supper. He disclosed some of his plans for the ranch, told her of his intention to add on to the cabin in the near future, and said that they would have to transfer her claim to Travis now that she would no longer be homesteading the land.

"I suppose you're right," she agreed, with a faint sigh. "The law is very clear on that matter, isn't it?" It troubled her a bit to realize that the land would no longer be hers, and yet she could not begrudge Travis and Beth the right to it. Still, she thought while her eyes filled with a twinge of sadness, she wouldn't have anything of her own. She had lost her independence forever; Ethan had seen to that. But somehow, that thought didn't distress her nearly as much as she would have expected. "I'll pay a visit to Mr. Calhoun tomorrow," she announced, rising from the table to begin clearing away the dishes.

"We can take care of it when we're in town for the wedding." He stood as well, then surprised her by helping. A slight frown creased his brow when he revealed, "I may have to be gone for a couple of days soon."

"Gone?" She turned to face him with an expression of bewilderment. "What are you talking about?"

"Sutton's asked for my help."

"Sutton. Isn't he the United States Marshal?" she asked, her eyes lighting with recollection. She watched as he nodded and moved across to the fireplace. Night had long since fallen, but the cabin was filled with the warm glow of the fire and the oil lamp.

"He's an old friend," said Ethan. "More than that, really. I used to be one of his deputies." He bent to place more wood in the midst of the crackling, smoke-curling blaze.

"But, why does he need your help?" She stacked the last of the dishes in the washtub.

"Because he'll be riding into the western part of the Territory. The Indians call it 'No Man's Land,' and for a good reason. It's rough country, uncivilized. That's why it's a popular hideout. I've been there more times than I care to remember. Sutton wants me to help him bring in some men who have been smuggling liquor on to the reservations."

"You mean you'll be going after outlaws?" Her eyes widened at the thought.

"That's the general idea," he responded, with a brief, sardonic smile.

"But it will be too dangerous," she protested impulsively. A dull flush crept up to her face when she saw the way his glowed with pleasure at her concern.

"It's no different than what I've faced before." His handsome features looked grim when he confided, "I'm not worried about myself, Lainey. I'm worried about you."

"About me? But why?" She stood near the table, uncertain about whether to join him in front of the fire or simply remain where she was. "I'm not the one who will be riding off into danger," she pointed out, her voice laced with unmistakable reproach.

"If Halloran knows I'm not here, he—"

"You needn't trouble yourself about Mr. Halloran," she insisted. Dismayed to feel telltale color washing over her, she spun about and hurried to take up a bucket. "I'm going to fetch some water."

"You'll stay with Travis and Beth while I'm gone," he decreed quietly.

"I most certainly will not," she disagreed, her eyes flying back to his face. "Why, they will have just gotten married, and I—"

"You'll do as I say."

"I am perfectly capable of looking after myself."

"Damn it, woman! Can't you ever do anything without a fight?" he charged, his tone holding both anger and affection.

"If you wanted a wife who would meekly follow your bidding, then you should have married someone else," she retorted, with considerable feeling.

"I didn't want someone else. I wanted you." His mouth curved into a slow, endearingly crooked smile as he folded his arms across his chest and teased softly, "You'll probably drive me to an early grave. But it will be one hell of a life until then."

His gaze locked with hers. She held her breath, certain that he meant to storm across the room and sweep her into his arms again. But he did no such thing. He merely strode forward, took the bucket from her, and announced that he would be back with the water soon.

Lainey stared after him for several long moments before releasing a sigh and crossing to her trunk. She opened the lid and searched for a nightgown among the closely packed contents. Musing in half annoyance, half excitement that her husband would probably remove it anyway, she nevertheless hurried to change.

Once she had donned the high-necked, white cambric nightgown, she belted a soft pink robe on over it and withdrew a book from the trunk. It was a beautiful, leather-bound volume of Shakespeare's sonnets. She opened it and began leafing through its thick white pages while crossing to sink down upon the bench in front of the fire.

Ethan returned with the bucket of water a short time later. He emptied the majority of it into the washtub, then poured the rest into the pitcher. His gaze traveled to his bride, and he smiled to himself at the sight of her sitting all prim and proper with her nose in a book. He began unbuttoning the clean, blue cotton shirt he had put on before supper.

"Maybe we can see about that cookstove when we're in town tomorrow. And a bed."

"What?" she murmured, drawing her attention from the stirring, romantic prose. She had been aware of him all along, of course, but hadn't wanted to give him the satisfaction of knowing that she could think of little else whenever he was around.

"A cookstove and a bed," he repeated, with only the merest suggestion of a smile. Peeling off the shirt, he sat down in her grandfather's chair and made short work of his boots and socks. She swallowed hard and tried to ignore the wild pounding of her heart.

"We could certainly use the stove. And it would be much more comfortable if we had two beds instead of one," she told him in a calm voice that belied the renewed turmoil within her.

"Not two beds," he corrected, pausing to blow out the lamp before moving slowly toward her. "One. The biggest I can find."

"Oh." Blushing, she shifted her gaze back to the book.

"Beth told Travis your father was a doctor." He dropped down on one knee before the fire and used the iron poker to rearrange the burning logs. A shower of sparks flew up the chimney.

"Yes, he was." She could not prevent her eyes from straying to his naked, powerfully muscled upper torso. "He was a very special man, and I miss him. It was hard on him when Beth . . . when Anna was born, but his love never wavered."

Oddly enough, it felt natural to be alone with him in front of the fire like this. She had even forgotten her embarrassment over what had happened beside the creek—though she certainly hadn't forgotten the pleasure of it.

"What about *your* parents?" she asked.

"They still live on the ranch where I was born." His gaze darkened for a moment. "I left a long time ago."

"Why did you leave?"

"I left because my father and I are too much alike. And because no man can make his mark living in his father's shadow." He drew himself upright again. "That's why Travis and I ended up here instead of back home in Texas."

"Perhaps I'll meet them someday," she said, without realizing the significance of her words. She commented archly in the next instant, "If you and your father really are alike, I'm sure your poor mother's life must have been an absolute misery."

"She knew how to keep us in line," he replied, with a low chuckle. "She'll be overjoyed to hear that I've finally taken a wife. Since I'm the oldest, I was expected to provide them with grandchildren by now."

"Have you ... any other brothers or sisters?" she queried, finding it increasingly difficult to think straight when he was standing so close and talking about children. It was the second time that day that the subject had come up; she couldn't help but marvel at the coincidence.

"I have. Two brothers, both not yet twenty. And a sister who's determined to keep chasing away the men my father brings home for her to marry."

"If that is true, then I'm sure I would like her very much. And it may well be that what she considers important in a husband is at odds with what your father wants for her." She wondered what her own father would have thought of Ethan. "Besides, I think every woman should have the freedom to make that choice for herself."

"Like you did?" he challenged softly.

"I—I didn't choose at all. *You* did," she asserted, lifting the book again.

"When are you going to face the truth?"

"I haven't the faintest idea what you're talking about," she denied coolly. She suffered a sharp intake of breath when, in a calm but authoritative manner, he took the book from her, placed it on the bench, and drew her to her feet in front of him.

"I love you, Lainey. And you love me."

"I do not."

"Yes, you do. And someday you're going to realize just how much. But until then," he said, his hands moving to the belt of her robe, "I'll have to settle for what you *are* willing to give."

"No." Coloring warmly, she tried to stop him. "Christopher Columbus, it cannot have been more than two hours since we—"

"You've got a lot to learn about men," he remarked, his tone laced with that combination of passion and humor she always found irresistible.

"And I suppose you think you're the one to teach me?" she tossed back defiantly.

"You'd better not have anyone else in mind to do it."

He slipped the robe from her shoulders and bent to lift her in his arms. Surprised that he had left her the nightgown, she did not struggle as he carried her to the bed. She knew it would do no good.

Lowering her to the mattress, he straightened again and began unfastening his trousers. She did not turn away, but watched while the soft golden firelight played across his magnificent, naked body. He joined her in the bed, pulling her close and claiming her lips in a gentle kiss that quickly deepened.

One thing led to another as nature took its highly agreeable course. Just as she had expected, Lainey soon found herself as naked as her husband. After he had kissed and caressed and tasted and stroked—and she had been every bit as willing a participant as he had hoped—he suddenly rolled to his back so that she was atop him.

She blushed at the unfamiliar position, but desire reigned supreme once more when he lifted her hips and brought her down upon his erect manhood. A cry of pleasure broke from her lips, and she grasped at his shoulders for support while meeting his thrusts. His hands moved back to her breasts. She rode atop him, her long hair cascading riotously about her and sweeping down across his broad, lightly matted chest. The fulfillment that soon followed was mutual and complete, tossing them both skyward before allowing them to drift slowly back to earth.

In the sweet afterglow of their passion, they lay entwined in the narrow bunk and listened to the sounds of the night. The fire was fast dying out, and the air inside the cabin was pleasantly cool. Clouds obscured the moon; their gathering thickness lent credence to Ethan's prediction of rain before morning.

Laincy's eyes swept closed as her head rested upon Ethan's chest. His left arm was draped possessively across her waist, while his right was bent beneath his head. She couldn't summon the energy to be angry with herself, or with him. And in truth, she reflected with a long, thoroughly complacent sigh, she was tired of fighting against something that was so wonderful.

I love you. Her heart stirred once more as his words echoed in her mind. Maybe it was true after all, she told herself, recalling with vivid clarity the way he always seemed to concentrate on her pleasure more than his own. She frowned and opened her eyes at a sudden thought.

"Ethan?"

"Yes?" His own eyes glowed warmly at hearing his name on her lips again. She said it like no one else.

"Have you—have you known a good many women?" she asked hesitantly.

"That depends on what you mean by 'know,' " he answered, his tone brimming with wry amusement. His hand moved down to trail lightly over the alluring curve of her hip.

"I think you know exactly what I mean."

"I'm thirty years old, Lainey."

"And?"

"And I've done my fair share of living," he confessed.

"I suspected as much," she muttered, tensing. How the devil *else* would he know so much about what they had just done? Her eyes flashed in spite of her body's contentment. Jealously shot through her, though she was still reluctant to acknowledge it.

"I've never been in love with anyone before," he declared solemnly. "Nothing else matters."

"I suppose you would hold the same opinion if I were the one who had done all the 'living'?" she challenged tartly, raising up on one elbow to fix him with a narrow look.

"Probably not," he conceded, with a soft, mellow laugh. He pulled her back down and dropped a kiss on the top of her head. "I can see right now you're going to make damned sure I walk the straight and narrow, Mrs. Holt."

"Only if you wish for me to do the same," she parried, settling her curves into a perfect fit with his virile hardness.

"You've nothing to worry about on my part. But if I ever catch you so much as looking at another man—" he started to threaten.

"For heaven's sake, Ethan Holt, I have no desire to contend with anyone else." That was certainly true. In fact, she couldn't imagine lying in any other arms but his.

"I'm glad to hear it."

"And even if I *did* decide to seek a divorce, I can assure you that—"

"By damn, you little wildcat! You're heading onto dangerous ground," he warned.

"There is no other kind where you are concerned."

Feeling a perverse satisfaction for the fact that she had managed to rile him, she sighed and closed her eyes once more.

The night deepened. They soon drifted off to sleep, their hearts beating as one and their breaths mingling in the cool darkness of the cabin. . . .

Chapter 15

Lainey rode homeward beneath a rain-washed sky, her deep blue gaze shining with emotion as she reflected that Beth was going to be the loveliest bride Oklahoma had ever seen. They had finished the alterations on the wedding dress, and now all that remained was to wait for the beautiful, late spring morning to edge into afternoon.

Ethan had told her that he and Travis would each be driving a wagon into town, for the purpose of hauling cookstoves and beds and whatever else they took it in mind to buy. She smiled at the memory of his promise to install a water pump and sink inside the cabin; they would eventually have a real bathroom as well.

It had never before occurred to her to wonder about his financial situation. She could only suppose that he had managed to save a portion of his earnings during his many years as a lawman. Indeed, it wasn't at all difficult to envision his former quarters—some tiny, sparsely furnished room where he did nothing more than sleep. Her heart twisted at the thought of him enduring such a lonely existence. But whatever his past had been, she had little doubt that he would make the ranch a success. And she would be at his side every step of the way.

The prospect filled her with more pleasure than she would have thought possible.

Arriving back at the ranch, she hurried inside, her

eyes alight with determination. The cabin was finally going to get the thorough cleaning it needed. To her way of thinking, it had gone without a woman's touch long enough. And it was her home now. She had a perfect right to bring order to the masculine chaos.

Tying on her apron, she proceeded to sweep and scrub and scour for the next hour, then finally set about unpacking the barrels and crates, which had been begging for her attention since the first night Ethan had brought her here. She found herself thoroughly intrigued by her husband's personal belongings, which she took the time to examine after having stacked the supplies neatly in one corner of the room.

Ethan found her sitting in the middle of the floor, with her legs tucked beneath her soap-splattered skirts, her beautiful face smudged with soot, and her wide, luminous gaze fastened on the old photograph in her hands.

"You've made a few changes."

She started guiltily at the sound of his voice. Jerking her head about, she colored a bit while her eyes flew to his face. He stood framed in the open doorway, his own gaze brimming with amusement.

"I—I didn't hear you come in," she stammered. She hastily climbed to her feet and raised her head in a proud, defensive gesture. "And it was high time someone made changes."

"You'll get no argument from me." Smiling, he negligently tugged the hat from his head and told her, "Travis and I will be wanting our dinner soon, if you don't mind. We've got a lot more to do before this afternoon."

"So you *did* marry me just to get yourself a cook," she accused saucily.

"Among other things." He strode forward and unexpectedly caught her about the waist. "Maybe we should forget about dinner and concentrate on those other things."

"Ethan Holt, you have a wicked mind," she scolded, though with an embarrassing lack of conviction. "What on earth would Travis think if we—?"

"Travis can think whatever he damned well pleases." He swept her even closer and applied the sweet, masterful pressure of his lips to her neck for a moment, then reluctantly conceded, "But I'm afraid it will have to wait." He gave her bottom a hearty, familiar swat before letting her go. "Get to it, woman. I'll be back for my dinner in half an hour."

"And what if I choose *not* to get to it?" she challenged, only half in jest.

"Then I'll send Travis off to visit Beth and we'll go for a swim."

She blushed fierily and narrowed her eyes at the broad, retreating target of his back. He closed the door behind him, leaving her to mutter an unladylike oath before whirling to fetch the required foodstuffs from the corner.

It was nearly four o'clock in the afternoon by the time they drove the wagon over to meet up with Travis, Beth, and Anna. The five of them set out for town, with Anna riding between her aunt and new uncle. Travis and Beth followed a short distance behind in the other wagon. The rains, which had come in the night and disappeared with the dawn, had settled the dust. The air smelled wonderfully fresh, the late springtime breeze scented with the wildflowers that would soon give way beneath the summer's heat.

"I think we should take Anna home with us for tonight," Lainey remarked, tightening her arm about the little girl's shoulders.

"Why?" asked Ethan. He handled the reins expertly as the wheels rolled across the damp earth.

"For the obvious reason, of course." She met his

warm gaze briefly, then looked away as faint color stained her cheeks. "Beth and Travis should be able to spend their wedding night alone."

"All right," he surprised her by agreeing.

"You mean you—you won't mind?" She raised her eyes to his face again, only to feel herself melting inside at the tender, loving humor she glimpsed within his magnificent turquoise gaze.

"We have the rest of our lives together, Lainey. I think we can spare a night." A soft smile touched his lips when he added, "But only one."

"I suppose they will have to accustom themselves to—to being together with Anna sleeping nearby."

"They will. At least until we can add on another room. It might interest you to know, Mrs. Holt, that I intend to enlarge our own cabin well before we're faced with a similar dilemma."

There it was again—*children*. She glanced down at her abdomen. If she wasn't yet carrying Ethan Holt's child, she mused with an inward sigh, it certainly wasn't for lack of the necessary "attentions." But how could she think about that when her feelings for him were still so unsettled?

She knew she didn't dislike him any longer. She wasn't sure she ever had. But was she in love with him as he had so confidently insisted? The possibility seemed far less remote than it had a few short days ago . . .

Upon reaching Guthrie, they headed down the main street toward the land office. Lainey regretted the fact that her sister would have to be married in the same small room where her own wedding had taken place, but she knew Beth was far too much in love with Travis to bemoan the lack of all the usual things most brides long for. At least Beth was wearing their mother's dress; seeing her sister in it brought tears to her eyes.

The ceremony was every bit as brief and unembellished as the other one had been—"short and sweet," Travis called it. Afterward, he pulled his new wife into his arms and kissed her until they were both praying for sundown to hurry. Lainey's eyes strayed toward Ethan, who was holding Anna on the other side of Travis. His gaze burned across into hers while his mouth curved into what she could have sworn was a triumphant smile. Another Holt brother had claimed another Prescott sister.

When Travis released her, Beth was glowing with happiness. She turned to embrace her sister.

"Oh, Lainey. I can't believe this is happening," she murmured breathlessly.

"I love you, Beth," Lainey whispered back. "And if you ever need me, you've only to let me know."

"I love you, too."

They drew apart, smiled at each other, and joined their tall, handsome husbands.

The newlyweds took their leave soon thereafter, driving away with a new iron bedstead and feather mattress in the back of their wagon. Beth had been reluctant to part with Anna. Lainey had assured her that they would return the little girl the next morning—but not too early.

Still holding Anna securely, Ethan took Lainey's arm and escorted her down the street to see about their own purchases. In no time at all, the wagon was fully loaded with a variety of furniture and supplies.

"I thought we were going to speak to Mr. Calhoun about the claim," Lainey reminded her husband immediately after he had lifted her up to the wagon seat again. He hoisted the sleepy toddler up as well. She cradled Anna in her lap and frowned at him in bemusement when he made no move to join them.

"You wait here," he instructed. "I'll go see Calhoun."

"But why—?"

"I need to have a word with Sutton, too."

"How do you know he is in town?" she asked. She

felt a sudden, sharp twinge of uneasiness when she recalled what he had told her about himself and the marshal.

"I don't. But it won't take long to find out." He gave her a brief, reassuring smile and tugged the front brim of his hat lower. "Just stay in the wagon. I'll be back soon."

She watched as he turned and strode away. Her eyes made a quick, encompassing sweep of the area. The wagon was parked in front of one of the town's several mercantiles. The building that housed it was still under construction, though the ground floor had been completed ahead of schedule. Guthrie was literally rising like a rough-hewn paradise in the midst of the wilderness, thought Lainey, smiling to herself at the bustling sights and sounds about her. Many of the initial boomers had moved on—either forced out by rival claimants or simply deciding to seek their fortunes elsewhere—but those who remained were finally bringing some semblance of order to the town.

"I was wondering when I'd see you again," a familiar voice spoke behind her.

Her throat constricted with dread at the sound of it. She instinctively drew the now sleeping Anna closer while Neil Halloran sauntered forward to confront her with a predatory smile on his face. He made no effort to disguise his lust as his gaze crawled hotly over her.

"Well, Mrs. Holt. When are you planning to return to the Palace?"

"I will not be returning at all, Mr. Halloran," she informed him in a furious undertone. Her eyes blazed vengefully across at him. "After what you subjected me to the last time, I could never—"

"Never is a long time." His smile faded. "We made a deal, remember?"

"The only thing I remember is your despicable behavior toward me." Worried that Ethan would return and find them talking, she demanded coldly, "Now please, go away."

"It doesn't have to be like that between us, Lainey," he said, edging closer. "With a little encouragement, I can be kind. And generous as well. I can give you a lot more than Ethan Holt can."

"Have you no principles at all? I am another man's wife," she reminded him. "I am no longer employed by you, Mr. Halloran, and if you ever—"

"Throw in with me, and what's mine is yours," he persisted, his swarthy features wearing a dangerously intense expression now.

Oblivious to the child sleeping in her lap, he lifted a hand to her arm. She felt sickened by the contact and would have jerked free, but did not want to startle Anna.

"Remove your hand at once, Mr. Halloran, or I will summon the authorities," she warned in a low, simmering tone.

"Someday, Lainey—and that day's coming sooner than you think—you're going to look back and wish you'd taken me up on my offer while you had the chance."

With that menacing prophecy, he finally lowered his hand and smiled again. The smile did not quite reach his eyes.

"You'll be back at the Palace soon. And when you do come back, it will be on *my* terms, not yours."

"Save your threats for someone else, Mr. Halloran," she responded, with a great deal more bravado than she actually felt.

His only response was to give a quiet, derisive chuckle. With a nod in her direction, he continued on his way down the street.

Lainey released a long, ragged sigh once he had gone. How could she ever have been so naive as to believe he possessed any notions of decency or honor?

Filled with loathing at the memory of his words as well as his touch, she gave silent thanks for the fact that Ethan had not witnessed the horrible little scene.

Ethan. Though she longed to tell him, to rest securely within the protection she knew he could offer her, she told herself it would only make matters worse. Halloran still wanted her. That much was painfully obvious. But if she confided in Ethan, the results might very well prove to be disastrous. No, she couldn't tell him. She could only avoid Neil Halloran and hope that, eventually, he would realize the futility of his desires.

"Calhoun sends his regards," Ethan relayed when he returned a short time later. He took his place on the seat beside her, cast an indulgent glance down at the angelic-faced child in her lap, and gathered up the reins. "He said he'll take care of the transfer right away. And it looks like his advice was sound after all—the other claims have been dropped."

"Oh, Ethan, that's wonderful," she exclaimed, her recent encounter with Halloran momentarily forgotten. "I'm so glad Travis and Beth won't have to worry about that. Did you find Marshal Sutton?"

"I did." He snapped the reins lightly together, the simple command prompting the team of horses to start forward.

"What did he say? Does he still require your help?" More than ever, the thought of him riding off into danger made her stomach tighten into knots. Neil Halloran's image suddenly rose in her mind again; she remembered Ethan's concern that the gambler might cause trouble for her in his absence. Until now, she had been inclined to dismiss his concern. She shuddered and dropped her gaze toward Anna.

"It will be a few days yet." He smiled briefly before telling her, "I got word that the cattle will be here tomorrow. Travis and I will have our hands full with the branding and marking, not to mention getting the fences done. In other words, Mrs. Holt, you may not see a lot of me for a while."

"Couldn't I help?" she offered, determinedly pushing all thoughts of Neil Halloran aside.

"Do you know anything about cattle?" he asked, another smile tugging at his lips.

"No, but I'm sure I could learn quickly. I've become a decent horsewoman, in case you haven't noticed. And besides," she admitted, with a sigh, "I have never been content to remain indoors for long. Beth was always the more domestic one. I did my share of the household chores, of course, but I became unbearably restless if I couldn't escape outside at some point during the day."

"Herding cattle is hard work, Lainey," he cautioned. "And branding is even harder."

"I have never been afraid of hard work," she declared proudly. Her eyes kindled with wholly feminine reproach when she charged, "Why is it that men think they are the only ones capable of physical labor? For heaven's sake, women work every bit as hard, sometimes even harder, taking care of a house, and raising children, and cooking and cleaning—"

"I'm convinced," he cut her off, his gaze full of amusement. "You've got the job."

"What job?"

"Starting tomorrow, you're going to start learning more than you ever wanted to know about raising cattle. Just don't expect to learn it all in one day."

"Why not? I happen to be a very good student."

"So I've noticed," he murmured, his eyes splendidly aglow as they traveled over her with bold, loving significance. "And I've no doubt that you'll be able to teach me a thing or two as well."

She grew warm and looked away again, her gaze drifting toward the horizon. The sun was already beginning to set, and she told herself she'd have to waken

Anna soon or the child would have difficulty sleeping that night.

Once they had arrived at the ranch, Lainey hurried inside with Anna to see about supper while Ethan began unloading the wagon. The cookstove would have to wait until Travis rode over to help the next morning, but he was able to lift the bed without any real difficulty. He carried the various pieces of the wooden four-poster inside, quickly assembled it, and set the thick feather mattress into place. After that, he brought in the supplies, then paused for a moment before returning outside to unhitch the team.

"It's . . . very large, isn't it?" Lainey remarked while surveying the new bed with him. Her face was becomingly flushed as she watched an ever-determined Anna trying to scramble on top of the mattress.

"Not so large that I can't find you," promised Ethan. He smiled and took himself back outside.

Lainey rescued Anna, placing her on the floor nearby with a collection of spoons and pots. The little girl took delight in banging the metal objects together, a very noisy undertaking to be sure, but at least she was safely occupied while her aunt finished preparing the meal.

Night was fast approaching when the three of them sat down to supper. Anna kept the two adults well-entertained, ate heartily, and promptly fell asleep a short time later after Lainey had tucked her beneath the covers of the bunk. Ethan had positioned the small bed between the larger one and the wall, so that they would not have to worry about the baby tumbling to the floor in the middle of the night.

"I'm going to check on the horses," he announced once they had finished clearing the table. Heading for the doorway, he suggested, "Why don't you put on some more coffee? I won't be long."

"Very well," Lainey consented agreeably. Her eyes sparkled when she realized that, only a short time ago, she probably would have told him in no uncertain terms that he could make his own coffee. It seemed that a startling transformation had taken place, she mused with an inward smile. And as she had discovered, Ethan Holt could be very persuasive when it came to getting his own way. *Very.*

Her skirts rustled softly as she crossed back to the fireplace. She reached for the coffeepot, her fingers curling about the cooled handle.

Suddenly the unmistakable report of a gunshot rent the stillness of the late evening air.

Lainey gasped sharply at the sound of it. Dropping the coffeepot back to the hearth, she whirled about, her eyes flying wide before filling with horror. *Ethan.*

"Dear God," she whispered. Sparing a quick glance to make certain that Anna slept on, she gathered up her skirts and raced outside. She did not pause to consider her own safety; her one thought was of Ethan.

She came to an abrupt halt in front of the cabin, her anxious gaze sweeping the yard before she hurried on toward the barn. Without warning, she found herself grabbed and flung roughly to the ground.

"What the hell do you think you're doing?" Ethan charged in a harsh, furious whisper, placing his body protectively over hers.

"Ethan?" she whispered back. Her whole body flooded with joy as realization dawned. "Oh, Ethan. I—I thought something had happened to you!" Lying on her stomach beneath him, she tried to rise, but he pushed her head back down to the grassy earth beside the barn.

"Keep still, damn it!" He silently cursed himself for leaving the cabin without a gun. His smoldering gaze narrowed as it traveled vigilantly about the yard and the surrounding hills. He had heard no hoofbeats, which led him to believe that whoever had taken a shot at him had done so from a distance. "Someone's decided to use me for target practice," he told Lainey, his low tone edged with sarcasm.

"Why would—?" she started to ask, her heart pounding in fear.

"Stay here," he commanded tersely.

"Where are you going?"

"To fetch my rifle." He pulled himself slowly up from the ground, his eyes constantly scanning the area. It was almost dark now, but the light from the cabin streamed forth from the windows and the open doorway to illuminate the yard.

"But you can't go," gasped Lainey, raising her head again. "What if they should decide to shoot at you again?" The thought brought with it an overwhelming rush of panic.

"I'll have to take that chance. I'm not about to let us get caught out here without protection." There was always the possibility that the unknown marksman would move in closer. He didn't think that would happen, but he had always made it a point to be cautious whenever he could. Furious with himself for getting careless about the gun, he muttered a curse underneath his breath and resolutely ignored the burning pain in his arm. Rage, white-hot and vengeful, shot through him when he thought about Lainey and the baby in danger. "Just don't move," he cautioned once more.

She offered no further argument, but instead nodded mutely. Holding her breath, she watched in heart-stopping apprehension while he made a run for the cabin.

Miraculously, no other shots rang out to interrupt his flight. He disappeared inside the cabin, only to emerge a moment later with the rifle in his hands. By then, however, he sensed that the gunman had fled. He strode back to where Lainey still lay beside the barn. As soon as he had pulled her to her feet and assured her that the danger had passed, she flung her arms about his neck.

"Thank God you're all right," she exclaimed tremulously. Pale and shaken, she was grateful for the support of his arm about her waist. "When I heard the gunshot, I thought—" She broke off and shuddered, closing her eyes.

"Let's get inside," he directed quietly. Still watchful, he led her back across the yard and up the steps.

"Why, you've been hurt," she announced once they were inside the cabin. Her gaze filled with both horror and compassion as she looked to where the left sleeve of his shirt was stained with blood. He threw the bolt and turned back to her with a faint smile of irony playing about his lips.

"His aim wasn't as bad as I'd hoped."

"You might have been killed!" The color drained from her face at the thought, but she composed herself and hastened across the cabin to fetch bandages and an antiseptic. "Sit down and I'll—"

"It's nothing more than a scratch, Lainey," he protested casually.

"Perhaps not, but it can still become infected without the proper attention," she insisted. She was satisfied when he moved to take a seat on the bench in front of the fireplace. Hurrying forward with the medical bag that had belonged to her father, she opened it and took out the bottle of iodine. "This may sting a bit," she warned, carefully rolling up his sleeve to expose the wound.

"I guess I should be glad I'm married to a doctor's daughter," he remarked, his eyes twinkling with wry amusement once more. "It might come in handy if this starts happening on a regular basis."

"How can you joke about something like that?" she scolded. She carefully applied the antiseptic, and was surprised when he didn't even wince. Frowning down at him, she withdrew a roll of bandages and began deftly winding the thin cotton about his arm. "Do you have any idea at all who might have shot at you?"

"I've made a lot of enemies through the years," he confided. Then he added, "Whoever it was, he wasn't much of a shot. Either that, or he never intended to kill me at all."

"Then why would he do it?" She tied off the bandage and sank down on the bench beside him. Having already breathed a sigh of relief to see that Anna had once again slept through all the excitement, she transferred her bright gaze to the dwindling flames. Her hands were shaking again, and she folded them in her lap while Ethan stood to take a stance before the fireplace.

"It may have been a warning," he told her, his features suddenly turning grim.

"A warning?" she echoed in bewilderment. "Against what?"

"Riding with Sutton, maybe. Or something else," he finished evasively. He turned his head to fix her with a steady, penetrating look. "Did Halloran ever say anything to you about his business?"

"His business? Why, no. He—he told me that there would be gambling at the Palace, but he said nothing else." She was dismayed to feel guilty color rising to her face. Hastily averting her gaze from the intensity of his, she murmured, "I never talked with Mr. Halloran very much."

"Did something happen between the two of you?" he demanded in growing suspicion. "Damn it, Lainey! Did he ever touch you?"

"Of course not," she lied, still desperately hoping to conceal the truth from him. "It's simply that I dislike him, and I . . . well, I am in truth glad that I no longer have to associate with him. You were right about him after all," she finished in a small voice.

"Are you sure there's nothing else?" His hands closed

gently about her arms, compelling her to look up at him again. "I know what he's capable of. Especially where women are concerned. And if I had reason to suspect that he had dared to try anything with you—"

He left the sentence unfinished, which made it sound all the more ominous to Lainey's ears. She swallowed hard and shook her head.

"No, Ethan. You needn't worry about him. He was perhaps a bit too attentive at times, but I did not hesitate to let him know that I would not welcome his advances."

"I'm glad to hear it. Because he's dangerous. I know I've told you that before, but I don't think you were of a mind to listen to me then." He released her arms and turned back to the fire.

"Do you think Halloran was the one who tried to kill you?" she asked, filling with dread again. The man had said he would like nothing more than to comfort her when she was a widow . . . Dear God, what was she going to do?

"No. He may have had a hand in it, but he's never been one to do his own killing. He's much too smart for that." His eyes glinted dully while his thoughts flew back to the two men who had come looking for him at Lainey's claim right after the run. They had once worked for Halloran.

"Why would he want to have you killed?" She was afraid she already knew the answer. But surely, she argued with herself, the gambler wouldn't arrange Ethan's death just because of his lust for her. There had to be more to it than that. There had to be!

"I'm not saying he does. But I saw the way he looked at you, Lainey." His features tensed at the memory. "Even if he hasn't made a move yet, there's no denying the fact that he wants you. And he still thinks he's got a score to settle with me. More than one, probably."

Feeling sick inside, she drew herself up from the

bench and lifted a hand to his uninjured arm. Her sapphire gaze was visibly troubled when it met and locked with his.

"Do you really think this will happen again?" she asked, a telltale catch in her voice.

"No," he reassured her. He placed his hand over hers. "But I can't spend my whole life looking over my shoulder. I learned a long time ago that if you go searching for trouble, you'll find it. Not that I don't intend to be more careful in the future," he added, still furious with himself for having left the cabin without his gun. He slipped his arm about her waist and pulled her close, then scowled reproachfully down at her. "By damn, you little fool! I ought to wring your neck for running out of the cabin like that. What the hell did you think you were doing?"

"I don't know," she admitted. "When I heard the gunshot, I didn't stop to think. I suppose I just acted on impulse." She bristled in the next instant, her eyes sparking with defensive anger. "But for heaven's sake, Ethan Holt. You ought to be glad I cared enough to find out whether you were alive or dead!"

"Do you care enough?" he challenged softly, his own fury evaporating. He smiled as he watched the rosy color stain her cheeks.

"I—I would never want anything to happen to you, if that's what you mean," she allowed. Her gaze fell beneath the searching warmth of his, and she made a halfhearted attempt to pull away. "Please, it's getting late."

"I'm still very much alive," he pointed out, his arm tightening about her.

"What?" she breathed.

"Don't you think it's time you said it, Lainey?"

"And what is it I am supposed to say?" she countered, feigning bewilderment—but not very convincingly.

"Tell me that you love me," he commanded. His

anger over the fact that she had so recklessly placed herself in danger had been tempered with fierce, undeniable pleasure at the evidence that she did indeed care. He knew he would never forget the way she had expressed gratitude to the Almighty that he had not been killed. "I know you love me. I want to hear you say it."

Lainey stared speechlessly up at him. And then, the truth struck her like a bolt of lightning. He was right. *She loved him.* That was why she had raced from the cabin to find him. And that was why she had been flooded with joy when she had discovered him to be all right. Dear God, she loved him!

There was no use in fighting against it any longer. Everything became clear to her at last: her inability to forget him after that first night in the boomers' camp; her instinctive desire to protect him from Neil Halloran; and her passionate response to his lovemaking. She wasn't wicked after all; she was simply a woman in love. Now she understood why she had felt such pain and distress at his apparent willingness to keep their marriage in name only. So many thoughts tumbled about in her mind as her heart and soul took flight together.

She loved him. She was his forever, just as he had claimed. Nothing else mattered anymore.

"Say it, Lainey," he prompted again, his deep voice little more than a whisper.

"I love you," she complied at long last. Her eyes shone softly up into his; she smiled. "It seems you have gotten your way once again, Ethan Holt."

"It's about time." His own heart soared with mingled happiness and triumph. Oblivious to his injury, he wrapped both of his strong arms about her trembling softness and answered her smile with a slow, thoroughly captivating one of his own. "I love you, you golden-haired wildcat. And I'm never going to let you forget it."

"Is that a boast or a threat?" she retorted saucily. Her head still spinning with the wonder of it all, she gasped in delight when his arms tightened about her.

"It's a promise," he assured her. His handsome features grew solemn. "You'll never have cause to regret marrying me, Lainey. God knows, I'm all too human, but I'll do my best to give you the kind of life you deserve."

"All I want is you," she declared in all honesty. She raised a hand to his face and smiled once more, sudden tears glistening in the brilliant blue depths of her gaze. "I love you, Ethan. I suppose I've loved you all along. Like you, it certainly wasn't something I had planned. But I am beginning to think that the plans we make have very little to do with the outcome of our lives."

"I happen to believe it's a combination of free will and Providence," he told her, with another smile. "And nothing would give me more pleasure than to exercise some of that 'free will' right now." He lowered his head toward hers, but she quickly moved her hand to his lips and cast an anxious look toward the child sleeping nearby.

"We can't! Not with Anna—"

"I'm only going to kiss you, Lainey. But come tomorrow, once we're alone again, I'll make up for lost time," he vowed masterfully.

"Do you suppose you'll ever get tired of me?" She sighed, only to color warmly when he smoothed his hands down to her hips and pulled her so close that she could feel the evidence of his arousal.

"Never," he asserted in a splendidly vibrant tone.

He kissed her then, his mouth claiming the sweetness of hers while she swayed against him in unspoken surrender.

Soon, they lay together in the new four-poster, secure in each other's love. There would be plenty of other battles between them, and well they knew it, but they had conquered the most important barrier of all. Pride no longer stood between them. And now that their hearts had been set free, their love would know no bounds.

Lainey pressed her body closer to her husband's warmth and smiled. The smile quickly faded, however, when her hand smoothed up his arm to encounter the bandage. Her gaze clouded at the awful memory of his brush with death, and her heart ached terribly. No matter what he had said, she feared the danger was not past. She loved him. She loved him more than she would ever have thought possible. And she could not bear to live without him . . .

Neil Halloran's face swam before her eyes. She knew then what she had to do.

Chapter 16

Her opportunity came the very next day.

After returning Anna safely to her mother's care, she rode into town alongside Ethan and Travis. She had been preoccupied with other matters, but she had not failed to notice the happiness in Beth's eyes. Travis looked equally contented, leading her to conclude that their marriage would be every bit as successful—and full of passion—as she knew hers and Ethan's would be.

She was relieved that the two men talked about business matters throughout the morning's all too brief journey. They both made an attempt to include her in the discussion, but she merely offered a smile and a noncommittal reply before lapsing into her unpleasant reverie once more.

Still praying that she could manage to get away long enough to visit Neil Halloran—without Ethan's knowledge, of course—she shifted in the saddle and tossed a glance heavenward. She could only hope that she was doing the right thing. But, what choice did she have? Either she told Ethan the truth and risked the consequences, or she took matters into her own hands and tried to reason with Halloran. She'd have to find out if he was indeed responsible for the attempt on her husband's life. And if her suspicions proved to be correct . . . then God help her, she'd have to think of a way to persuade him against any further aggression.

She heaved a disconsolate sigh. The day promised to

be another bright, pleasantly warm one, but she was far too troubled to care. Her spirits sank lower with each passing minute as she pondered what lay ahead. The prospect of coming face-to-face with Neil Halloran again was a dismal one.

Glancing up again, she noticed that she had fallen behind a bit. It was important that Ethan not suspect anything. With a heavy heart, she urged her horse into a swifter pace and caught up with the men.

It was midmorning when they reached Guthrie. Ethan led the way toward the depot. The cattle were being transported by railroad; it was considerably more expensive than relying upon the old-fashioned drive, but it was also faster and subjected the animals to far less wear and tear. Travis had mentioned to Lainey that they had purchased the cattle from a friend in Fort Worth. She thought about Ethan's family once more and vowed to meet them someday—perhaps in the near future, if she could convince Ethan to go. It might help matters if they were to leave Oklahoma for a while . . .

"You can wait inside," Ethan told her as he dismounted in front of the depot and strode around to lift her down as well. "The train probably won't be in before eleven. Travis has some business to take care of elsewhere, and I've got to pay a visit to the city marshal."

"The city marshal?" she echoed, frowning up at him. "Are you going to tell him about last night?"

"We've got several things to talk about," came his evasive reply. He smiled briefly and relented enough to explain, "I've been able to give him a few leads about the claim jumping and other crimes taking place around here. Some of the men responsible are familiar to me."

"Oh, Ethan. I wish you would stop involving yourself in these matters," she pleaded earnestly. "I don't think I could bear it if someone else took it in mind to shoot at you."

"As long as I've got you around to patch me up, I'll be fine," he teased. "Now go on inside. I won't be long."

"I think I'll take a walk first." Striving to keep her tone casual, she forced a smile to her lips and assured him, "I will return in plenty of time to witness the train's arrival."

"Good. Lesson number one will be helping to make sure the cattle are unloaded without a stampede."

"Lesson number one?"

"You're going to start learning how to be a rancher today, remember?" he reminded her. "A rancher's wife, that is." His eyes were alight with loving amusement as he turned away.

She stood and watched while he and Travis headed down the street. Once they had disappeared into the crowd, however, she sprang into action. She gathered up her skirts and hurried toward the Palace, her heart pounding in her ears. An awful combination of guilt and apprehension plagued her as she reached the theater and slipped inside through the double swinging doors.

There were already several customers bending their elbows at the bar, even though it was not yet noon. Lainey came to an abrupt halt just within the doorway and cast her wide, searching gaze anxiously about the room.

"I'm afraid we don't serve ladies, ma'am," the bartender advised her, with a deep frown. He was new to the job, and had no idea that she was the singer everyone kept talking about. "You'll have to—"

"I am looking for Mr. Halloran," she informed him coldly. "Will you please tell me where I may find him?"

"Halloran?" He hesitated for a moment, wondering if she was one of the whiskey-hating females who had been threatening to smash up Guthrie's saloons. She certainly didn't look like the kind who'd take an ax to the place. What the hell, he finally decided, she was pretty enough so that it didn't matter. "Upstairs," he directed, nodding curtly toward the staircase at the far end of the bar.

"Thank you."

Instinctively squaring her shoulders, she sailed across the room and up the stairs. The wooden steps were uncarpeted; there were still a great many details to be seen to before the theater would even begin to approach the degree of elegance Neil Halloran envisioned for it. But business was even better than he had expected. And his other interests were starting to pay out as well.

At the top of the staircase, Lainey discovered a narrow corridor flanked by several doors. None of the doors bore either a number or any other indication of the room's purpose. She frowned to herself as she wavered indecisively for a moment, then decided to try the first door to her right. There was no response to her knock, so she continued to the next door. She was just raising her hand when her former employer emerged from one of the rooms on the other side of the hall.

"I knew you wouldn't be able to stay away," he proclaimed, his hawkish gaze gleaming with mingled desire and triumph at the sight of her. With deceptive nonchalance, he looped his thumbs in the pockets of his satin brocade vest and strolled forward. "What a pleasure it is to see you again, my dear Mrs. Holt." His voice was laced with sarcasm.

"I would like to have a word with you, Mr. Halloran!" she insisted, her own voice quavering a bit in spite of her firm resolve to conceal her emotions. She had chosen to wear one of her most modestly styled gowns, and yet she still felt as though he were undressing her with his eyes.

"Of course." He was all too willing to comply. "Let's step into my office. We'll have some privacy there."

He led the way back down the hallway, stopping in front of the last door on the left. Lainey held herself proudly erect as she swept past him and into the room. It was all she could do to prevent herself from shuddering at his proximity.

There was no desk inside, but rather a red velvet upholstered sofa, a matching wing chair, and several boxes and crates that had not yet been unpacked. Heavy gold satin draperies already hung at the window, while overhead was a small crystal chandelier. The walls were papered in a gold leaf pattern. An expensive Oriental rug, its rich hues casting a dark, almost oppressive glow about the room, covered the floor.

"Well? What do you think of it?" Halloran queried, with unmistakable pride, as he followed her inside and closed the door. His eyes glinted with satisfaction when he boasted, "This is only the beginning, Lainey. Before I'm through, the Palace is going to be the finest theater in all the West."

"You mean 'saloon,' don't you?" she disputed sharply.

"Call it whatever you like." He smiled again and extended a hand toward the sofa. "Have a seat and tell me what's on your mind."

"I prefer to stand, thank you." Filled with dread at being alone in the same room with him, she wasted little time before getting to the heart of the matter. "I have come to ask you something, Mr. Halloran, and I can only hope you are man enough to admit the truth."

"That depends upon whose 'truth' you want," he parried, with a quiet, scornful chuckle. Folding his arms across his chest, he allowed his gaze to flicker boldly over her before asking, "What is it you want to know?"

"I want to know if you had anything to do with what happened last night."

"I don't know what you're talking about," he denied smoothly.

"Someone tried to kill my husband," she exclaimed, her eyes narrowing at him in visible accusation.

"Tried?"

"He was only injured, thank God. Whoever shot at him was too much of a coward to show his face," she went on to reveal in a low, furious tone. "It occurred just after sundown. But then, I expect you already know that."

"I don't make it a habit to ride across the countryside shooting at people, Lainey," he said, with one mockingly raised eyebrow. "Not even if the people in question are enemies—old or new ones. That isn't my style." His voice was full of derisive amusement, and he had wandered over to examine the contents of one of the boxes as though he didn't think the subject worthy of his full attention.

"And is it your 'style' then, Mr. Halloran, to hire other people to do your dirty work for you?" she demanded. Still uncertain whether he was responsible for what had happened, she pressed on. *"Is it?"*

"Why would I want to kill your husband?"

"Perhaps because of me," she suggested, her eyes blazing wrathfully. "You have certainly made no secret of your—your desire for me. And you did make threats, however subtle, about what would happen if I told Ethan."

"Did I?"

"You know very well you did. I am all too aware of the fact that you and my husband are old acquaintances. You seem to hold him to blame for some of your past troubles, even though he was only fulfilling his duties as an officer of the law. That ill will you bear him, combined with your actions toward me the other night, led me to conclude that you might be involved."

"Since you obviously believe me guilty, what do you propose to do about it?" he startled her by challenging. He looked back to her while a slow, contemptuous smile spread across his darkly attractive features. "I admit nothing, of course, but I'd like to hear what you'd be willing to do to ensure that Ethan Holt remains alive."

"What?" she gasped, a warning bell sounding in her brain. She couldn't tell if he was merely toying with her, or if he was actually serious about making some sort of deal. "I don't understand," she said, shaking her head. "If you deny that you had anything to do with the attempt on his life, then what good will it do to discuss—?"

"I hold a lot of influence here in Guthrie. I could see to it that your husband had some measure of, shall we say, 'protection.' " It was an offer he had no intention of honoring, of course.

"And what would I have to do in return?" asked Lainey, then felt her pulse leap in alarm when she glimpsed the strange light in his eyes.

"Resume your performances here at the Palace."

"I cannot do that," she adamantly protested. "You always seem to forget, Mr. Halloran, that I am a married woman. My husband will never allow me to return."

"Then you'll have to find a way to do it without his knowledge."

"But that's impossible."

"Not if you want it badly enough," he countered. He moved closer, his face taking on a hard look. Before she could prevent it, his hands had shot out to curl about her arms in a forceful, punishing grip. "Did Holt send you here to get information from me?" he demanded ruthlessly, his gaze boring down into the wide, apprehensive depths of hers.

"No. No, he—he doesn't even know I'm here," she gasped out, stunned by his attack.

"How do I know you're telling the truth?"

"You don't," she retorted, indignation overcoming fear. She pushed spiritedly against him, but did not have to struggle for long. He released her in the very next instant, his mouth curving into a faint, humorless smile.

"Strangely enough, I believe you. And you'll have to believe me when I tell you that either you agree to return to the Palace, or face the possibility that your refusal will mean your husband's death."

"But that's blackmail!"

"I prefer to call it a simple matter of business."

"I could go to the authorities, Mr. Halloran," she warned, still desperately hoping to find a way out of the terrible dilemma. Too late, she realized that it had been a mistake to come.

"And what would you tell them?" he responded, unconcerned. "You haven't got any proof, Lainey. It would just be your word against mine, and though it would be ungallant to call a lady a liar, I couldn't allow you to interfere with my plans."

"What plans?"

"I'm going to end up running this town," he vowed smugly. "And there's not a damned thing your husband or any of those other interfering bastards who hide behind their badges can do about it. They tried to stop me before," he recalled, his eyes glittering with hatred at the memory. "But they're not going to stop me this time."

"Dear God, you truly *are* without scruples, aren't you?" she said in dawning horror, her eyes growing very round.

"Scruples are for poor men. And I have every intention of being rich. Very, very rich." He raised his hand toward her again, but dropped it in a gesture of uncertainty. It wasn't at all like him. But then, he had never felt this way about a woman before. He had experienced more than jealousy when he had learned of her marriage—before that, he had actually considered making her *his* wife.

Ethan Holt had changed all that.

"Do we have a deal?" he asked Lainey, his voice cold

and clear now. "Your husband's life for a song. It's appropriate, don't you think?"

"If I should agree, how can I know that you are really able to guarantee his safety?"

"You'll just have to take that chance."

"Just as I'll have to take the chance that you won't try and force your attentions on me again?" she demanded bitterly.

"That's right."

Lainey glared across at him. God help her, what should she do? The man had never once admitted his guilt. He could offer her no real assurances—and there was every likelihood that once she returned to the theater, he would seek to take advantage of the situation. Her common sense told her to leave, to run from the room and forget that the ill-fated meeting between them had ever taken place. But her heart would not allow her to do that. She loved Ethan. She loved him more than she had ever loved anyone. And if it was even remotely possible to keep him from harm by striking a bargain with an evil, rapacious man like Neil Halloran, then she had to do it. *She had to.*

"Very well," she finally acquiesced. "But I won't be able to perform more than once a week. And it will have to be much earlier in the evening, well before nightfall." With summer approaching, the days would be getting longer. She knew Ethan would never allow her to ride alone after dark.

"That's not good enough," Neil told her, a dull flush of anger rising to his face.

"Take it or leave it, Mr. Halloran!" she shot back. Not at all certain how she would manage to get away even once, let alone on a regular basis, she prayed that some other solution would present itself soon. For now, she had no choice but to agree. Neil Halloran had backed her into a corner, and they both knew it. She had to buy herself some time, at least until she could think of a way to keep Ethan safe *and* make sure that she never had to go near the Palace again. "Well?" she prompted, anxious to put an end to the present torment.

"All right. You win." He resisted the impulse to touch her again, consoling himself with the thought that, soon, he'd have her exactly where he wanted her. What started out as a weekly rendezvous would turn into a hell of a lot more than that in the near future, he vowed. And by the time Holt found out, it would be too damned late. "I'll expect you here on Saturday, at seven o'clock. Any earlier than that," he cautioned, anticipating her objections, "and we might as well forget the deal altogether."

"We'll have to take care that my husband does not hear of my performance," she insisted, feeling as if she had just made a pact with the devil himself. "In other words, you will make no mention of my name on the handbills or other advertisements, is that understood?"

"Why should I care if he finds out?" It might fit in better with his plans if Holt *did* come gunning for him, he mused silently. He'd have witnesses that way, witnesses who could attest to the fact that Holt had started the fight. Someone else would finish it, of course. And he'd have to make sure the next man he hired didn't botch the job like that son of a bitch Payton had done last night . . .

"If Ethan finds out about our agreement, Mr. Halloran, I will never be able to come at all," she pointed out. With a composure that belied the painful chaos within her, she turned and lifted a hand to the doorknob. "And if he ever discovers that you touched me," she paused to warn, slicing a narrow, loathful glare at him over her shoulder, "he will kill you."

Wrenching open the door, she finally escaped from the room. Neil Halloran's last, mocking words followed her as she fled back down the corridor.

"I'll be counting the hours until Saturday, Lainey."

A shiver coursed down her spine. She hurried downstairs and out of the theater, feeling perilously lightheaded by the time she had reached the depot once more. Her stomach churned at the memory of what had just transpired, but she fought down a fresh wave of nausea and prayed that Ethan had not yet returned.

She breathed a long sigh of relief when she stepped inside and found no sign of him among the dozen or so people who filled the waiting area. Her troubled gaze shifted to the clock on the wall above the ticket window. The train was not due to arrive for another twenty minutes yet.

Her legs suddenly felt weak, and she was dismayed to realize that she was trembling all over. Making her way over to one of the benches, she sank down beside a woman who was singing softly to the baby in her arms. Gazing at the innocent young child, Lainey was reminded of Anna and felt tears start to her eyes. She furiously blinked them back, but her heart twisted when she reflected that men like Neil Halloran would always exist to prey upon those smaller and weaker than themselves. Ethan did not fit into either of those categories, but she certainly did. And her "employer" was taking full advantage of it.

The thought filled her with rage. She had never been one to accept defeat easily, and she wasn't about to start now. Come Saturday, she would sing at the Palace—but she would not meekly allow a repetition of what had happened on the occasion of her last performance. This time, she would not be caught unprepared.

Saturday. She silently repeated the word over and over again, her mind racing to think of some excuse, some reason she could give Ethan so that he would allow her to ride off alone. If she could just make it through that one night, then there was still a chance she'd be able to come up with a better plan before the next Saturday rolled around.

There was always the possibility of going to Travis for help . . . But no, she told herself with another sigh, he would be every bit as hotheaded as his brother. The local marshal might listen to her, but it would be as Halloran had said—her word against his. Even though she was the wife of a former lawman, she'd have to have some kind of proof, some evidence that would incriminate the man.

God help her, she was trapped! She despised Neil Halloran, both for what he was doing to her and for what she still suspected he had tried to do to Ethan, and yet she would have to play along with him for now. . . .

"Lainey?"

She started guiltily. Her eyes flew up to Ethan's face as he stood towering above her. He smiled and drew her to her feet before him.

"What were you thinking about?" he queried.

"I—I was thinking about several things," she stammered weakly. She avoided meeting his eyes, and clasped her hands together in front of her so that he would not see how they were shaking. Facing him again after the meeting with Halloran was proving to be more difficult than she had imagined. "Where is Travis?" she asked, hoping that he would not be able to detect anything of the nervousness she was feeling.

"He isn't back yet," said Ethan. His brows knitted together in a slight frown while his gaze narrowed imperceptibly down at her. "What's wrong, Lainey? Did something happen while—?"

"No," she was almost too quick to deny. She forced a rather wan smile to her lips and finally raised her eyes to his. Deception had never been a particular skill of hers, and yet she prayed to be convincing now. "I'm sorry, Ethan. It's just that I was troubled about last night again. I know you don't want me to worry, but I cannot help it. Did you tell the marshal what happened?"

"I mentioned it," he replied, leading her outside to the platform.

"And is he going to launch an investigation?" she asked hopefully.

"He'll do whatever he thinks best. With all the crimes taking place in and around Guthrie these days, I doubt if it will be his top priority," he told her, with a faint smile of irony. "Let's just forget about it for now."

"How the devil am I supposed to do *that*?" she demanded. Lowering her voice so that the other people waiting on the platform wouldn't hear, she informed him with considerable feeling, "I am not at all accustomed to having my husband shot at."

"Then it's a good thing we didn't meet a few months ago."

"I'm serious, confound it." Her eyes were full of such distress that he was immediately contrite. He slipped a comforting arm about her shoulders.

"I know you are, Lainey. And I'm sorry it had to happen. But it won't do any good to worry. What's done is done. We've got plenty of other things to think about."

"Will you at least ask the marshal to try and find out who's responsible?" she pleaded, her nerves strung so tight she could scarcely breathe.

"He's already promised to do that. I told him to start with Halloran."

"With Halloran?" she gasped, stiffening.

"Sooner or later, Neil Halloran is going to make the one mistake that finally brings him down. And by damn, I hope I'm there to see it happen," he concluded, his deep voice edged with vengeful fury.

Lainey drew in a ragged breath and hastily looked away again. She closed her eyes for a moment, offering up yet another silent, heartfelt prayer that the nightmare would be over soon.

The train pulled into the station a few minutes ahead of schedule, bringing with it more people, stock, building supplies, and merchandise to fit nearly every demand. All would contribute to Guthrie's rapidly spreading reputation as a gold mine of opportunity. Unfortunately, too many of the "opportunists" were the kind who would add to the other, far less agreeable reputation it had earned, the one the town's newly elected—or self-appointed—officials would just as soon forget about.

Travis got back to the depot just in time to help Ethan supervise the unloading of the cattle. The two of them mounted up to herd the frightened animals away from the train and out of town, while Lainey followed their example as best she could. She was glad she had learned to control her horse; it was no easy task to prevent the cattle from straying or breaking into a run as they headed westward across the open prairie. But just as she had claimed, she was a quick learner. They hadn't traveled far before she began to feel more confident, taking the initiative whenever she spied a cow trying to veer off from the others.

There were only a hundred head in all; Ethan had told her that it was a good number to start with. As time went on, he planned to buy more land and enlarge the herd. She vowed to do everything in her power to help him achieve his dream of a big spread.

The journey back to the ranch served to take her mind off her troubles for a while. She rode behind the noisy, slow-moving group of animals, while Ethan and Travis assumed a vigilant position on opposite sides of the herd. They were constantly in motion, their sharp commands adding to the excitement of her first cattle drive. She watched in admiration as the two of them expertly guided their horses to-and-fro. Her heart swelled with love and pride whenever her gaze fastened on her tall, handsome husband. He looked every inch a rancher, and she found herself musing once again that he seemed to have been born to the saddle.

But thoughts of Neil Halloran would not stay away forever. Much later that day, after Travis had gone home and the cattle were penned in the corral on the far side of the barn, Lainey sat drying her newly washed hair before the fire while her gaze drifted toward the window.

Darkness had already begun to cloak the earth. Ethan was still outside. He had told her that he would wash up in the creek and check on the stock while she bathed. It was impossible for her not to worry about him. After all, what if the deal she had made that morning proved useless? What if there was no "protection" to be had?

She wondered how it was possible to feel so happy and so utterly miserable at the same time. Her heart would soar whenever she thought of her husband and the love they shared, but it would plummet to the very depths of despair in the next instant as Halloran's words returned to haunt her.

The door swung open behind her. Rising from the bench, she turned to face Ethan, her troubled gaze softening when it met the deep, affectionate warmth of his.

"We had no visitors tonight," he informed her, with a brief smile, having known that she would worry in spite of all his reassurances. He closed the door and threw the bolt. "Unless something happens to set them off, the cattle shouldn't keep us awake tonight."

She watched as he hung up his hat and unbuckled his holster. His hair was damp, he wore no shirt, and his upper body gleamed bronze in the soft lamplight. Looking at him, she felt a sudden lump rise in her throat. She had never thought she could love anyone the way she loved him. He had truly gained possession of her heart, her body, and even her soul. Dear God, how could she bear it if anything happened to him?

He crossed the room and gently drew her close, his strong arms slipping about her. She wore only her robe, and she felt her whole body quiver when she pressed herself against his virile hardness.

"Lainey, I'm afraid I'll have to go away sooner than I expected," he suddenly revealed, his tone low and level. "As a matter of fact, I have to leave the day after tomorrow."

"The day after tomorrow?" she echoed in dismay. She lifted her head and tilted it back to face him squarely. "But I thought you said it wouldn't be for several days yet!"

"There's been a change of plans. Sutton wants me to meet him elsewhere."

"I don't understand," she exclaimed, shaking her head. "When did you find out about this?"

"Today, when I went to the marshal's office. He gave me the message." His features looked grim, and his eyes were glinting dully when he said, "The timing's not the best, but I have no choice."

No choice, she repeated silently. It was ironic, in a way. Neil Halloran was forcing her to do his bidding, while Marshal Sutton was using less sinister—but equally persuasive—means to get Ethan to do his.

"Why didn't you tell me this before now?" she demanded, her sapphire gaze kindling with a touch of reproach. "You've known about it all day, and yet you're just now—"

"I wanted to wait until we were alone." He reluctantly let her go and moved to the fireplace. "Damn it, Lainey. The last thing I want to do right now is leave you. At least I know you'll be safe with Travis and Beth."

"How long will you be gone?" she asked, her voice little more than a whisper. The prospect of his absence made her heart ache terribly, and she knew it was not simply because she would miss him. He would be in danger. And as if that weren't enough to make her pulse leap in panic, she realized that she would be facing a different kind of threat. Once again, Neil Halloran's face swam before her eyes.

"I don't know," he admitted, with another frown. "Two or three days, maybe more."

"Then you—you won't be here on Saturday."

"No. I doubt if I'll be able to make it back before Monday. It all depends on how far we have to ride before we find the men. And what happens when we do."

"Oh, Ethan. Please don't go," she blurted out, whirling about to fling her arms around his neck. Her wide, luminous gaze was full of a desperate entreaty as she murmured tremulously, "I couldn't go on living if anything happened to you."

"Nothing's going to happen to me," he asserted, touched by her concern and yet suffering his own private hell at the thought of leaving her. A soft, crooked smile played about his lips when he decreed, "You're stuck with me for another fifty or sixty years. You can be damned sure I'll come back in one piece."

"And will you have to go away again?"

"No. I promise you, this will be the last time I ride with Sutton." He pulled her close again, tenderly cradling her head on his shoulder. "Once this is over with, I'll never leave you again," he vowed.

They lapsed into silence for several long moments. Lainey's eyes swept closed as she tightened her arms about his neck. More than anything, she wanted to tell him the truth, to admit her deception and plead with him to find a way to ensure that Halloran's evil plans were thwarted once and for all. But she battled the impulse, calling up the memory of the man's heartless, cold-blooded attitude when he had warned her against refusing his offer.

"I would still rather stay here while you're gone," she declared, finally stirring in Ethan's embrace.

"No," he reiterated firmly. "I've already spoken to

Travis. There's no one I'd trust more to keep you safe. And you know Beth will welcome you with open arms."

"But I don't see—"

"No more arguments," he cut her off. "It's getting late. We'll need to get an early start with the branding tomorrow. And besides, I seem to recall that we've got some lost time to make up for." His magnificent, blue-green gaze smoldered with the promise of passion as it traveled over her upturned countenance.

"Don't you ever think of anything else, Mr. Holt?" she admonished weakly, in truth longing to forget about everything else but their love.

"Not with a wife like you. You'd tempt a saint," he remarked, his voice laced with amusement as well as desire. "And in case you haven't noticed, Mrs. Holt, I'm only flesh and blood."

"I've noticed," she whispered. Her eyes held all the love in her heart, while her lips parted in a silent invitation.

Ethan scooped her up in his arms, pausing only to blow out the lamp before carrying her to the bed. She lay perfectly still and waited while he quickly stripped off the rest of his clothing. He lowered his naked, hard-muscled body to the feather mattress. But when he reached for her, she surprised him by eluding his grasp and pressing him back down.

Without a word, yet with a faint smile that was at once mysterious and seductive, she knelt on the bed beside him and slowly untied the belt of her robe. He watched, his blood turning to liquid fire in his veins as she peeled off the robe and thereby revealed that she wore nothing beneath it. Her beautiful, silken curves were fully exposed to his branding gaze in the soft firelight. His eyes raked hungrily over her naked breasts, then flickered downward to the alluring curve of her hips and the triangle of golden curls at the apex of her thighs before returning to her face.

"I love you, Ethan," she told him, a bit shocked at her own boldness but filled with the sudden, desperate need to show him how much she cared.

"I love you, too," he replied huskily. He tried to pull her close, but she was determined to be the aggressor this time. It was not a role she had ever played before, and she wasn't at all certain she would be able to see it through. Still, she yearned to give him pleasure, to let him know that nothing else mattered but the love they shared. She pushed thoughts of danger and blackmail and deception aside; for the moment, there was only Ethan.

His heart swelled with love while his body literally burned to possess her. Curious to see just how far she would go, he lowered his head to the pillow again and waited for her to make the next move. He knew she was troubled—he told himself it was because of last night's incident and his upcoming trip with Sutton. But, like her, he wanted to forget about everything else for now. They had the rest of the night, and tomorrow night as well, to spend together before he had to leave. And he had no intention of wasting a minute of that time.

Trusting in her womanly instincts, Lainey smoothed a hand up the sinewy length of his arm and leaned down to brush his lips with hers. It was a sweet, tantalizing kiss, but she did not allow it to deepen. Coloring faintly, she straddled his hips and moved her hands to his shoulders. She leaned down again and began to press a series of warm kisses along his neck. Her long hair tumbled freely down about her shoulders, teasing at Ethan's feverish skin, and he inhaled sharply when her full, rose-tipped breasts made contact with his chest. The scent of her was intoxicating. It was all he could do to keep from sweeping her into his arms and kissing her until they both begged for mercy.

His hands came up to close about her waist as she continued her delectable assault. She trailed her lips provocatively downward, across the broad, muscular expanse of his chest, then moved lower still. Her tongue dipped into his navel, and she was satisfied when he suffered another sharp intake of breath.

"Lainey . . ." he murmured gruffly.

"Don't you like it?" she asked innocently.

"You're driving me mad," he warned, with a faint, wry smile.

"Oh." Her eyes sparkled with wholly feminine triumph as she bent over him again. It was her turn to gasp when his hands moved to her breasts, but she was not yet ready to stop exerting her newfound power. She seized his wrists the way he had done to her so many times, urged his hands away from her breasts, and lowered her head purposefully toward the tight cluster of dark curls between the lean hardness of his thighs—and the throbbing instrument of masculine passion that seemed to beckon her onward.

Ethan groaned, his whole body tensing at the first touch of her lips upon him. He tangled his hands within her thick, luxuriant tresses and felt his desire blazing nearly out of control.

"Damn it, woman, *enough!*" he ground out, though not with any anger.

Lainey gasped again when he suddenly pulled her full length atop him, wrapped his arms about her, and then rolled so that she was beneath him. His mouth descended upon hers with such fierce possessiveness that she trembled from head to toe. One of his hands claimed the pleasure of caressing her breasts, while the other sought the delicate, soft pink flesh between her thighs. In no time at all, her desire was blazing every bit as hotly as his own. He plunged into her at last; she could have sworn he touched her very womb.

The fulfillment that met them was fiery and complete, a glorious acceptance of the union God had intended. Afterward, Ethan swept his delightfully emboldened wife close against him and smiled.

"I told you I'd be able to learn a thing or two from you," he teased, his rich, mellow voice sending yet another tremor through her.

"I'm quite sure, Ethan Holt, that there's little you don't already know," she retorted saucily, then grew serious. "I wish you weren't going away."

"I can remember a time not too long ago when you would have been glad to get rid of me for a few days—or even forever."

"Things have changed." She sighed. She smoothed a hand lovingly across his chest. "I never counted on being married at all, much less being married to someone like you."

"I can't imagine you as an old maid," he said, his own hand resting warmly upon the curve of her hip. "But I can't imagine you as another man's wife, either."

"Do you think we'll always love each other as much as we do now?" she murmured.

"No." He smiled again when she raised her head to stare down at him with an expression of wounded surprise. "It will only get better as time goes on."

"No matter what happens?"

"Did you have something particular in mind?" he challenged softly.

"No, I—I just know that things *will* happen, whether we want them to or not." She lay back down, her eyes clouding as she was once again plagued with the uneasiness she had earlier set aside. "You told me once that we cannot truly appreciate pleasure unless we have suffered pain."

"Did I?" Settling her well-loved curves into even closer contact with his hard, lithely muscled warmth, he allowed a brief frown to crease his brow. "I think I also said that it's bad luck to go looking for trouble. I wish you'd stop worrying, Lainey. Nothing's going to happen to me," he assured her once more. Then he commanded at a sudden thought, "You're to stay away from town until I get back."

"But why?" She stiffened, a knot tightening in her stomach as she wondered if she had given him cause to suspect anything.

"I don't want Halloran to know I've gone. I wouldn't put it past him to try something."

"What makes you think that?" she asked, her voice scarcely audible in the firelit darkness of the cabin.

"Instinct. And I've had dealings with him before, remember?" His gaze darkened when he added, "The man doesn't have a conscience, Lainey. Whatever he does, he does to serve his own purposes."

"I'm afraid you're right." Closing her eyes again, she released another long, pent-up sigh. She couldn't allow Neil Halloran to ruin what little time she and Ethan had left together before he rode away into certain danger. No, by heaven, she decided, she wasn't about to give Halloran that victory as well . . .

"You still haven't given me your promise," Ethan reminded her.

"What promise?"

"To stay put at Travis and Beth's while I'm gone."

"What happens if I refuse?" she countered, trying to keep her tone light and playful.

"I mean it, Lainey," he warned grimly. He cupped her chin and forced her to look at him. "I'll tell Travis to keep you under lock and key if I have to."

"That won't be necessary," she replied, her tone edged with indignation. Her eyes flashed up at him. "If you really loved me, you would trust me." She felt a sharp pang of guilt the moment the words were out of her mouth.

"I love you. I trust you, too. It's Halloran I'm worried about. And any other man who might decide to try and take what's mine."

A soft gasp broke from her lips when he suddenly

pulled her all the way atop him. He kissed her, his mouth sweetly ravishing hers while his hands set up another bold, masterful exploration of her supple curves. She did not protest when, several moments later, he rolled over and trailed his lips downward across her body, seeking out every hill and valley while she squirmed and felt her head spinning. Nor did she offer up any objections when he turned her facedown in the bed and paid loving tribute to her backside. But when he urged her up to her hands and knees and knelt behind her, she cast a bemused, passion-laced glance over her shoulder at him.

"Ethan?" she gasped out, dazedly wondering how he was going to take her when he had yet to turn her around. She was so on fire for him that she was almost beyond caring *what* he did, so long as he did it soon.

The wait was mercifully short. In the next instant, Ethan thrust into her from the rear, his manhood sheathing expertly within her feminine passage. She gave a soft cry of pleasure and strained back against him, her hips matching the age-old rhythm of his. His hand sought the secret place between her thighs again. She moaned and lifted her arms, her hands curling about the corded muscles of his neck. The position was altogether new and probably quite wicked, but she was not in the least inclined to put a stop to the exquisite madness.

Swept away on a flood tide of love and desire, and safely ensconced within their own private world, the two of them felt their passions spiraling upward, higher and higher. It wasn't long before the thrilling, unequaled splendor was theirs once more.

Lainey soon fell asleep in her husband's arms, knowing that tomorrow would pass all too quickly ... and that Saturday would come with the same unrelenting swiftness.

Chapter 17

Travis rode over with Beth and Anna just after breakfast, which had followed the dawn by scarcely half an hour so that the two brothers could get an early start with the branding. Lainey was glad for her sister's and niece's company, but she still insisted upon taking an active role in the work. Beth had favored her with a warm, indulgent smile and agreed that their husbands would be grateful for her assistance. She, on the other hand, would content herself with watching Anna and seeing to dinner.

Ethan had already built a fire where the branding irons would be heated, and Travis stood coiling up a length of rope in preparation for the task ahead, when the women approached the corral. Anna darted ahead, only to be caught up in her new father's arms and warned against going too near the fire. She responded with a laugh and an exclamation that was intelligible only to herself, and it was clear from the look on Travis's face that she already had him wound about her tiny finger.

Lainey's attire had earned her crooked smiles from the men, and a surprised, mildly disapproving frown from Beth. It was the first time she had ever dared to wear trousers. They were Ethan's, as was the shirt she had donned. She had found it necessary to roll up the legs of the pants and cinch the waist with a belt, while the shirt, the same one she had borrowed from Ethan the day of the run and for some reason never returned, had also required a great deal of adjustment. Her appearance was undeniably odd, but she knew that she'd be able to move about more freely and therefore be a help instead of a hindrance.

The work began. Throughout the morning, the hapless animals were systematically roped and branded, the CIRCLE H burned into their tough hides. The smell was far from pleasant, and the cattle bawled loudly even though Ethan assured the three worried females that the process was not at all painful.

Lainey did her part by keeping the fire stoked and occasionally helping Travis hold one of the calves. The work kept her mind well occupied, but she still felt as though some terrible cloud were hanging over her head. No matter how hard she tried, she couldn't forget that Ethan would be leaving the next day, nor that she would be singing at the Palace the day after that. Both prospects were dismal, and she realized that she'd never had to deal with such overwhelming turmoil before, at least not since Beth had suffered Jack's betrayal and an entire town's judgment. But even then, she mused disconsolately, her pain had not been as great as her sister's. Now it was her own life that was a maelstrom of fear and uncertainty . . .

By the time noon came, they were ready for the meal that Beth had prepared on the new cookstove. They ate heartily of the fried chicken, boiled potatoes, baked apples, and hot buttered corn bread—and then it was back to the branding. The day wore on quickly; once all the animals were marked, they were released from the corral and herded to a site just west of the ranch where there was plenty of water and thick, fragrant grass.

Each day, until the fencing was completed, the cattle would have to be checked on to make sure they had not wandered too far away. While Ethan was gone, Travis would handle the task himself. Lainey offered to help, but her brother-in-law insisted that she could do more good at home with Beth and Anna. She declared with a sigh of exasperation that he was every bit as domineering as the Holt she had married.

Finally Lainey and Ethan were alone again. She wasted little time in heating water for a bath, while he followed his own daily ritual of heading for the creek. The night ahead promised to be clear and moonlit.

Lainey poured the last of the water into the tub and hurried to strip off her dusty, borrowed clothing. She wound her single long braid of hair upward, pinned it securely, and lowered herself into the tub.

As if on cue, Ethan swung open the door. Lainey shivered as the cool air swept across her nakedness. She blushed, in spite of her resolve not to, and raised her eyes to meet her husband's boldly appreciative gaze while sinking lower into the water's warmth.

"You did just fine today, Mrs. Holt," he pronounced, casting her a brief smile as he closed the door and set his things aside.

"I'm glad my efforts met with your approval." She took up the cake of soap and the sponge. Attempting to keep her tone casual, she asked, "I suppose you've packed everything you'll need?"

"I won't need much." He slowly crossed the room to stand gazing down at her with an inscrutable expression on his face. His eyes, however, were warmly aglow as they roamed over her face, and then dropped to linger on her full, glistening breasts. "I'll have to leave at first light."

"I know." She cursed the tears that suddenly sprang to her own eyes. It was so difficult to behave as though nothing was wrong when, in only a few short hours, he would be riding away and she would be left to agonize over whether or not he would return safely. *And whether or not her deal with Halloran would prove di-*

sastrous. "I—I'll be finished in a moment," she faltered.

"There's no hurry." He bent his tall frame downward, kneeling beside the tub. "Here. I'll do that," he offered in a low, vibrant tone.

He reached for the sponge and smoothed it gently across the silken planes of her back. She shivered, albeit not with cold this time, and gave herself up to his tender, loving ministrations. Her eyes swept closed as his hand dipped below the water's surface, gliding the soapy sponge over the rounded curve of her hips before trailing it back up to her shoulders.

He transferred his attentions to the front side of her body, though he now allowed the sponge to slip from his grasp. She inhaled sharply when his hand caressed her breast. Her eyelids fluttered open, and she felt a delicious warmth stealing over her when she saw that his gaze was brimming with that irresistible combination of amusement and desire she had come to know so well.

"You've got beautiful breasts, Lainey," he murmured huskily, the merest ghost of a smile tugging at his lips.

"And you, confound it, probably have a great deal of experience upon which to base your comparison," she retorted. A small, breathless cry of surprise escaped her when his strong arms suddenly plucked her from the tub. "Ethan! I'm dripping wet!" she protested, though she could not help laughing softly.

"I like you that way."

He carried her off to bed, where they spent the next two hours making love, and trading dreams and memories. Then, unhappily aware that morning would come sooner than either of them wanted, they forced themselves to try and get some rest. Lainey was tired after the long day's work, but it was still quite some time before she managed to drift into a troubled, restless sleep.

She watched Ethan ride away just after dawn the following morning. He had held her close while saying good-bye, and she had clung to him as though she would never let him go. After offering one last final promise to return soon *and* in one piece, he had reluctantly but firmly set her away from him and mounted up.

Heartsick at his departure, Lainey returned inside once he had disappeared from view and flung herself facedown on the bed. The tears she had held back these past two days finally burst free, and she cried like she had not done in years. The storm of weeping did not pass until several minutes later, at which time she dragged herself from the bed and got dressed.

Her eyes swept the cabin one last time before she stepped outside and closed the door behind her. Heading into the barn, she quickly saddled her horse. She knew Beth would be expecting her.

Her spirits still perilously low, she rode away from the ranch. She had packed the things she would need for the next few days into her carpetbag—including her blue silk suit. Since the green velvet gown had suffered what was probably, in retrospect, a well-deserved fate, she would have to wear the suit when she performed tomorrow night. She had no intention of relying upon Neil Halloran for another costume. In fact, she was fervently hoping that she would not have to speak to him at all.

Beth and Anna welcomed her with open arms, just as Ethan had predicted. She spent the remainder of the day in their benevolent company, helping her sister with the household chores and playing outside underneath the trees with the chattering, vivacious Anna. Thoughts of Ethan filled her mind every minute . . .

That night proved to be almost unbearably long. She yearned to be at home in her own bed, with Ethan's arms about her. Her heart called out to him as she lay beside Anna in the narrow bunk. *Please God*, she prayed with every fiber of her being, *watch over him*.

And then, all too soon, Saturday evening arrived.

Lainey had finally thought of what she hoped would be the perfect excuse to go riding off alone so late in the day. She hastily donned the silk suit, pinned her hair into a simple but elegant chignon, and ventured outside to find Beth. Her color was a bit higher than usual, and her eyes were perhaps too bright with determination, but she managed to conceal her nervousness quite admirably as she gathered up her skirts and forced a smile to her lips.

Fortunately Travis was away tending to the herd at the moment. He had said he would not be back until suppertime or perhaps even later. Beth was sitting beside the creek with Anna when Lainey approached them. Her opal gaze widened with surprised bewilderment at the sight of her sister.

"For heaven's sake, Lainey. Why are you dressed like that?"

"I'm going to pay a visit to a friend."

"What friend?"

"Alice Bennett. Or rather, Alice McNeill. I told you I saw her in town last week, remember? She invited me to supper." It was not a complete lie, she consoled herself silently.

"But, why didn't you tell me you were planning to go tonight?" asked Beth, her brows pulling together in a slight frown. She stood and lightly brushed the grass from her skirts. "I'm not at all sure you should go alone."

"Why not? It will only be for a couple of hours. In fact, I should be back before nightfall. And I didn't tell you before now because I knew you would worry. She only lives a few miles away, Beth," Lainey reassured her.

"Maybe so, but I don't think Ethan would approve. After all, he did charge Travis with looking after you—"

"Oh, please. Not you, too," she exclaimed in mock

reproach. "I am a grown woman, not a child, and it's high time your husband and mine realized it." She smiled again and pressed a warm kiss to Beth's cheek. "I'll be fine. If Travis decides to scold you for not locking me in the cabin, you may kindly tell him for me that he'll pay for the offense when I get back." Relieved to glimpse the light of amusement in her sister's eyes, she turned away and moved calmly toward the half-finished barn to saddle her horse.

The ride into town would have been a pleasant one if not for her extreme reluctance to be going at all. She could only hope that the next two hours would pass quickly, and that nothing would occur to delay her return. Just as she had earlier resolved, she would not be caught unprepared if Neil Halloran should decide to try and assault her again—it was to this purpose that she had slipped one of her father's scalpels into her boot. Though she did not possess a truly violent or bloodthirsty nature, she was fully convinced that she could use it if the need arose.

Ethan's face swam before her eyes as she dismounted behind the theater. Guilt and trepidation joined together to make her heart pound wildly within her breast. She headed inside, her legs feeling heavier with each step she took. She gave an inward groan of dismay when she discovered that the one person she had hoped to avoid was waiting for her just within the doorway. Filled with revulsion at the sight of him, she lifted her head to a proud, defiant angle and tried to sweep past him without a word.

"Did you have any trouble getting away, Mrs. Holt?" Neil Halloran challenged derisively, moving to block her path.

"It is nearly seven o'clock, Mr. Halloran. Will you please step aside?" she requested in a low, seething tone.

"Not until you've answered my question."

"It doesn't deserve an answer!" Her eyes blazed venomously up at him. "You knew it was going to be difficult for me to deceive my husband."

"Ah, but not so difficult when he is away from home," the gambler drawled in response.

"Wha—what are you talking about?" she stammered, her pulse leaping in alarm. She watched as his mouth curved into a slow, predatory smile.

"I know he's gone, Lainey. I even know where he's headed."

"But, how—"

"Let's just say I have my sources." His gray eyes darkened with mingled lust and displeasure as they flickered up and down the length of her body. "Why aren't you wearing your costume?"

"I have no desire to attire myself in anything of *your* choosing. Now, if you will excuse me, I have a performance to give," she reminded him coldly.

Her senses were still reeling at the news that he was aware of Ethan's absence. It occurred to her that he might be involved somehow. She cautioned herself against jumping to conclusions, but her present state of mind was ripe for further chaos. Dear God, she thought in growing dread, what if Halloran was actually responsible for the smuggling? He had boasted that he would be running Guthrie someday, and that he would be rich. It wasn't difficult to imagine him using whatever means it took to achieve his goals . . .

"I need to have a word with you in my office afterward," he insisted, his voice drawing her from her increasingly anxious reverie.

"Absolutely not," she was quick to refuse. The prospect of being alone with him flung her emotions into even deeper chaos. She had known for some time that he was unscrupulous, but she was just now realizing how truly evil and menacing he could be. *Oh, Ethan.*

What am I going to do? she implored silently, her heart twisting as his image rose in her mind again.

"May I remind you, my dear Mrs. Holt, that you're not in a position to argue?" offered Neil. He smiled again, his teeth flashing white in his swarthy countenance. "I'll expect you immediately following your performance."

He sauntered away, leaving her to glare after him in helpless fury. She whirled about in the next instant and hurried into the dressing room to smooth down her skirts and tidy her hair, then assumed her usual position to the left of the stage while waiting for her cue to go on. Mr. Bloomfield's portly features broke into a grin when he saw her, but she favored him with nothing more than a curt nod before drawing in a deep, steadying breath and offering up one last prayer for the ordeal to end soon.

The musicians struck up a lively tune to announce her entrance onto the stage. As if in a daze, she moved forward. Her preoccupied gaze swept across the sea of faces before her while the thunder of applause drummed in her ears. She was afraid for a moment that she would be ill, but she squared her shoulders and drew herself rigidly erect.

With a quick glance toward the orchestra, she began to sing. She had never felt less like singing in her whole life, particularly when the mournful words of the ballad reminded her of the danger Ethan was facing. Yet she managed somehow to complete the song, and then another one as well. Her eyes strayed up toward the second floor of the building as she finished. She thought once again of the weapon she had hidden in her boot.

When the performance was over with at last, she did not linger on the stage, but instead gathered up her skirts and brushed past Mr. Bloomfield on her way toward the staircase. One of the more appreciative members of the audience, having imbibed too freely of the illegal whiskey served by the Palace and a number of other "theaters" in town, seized advantage of the opportunity to press her for a few moments of her company. She gasped when he planted himself in her path and swept the hat gallantly, but rather unsteadily, from his head.

"What's your hurry?" he asked, with a lopsided smile. "I'd like to . . . buy you a drink, ma'am," he then offered, his speech slurred. He appeared to be very young, and there was nothing more than simple admiration in his bloodshot eyes.

"Please, you mustn't—" she started to caution, only to be cut off when two burly, coarse-looking men came forward to seize her admirer. She watched in horror as one of them roughly yanked his arms behind his back while the other brought his fist smashing up against the young man's unguarded chin.

"No, don't," she cried, her voice lost in the din of the smoke-filled room. Her protests were futile. The man was hit twice more, then dragged outside, his battered, unconscious body dumped into the street. No one seemed to care; the drinking and laughing and gambling continued almost without interruption.

Shuddering, Lainey turned and headed up the stairs again. She wondered how she had ever allowed herself to become associated with a place like the Palace Theater—and with a man like Neil Halloran. If only she had listened to Ethan in the very beginning. He had warned her, but she had been too proud and stubborn, too damnably foolish to believe him. She was paying for her mistake now. God help her, she was paying dearly.

The upstairs corridor was ablaze with light. Men's voices drifted outward from behind the closed doors of the rooms where the higher stakes games of poker and blackjack were played each night until the early hours of the dawn. It was uncomfortably warm on the second floor, in spite of the open windows, and the air was choked with the smell of cigars and unwashed bodies. The music and laughter from below added to the overall feeling of depravity.

Fervently wishing she were at home where she belonged, Lainey forced herself to walk down the hallway. Fear gripped her heart as she approached the last door on the left. She knew that Halloran was waiting for her inside. And she knew that she had to face him. For Ethan's sake, she would do anything. *Anything.*

Gathering her courage, she reached for the doorknob. She did not bother to knock, but swung open the door to confront the man who was in all probability going to demand a great deal more from her than a few songs every week.

"You sang beautifully tonight, Lainey," Neil told her as he strolled forward to greet her. "But then, you always do. Come in and close the door."

"I prefer to leave the door open," she insisted firmly. She was almost too distracted to notice that the room had undergone a transformation since her last visit. The boxes and crates were gone, there were several paintings hanging on the walls, and a polished, carved mahogany desk sat near the window.

"Nonsense. We don't want anyone else listening in on our private conversation, do we?" His tone was laced with sarcasm, and his eyes were full of malicious amusement as they crawled over her tense body. He moved unhurriedly past her to close the door himself.

Lainey resisted the impulse to flee. She instinctively stepped away from him, anxious to keep a safe distance between the two of them. Longing to get this latest, thoroughly distasteful encounter over with, she waited until he had returned to the desk and then flung him a chilling glare.

"I have fulfilled my part of the agreement, Mr.

Halloran. I should like to go home now, so if you will please tell me what—"

"You're not going anywhere yet, *Mrs. Holt*," he countered, his voice heavy with meaning. He leaned his hips back against the edge of the desk, and, in a gesture of smug satisfaction, folded his arms across his chest. "There's been a change in plans."

"A change?" she echoed. Her throat constricted with alarm. "What are you talking about? We made a bargain—the continuation of my performances in exchange for my husband's protection."

"That was indeed the bargain we made," he agreed smoothly. Then he added, "But that was before your husband decided to interfere in something that wasn't any of his concern."

"What do you mean?" she demanded, fearing that she already knew the answer.

"He should have known better than to ride off with Marshal Sutton," the gambler opined, with a faint smile. His eyes glittered hotly in the next instant. "I thought maybe he'd finally decided to wise up. When he handed in his badge, I expected him to let go of the past. Obviously, I was wrong. This time, he and Sutton have made a serious—and perhaps even fatal—mistake."

"*Fatal?* Dear God, what are you—?"

"The whiskey smuggling has been a very lucrative undertaking, to say the least," he went on to boast. "The Indians get what they want, and I get what I want. It's a simple arrangement, one that's worked quite well. And it will continue to do so just as soon as I take care of this 'inconvenience.' "

"But Ethan was only repaying a debt to Marshal Sutton!" Lainey pointed out, panic rising within her. She couldn't believe what she was hearing. "He didn't want to go. Please, you can't—"

"Believe me, my dear Mrs. Holt, I can. I have a number of men on my payroll who wouldn't think twice about it, badge or no badge."

"Then you *were* the one who tried to have Ethan killed!" she said in dawning horror.

"I'm reluctant to take credit for that. It was a botched job. And you can rest assured that the son of a bitch who missed has been dealt with," he declared ruthlessly. He straightened from the desk and began advancing on her with slow, measured steps. "It's time to strike a new deal, Lainey."

Her breath caught in her throat as she felt very real terror coursing through her body. She opened her mouth to speak, but no words would come. *Ethan!* Her heart cried out to him once more. She closed her eyes for a moment, hot tears stinging against her eyelids while she prayed that he was all right. She told herself that he was still alive, that she'd know if anything had happened to him. But Halloran's threats could not be denied. She realized now that he was capable of anything—even murder.

"What—what do you want from me?" she finally choked out, her bright gaze widening as she edged toward the doorway. An inner voice screamed at her to take flight, to escape before it was too late, but she would not yet heed it. She dropped her arm to her side, her fingers ready to make a move toward the small knife concealed within her boot.

"I think you know. In fact, I think you've known all along that it would come down to this." He paused mere inches away from her, his features turning ugly with lust and triumph and menace. His gaze seared mercilessly down into the fiery, deep blue of hers. "I told you once before that you'd be mine, Lainey. It's going to take a lot more than a song to save your husband's life this time."

"No," she gasped. Shaking her head in a vehement

denial of his words, she battled the fear that threatened to overwhelm her.

"Don't be so quick to refuse me," he warned, confident that he would win. She would be his at last. And Ethan Holt would finally get what he deserved—if he hadn't already. The thought that his old adversary might be lying dead in No Man's Land at this very moment gave him considerable pleasure. "I've always found your loyalty to your husband to be quite touching," he lied. "Surely you don't want to run the risk of losing him now?"

"You know what you are demanding is impossible," she proclaimed furiously. "I could never—"

"You can and will," he insisted. "I've waited long enough, Lainey. Too long. I should have taken you back when I had the chance. Maybe then Holt wouldn't have been the first to bed you—assuming he *was* the first," he sneered. "But it doesn't matter anymore. You'll be mine now, and I have no intention of sharing you with anyone else. If you won't be a widow, then I'll settle for whatever term you care to apply to yourself."

"You're insane," Lainey whispered hoarsely. She loved Ethan, loved him more than life itself, but how could she possibly give herself to this man? The very thought of allowing Neil Halloran to take what she and Ethan had shared in love sent a sharp pain slicing through her heart. Her stomach churned, and she cast another desperate glance toward the doorway.

"How about a kiss to seal the bargain?" It was more of a command than a request, and they both knew it.

"I—I have not yet agreed," she stammered, backing away from him as he began to advance once more. She had believed herself ready to do whatever was necessary to protect Ethan. But now that the moment of truth had arrived, she felt her courage and determination abandoning her. There was no way of knowing if Halloran had as much power as he claimed, no way of knowing if he would honor his part of the deal even if she were to comply with his demands. He wasn't a man to be trusted. *Dear God, what should she do?*

Neil Halloran made it painfully clear in the next instant that he was through playing games. He lunged forward, caught her about the waist, and yanked her up against him with such force that the breath was knocked from her body.

"*No!*" came her strangled cry of protest, every instinct telling her to fight. His arms tightened about her with surprising strength, while his eyes glinted down at her like cold steel.

"Scream all you like," he told her. "I've left orders not to be disturbed."

"Let me go!" She struggled in his cruel grasp, raising her hands to push at his chest. He caught her wrists and jerked them behind her back. Tears of helpless rage started to her eyes. "No, damn you, no!"

"I'll make you beg me for it, Lainey," he vowed, his voice heavy with desire. "I'll make you forget all about Holt."

She squirmed and twisted violently against him, but he bore her over to the velvet upholstered sofa, and flung her down upon it, his body falling heavily upon hers. Wincing in pain as her shoulders strained at their sockets, she kicked in a futile effort to prevent him from dragging up her long skirts.

A shrill, breathless scream broke from her lips when she felt the cool air upon her skin. No matter what he had said, no matter what he had threatened, she couldn't willingly submit to this degradation. *She couldn't!*

Summoning every ounce of strength she possessed, she managed to pull one of her wrists free. She bent her knee and lifted her foot upward, her hand searching for the scalpel in her boot. Her fingers closed about the handle, and she withdrew the knife.

She raised her arm again. Without hesitation, she

brought the thin, silvery blade in her hand slashing downward. Halloran jerked his head about at the last moment, so that the knife cut across his face instead of imbedding within his neck as she had intended.

He cursed in pain. Then, filled with vengeful rage, he grabbed her wrist again and squeezed until she was forced to drop the scalpel.

"Stop it," she gasped. Blood dripped from his wound onto the bodice of her suit, and she raised her eyes fearfully to the narrow intensity of his.

"You're going to pay for that," he promised in a harsh, sinister tone. He abruptly climbed to his feet and yanked her up beside him. "*Later.* But now, it's time to go. And while we're on our way, you can think about that husband of yours lying dead out on the prairie with his throat cut!"

"*No!*" came her strangled cry of denial. It couldn't be true. Dear God, Ethan couldn't be dead!

"It's already too late," Neil ground out. With a swift and furious brutality, he caught her hands up and bound them together with a silken cord. Her protests were quickly muffled when he tied a thick cloth across her mouth. She struggled in vain, her skirts tangling about her legs while Neil literally dragged her from the room. He propelled her down the back staircase, and outside to where another man stood waiting with three saddled horses.

Lainey inhaled sharply when she saw that it was none other than Vince, the same man who had attacked her on the day of the Run . . . the man with whom Neil had denied anything more than a passing acquaintance. He ignored the silent appeal in her eyes and darted a quick, narrow glance toward his employer.

"What happened to your face?"

"Mount up!" Neil bit out impatiently. Although Lainey kicked and twisted within his grasp, he tossed her up onto one of the horse's backs. She managed to pull the gag from her mouth, calling out for help as she tried to scramble down, but Neil mounted behind her. He clamped an arm about her waist and rasped close to her ear, "*Quiet!* We've a long ride ahead of us, Mrs. Holt. I have 'friends' who will be only too happy to make us welcome for a few days. Now keep still, or you'll never have a chance to enjoy your widowhood!"

Lainey shuddered involuntarily at the threat, but the terrible dread gripping her was on Ethan's behalf, not her own. *It's already too late.* She choked back another sob at the memory of the words Neil had uttered with such a cruel and taunting certainty. It was a lie! she told herself. Neil had lied in the hope that she would surrender. She'd know if anything had truly happened to Ethan. She'd know because her heart would have broken in two . . .

Neil reined the horse about and urged it into a gallop. Lainey battled a fresh wave of light-headedness as the animal thundered away from the bright lights of the theater. Vince kicked the flanks of his own mount and rode after them. In a matter of moments, the town was only a speck in the distance behind them.

The sun was sinking low upon the horizon by now. Darkness approached, and with it the promise of a beautiful starlit night. The minutes that passed seemed like hours. Lainey strained forward in the saddle, struggling for breath while Neil's arm tightened like a vise about her. She had to find a way to escape, to get to Travis and warn him about the danger to Ethan. Please God, *she had to*!

The anguished prayer burned in her mind as her gaze swept the prairie for any signs of life. She saw nothing but the rolling, grass-mantled hills, the endless sky above—and the beckoning waters of the river just ahead. They were headed straight toward it.

Her eyes lit with purpose. There was no time to

think, no time to plan or falter. She simply obeyed a sudden impulse to act.

Jerking abruptly backward, she brought her right leg up to curl about the saddlehorn and grabbed at the reins. The horse gave a shrill whinny of protest. Slowing its frantic pace, the animal reared up on its hind legs, then began careening wildly toward the tree-lined banks of the river.

Neil growled an oath and fought to regain control of the horse, but it was too late. Behind them, Vince shouted a futile warning.

The horse plunged through the trees and into the water. Sucking in a deep breath, Lainey tumbled deliberately downward. Neil's hand shot out to tangle in her skirts. She was torn away from him by the river's swift current.

She heard him call her name. She could have sworn she heard a gunshot as well.

But there was no time to think about that. The coldness of the water was a shock. It was difficult to keep her head above the surface, difficult to find enough air to breathe. Struggling desperately against her bonds, she tried to swim for the riverbank. Panic rose within her as she felt her wet skirts threatening to drag her under for good. Her lungs were already near to bursting.

A blackness threatened to close about her. Ethan's face rose in her mind. *Ethan.* She had to save him!

With renewed strength, she kicked and turned, fighting her way to the surface once more. Again and again, she burst forth into the life-giving warmth of the air, only to be mercilessly snatched back down in the next instant. Mere seconds became an eternity . . .

Suddenly someone caught her about the waist. She coughed and spluttered, battling to remain conscious as she was hauled once and for all to the surface. Strong arms bore her quickly through the water now, to the safety of the riverbank. She was set gently upon the ground. Still coughing, she lifted an unsteady hand to rake the wet, streaming tresses from her face. Her eyes had difficulty focusing as she looked up at her rescuer.

"Ethan?" she choked out in disbelief. She blinked hard, then realized that it was true. He was alive! Her whole body flooded with the most profound joy and relief she had ever known. *"Ethan!"* She sat up and threw her arms about his neck, only to gasp in startlement when he drew away and climbed to his feet.

"I'm going after Halloran." His expression was dangerously grim. His eyes moved to where his brother stood watching them from the opposite side of the river.

Lainey's gaze followed the direction of his. She saw Travis, and saw that Vince sat on the ground nearby, groaning in pain from a bullet wound to the chest. Neil Halloran was nowhere in sight.

"Look after her!" Ethan commanded his brother. Travis responded with a curt nod.

"Ethan, no!" Lainey gasped hoarsely, her stomach knotting in alarm once more. He had already turned away, but she staggered to her feet and clutched at his arm. "He'll kill you!"

"No, he won't." His eyes burned down into hers. "I'll be back." Giving her the merest ghost of a smile, he set off down along the riverbank. She stared after him in mingled dread and confusion, wondering how he meant to catch up with Neil on foot.

There was only one way to find out.

Although her legs still felt perilously weak, she gathered up the sodden folds of her skirt and followed Ethan's trail. Travis could do nothing more than shout at her in dismay.

"Lainey, don't!"

She ignored him and made her way as quickly as possible through the trees. It wasn't long before she heard voices—*Ethan's and Neil's.* She ran forward without regard to the danger, desperate to see what was happening

. . . still resolved to do whatever she could to save Ethan.

Having crossed the river by this time, Neil had dismounted and taken cover behind a tree. The Holt brothers' appearance on the scene had proven an unhappy surprise. But surprise had quickly given way to a cold-blooded determination to see Ethan Holt dead.

"Give it up, Halloran!" Ethan ordered from his own cover a short distance away. He knew his gun would do him little good; the soaking in the river had seen to that. "It's over!"

"Is it?" retorted Neil. He held a rifle in his hands, shouldering it in readiness.

"The men you hired to do your killing for you didn't last long once they saw they were outnumbered. And they talked. Sutton knows you were behind the claim stealing."

"The charge will never stick and you know it. I've got too many well-placed friends!"

"Not for long. There's a new Territorial judge coming in to clean up the town."

"You think I give a damn about that?" Neil countered scornfully. "You're out of your mind if you think I'll give anything up—*including* Lainey!"

Ethan's jaw clenched, his eyes glittering hotly. The thought of what Lainey may have suffered at the bastard's hands filled him with a vengeful, white-hot rage.

"I'll see you in hell first," he promised, his tone one of deadly calm.

"You'll be there soon enough!" snarled Neil. With that, he finally took aim and fired.

Ethan crouched low; the bullet narrowly missed him. He swore underneath his breath and tightened his grip on his six-shooter.

Lainey had almost reached them now. She paled at the echoing report of the gunshot. Sick with the fear that Ethan had been hit, she whispered another frantic prayer before stumbling onward through the underbrush.

"Dead or alive, Halloran—I'm taking you in," vowed Ethan.

"I should have killed you a long time ago, you son of a bitch!" Neil flung back. He was preparing to fire in the same direction again, when a sudden movement out of the corner of his eye caught his attention. He jerked about, his finger squeezing the trigger.

A sharp, breathless scream broke from Lainey's lips. She felt a sudden burning in her left shoulder, felt her legs giving way beneath her. She was only dimly aware of Ethan calling her name as she collapsed onto the ground.

Her name was on Neil's lips as well. Momentarily stunned by the realization that he had shot her, he lost the advantage. His grip on the rifle relaxed.

A murderous Ethan immediately closed the distance between them. He lunged at Neil and sent him crashing to the ground with bone-crushing force. His fist smashed into the gambler's face again and again. Neil suddenly rallied, landing a blow to Ethan's chin. He scrambled onto his hands and knees, but Ethan caught him and pulled him back.

The two of them grappled for a moment longer. There was little doubt who was the stronger of the two. Neil could feel himself weakening, could feel the blood rushing to his head as he tried, in vain, to break free.

And then, he remembered the knife he had concealed within his boot. His hand shot downward. He snatched at the weapon, his fingers closing about the hilt. With a low, feral growl, he raised his arm and plunged the blade downward.

Ethan's reflexes were quick, but not quick enough. He tensed, muttering an oath as the blade cut down across his arm. The fury in his eyes turned even more lethal. His hands curled about the other man's throat.

He might well have killed him there and then, if not for his concern over Lainey. *Lainey.*

Leaving Neil sprawled bleeding and unconscious on the ground, he climbed to his feet, caught up the rifle, and hurried across to where Lainey lay beneath the trees. He dropped to his knees beside her.

"Lainey?" His anxious gaze fell to the blood seeping from the wound in her shoulder. Though his heart twisted at the sight of it, he wouldn't allow himself to fear the worst. He quickly took his bandanna and pressed it to her shoulder in an effort to stop the bleeding. She gave a soft groan. "Lainey, can you hear me?" he asked her.

"Yes," she answered feebly. She opened her eyes, and a shadow of mingled pain and apprehension crossed her face. "Oh, Ethan. Are you—?"

"I'm fine."

"And . . . Neil?"

"Still alive. For now, anyway."

He could hear someone coming toward them. He leveled the rifle, then saw that it was his brother hurrying through the trees. Travis was leading one of the horses along behind him.

"I got here as soon as—" Travis started to explain, only to break off when he saw what had happened. His gaze flickered briefly to where Neil lay a few feet away.

"Stay here," Ethan told him. "I'll send help from town." He lifted Lainey gently in his arms and stood up. She inhaled upon an audible gasp, trying without much success to ignore the pain.

"Where are we going?" she murmured, her head spinning.

"We've got to get you to the doctor." He carried her toward the horse, allowing neither his voice nor his expression to betray the terrible worry that gripped him.

"Ethan?" she whispered.

"Yes?"

"I love you . . ." Her voice trailed away as she slipped into the darkness.

Her eyelids fluttered open. Her head slowly clearing at last, she heaved a sigh and allowed her gaze to move about the small, sun-filled room. She frowned at the unfamiliarity of her surroundings. Her pulse raced with a momentary alarm, until her eyes fell upon the tall, solemn-faced man who stood staring out of the window a short distance away. She felt her heart stir at the sight of him.

"Ethan?"

He turned his head. His eyes met hers, his face lighting with a visible combination of joy and relief as he crossed the room in two long strides.

"I was beginning to think you'd sleep forever." The teasing lightness of his tone completely belied what he had suffered. He resumed his seat in the chair beside the bed and grasped her hand within the strong warmth of his.

"Where am I?"

"At the doctor's house. You've been here nearly three days."

"Three days?" she echoed in surprise.

"The doctor says you're going to be fine. But you'll be sore for a while."

"True enough." She sighed, wincing slightly when she eased upward upon the pillow. She looked back to Ethan, then frowned again when she took note of the dark circles underneath his eyes and the telltale stubble on his face. "You look as if you haven't slept for days."

"I haven't." His hand tightened about hers, his features sobering. "You've put me through hell, Mrs. Holt."

"I didn't mean to." Sudden tears started to her eyes, and she felt her mind whirling anew at the memories that came flooding back. "Oh, Ethan. How did you find me? You were supposed to be away—"

"Halloran set up an ambush. We didn't have to ride as far as we planned. After Sutton was injured, I brought him—and the prisoners—back to town." He had finally repaid the debt.

"But how did you know where I was?"

"It didn't take long to discover that." His eyes darkened at the memory. "And you weren't hard to track." He lifted his other hand and smoothed a wayward strand of hair from her face before demanding quietly, "Why did you disobey me, Lainey?"

"I—I had no choice," she stammered. "I suspected that Neil was the one who tried to have you killed, and I certainly couldn't let him try again. He told me he would make sure you stayed alive if I resumed my performances. But then, after I sang, he told me I would have to—" She broke off, her gaze falling beneath the steady, loving intensity of his. "He confessed his part in the smuggling. And he said the only way he'd let you live was if I agreed to be with him."

"You didn't—?" Ethan started to demand, his gaze smoldering as he searched her face.

"No!" she hastened to deny. "God knows, I thought about it. But I couldn't give in to him." She heaved another long, ragged sigh and asked, "What will happen to him now?"

"He'll be hanged, most likely. Sutton will see to that."

"Then . . . it's really over."

"It's over." His eyes burned down into hers, and she trembled when his fingers glided tenderly, possessively, across her cheek. "Damn it, Lainey. You almost got yourself killed!" he accused, his tone low and brimming with emotion. "Will you never learn to do as I tell you?"

"Probably not," she replied, then smiled softly. A

sweet warmth spread through her at the sound of his quiet, vibrant chuckle. "But you can keep trying all the same."

"I will," he promised. He leaned forward and brushed her forehead with his lips. *"I will."*

Chapter 18

One year later . . .

"It's going to be beautiful, Lainey," said Beth. She smiled as the two of them stood surveying the large, half-finished frame structure that would feature the columns and gables Lainey had always dreamed of. Ethan was making good on his promise to build her the finest house in the Territory.

"Yes, it is," Lainey agreed, then gave a rather wistful sigh as her own gaze moved back to the nearby house of logs. "But I'm afraid I'll miss the cabin."

They had known such happiness there this past year. Recalling how Ethan had enlarged it to include a second bedroom, a separate kitchen, and a real bathroom, she felt a sudden lump rise in her throat and instinctively tightened her arms about her sleeping son, now three months old. Ethan had teasingly remarked on more than one occasion that the baby would have been born a day sooner if she hadn't delayed their wedding night. Jacob Holt was already the spitting image of his proud, handsome father.

"Travis has insisted that we will have a new house as well, but I'm not at all sure I want one," Beth admitted. She lifted a hand to her well-rounded belly, her eyes shining softly. "Of course, once the baby comes, I may feel differently."

Anna called out to them from the bunkhouse, where

she was visiting with the half dozen young cowboys her uncle had hired to tend to the ever-increasing herd. Lainey and Beth both turned to respond with a smile and an affectionate wave, though Beth's smile faded when she viewed the mud splattered all across her little daughter's red gingham dress.

"I'm beginning to think she cannot remain clean for any time at all." Beth sighed in maternal exasperation. "Jacob will probably be far worse."

"Perhaps, but I think you are very well suited to raising boys. You have always possessed far more spirit than I, you know," Beth reminded her, with a soft laugh.

"I hope you're right," replied Lainey. Her mouth twitched when she confided, "Ethan wants to have a dozen of them."

"And what if one should turn out to be a girl?" her sister queried archly.

"Then God help the man who someday comes courting Ethan Holt's daughter." Her sapphire gaze sparkled with wry, loving amusement at the thought.

Ethan and Travis returned from town a short time later. Guthrie had changed considerably in the past twelve months. Brick structures and impressive false-front buildings had taken the place of the tents, the saloons had given way to churches and banks and stores and hotels, and a school had even been started. As Oklahoma's first Territorial Capital, the onetime boomtown had settled into a peaceful, prosperous existence that belied its violent and chaotic beginnings.

Travis soon collected his wife and daughter and drove them home in his newly purchased buckboard. He had made similiar improvements to the cabin where he and Beth had shared a year of love and laughter. Since he and his brother were equal partners in the ranch, his share of the profits were more than enough to provide his own family with a new, much grander house. He was confident he'd be able to talk Beth into it. His eyes glowed warmly when he mused that he was always able to talk Beth into what he wanted sooner or later.

That night, after Jacob had been fed and tucked into his cradle, Ethan pulled his wife down onto his lap as he sat in a rocking chair before the fire. The late spring air was unseasonably cool, but the comforting blaze chased away the chill inside the room. A clock chimed softly on the mantelpiece above the flames.

Lainey settled contentedly against Ethan's hard warmth and entwined her arms about his neck. She lifted her head to favor him with a secretive little smile.

"What is it?" he asked, his suspicions aroused. His deep-timbred voice was brimming with humor.

"I just thought you might like to know that your parents are coming for another visit as soon as the house is finished."

"Damn it, woman! Did you invite them?" he demanded accusingly, though without any real anger.

"Yes, I most certainly did," she confessed, unrepentant. "It's only right that they see their grandson as often as possible. And besides, since you and your father did not kill each other off during their last visit, I see no reason why there should be any danger of your doing so this time."

"Sometimes, Mrs. Holt, you're every inch an interfering female."

"And *you* are every inch a bullheaded, overbearing male!" she retorted saucily. She was delighted when his arms tightened about her. Her eyes glowed softly up into the penetrating, blue-green intensity of his when she added, "But in truth, I wouldn't have you any other way."

"Keep looking at me like that, you little wildcat, and you'll find yourself in bed with your skirts tossed above your head," he warned in a low, vibrant tone.

"Is that a threat, Mr. Holt?" she challenged, her manner even more seductive.

"It's a promise."

"And you are, after all, a man of your word."

"Don't ever doubt it," he murmured huskily, his lips descending upon hers at last.

Her heart took flight as passion flared deep within her. She knew it would always be so . . . For the rest of her life, she would love, and be loved by, this tall, devilishly handsome Texan who had taken her by storm. Fate had decreed it, and the heavens had smiled. In his arms, she was truly home.

Catherine Creel

**Published by Fawcett Books.
Available in your local bookstore.**